Unlovable but Maybe Not

Gina Marie Adkins

Copyright © 2023 by Gina Marie Adkins

The story, all names, characters, and incidents portrayed in this production are fictitious. No identification with actual persons (living or deceased), places, buildings, and products is intended or should be inferred.

Book Cover by Nicholas LaPrade

First edition 2023

Dedication

Dedicated to the best Papa anyone could have, Jessie Ford Trent. Love and miss you.

Chapter 1

The muffled roar of the crowd hummed backstage. Park Mal-Chin recognized K-pop group Beast's fan chant. He knew it by heart at this point. Mal-Chin's stomach hurt. Maybe too many crunches while trying to forget how Arin slept with him one last time before breaking up with him. It could just be his nerves. The crowd hushed as their warmup act, Exhaust, a freshly debuted group, took the stage.

Mal-Chin fought the urge to run his hands through his perfectly styled hair. His eyes closed as the make-up crew dabbed color onto his lids. The eye shadow and his dark blue hair gave the striking effect that his fans went wild for. Mal-Chin used to think the dab of the makeup sponge on his chest tickled, but over the years he had gotten used to the sensation. It was just a regular part of his show prep now. There was a certain spot on his side that still made him jump when they tapped too hard there. Makeup was always the longest part for him. They covered his whole upper body in it preparing for him to rip his shirt off later in the show. Mal-Chin's real skin color was a bronze tone that he preferred over the porcelain color the makeup artist lightened his skin to. In his mind, his real skin tone looked more manly, but the beauty standard was pale.

Tonight was the final concert of Beast's international tour. The members of Beast did their best to joke around and keep the energy up as they went through their warmups. As always, they saved their home, Seoul, South Korea, for last. It would be their last concert as six. Suho, the only member with a natural hair color right now, patted Mal-Chin on the back. "Are you ok?" Suho's eyes scanned Mal-Chin's face. Mal-Chin just nodded. "Remember your fans. It's just a normal concert. Try not to think about the rest."

Mal-Chin fought the urge to press his mouth into a line. *He could do this*. He could get through this concert without showing even a hint of what was happening. To people outside their fan base, Park Mal-Chin was just the beefy eye candy for the group; Beast's fans loved Mal-Chin for his bright smile and goofy personality. He needed to deliver all of that, plus perfect vocals, tonight. If he didn't his fans would be let down. He would do that enough for them in a few minutes anyway.

Exhaust finished. Beast congratulated them on a job well done. They remembered being where Exhaust was. The old knots in their stomach that was now just excitement. The warm-up act bowed to them glad to have been included as Beast's fan chant started again; Mal-Chin could hear it better now from his spot on the lift stage. The hair and makeup crew did last minute spot checks, fidgeting with pieces of hair, brushing invisible lint off costumes and just, essentially, looking like parents trying to make their kids presentable. Mal-Chin adjusted his microphone headset as he waited. Sharing the same lift, Kang Dae-o hopped from foot to foot before leaning his elbow on Mal-Chin's shoulder for their starting pose. Dae-o and Mal-Chin were rarely shown interacting even though they were good friends. Their fans liked this starting pose at every concert. Without looking around, Mal-Chin knew the others getting into position. How would they pose once they were a member down?

He let his performance persona take over.

The floor lifted them onto the stage. The lights showing only their silhouettes. They were greeted by screams as fans waved their official Beast light sticks. It always reminded Mal-Chin of the city lights from the plane windows. City lights that were now chanting their names.

Eoguem Suho, Yun Minkyo, Park Mal-Chin, Cho Jeong-hui, Kang Dae-o, Lee Ryu

The crowd screamed as Beast became visible, expertly posed. "Seoul! We're back!" Cho Jeong-hui – J.E. was his stage name—yelled into his green hand-held microphone. The others yelled similar phrases greeting the crowd as they casually moved into position for their first song.

Midnight Lover was their latest big hit. The fans called out the song's chant and squealed at every hip thrust and body roll. The screams hit a new level when Ryu did his signature face caress while making eye contact with the camera instead of the hand motion that usually accompanied that part of the choreography. Mal-Chin put his problems aside as they performed for the adoring crowd. Focusing on anything else was difficult when the crowd's energy was so high.

Instead of an intermission, the group stopped to play games and talk to the crowd. This was a popular section of any k-pop concert and dozens of videos of it would appear online tonight. Mal-Chin got a short break while J.E. and Ryu performed a rap song. Ryu was practically screaming his verses at one point. A part of Mal-Chin wanted to be out on stage vibing with them. The backstage crew surrounded the vocalists with portable fans to quickly cool them. Mal-Chin barely noticed the team drying his body. Beast had been running around freely during the last song and at some point Minkyo poured a bottle of water down Mal-Chin's back after he splashed the crowd. Mal-Chin held out his hand to receive a handful of baby oil. He rubbed the oil onto his dry chest. The shirt would not last too much longer. He needed to have a perfectly shined chest when it was gone. The vocalist rushed back to the lift stage as J.E. and Ryu finished. Mal-Chin hurriedly buttoned his shirt back and pulled his jacket back on.

No matter how many times Mal-Chin was lifted high into the air, it still made him nervous. He tried to not notice how far below the crowd was. The fans knew of Mal-Chin's fear of heights. The sound of Suho's dynamic voice as he belted out the beginning lines kept Mal-Chin from breaking his professional face. The slow song felt like an eternity. Mal-Chin breathed a sigh of relief as the lift lowered to the main stage. The whole group returned to the main stage. The vocalist removed their jackets. It felt good, the jackets combined with body heat and lights was too hot. The music began slow but quickly picked up an almost techno beat. Mal-Chin danced front and center as the music made a loud bang. At the same moment, he ripped his shirt open revealing perfectly sculpted muscles. What followed was his favorite sound. The crowd screaming and squealing all for him. The sound would have been deafening if not for Mal-Chin's earpiece. He knew all the big screens were on him right now as well. Flirting with every camera that caught his eye, Mal-Chin enjoyed this moment in the spotlight. Sure, concert attendees had been calling his name all night, but right now every voice in the audience was just for him.

Then came the moment Mal-Chin had dreaded for days. The moment he had tried to put out of his mind. They performed their last song in the tour t-shirt, everyone looking cool and refreshed, then began to say their goodbyes to the audience. He waited patiently while the others spoke. Mal-Chin could not pay that much attention to them. It was the same rehearsed lines they said through the whole tour with a few extra throw-ins to make it personal. He was the last to go.

"Beauties," he started, that was their fandom name. They cheered his name. This time the sound left him feeling hollow; he was about to hurt these people that loved him. Fans would later say that they saw the news on his face before he spoke. The light dimmed in his sparkling eyes. If he looked behind him, he knew the big screen was showing his sweat covered form. He shifted his gold microphone between his hands suddenly unsure of what to say. "I'm sure you've heard what's being said about me on the news," he paused, his eyes felt strange. The crowd yelled motivation to him, Minkyo patted him on the back. "While we know it's false," he pressed his lips together holding back tears, "there are many who are judging Beast for it so," the words were harder to say than he thought; they caught in his throat, "I've made the decision" his voice faltered, tears began to fall, the crowd made a collective noise of sympathy, "to leave Beast after tonight's concert."

Mal-Chin felt the life suck out of the room. People were begging him to reconsider, telling him how much they loved him, how much they would miss him. This made the flow of tears worse. The rest of the group descended on him trying to comfort him. Suho and Dae-o where practically holding him up. They knew it was coming but it was still a shock to the system to hear. Mal-Chin found himself apologizing to the other members and to the fans. "When this is all over. I'll come back to you. I promise," was the last thing he said between broken sobs.

An hour after the concert, the news was online with videos of his tearful goodbye. The urge to call Arin hit him, he was already imagining the comforting way she stroked his back when he was upset. Remembering how she left soured his memory of Arin. He thought they had a future. Past girlfriends wanted his money, body, or fame, but Arin did not show interest in any of that. She had money and fame all her own. He believed she loved him and he had fallen hard. The truth was she was using Mal-Chin to climb the ranks of celebrity. Now that he was losing his status she was gone.

The makeup and hair dye swirled down the shower drain as he wondered what he kept doing wrong in his relationships. Letting the warm water run over his face, he tried to forget it. He wasn't going to let himself spiral into self-pity tonight.

Chapter 2

Attention was short even for a Friday. Ms. Sophie Gregory could not blame her seventh-grade students. Organizational Patterns were not the most entertaining topic, especially the second time around. They were in that time of year Sophie Gregory called "Review Mode." SOL's, Virginia's standardized tests, were approaching faster than anyone wanted to admit. Teachers were pushing harder than normal this year and the school board was breathing down administrations' collective necks. If the school did not pull up scores this year, then the state would be sending in "experts" to "fix" things. That boiled down to more meetings, professional developments, test for the kids, and strategies that people who last taught 30 years ago think will work but don't. There was a rumor going around that teachers would get fired. Sophie knew that meant her. She was young and relatively new.

March had been a long month with no days off. The weather dragged from one cold day to the next. Earlier in the week, they were teased with the feel of milder temperatures, now the word snow was being said again. Sophie needed the break as much as the students did. The idea of an unexpected break sounded great right about now. She toyed with taking a day off for herself, but just the idea made her feel guilty. Her sick days were reserved for migraines, the only thing that tended to lay her low. About this time every year, the seventh graders went through a change, the older teachers blamed hormones, they became overdramatic, disruptive, and hyper. Every day was something new and eventually resulted in administration having to crack down on rules, only causing more problems as students adjusted. Somedays, Sophie swore she could feel the brown hair at her temples turning gray.

She checked the time on her outdated Fitbit, almost time to go. Looking out the window, she took a deep breath, which drew the attention of her students. It was her sign that she wanted to say something unexpectedly. How that worked, she still was not sure. They could be working loudly in groups and all she had to do was stand in her favored spot, make a face, and take an opened mouth breath. "Anyone got any plans for weekend?" Sophie asked as she took up papers. She got replies such as video games, sleeping in, four-wheeling, and other outdoor activities. The school was located in a rural part of the county with numerous farms and most of her students lived on farms or in low-income apartments. There was little for students to do here without travelling almost an hour away to Danville or Lynchburg. Unless their family had money, most of her students' weekends were spent at home. Sophie worried about what some of them did on the weekend. They avoided answering that particular question and seemed to always return in a bad mood.

Announcements started with the usual "Good afternoon, Falcons!" from Mr. Motley. He read off the list of upcoming events and reminded teachers of the faculty meeting Tuesday. When he finished, he released car riders to leave. A few kids rushed out the door as Sophie yelled at them to have a good weekend. At 3:15 the last load of bus riders hurried out the door. The hall became quiet and calm. Sophie chatted with the other teachers for a few minutes, mostly about the latest incident that had them shaking their heads. Today's was an intentionally clogged toilet that overflowed and flooded the hall. The water almost reached her room, she thanked her luck that it had not. The water may have been clean, but the thought of it coming out of a bathroom and into her room disgusted her. Sophie thought she could still smell toilet water in the hall. The day janitor was understandably upset. Surveying the colorful poster clad walls and group crates, Sophie made sure everything was back in place before the tiredness of the day set in. She made a mental list of the things she needed before packing her teacher bag: purse, lunchbox, student work, recent test data, pens, highlighters, cardigan, water bottle, heavy jacket, keys, and phone. In the back of her mind, Sophie knew she would do little work over the weekend but she lugged it home anyway. She feel guilty if she did not take it all with her.

On the way out, she crept by the data analyst's room hoping the woman would not come out to hound her about the recent test scores. Their data analyst, Mrs. Barbour, was a school board member assigned to bring up SOL scores but just bullied teachers and caused more stress; Sophie was a favorite target as she was the youngest teacher in the building. Mrs. Barbour had not taught since before Sophie was born and did not have a clue about what went into modern teaching. That was a common strain between the school board and teachers. Luck was on Sophie's side again today and she slipped by without a visit.

Crossing the parking lot, she made the mental shift from professional teacher Ms. Gregory to shy 27-year-old Sophie. The drive home took about 40 minutes depending on how fast Sophie drove or how many stop lights caught her. Fridays were grocery day so her trip would take a bit longer. No sooner than Sophie hit the highway, was she singing along to a song on her car's Bluetooth radio. She could not sing but she knew every word and back up. While there was a decent mix of pop and rock music, no country or hard rap, there was one specific type of song missing from her playlist. Her playlist lacked love songs. Sophie removed them all a few years ago when she gave up dating. Admittedly, it was an embarrassing moment of self-loathing that caused the purge. They represented something that she would never have.

The grocery store visit was quickly completed. She knew what she was after for herself and her grandparents, and where to find it. She exchanged polite conversation with the cashier whose daughter had gone to school with Sophie, while she checked out then made the short trip down tree lined side streets to get home. Sophie lived with her mother but, between work schedules and their need for alone time, they rarely spent time together.

Sophie unpacked her things then was out the door to her grandparent's house, just three houses down the street. Sophie struggled to pull the screen door open while holding the grocery bags. In the end, she let the screen door rest against her back as she nudged the door open with her foot. Even though they were expecting her, Virginia and Ford Coleman looked up at their granddaughter with surprise.

"Hey, gotcha some stuff," was all Sophie said as she headed into their kitchen to unpack. Virginia followed behind her looking at everything before Sophie could put them away. It was not much, Virginia usually went to the grocery store on Saturday mornings, but Sophie ate with them almost nightly, so she wanted to contribute. They never gave her a list. She just bought what she knew they needed. Being useful to them made her feel proud. "Oh, I got y'all a surprise too." Sophie held up their favorite candy bars and shook them absolutely pleased with herself.

"Ooh, ooh," Ford said pointing at his, "bring me that."

"Calories, Calories," Virginia reminded as she watched Sophie open a candy bar for herself. Sophie was suddenly too aware of the pooch of her lower belly. She could not seem to get rid of it no matter how much she worked out or how many calories she cut. She'd once gone so far to cutting down to nine hundred calories and almost passed out in front of her students. Sophie realized how messed up that was as soon as it happened. Her grandparents closely monitored her food intake for a few months until they were sure she was eating enough. This candy bar was intended to be split up over several days. "Oh, did I tell you what James has done now?" Virginia began. James was Sophie's uncle's brother-in-law and the family was having some drama over a misunderstanding that happened months before.

"No, what?" Sophie answered. Over the last few weeks, Sophie had grown tired of hearing the latest development in this drama, usually multiple times in a row. But, Virginia liked to tell it and had probably waited all day to do so. The whole thing had become petty name calling and annoyances.

Their day fell into the usual Friday rhythm. The three ordered take out from Mama Possum's, a local burger joint, like they did every Friday and watched the same shows they watched every night. A wrapped burger in hand for her mother, Sophie went home about 9. For 40 minutes, Sophie practiced yoga on the living room floor and tried to think only of the movement of her body and not replay a list of everything she could have done better that day.

Nothing was exciting anymore. Getting out of this town was the goal. There was more to this world than this town and the small beach they visited every summer. She loved the comfort of small town living but her daily life was too routine. Sophie dreamed of distant shores with blue water and white sand, Greek villas and cherry blossom lined streets. Her Instagram had a few travel bloggers so she could live through them. Sophie would have to go alone, but even surrounded by the constant crush of family Sophie was alone here. What was the difference? Planning her escape caused her a tinge of guilt. Her grandparents relied on her for more than the rest of the family would admit. They would be left behind. As much as she wanted to escape, she could not do that. Maybe, just maybe, she could move somewhere close enough to return when needed, like the little town of Chatham that was only 20 minutes down the road.

Chapter 3

"In other news," the news anchor began, "former member of idol group Beast, Park Mal-Chin, is reported to be leaving the country for rest after stepping away from Beast. The scandal involving-" The T.V. turned off just as a video of his teary goodbye to fans was being shown silently in the background of the news broadcast.

Kang Dae-o tossed the remote onto the end table. "Don't they have anything better to report on?" He spat out as he settled back into his spot on the end of Mal-Chin's couch. "So, are you still going to Danville in the morning?"

Mal-Chin nodded; he leaned his head onto the back of the couch. One of his cats, Aruem, was staring at him curiously. "Yes, our manager already has a place ready for me." He began to flick the cat's ear. Pouting while flicking a cat's ear didn't work too well. Mal-Chin just thought the ways its ear moved was too cute.

"Minseok said he'd meet you there," Dae-o stated.

"Is he still in school? Will he have time?" Mal-Chin questioned. Beast met Dae-o's brother, Minseok, once while he was still in the early stages of his college years. Beast had performed at a music festival in the United States and Dae-o used the opportunity to visit. At the time, the band never thought they would regularly do international tours. Mal-Chin remembered Minseok as an awkward guy with dark circles under his eyes. He could not remember if this was the same town they visited.

"He's just starting a residency at the hospital," Dae-o answered. Mal-Chin's eyes focused on one spot of the ceiling. Absentmindedly, he patted the cat's head. Dae-o decided to leave him to his thoughts as he turned the T.V. back on and began to channel surf.

The room soon filled with noise and excitement as the other members of Beast arrived. They brought food and alcoholic drinks. Mal-Chin's cat disappeared. No one wanted to officially admit it but this was his going away party. His family was invited but declined in favor of the lunch they had earlier in the day. Beast, current and ex-members, crowded around the living room table. Drinks flowed freely as they chowed down on spicy chicken and all of Mal-Chin's favorite side dishes. Their first shot followed a shout from Jeong-hui of, "Fuck Kim Eun Jung!"

"Who is this woman anyway?" Minkyo asked. "That name sounds fake."

"I've never heard of her." Mal-Chin added. The shot of whiskey was still burning his throat. He barely registered what Ryu poured him until it was running down his throat. "Do you think she's one of those serial scandal starters?

The mood dipped with this conversation. Ryu refilled all their glasses, Jeong-hui turned on an action movie and Minkyo began to scroll through his phone. No one wanted to mention the scandal. They wanted this to be a happy send off.

"Are you all packed?" Suho asked taking a glance around the apartment.

"Yeah, just need to pack the last-minute things and the cats." Mal-Chin replied. The question brought him back down to reality. "I want to stay but I guess it's too late for that."

"It'll be good for you," Suho commented. "You need to get out of here for a while." Mal-Chin had pouted around his apartment for weeks. If he went out the media hounded his every movement asking questions he could not answer. Maybe they were right. In the U.S., he was less likely to be spotted and the Korean media would take some time to find him.

"Maybe you can catch a busty American woman," Ryu added momentarily interrupting the argument he was having with Jeong-hui. "Aren't women in the southern states supposed to be extra sexy?" Jeong-hui took up the lead rambling about short-shorts and tank tops. Mal-Chin shook his head, Arin popped into mind again. He needed more time.

Minkyo stopped scrolling through his phone and suddenly spoke, "Oh! They've got a bowling alley." The conversation about Southern girls was dropped in favor of excitement over bowling.

"Dude!" Jeong-hui called out. They started scrolling through the attractions in the small town.

Before any of them knew it, the night had gotten late and they all had a little too much to drink. Their driver picked up the members of Beast. They had to sneak out to avoid the media. Mal-Chin flopped down in bed and debated texting Arin. *I'm leaving tomorrow. Can I see you one last time?* That sounded too desperate. A part of him was shocked she had not shown up for one more final fling. They had done this several times in the past: break up, jump into bed, get back together. Mal-Chin's eyes squeezed tight as he wondered how he'd been so dumb not to notice something unhealthy in that pattern.

Chapter 4

Sophie was already having a rough day and she had only finished her first two classes. A throbbing in her head was threatening to turn into a migraine that would take her out of commission for the rest of the day and probably tomorrow. This, of course, was the day when her students were their loudest. The rumor of drama and the possible resulting fight kept the students on edge. They all wanted to discuss what would happen. Sophie stopped conversations about it multiple times.

Her worst behaved students were extra wound up. No matter how many times she told students to sit down, stop talking or pay attention they just were unable to. One particularly hyper student would not stop bad mouthing her. He ended up going to the Behavioral Management Center. Sophie suspected this was his plan. The Behavior Management Center was supposed to be a punishment where students went to separate them from their classmates. They were supposed to sit in silence and do work until the class period was over. The problem was that students went there, went to sleep, and avoided doing their work. The teacher watching the room did little in the way to keep them on task. Sometimes she'd talk to students and try to work them through their problems.

On the way to their extracurricular classes, Sophie held onto one of the students that was going to fight. She told the student, one that was usually good, it was so he wouldn't run into his classmate. "So, what's going on?" Sophie asked him as they waited for the last of the students to pass.

"He's just talkin' mess and I ain't gonna put up with it." The boy answered. His lips puckered out with anger.

"What did he say?" Sophie asked as they stepped into the hallway. They started walking side-by-side down the hall.

"That my sister is something that she's not because his sister and my sister like the same guy and they got issues. So now he's causing trouble with me. So, now we gon' fight," The boy's eyes stay glued to his shoes as he talked.

"So you're trying to stick up for your sister," Sophie summarized. The boy nodded. "And he is trying to stick up for his?" Sophie added.

The boy hesitated for a moment, "I guess so,"

"So if you're both just taking up for your sisters, can you try to work it out peacefully? It isn't your drama."

"But I gotta *protect* my family," The boy insisted.

"And I respect that," Sophie nodded, she slowed them down. They were getting close to his classroom and this conversation was not over. "But is it worth the suspension?"

The boy nodded. "I *gotta* protect my family, Ms. Gregory" He restated to make his point.

"I get that but is *he* worth the suspension? I know you're upset but is he worth getting in trouble for." Sophie added, "A week's suspension."

The boy thought it over looking at Sophie, "I guess you're right Ms. Gregory. What should I do?"

"Well, just avoid him. Try not to talk to him and if he tries to talk to you just walk away from him." Sophie shrugged. They reached his classroom and she informed the teacher that she'd "borrowed him" for a minute with a smile on her face.

Back in her classroom, she took an Excedrin for her head and turned off the light hoping the combination would help. Mrs. Barbour, the data analyst, let herself into the room as soon as Sophie settled into her desk chair. Sophie plastered on a pleasant smile.

"Ms. Gregory," Mrs. Barbour started as she took in the anchor chart of the board, "I noticed you working on this chart today. Why did you pick this chart over a slide presentation?"

"I've noticed they do a little better with visuals than just rote memorization. Plus, it keeps the information short and concise. All the examples on it are made by the class so it gives them a chance to interact with the lesson."

Mrs. Barbour just nodded and started looking through the worksheets that accompanied the day's lesson. Sophie got the impression that she was looking for something to criticize. "This work looks under grade level. Why did you choose it?"

"They've been struggling with the concept for a while so I'm giving them an easier assignment to build understanding and hopefully confidence. The next assignment will be on grade level with a partner. I'm trying to scaffold them back on track."

"Well, you don't understand scaffolding." Mrs. Barbour launched into a lecture on what The Scaffolding Approach was. It was exactly what Sophie was doing; offering support and lessening it as their ability built. By the time Mrs. Barbour left, Sophie's head was pounding worse. Sophie slipped across the hall to Mr. Worley to see if he got the same criticism. They were using the same worksheets. Mr. Worley just shook his head frustrated before they began to whisper about the insanity of it.

When the last load of bus riders left, Sophie let out a sigh of relief. Her head was no better and she was beginning to feel weak. She rushed to get home before the migraine hit in full. Vision blurred and a prescription medicine in her system, she flopped into bed having stripped off her work clothes. Her mind flipped between what she needed to do that afternoon and what she had done during the day. It was a jumbled mess that barely made sense in her head. Sophie curled up into a tight ball and squeezed her eyes shut. The light through the window was beginning to hurt. She fell asleep this way.

When she finally awoke, she lay in bed wondering what time it was and fearing the pain would return if she turned on a light. Her whole body felt heavy. Eventually, she worked up enough nerve to crawl out of bed. In the kitchen, she quickly found a soda to drink, not having the energy to start the coffee maker. The bright lights agitated the migraine and caused it to return. Pack of Tuna and soda in hand, Sophie retreated to the lower lights and silence of her room to eat. She took the next day off of work to fully recover.

Chapter 5

Mal-Chin awoke early in the morning to the realization that he would be gone for much longer than a tour. He did not have a return date. A hollow sinking feeling flooded him. For all he knew, he would be permanently restarting his life in the U.S. That thought made him want to sleep in, but he needed to finish a few things. Notably, catching and packing the cats into their crates. This turned out to be a much more difficult task than he originally thought. The two creatures hid from him and fought going into their crates. "You're not going to the vet, calm down," Mal-Chin mumbled.

Hoping to conceal his identity, Mal-Chin put on all black including a ball cap and surgical mask. The ball cap also helped hide the fading blue in his hair. If he wasn't going to be in public view, he would let it just fade out and not have to waste time dying it again. A man carrying two cat crates with complaining occupants was hard to miss. Being built like a living Hercules statue did nothing to help the situation. The media descended on him as soon as he walked into the airport. He ducked his head trying to hurry to his plane. Mal-Chin path was blocked by journalist trying to get his picture and asking him questions. A few were bold enough to stick their cameras directly in his face. Fans begging him to stay soon followed the journalist and his manager, Kim Chanyeol, was no longer able to clear Mal-Chin's path on his own. Security escorted him the rest of the way to his gate. The mask hid Mal-Chin's irritation. He did not relax until he was safely onboard the plane.

Before booking his flight, Park Mal-Chin had done his research. For the cat's comfort, he chose a flight that would allow his cats to ride up front with him; the idea of having them packed away in the cold cargo bay was horrifying. A longer flight with several layovers allowed him a chance to check on his companions. There was no hurry. No strict schedule to keep. All he needed to worry about was making his flights. Throughout the trip the flight attendants offered treats and water. Cats got special treatment when they fly first class.

Landing in Lynchburg, Virginia, Mal-Chin searched for his ride. His items, except what was in his carry-on bag, were waiting for him at the house Mal-Chin purchased. He was supposed to rent a car or get a taxi but he was struggling to find one. Uber would not take him that far and taxis were scarce. This place was already frustrating him. When they visited years ago, it was not this difficult, but Beast was touring in a van then.

Just as he was heading to the car rental center, he caught a sight of a Korean man. At first, Mal-Chin thought it was Dae-o. He'd been relieved to see a familiar face. Then he realized it wasn't Dae-o. This man's hair was cut too short and he had a bit of a mustache. The man headed toward him. "Park Mal-Chin-*nim*?"

"Ah, yes." Mal-Chin nodded. "Are you Kang Minseok-*ssi*?"

"Yeah, nice to meet you. Did Dae-o forget to tell you I was coming?" Minseok asked.

Mal-Chin had forgotten about him, "No. I wasn't expecting to see you till later." A group passed them giving them dirty looks.

"Right. Do you need a hand with that?" Minseok gestured toward the two cat carriers and carry-on bag that Mal-Chin was trying to juggle. Mal-Chin gratefully handed over the carry-on bag still reluctant to let go of the cats.

Minseok was parked a distance from the airport, but the car was still warm when they reached it. The parking lot was much colder than Mal-Chin expected. The car they were riding in was beat up, far removed from the luxury vehicles he was used to, but Mal-Chin was just happy for a ride. When they put the cats in the back seat, Minseok ran a seat belt through each of the carrier tops and buckled them in. Mal-Chin questioned the action. "Oh, a friend taught me to do that. It was in desperate need of a vet and she didn't have a car. Poor thing didn't make it." Minseok told the tale as he climbed into the driver's seat.

"Good idea. Did you like her?" Mal-Chin asked trying to forget dead cats. Dae-o hinted to him to be as nosy as possible. It seemed the brothers were not as close as Mal-Chin thought.

They backed out of the parking spot, and were heading for the exit before he answered, "No, not my type. How's my little brother doing anyway?" Minseok adjusted the radio as they pulled out into the road. A commercial in English sounded strange to Mal-Chin's ears.

The drive to Danville was long, not to mention rough in Minseok's old car. The sky overhead was a dreary slate gray, everything looked dead. They drove for miles on a highway lined with dead trees, passed an abandoned church and exited the highway. Minseok informed him that they were in Danville at this point even though they were not in the city limits yet. A large lot selling mobile homes came into view. At first, Mal-Chin thought that it was a community of average houses with terrible lawns until he saw the sign. He was fascinated with the idea of mobile homes. He always envisioned the classic trailer style home like he saw in movies, but these looked nice. Farther into town, they passed the tank museum. There was an actual tank parked outside. Mal-Chin questioned if he would be allowed to get inside of it and look around. Minseok never visited it and did not know. The place was closed often.

More twists and turns took them out into the country. Trees hung close over unlined roads that snaked along hillsides. Minseok was navigating by GPS. Mal-Chin worried they would get lost. They finally turned down a dead-end street and came to a red brick house at the very end. A black luxury car was parked in the driveway. Mal-Chin wanted to take it for a test drive; he just needed to find the keys. Later, he would inspect the car carefully, for now he needed to get the cats inside.

The inside of the house was all bright white walls and hardwood floor. There were no personal items sitting around to make it look properly lived in. He would do that later, maybe. The cats crept across the floor as Mal-Chin and Minseok looked around the house. Every time Mal-Chin caught a glimpse of a cat or heard it, he made little noises to lure it out. There was a large master bedroom with sheets that were exact copies of those in Mal-Chin's Seoul apartment. One of the bedrooms had been turned into a studio and the other was furnished with basic white sheets. He was not expecting overnight visitors, but it was a nice touch.

A notebook with important information lay on the coffee table. Minseok added notes to this as they looked through them, scribbling in Korean. Mal-Chin's head began to spin, his neck felt tight. There was so much to take in at once that he struggled to comprehend it all. Minseok excused himself saying that Mal-Chin was probably tired. They exchanged numbers just in case Mal-Chin needed him for anything.

Mal-Chin looked out the large back window. In the summer, this was probably a nice view but everything looked cold and dead. It did, however, make a good backdrop for a selfie. He posted the picture to his official Instagram with the caption "*Landed safely. Time for a nap. It's cold outside stay in with me and stay warm!*" Within a few seconds comments began to pour in.

*Congratulations on a safe trip! Remember to eat well! - **@Imkiki***

*Our king is safe! - **@unofficialPMCfanpage***

*You look tired my sweet boy. Please get some rest. **@Beauty4life***

The comments put the first real smile of the day on his face, even if some of them were a little strange. No matter where he went, his fans could always be relied on to be there for him.

Over the years, he had gotten used to sleeping in hotel beds so going to sleep in a strange place did not bother him. It would be dark before he awoke to find the cats curled up with him. The poor creatures had gone through so much the last few days on the trip here. He ran a hand down each one trying to be comforting. He did not know if it worked, but he hoped so. They had never traveled with him before.

Days passed slowly for Mal-Chin. The notebook was turning out to be of little help. Yes, it told him where the stores were located, but did not help him find what he actually needed there. When he did find it, Mal-Chin had to deal with impatient clerks and customers. They were constantly annoyed with his struggle to make the correct change or his lacking English. He began to pick the clerks who either just ignored him or were kind to him. Mal-Chin learned that if he went to the grocery store early Saturday mornings that the elderly people shopping were more than willing to help and give him recipes. In exchange, all Mal-Chin needed to do was have a short talk with them and help load groceries into their cars.

Lonely. That's the only way that Mal-Chin could describe his days. He was used to the noise of the dorm he had shared with the other members of Beast. The sounds of video games, music in creation, arguments and laughter had filled his world. This was all backed by the sound of a city constantly moving. But, here, on a back road of a small Virginia town, everything was constant silence. For the first month he struggled to sleep; it was so quiet. This house was too big for one person. Minseok visited often and would sometimes bring his roommate John, who Mal-Chin suspected was not Minseok's roommate, but he did not feel comfortable asking. That broke the monotony of his days but still left him wanting.

What disturbed him more than the silence at night was when there were noises outside. It was never the sounds of cars but something moving in the yard. Like a creature stalking outside the house. One night he heard a sound like a little girl giggling; his mind ran to all the ghost stories *Halmeoni* Hayun told him as a child. The sound sent a shiver up his spine.

The highlight of Mal-Chin's days became his gym visits. The music blared through the building's personal playlist, which he drowned out with his own headphones. Common interest made it easy to fall in with the male regulars as they swapped advice. They were friendly and did not mind stopping to talk or working out alongside him. His accent seemed not to bother them. The exercise exhausted his body enough to keep his mind off his situation.

What excited Mal-Chin the most about going to the gym was not the exercise or the new acquaintances, but a woman. There were plenty of women there that readily gave him attention but this one was different. At first, he paid no attention to her. She moved about like a ghost, always in the background, passing behind him in the mirror, ducking her head as she passed a talking group. Then one day, she caught his attention and kept it. On his way in, he held the door for someone coming in behind him, not looking back to see who it was. A sweet "Thank you" in a soft accent reached his ears. He must have stopped dead in his tracks as he looked to see who it was. Bright green eyes looked up at him in surprise, half from his sudden stop and half from the way he was staring at her. She shifted, mumbled a polite hello then ducked her head and scurried around him. Briefly, the idea came to him that she was a fan or with the media but he soon gave this up.

"Who is that?' Mal-Chin asked one of his new gym friends. The small group turned to look at the woman, who glanced at them then away quickly.

"No clue." One answered, "She comes here all the time, keeps to herself though."

"I mean, she's cute and got all those curves but, come on." Another said. Something like jealousy flashed in his eyes. "You've got half the girls in this place chasing you. You can do better."

"She's just different looking." Mal-Chin added, noncommittally. Curvy was a good way to describe her. She had an hourglass frame, a little bit of a tummy and legs that perfectly shaped a pair of leggings. *Don't stare, don't stare.* Her face was always calm, no matter how red it got from exercise she never looked pained. At most, she expressed mild discomfort. Mal-Chin was fascinated by the calmness of her face. He wanted to know what as going on under the surface. The expression left little room to tell if she was tired or concentrating and the smile she gave in passing was washed out like she was smiling because she had to.

For a week, he puzzled over how to approach her. They had no friends in common to introduce them. Finally, Mal-Chin settled on doing this the American way and approaching on his own. He tried to talk to her. Usually her earbuds were in, the universal sign of "leave me alone," or she would hang her head and hurry past like she did not see him. He got his chance one day when she could not reach the pull-down cable to put the handle on it. Casually, he pulled it down for her, making sure to flex his bicep at eye level for her. It did not work. She taken the cable, looked at him curiously, and thanked him. All the flirty lines he thought up fell away and he mumbled a "you're welcome" before leaving. The incident did cause her to not shut him out as much. He would get a nod, a moment of eye contact and sometimes a quick greeting. Mal-Chin found a mystery. A woman that stole his words.

Chapter 6

Taking a deep breath, Sophie tried to let go of Virginia's comments right before she left for dinner. Virginia ridiculed her outfit as being too tight in the legs and making her tummy look big, she added that the red lipstick Sophie wore made her look older. That particular shade got Sophie compliments every time she wore it out. The outfit in question was a burgundy peasant shirt with ruffles around the neck and black fleece lined leggings that accentuated the fullness of her thighs. The top hit her breast and hung loose over her stomach. Virginia had no issue with it until Sophie wore it to a family gathering and her aunt turned up her nose at the outfit. Tonight, Sophie thought she looked good, until Virginia stepped in. Sophie let a breath out as she crossed the parking lot. Black heeled boots clacked as she walked, soreness already forming in her legs and butt from today's workout.

Late. Sophie was usually one of the first to arrive. The smell of cooking food and music sung in Spanish greeted her as she entered. It did not take her long to find the almost full circular booth where her college friends were seated. Faith and her wife, Sarah, were in the center, Anne with her signature slick backed ponytail and Scotty whose red frizzy hair matched his beard sat on one side. Sophie was trying to decide where to sit even before she reached the table. There was space for two more on Anne's side of the table so that was an option. If Minseok and John were on the other side she would sit there so Eileen and Devon, the newlyweds, could sit together. Not to mention John always told the best stories and made her feel included when she started to fade out. She could see Minseok talking to someone as she got closer. John was here. Her seat was decided.

Faith greeted her as she reached the table, "I was just thinking you won't comin'."

"Sorry I was icing a cake for Granny," Sophie swung into the booth on the side Minseok was on. As soon as she sat down, she realized that it was not John beside her. His body heat and presence were different. He felt safe, a rare occurrence for Sophie. The stranger stared at her just as surprised as she looked. "Oh, hi." Sophie recognized him. He was the new guy from the gym. The one with the nice butt that helped her with the cables. He nodded in reply.

"Sophie, this is my brother's friend, Mal-Chin. Have you two met?" Minseok glanced between them.

"We use the same gym," Mal-Chin replied. His eyes were glued to Sophie in a way that should have been uncomfortable, but Sophie could not look away from him either. Now that she was actually looking at him, Mal-Chin was the handsomest man she had ever seen. The skin of his oval shaped face was flawless, not an acne scar or blemish in sight. His dark doe shaped eyes were soft. Everything about him radiated a gentle presence, but his body looked hard and strong.

Eileen and Devon swung into the booth seats across from them. Sophie turned her attention elsewhere suddenly embarrassed. From across the table, Anne was giving her a mischievous grin. The group talked about the book they were all supposed to have read. Only Sophie, Faith, and Scotty had read it; Anne said she was not finished it. This dinner was supposed to work like a book club. It was really just an excuse for the group to get together. It was one of the few events that Sophie received an invite to. She tended to be on the outside of the group. Mal-Chin sat in silence watching all of this. They soon became the loud table but their waiter didn't seem to mind as he laughed and joked along with them.

As they ordered food, Sophie noticed Mal-Chin was struggling and made a few suggestions of what she thought was good. This gave her an opening to help him pick something, he was getting stuck on words like "smothered" and "sauteed". The boyish smile that lit his face was cute.

"Girl, it's Saturday. Stop teaching." Faith called out to her.

"Can't help it. How's teaching at Boon going?" Sophie asked. Sophie student-taught there in college and was convinced she did not want to teach middle school. She was wrong.

"I love it." Faith answered. The teachers in the group, and there were several, started swapping teaching stories. Once the food arrived, the conversation grew louder. Mal-Chin listened to it all trying to keep up with the conversation.

"So, how have you liked it over here so far?" Sophie asked Mal-Chin, she had been leaning around him to talk to Minseok and remembered what it felt like to be the outsider in a group of friends.

"It is different." Mal-Chin started, "Very quiet. My cats like all the animals outside."

Sophie's face lit up, "You've got cats?" Nothing better than a potential friend that liked cats.

That was all the invitation Mal-Chin needed to pull out his phone and show them off. Sophie tried not to notice all the shirtless selfies and suggestively angled pictures as he scrolled. There were even a few where he was seated and the camera was at crotch level. "The white one is Aruem and the" he looked to the right word, "lined one is Ramyun." He got embarrassed. "He was named that when I got him. I like noodles. I needed the cat named for noodles." Sophie cooed at how cute they were. She was patient with him as he told her all about struggling to get them over here.

Eileen pulled her attention away from their conversation, "That pose in your last Instagram post was impressive." Sophie bashfully thanked her.

"What post?" Scotty asked, he was tucking his phone back into his jeans pocket after checking on his son. Eileen pulled out her phone and showed him. In the picture, Sophie was standing on her yoga mat with her arm hooked under her leg and her leg up in the air almost pointing straight up. It was a bird of paradise pose. What they could not see was how long Sophie fought to get her balance then get her leg straight as possible for that picture. It still was not as impressive as the yoga people she followed on Instagram, but she was getting there. "Damn," was all Scotty said.

Anne leaned over looking at it, "Oh, I should learn to do that. I can think of a few people that would like it." She smiled naughtily, her eyebrows raising and falling.

"So, does that mean you're seeing someone new?" Sarah shot across. Anne just smiled in response. She tried to keep her love life private now. In college, Sophie met Anne after they sat together at lunch and Anne told her too much about her sex life.

"But, like, we should all go take a yoga class together," Eileen added giving Sophie an enthusiastic smile.

"Oh, hell no," Faith disagreed, "Y'all ain't getting me all pretzeled up."

As they were having this conversation, Devon and Mal-Chin began a discussion about weightlifting. Devon was a personal trainer and wanted to know what program Mal-Chin was following to get in such good form. They soon pulled Sophie and Eileen in as the only other gym rats at the table.

Once all the food was eaten, and the conversation hit a lull the group paid their bills and headed outside. In true Southern fashion, they stood around in the parking lot chatting before saying their goodbyes. Sophie hunkered down into her jacket trying to hide from the cold night air as she traded numbers with Mal-Chin. "If you need help with anything, let me know," Sophie offered politely. It was an empty promise, one that she expected him not to actually use. Sophie said her goodbye's and hurried to her car. It was still too cold for her. She spotted Mal-Chin in her rear view.

A bubbly feeling ran all over her and a grin lit her face for a second. She took a breath. *Calm down. He just wants a friend. He's just nice, and lonely.* By the time she reached the stop light at the bottom of the hill, the bubbly feeling was gone. Something sank out of her chest into her stomach. She pressed her lips into a tight line, her fingernails biting into the steering wheel before she realized she might leave a mark. The car was not paid off yet and needed to last her many years.

***

Sundays were the day that Virginia Coleman cooked a large family meal. Occasionally, Sophie would show up and try to help, but Sunday dinner was Virginia's territory, and she would accept no help. It was a casual affair, there was no set time but everyone tended to show up around 12:30 as soon as Virginia finished cooking.

Robbie and his daughter, Jessica, started talking the moment they stepped through the door. They did not stop even as they ate, even as others tried to add to their monologues. Jessica was the family beauty. She was a pretty child and had grown up to be broad shouldered and heavy set. Jessica's blonde hair, rosy cheeks and blue eyes held her status as the pretty grandchild. Sophie quietly listened as Robbie droned on about the new expensive tool he was going to buy, for reasons that Ford would later say did not make sense, and Jessica talked about everything she was going to purchase at Target and why. When Robbie's wife, Carol, and their son, Conner, arrived the group grew even louder.

"Oh," Carol said suddenly, "you won't believe what my brother said now." She shook her head blinking her eyes rapidly, her nose held up in the air.

"He's an asshole," Robbie yelled over everyone else, "I wish he would call me, I'd tell him where to go. Jessica, tell 'em what he said."

Jessica began telling the same story that Virginia told Sophie Friday afternoon. Sophie began to zone out. She nodded at the right moments and left comments like "That's crazy" and "Wow" so she would not hear about being rude to them later. Ford looked about as bored as she did, but he somehow was above reproach for not listening.

In the middle of this, Sophie's phone went off; the message header read "Mall Shin." A small smile graced her face as she opened it, "*Are you going to the gym today?*"

"*No, rest day.*"

"*Okay. I was thought we could together,*" Mal-Chin replied. It took Sophie a second to catch his meaning. She nodded to herself when she figured it out.

"*Sorry. Yoga tomorrow.*"

Mal-Chin replied with a picture of him sitting on one of the gym benches with a handlebar mustache drawn on his face. Sophie chuckled to herself; Robbie shot her a look. She did not notice the glare, but she noticed Mal-Chin's shorts that were pulled up enough to show off his muscular thighs. She looked away, and reminded herself she should not have been looking. *"Lol why did you ask me if I was coming when you're already there?"*

"Just wanted to know. Tell me about yoga class."

Sophie sent him the information about how to sign up for yoga and how to get there. She stopped listening to her family completely at this point. A smile unknowingly climbed onto her face, and she got that forward slouch that people get when engrossed in their phones.

"Who are you texting so much?" Virginia asked, there was an annoyed edge to her voice.

"Oh, Mal-Chin. Just moved here. Minseok brought him to dinner last night." Sophie answered.

"Sophie went to that Mexican place up on the hill with her Averett friends." Virginia told the rest of the group. Virginia struggled to remember the names of the Mexican restaurants and called them by their locations.

"Oh, fun. Anyway..." Carol went back to talking about whatever the current subject was. Sophie felt tension release when they did not question her on the outing, yet at the same time she wanted to share. They moved on to bad mouthing someone named Mary who may not have been legitimate and lived next door to her sister, neither of who Sophie knew. Sophie enjoyed good gossip, but only if she knew who was involved. Her co-workers usually brought her all the workplace gossip because they trusted her not to tell and she listened well.

Sophie left the table and took up her favorite spot in the living room, a rocking recliner. As a distraction from the gossip in the other room, Sophie scrolled through her Instagram feed. She checked the likes on her last gym selfie then looked at the story feeds. Minseok posted pictures from last night's group dinner. Oddly, he left Mal-Chin out of all the pictures. That wasn't like Minseok. A grimace came to her face as she realized how large and ugly she looked.

The rest of the family migrated to the living room at some point during all of this. There was a lull in the conversation. "Oh, Sophie," Carol started, she settled on the couch with her legs crossed and a piece of cake on a Styrofoam plate balanced on her knee, "Rob has a work friend he wants you to meet." She shook her head like she was trying to shake her hair from her eyes, "He's got Thursday off and wants to meet you then."

Sophie sighed internally, "I'm not really dating right now."

"Ugh, well," Carol's nose literally stuck up into the air, "we already told him you'd be there."

Chapter 7

Beast's new album and music video released late Sunday night. Fans posted online that Mal-Chin's name had been removed from the list of musicians. The album was recorded before he left and his voice was still on the tracks. Even the music video contained his voice; they tried to hide that it by having Minkyo walking away from the camera as his lines were played. Minkyo sang his lines in the live performances as well. He'd been removed from the photo album and edited out of the group pictures. The outcry from his fans over what they called an injustice was immediate. When the usual rounds of variety show performances started, there was no mention of the scandal or Mal-Chin's disappearance. He had become a taboo subject.

It was spite that moved his feet to the makeshift studio set up at the back of the house. Putting everything else aside, except for the hungry cry of his cats, he got to work. He ignored the ping of his phone, the time, the changing lights and worked. The words flowed at a fevered pitch. Whether they were songs worth producing or not would have to wait till later. Mal-Chin needed to do this, needed to get his career back.

The room was soon only lit by the light of the computer screen. He checked the time finding that it was late at night. He stood up. The breath he took felt like the first in hours. Stretching his hands over his head, a few muscles popped. Stretch. He had forgotten. Quickly, he checked his phone and found a single message from Sophie, *"Did you still want to go to yoga?"* It was too late now. The class was well over. Mal-Chin missed his chance.

He made instant ramen as he replied, *"I lost time. Sorry."* His mind was already trying to formulate some excuse. Maybe he could just say his phone had reset to Korean time. It was a flimsy excuse, but better than nothing if needed. Somehow saying he was working did not sound good enough, especially since no one here knew he was a singer. With the mood he was in today, he was liable to tell everything.

"It's ok," was her only reply. What did that mean? No emojis, no punctuation. Just those two words. Arin would have told him off by now. His relationship with her was different and their time had been very limited. Maybe Sophie was mad, just in a different way. He slurped the noodles trying to let it go.

***

The gym was empty for a Tuesday afternoon. The chilly rain was the deciding factor keeping most people home. Mal-Chin picked a lull in the rain to go. He was there for 2 hours. Every muscle in his legs and butt was already screaming. The distraction was good. If he just worked hard enough, he wouldn't think of Beast's new album. The sound of the rain slowed so Mal-Chin picked that moment to pack his things hoping he could get out before the rain picked back up.

By the time he left the men's locker room, the rain was pouring again. Mal-Chin stood in front of the window and watched the rain coming down so hard that it hid the parking lot. The occasional flash of lightning gave the parking lot an eerie glow. His umbrella was going to be of little use in this downpour. "Hey, I'm gonna be late..... it's pouring..... yeah it's bad here...." A sweet-sounding voice spoke to someone; he recognized it. "No.... I think Carol still has it..... ok.... I will... be there as soon as I can." Sophie hung up the phone. She was sitting at one of the counter height tables as she looked out over the gym. Mal-Chin was certain she had not noticed him. He wondered how he did not see her on the gym floor.

All the color was drained from her face and, if it had not been for the sheen of sweat coating her body, Mal-Chin would have thought she'd just arrived. That pale look was familiar to him, it was the look of someone who had overdone it. The fingers of one of her hands were absentmindedly massaging her left temple. Well, his legs were tired. "Can I join you?"

Sophie stopped scrolling with a panicked expression on her face. Once she realized it was him, she relaxed a little, "Yeah, sure." She laid her phone down next to her almost empty water bottle. "Are you waiting out the rain too?" It was a silly question.

Mal-Chin sat facing the window. "Yes, umm... sorry about yesterday."

"It's fine. I figured you didn't feel like getting out." She took a sip of water as she turned her head to look out the window. "I go every Monday if you change your mind."

Mal-Chin's eyes followed a stray strand of hair as it fell over her shoulder and ran down her chest. *Don't look, don't look.* Mal-Chin told himself mentally. The green spaghetti strap top did little to hide her ample cleavage. He tried to find something else to look at. But, damn, it was a lot. Mal-Chin looked at the T.V. over the reception desk. His ears were turning red.

He started digging through his gym bag, "Another time then?"

Sophie looked at him like she forgot what he was talking about, "Oh, yeah. Just text me when you want to."

He came back with two white flavor packets with Korean writing on them. "Here." He offered both to her and she picked one.

"Thanks" she turned it over in her hands, "What is it?"

"Electrolyte pack," He demonstrated opening his and sucking the contents out.

Sophie looked at it skeptically. She copied his actions. Her nose scrunched up and her bottom lip pouted out as she fought not to spit it out. Sophie's hand covered her mouth before she took a big gulp of water. It was the most expression she had shown. Mal-Chin was cracking up next to her. Sophie gasped her hands started to flap up and down at the wrist, her fingers stiff, "That's nasty!" She took another sip of water. Mal-Chin laughed harder his eyes and nose scrunched up. The rain slowed to a drizzle, but they did not notice.

"I-I forgot mention that," Mal-Chin spluttered out. "What was this?" He mimicked her hand flap.

Sophie was laughing now too. "I don't know." They calmed. Sophie took another sip of water. "Ugh! I'm never gonna get that taste out of my mouth!" Mal-Chin cracked up again.

Mal-Chin leaned back in his chair and looked at her. "Since I gave you something nasty. Can I buy you dinner?"

Sophie looked surprised and shifted. "Oh, I can't. Granny is having family dinner night," she looked at him apologetically.

"I understand. Another time." He nodded then looked out the window. "The rain has slowed down."

Sophie looked over at the window before hopping down from her seat. She gathered her things, "Guess I won't be too late." She pulled her hood over her head as she stepped outside.

"Where's your umbrella?"

"Oh, I don't have it."

"You can use mine."

"No. You need it and its barely raining now. I'll be ok." Sophie reassured.

He opened the umbrella even though they were still under the awning, "Let me walk you."

Sophie looked out at her car then back at him. It was a short walk; she could handle a short walk close to him. "Ok." She nodded at the surprised look on his face. They repositioned their bags to be on the outside of them, moved in close. Sophie's shoulders pulling in before they stepped into the rain. Mal-Chin adjusted his stride to match hers.

They were soon at her red car. Her keys jingled in her hands as she spoke, "Thanks. Sorry again about turning you down." She opened the car door and threw her bag into the passenger seat.

"It's ok. Another time." Mal-Chin nodded then watched as she climbed into the car and backed out.

Chapter 8

She had never been one to obsess over idols. They were larger-than-life characters to her. Someone on the screen to look at, to listen to but who had very little impact on her life. Throughout most of her middle and high school years she never understood the fanatics of her classmates as they swooned over their bias, plastering pictures of them on their personal belongings. It was all nonsense. Silly people pretending to have something they could not.

Then she laid eyes on Park Mal-Chin. Beast was appearing on her mother's favorite talk show after the release of their second album. Suddenly, she understood. She could not take her eyes off him. From the muscular build to the sweet goofy smile, all she could see was perfection. Usually, she hated blond dyed hair on men, but it brought out the deep brown of his eyes. When he winked at the camera, she just knew that it was meant for her. By the end of the week, she learned to pick out Mal-Chin's voice in Beast's songs and was working her way through every YouTube video she could find of him.

That was five years ago. Now, the walls of her room were covered with his posters and fan cards. Any merchandise she could get with Park Mal-Chin's face on it she bought. Once she went to a fan meet and got his signature. Too nervous to speak, she barely garbled out an "I love you." She left with a thrumming heart when he made a finger heart, given that big bright smile and told her he loved her too. That was all the proof she needed. She heard the message loud and clear. As other girls greeted him, she realized they were in her way. She would have to get rid of them.

As soon as Mal-Chin left Beast, she turned her back on the group. Their only use was to get information about Mal-Chin, but it seems they were not allowed to talk about him. They avoided any mention of his name and did not read questions about him during their V-lives. Useless. He always deserved better than this fake group that pretended to be his family. Beast was out of the way for now. That was step one. She hated that he was alone but that wouldn't be for long.

Rewatching videos of him boarding the plane from multiple angles, she tried to figure out where he had gone. It was becoming frustrating. The only other clue was the picture he posted once he was settled in his new home. After wishing she could really be there to stay in with him like his captioned stated, she analyzed the background but only found trees. Her poor baby, alone in some terrible house with dead trees outside his window. She would not let him be alone for too long.

Chapter 9

Today was exhausting. Sophie Gregory's students were rowdy all day and it just got worse as the day dragged on. Half seemed to have eaten too much sugar, and the other half were in the mood to argue. The students were beginning to feel the pressure as teachers put more emphasis on computer test scores and released practice SOL tests than they had in past years. She pitied their situation. No middle schooler should have this much stress on them, but she did not know what to do to relieve the situation.

There was no car dancing on the way home today, just exhaustion. Sophie's ears tuned out the music. All she wanted was a nap. With a groan, she remembered she was supposed to go meet Robbie's friend from work. Maybe she would have time to at least get a quick nap before she went. As soon as she was home, she took off her work clothes and flopped into bed, setting her alarm to get her up in time to go. Sophie debated not going. Coming up with a good excuse seemed like more trouble than just going. Besides, it would just delay the inevitable.

The night air was still cold enough for Sophie to need a jacket. Noah picked the restaurant; it was a chain sports bar known for its chicken wings. Sophie took that to mean it was a casual event. She'd simply freshened her makeup and dressed in jeans and a floral pattern top. It was the type of outfit she wore to family events. She looked Noah up ahead of time, he was an average southern boy, slightly pudgy with a scruffy beard and, in most pictures, clad in camo.

He greeted her as she arrived at the table. The smell of his cologne met her before he did. He put some effort into cleaning himself up, his hair parted to the side and gelled over and his clothes the standard khaki pants and polo. Noah was generically handsome in that way that he looked like a contestant on the Bachelorette but with a belly instead of a six pack. He looked her over like she was a prize-winning cow as she settled into the booth opposite him. "Remind me to thank Coleman for this." Noah said with a big smile on his face. Those eyes were not on her face. Maybe he was not looking where she thought.

"Oh, um, thanks." Sophie shifted and looked around not sure what to talk about. "So, you work with my uncle?" That was the best she could come up with. Strangers were difficult for her to talk to, and dates made it worse. What did she know about this guy?

"Yeah, Coleman's been training me," Noah launched into talking about what he learned from Robbie then backed up into talking about how he got the job at the factory and what he did before that. It did not take much to keep him talking. Just nod at the right time and leave a comment or two. From the corner of her eye, she saw Minseok, Scotty, Devon, Mal-Chin and John take a table not too far off. Seeing John and Minseok on a rare outing together made her happy. With their hectic schedules the two did not get much time together. Though, she did think it was odd that they were out with the guys instead of a date together.

Noah was rambling about four wheeling now. Sophie made a comment about her students liking to go riding. "Oh, I forgot you were a teacher." Noah commented around a mouth full of food. "Wish my teachers would have looked like you."

Sophie looked at him stunned. Had he really just told her that? Was it supposed to be a compliment? "I'm sure you wouldn't think that if I was your teacher."

"Nah, all of my teachers were old and ugly. Oh, god, I remember Mrs. Strader was the meanest thing I've ever met. She used to stay on me all the time; sit down, stop talking, hands to yourself," he laughed. Sophie did not really respond. So, he had been one of those kids. Thankfully, he was distracted by whatever was on the screen in the corner of the room. He got up suddenly, "I gotta piss. Be right back." Sophie tried her best not to let her nose curl as she nodded her head in acknowledgment. Sophie sunk into the booth with a sigh when he walked away. He was exhausting. Her ears felt full. She debated just quickly paying the bill and disappearing. That would have been rude. Maybe fake an emergency to leave? No, he knew her family. Noah could just ask them about it later.

"Girl, what on earth?" John was leaning against her side of the booth. He was still dressed in his button up from work. "What happened to you not dating?" He put a hand on his waist.

Sophie let out a sigh, "My aunt and uncle set me up. He won't shut up." Time to think up another escape plan.

"Hm, I noticed that. He looks like a creep," John looked in the direction of the bathroom. "Will you be ok? You can come join us if you need to." John nodded his head toward the table. They were all watching Sophie and John.

Sophie's chest suddenly felt tight. "Um, I'll be ok. It's only once, right?" She put on a brave face. Noah was coming back now; he was looking at John confused.

John suddenly said goodbye and returned to their table. Noah gave him the side eye as he slide back into their booth. "Who was that? Looks fruity."

"Just a friend from college," Sophie answered with a shrug. Noah rolled his eyes at this comment. Mentally, she was imagining stabbing Noah with a fork for that comment about John. That wouldn't have ended well.

When the check finally came, Sophie insisted on splitting the bill. There was no way she would allow him to have a free meal to hold as collateral. Noah tried to exchange numbers with her, which she dodged with precision. She used the excuse that her phone was dead and that she could not remember her number off the top of her head. It worked, for now. "So, what are you doing the rest of the night?" Noah asked suddenly, his eyebrows raising.

Sophie mentally rolled her eyes, "I've got papers to grade and work tomorrow so, that."

***

Bing, Bing, Bing. Sophie did not even reach her classroom door before her phone was going off again. She left the sound off when the students were in the room. They could not have their phones so, in her mind, it was only fair that she did not use hers either. She pulled the phone out of her jacket pocket as she headed down the hall. Her watch used to display messages for her but the software was outdated and that function no longer worked.

It was Noah, all three times *"Hey, it's Noah. I had a good time the other night,"* Then, *"Haven't heard from you since Thursday. Been a few,"* followed by, *"What are you up today?"* Finally, *"I bet them kids are driving you crazy. We should get some drinks."* To her annoyance, Robbie or Carol had given out her number. *"What time do you get off?"* The next one read. Sophie did not answer any of Noah's messages, but he just kept texting her. Part of her wondered if she was being a bitch and should answer at least one of them. Maybe she got the wrong impression Thursday.

Bing. Maybe he was just annoying.

She rolled her shoulders and neck listening to everything pop. Today was a stations day, meaning lots of noise and movement. The largest part was keeping groups on task. She tried to separate the buddies, but some kids could get a wall off task. Fifteen minutes to finish seven stations was never enough time. They would have to finish tomorrow.

"Ms. Gregory," Mrs. Barbour called from the seventh-grade lounge door. *Damn, caught.* Sophie peeked back into the lounge. She was standing outside reading the multiple texts so she could not pretend she did not hear her. Mrs. Barbour was sitting at one of the computers that lined two of the walls in the lounge. She had obviously been either waiting for Sophie or on her way to meet her.

"Yes?" Sophie tried to discreetly look at the screen to get an idea of what Mrs. Barbour was looking at. School Assessment, the program they used to give tests online, was open to her information. It was redder than Sophie remembered.

"I was just looking at your last test scores. Have you seen them?" Mrs. Barbour gestured to the screen, the multiple bracelets on her wrist jiggled.

"Yeah, they really struggled with the second passage."

"Why do you think that?" Mrs. Barbour crossed her legs and hooked her arms around the top knee.

"Well, it's an older passage, like maybe 19th century old. It's lengthy, there was a lot of words they didn't know and some of the concepts they just didn't understand." Sophie already talked to Mr. Worley, whose students struggled as well. He agreed with her.

"Well, what are you going to do about it?" Mrs. Barbour cocked her head to the side.

Sophie's breath caught for a second. Incompetent. That's how this woman made her feel all the time. "We're doing stations today and tomorrow to cover the most missed SOL strands," that was a favorite phrase for Mrs. Barbour. "Probably, when we finish stations tomorrow, I'll take some time to go over that passage and explain parts they didn't understand."

Mrs. Barbour questioned her on why a few students' scores came down. One was not feeling well, one was just having a bad day, and another was burnt out from testing. That was not the correct answer. In Mrs. Barbour's mind, these students should be able to perform at any given time. Sophie wanted to scream *THEY'RE KIDS!* To the school board, and Mrs. Barbour, they were just test scores and numbers on a paper. That made Sophie's blood boil.

The sun was beginning to set as Sophie drove to her yoga studio. Another message came in from Noah, her car read it for her, *"I know u r busy ill meet you. Where u @"* Sophie rolled her eyes. She was not going to answer that one either. Her shoulders tensed just thinking of him showing up at her yoga studio.

She paralleled park up the street, almost at the next stop light. Firefly Yoga was on the second floor of a small building. On the first floor was a small women's clothing boutique. The outfits hanging in their window were pretty. Sophie debated going inside but they were closed when she arrived. The store looked expensive and, she reasoned, the clothes probably would not fit her frame or would not look good on her.

"Sophie?" A man's voice called from behind her. Sophie tensed before turning.

Chapter 10

Park Mal-Chin looked over his work disappointed. Nothing he had written in his spite driven frenzy last week looked or sounded right anymore. He picked out a few pieces he thought were salvageable and set to work. With no album theme, Mal-Chin was free to create whatever he wanted. He picked up one of the songs, it was sad, but he saw potential in it. Right now, it was a base level heart break song, based on his loss of Arin but he dug deeper. Mal-Chin brought out the worst pain he felt. The break from his band, the loss of his fans. He used the emotion from that to rewrite the lyrics.

Leaning back, he thought about what beat to put to it. He wanted something slow, something that would convey the heartbreak he felt. He looked up at the ceiling. Was it too much? What if it was too sad and made his fans cry? He did not want to do that. But the songs needed to be something new, something different to impress the CEO and to not lose his job. If he made something that sounded completely different than his style with Beast, he could prove to the CEO that he was worth keeping. His legs started to fidget.

Overwhelmed, he removed himself from the studio. He flipped through Netflix for a movie to watch, scrolled through his social media pages. but only came across pictures of Beast and Arin living their lives seemingly happy as could be. They abandoned him in this boring town. Relax. He just needed to relax. What time was it? Mal-Chin checked his phone. There was enough time, it was Monday. Dressing quickly, he hurried out. GPS sent him to the wrong side of town. The librarian at the university was nice enough to give him directions. He finally found the right place and a parking spot a block up.

The air felt sticky but somehow refreshing as he made his way down the store lined street. Wedged between two antique shops, an Italian restaurant played classic rock music for its empty outside dining area. The smell of pizza floated into the air. J.E. popped into his mind; he liked old American rock music, and this place gave off his type of vibe.

That was when he spotted her. Mal-Chin was so preoccupied with the building fronts that he had not notice the familiar figure in the purple jacket. "Sophie?" He watched her tense before turning around.

Her whole body relaxed. "Oh, hey. You decided to come." She wore a pastel purple tank and yoga pants. The combination was a stark contrast to her usual dark gym clothes. It brought out a different tone to her skin.

"I got lost but I made it. But," he looked around, "but where is it?"

"Upstairs." Sophie opened the door that looked like it should have led into the clothes store. It opened to a stairwell. Sophie hurried up the steep stairs. Mal-Chin followed unsure of the wall that had gaps between some of the bricks. They turned right at the top. The studio was one long room with a practice floor partitioned by a curtain on the right and a sitting area on the left. There was also a set of steps that went up another floor, but they had merchandise blocking access to it. Mal-Chin wondered if there was another business up there. The roof creaking throughout their class confirmed this for him until someone made a joke about the ghost upstairs.

A hostess in gym wear greeted them warmly. Sophie signed in on a wall-mounted tablet, but Mal-Chin needed to register in person and sign some paperwork practically stating that he would not sue them if he got hurt. That was worrying. *There was no way to get hurt doing yoga. It was just stretching right?*

They deposited their belongings and phone into little cubbies to the left of the hostess's station. Barefoot, they padded into the practice area, Sophie rolling out her black moon phases mat next to his rented mat. As far as yoga classes go $13 wasn't too bad. Mal-Chin remembered the dancer he used to date paying the equivalent of $20 for a class.

Mal-Chin sat cross legged on his mat, taking in the view from the large windows in front of him. It was all old brick buildings; one had an old Pepsi logo painted on the side. Later when they were standing, he was able to see the fro-yo place across the street. His eyes wandered around the room trying to find something to look at. The few chakra tapestries on the wall got boring quickly.

He took a deep breath; his body was already relaxing. The sound of others arriving whispered through the air just above the low murmur of music. A row was added right against the wall with the windows, a single mat in the center was left unoccupied. Sophie leaned back on her hands, her legs out in front of her as she pedaled her feet up and down. The sides and bottom of her feet were bright red. Mal-Chin didn't ask, his feet looked like that at the end of dance practices.

"I'm glad you decided to join me."

"Ah, I just needed to get out."

"That makes sense," Sophie agreed then waved at someone across the room.

The instructor made her way to the front of the room. She was a tall slender woman with thick curly hair in maybe her mid 30's. The low murmur in the room quickly ended, Sophie turned on her activity tracker and sat up crossing her legs. The instructor introduced herself, told that the class was multi-level meaning there was beginner to advanced practitioners in the room, and a few other pieces of information including that something called child's pose was always available if they needed it. He had no clue what that meant.

They were instructed to take slow measured breaths; the instructor counted out the breaths until they got the rhythm of it. The collective sound reminded Mal-Chin of the ocean. They were asked to set an intention for their practice if they wanted to; the instructor would cue them to remember this intention throughout the practice. Mal-Chin just wanted to relax, so he set an intention to find peace. If he was going to do this, might as well go all the way. Peeking at Sophie he wondered what her intention was. The class was soon flowing through rounds of vinyasas and into warrior poses. Mal-Chin felt a tension he did not know he was holding release and heard a few pops in his muscles as well. He did not realize how tight his muscles were. After a particularly loud pop, he heard a soft snorted laugh leave Sophie. A wince graced his face as he tried to get the poses perfect. The instructor reminded them to relax their faces and use the cork blocks as needed. About halfway through, the instructor gave them time to play around with crow pose; a hand balancing pose involving curling your legs up to your chest while balancing on your hands. Mal-Chin did not try it; it just looked hard. Sophie nearly face-planted but caught herself at the last second on her forearms. Mal-Chin moved to catch her, practically throwing his water bottle down. She sat back onto her feet with a look of accomplishment before trying it again. The instructor soon cued them to move on. Sweat was falling in beads down his neck and chest.

Night had fallen and the room was lit only by the overhead tea lights by the time they laid back in savasana. Mal-Chin thought he could melt into the floor and just rest there all night. He was so relaxed.

"When you're ready, roll onto your favorite side," the instructor's voice was barely a whisper yet carried throughout the whole room. Mal-Chin rolled to his left. He was not ready to get up but rolling over did sound nice. His eyes opened slowly. Next to him, Sophie rolled to her right and was curled peacefully. Sophie could have been asleep. When her eyes finally opened, a big smile painted across her flushed face. His heart thumped erratically.

The group sat up crossing their legs, then bowed to the instructor with a mumbled "Namaste". The magic was broken. The instructor went over upcoming events as students rolled up mats and returned yoga blocks that were not needed for the next group. The hostess took Mal-Chin's mat.

Out of the practice area, Sophie and Mal-Chin retrieved their belongings. The instructor chatted to Mal-Chin awhile, getting to know him better before getting distracted by the next class trickling in. Sophie and Mal-Chin ducked out the door to avoid the arriving class.

"So, what do you think?" Sophie asked as they stepped into the chilly night air.

"Ah, it was fun," His heart was still doing flips. "I'm hungry. Are you hungry?"

"Trying to get that dinner you promised out of the way huh?" Sophie joked. Mal-Chin just scratched the back of his head. He was surprised by how sweaty it was. "Ok, do you like pizza?" She gestured toward the Italian restaurant Mal-Chin had passed on the way in, "Or, you know, Italian food in general."

Dellano's, the restaurant that was playing classic rock, was dark on the inside. The framed pictures on the wall were lit from inside and the chalk menu with today's specials had an almost neon glow to it. It was a narrow restaurant with a line of booths on one side and a line of tables pushed up against the other side. Instead of a hostess desk, there was a small bar at the front. Mal-Chin and Sophie were seated at a booth about mid-way back. Sophie deposited her yoga mat in her car and sat her wallet and silenced phone in a little pile on the table. Sophie took a moment to fix her ponytail so that it wasn't as messy. Unknowingly, she started humming off tune to the rock song that was playing. The dried sweat on them left both feeling gross and like they shouldn't be sitting in a restaurant right now.

They discussed pizza toppings as they read through the menu. Sophie closed her copy, "You decide, surprise me."

"What if I pick something strange?"

Sophie's face went blank for a second, "Didn't think of that. But you could only get so weird." She shrugged.

Mal-Chin raised an eyebrow like that was a challenge. A little mischievous smile crossed his face. When the waiter came, he ordered pepperoni, ham, onions, green peppers, spinach, mushrooms, and broccoli. "Weird enough?" He smiled playfully.

Sophie nodded, "At least you didn't order pineapple."

"Almost did but," he made a face of disgust, "I just couldn't."

"Have you tried it?"

"No, you?"

"No, but it sounds nasty."

"Does it sound," he flapped his hands his fingers stiff, "nasty?"

Sophie laughed embarrassed; she thought he had forgotten that, "My babies pick on me for that too."

"Babies?" Mal-Chin stopped flapping his hands.

"Oh, no." Sophie shook her head, "My students. I teach middle school. One time, I had a group get into an argument about what leeches looked like," A sparkle filled her eyes as she spoke. Mal-Chin could have listened to her talk about anything as long as that light was in her eyes. "So, I looked it up to end the argument, which the girl was starting to get super frustrated, and I did that" she flapped for effect just as the waiter brought their food. They giggled like kids almost caught doing something they were not supposed to when the waiter walked off. "Sorry, I get too excited about work sometimes," Sophie added before taking a bite of pizza. The restaurant made a good base pizza and, while the broccoli was an odd edition, the toppings were tasty. "What about you? What do you do?" Sophie looked him over.

Mal-Chin froze. If he told her he was a musician she would be able to look up his scandal. Sophie might not want to be around him if she believed it. "I'm in media."

"Media?" Sophie questioned around a mouth full of pizza. "Like you're a camera man?"

"Sort of. I help on shows."

A family of four walked past. A tall broad-shouldered blonde girl did a double take when she saw Sophie, who waved at her. It was the distraction Mal-Chin needed. Hearing Jessica speak, the rest turned to see who she was talking to. "What are you doing here?" Carol asked, her eyes cut to Mal-Chin long enough to register that he was not Noah.

"You had yoga tonight." Connor, the 13-year-old, added. Connor was red faced and sweaty from football practice.

"Yeah, we decided to get pizza, Oh," Sophie made quick introductions.

"The hell did you get on that pizza?" Robbie blurted out.

"She said surprise her." Mal-Chin stated looking pleased with himself.

"Looks, interesting," Carol added, her nose visibly curling up. "We'd better get to our table. Nice meeting you," they left quickly.

Sophie was already anticipating the lecture that would come from this run in. Her fingers crinkled up her napkin, "Oops...." She mumbled this to herself.

"What?" Mal-Chin asked around a mouthful of food. He noticed the change in her. The walls were back up.

"Nothing."

Reaching across the table. Mal-Chin lightly ran his fingers over the hand that was worrying the napkin. Confusion came over her face as she watched his calloused fingertips run the length of her hands then reverse. The waiter returned and they separated. Sophie could feel the ghost of his touch on her skin. It felt nice. His fingers were warm and gentle.

On the way back to his car, Mal-Chin received a text from Minkyo asking him if he had looked at the gossip columns today. Mal-Chin had not but now he was curious. He told Minkyo as much before driving home. The reply surprised him.

Minkyo sent him a link to a Dispatch article. Arin's smiling face appeared beside that of S.J., the leader of the biggest boy group in the world right now.

S.J of SLS announces relationship with Purple-Pink's sweet-heart, Arin.

He wanted to throw his phone across the room. That was quick. Most idols did not announce relationships unless they were serious or were caught. Mal-Chin's mind went back to the night she'd left him. Were they already together then? Dispatch tended to run scandal articles but this one looked trustworthy. The pictures attached looked more than friendly. They did not seem to be trying to hide it either.

"Is this real?" Mal-Chin texted.

"Seems to be. It's all over the news." Minkyo replied then added *"Your scandal hasn't been mentioned since. So, that's good."*

"Great." Covering his eyes, he sank onto the couch. Mal-Chin had thought, if he successfully launched a solo career, Arin would come back to him. His future was with her, then she walked out on him for the last time. Now, there was no plan. Beast was moving forward and so was Arin. There was no space left in their worlds for him. Sophie's unguarded smile flashed into his mind. *Is that really what I want now?*

Chapter *11*

It started innocently enough. A phone call, a mumble in Korean and a hang up. Wrong number. No question as to who answered. The speaker on the other end did not recognize his voice. Mal-Chin put the call out of his mind. Then the text messages started. The first was simple enough. It was a cute picture of ducks in the river. He smiled at it then realized it was an unknown number. He texted back *"wrong number"* and went back to sleep. His phone blew up. Message after message lit up his night darkened room. Pictures and declarations of love flowed in one after another.

Mal-Chin felt a knot in his stomach. He was not dealing with a wrong number; this was a *sasaeng*. *Sasaengs* were crazed fans that would go to any length to be near their favorite star. South Korean media was flooded with stories of *sasaengs* breaking into celebrities' apartments or tour buses. Suho's family was stalked during an outing. Ryu's phone was stolen early on in their career. On the way into a variety show, Minkyo was tackled by a surprisingly fast woman. Mal-Chin had to move after coming home to one standing in his living room. All of them were followed at some point and received phone calls from them. Even SLS was mobbed by fans overseas and had their clothes torn.

There was little they could do to protect themselves. Security guards and key code buildings only went so far. When you never knew where they were going to pop up it's hard to prepare. The security guards knew the faces of repeat offenders, and some were blacklisted from buying concert tickets.

Phones were the tricky part. Constantly changing numbers because a *sasaeng* called was tiring. All celebrities would do was update their phone numbers. Plus, a few particularly crafty fans texted them that they were a band member with a new number. They just blocked the number and hoped it was enough to put the fan off. Mal-Chin did that now. He tried to go back to sleep but just could not. His heart was racing. Even if it was just a phone call, an encounter with a *sasaeng* always set his nerves on edge.

A walk would probably calm him. Mal-Chin headed to get changed then remembered where he was. In Seoul, going for a walk at 3 in the morning was not a big deal. People were still up and moving, all he had to do was step out of the apartment building and pick a direction. Unless he wanted to wander the woods, and he did not, there was nowhere to go here. Not this late.

Mal-Chin stepped out onto his back porch. It was still too chilly to be out at night without a jacket but right now the cool air felt good. He began to feel the creeping sensation of being watched from the darkness of the woods and headed back inside. *Just your imagination.*

***

Movie night with Minseok and John was awkward. It was only the three of them in Minseok's apartment. Mal-Chin got the feeling that they invited him because they were concerned about him being lonely. He was. Mal-Chin had barely spoken to anyone since Monday. The trio chatted throughout the movie, which Mal-Chin did not mind because he was having some trouble keeping up with the plot. Subtitles would have been nice. It was a base level horror movie but the plot was some kind of experiment gone wrong.

"How do you date here? It seems so different than in Korea?" Mal-Chin awkwardly asked. "I've been trying to date someone but it's just not working. I even gave her my best moves and she didn't bite. And, all she does is smile and-" Mal-Chin's ears turned red. His mind flashed back to the way Sophie smiled after yoga. "She's just so cute."

"Well," John's eyes cut to Minseok, "You're kinda asking the wrong people here," John laughed. John and Minseok tried their best to guess who it was. Mal-Chin would not cough up an answer. "Well, let's just go through the list. If it's Anne, just be a country boy with a dirty mind. That's common here. Eileen is married so that's a no-go. If it's one of your gym girls, probably open with some compliments. You know, just be real. They like real. Just don't be creepy," John shrugged. "I guess that's what they'd like."

"Unless it's Sophie," added Minseok.

"Unless it's Sophie," John agreed with a nod. "Then just give up."

"Does she like women?" Mal-Chin started to feel disappointment setting in.

"No. Just gave up," John answered. He seemed to be hiding something. Mal-Chin tried to wrap his mind around why someone would just give up on dating. He turned back to the movie. "Oh hell, it's Sophie," John started, "I'm sorry."

The house was dead quiet when he returned. His nerves were jangled just enough to see monsters in every corner. Mal-Chin spent too long trying to figure out what the cats were staring at out the dining room window. The feeling of being watched crept over him. What could be hiding in the darkness? *Halmeoni* Hayun's stories came back to his mind again. This time accompanied by the monster from Minseok's movie night. Mal-Chin never understood how people could watch those and not be scared.

He shut the blinds. Areum was not happy about this and complained while glaring at him. Mal-Chin grumbled at her for being so noisy this late at night. She finally slipped behind the blinds, her fluffy tail sticking out.

Logically, his mind told him that he was safe. He was inside with the doors locked and the blinds closed. Yet, his mind was still telling him something was stalking around in the night. He suddenly felt trapped in his house.

Just when Mal-Chin had shaken the idea from his head, his phone went off. Startled, he jumped before seeing the video chat request from his sister and quickly answered.

"Chinnie *samchon*!" Hyeonuk called as soon as the video turned on.

"Hyeonukie!" Mal-Chin yelled back seeing his toddler nephew on the other side he barely registered his sister in the background, "Did you miss me?"

"Yes, and your cats." Hyeonuk answered. Both the adults laughed. Mal-Chin put the phone down long enough to collect both cats, Ramyun looking annoyed and Areum openly complained. He brought them in view of the camera. "Where are you?"

"I'm in America. Do you know where that is?" Mal-Chin smiled; Areum was trying to escape. Hyeonuk shook his head no. "It's all the way on the other side of the globe. And you know what? The weather is the same, but it's nighttime here." Hyeonuk thought that was funny but did not believe Mal-Chin, so he showed him. Mal-Chin asked him all the questions that adults love to ask little kids. Hyeonuk spent a good amount of time telling him all about the field trip his daycare had taken to see the dinosaurs at the museum. Mal-Chin ate every second of it up.

"*Samchon*, how long are you going to be on tour?" Hyeonuk suddenly asked. Mal-Chin's throat caught.

"I'll be gone a while longer, but I promise I'll come visit as soon as I get home."

Hyeonuk clapped his tiny hands, "Ok, I'll see you then." Hyeonuk tried to hang up the call, but his mother moved the phone out of his range and told him she wanted to talk to Mal-Chin too. She checked on his wellbeing and apologized for calling so late. Mal-Chin promised her that it was the best part of his day. They checked in on their daily lives before hanging up.

Mal-Chin went to bed with a smile on his face and a hollowness in his chest. Ramyun's content purr vibrating against his side did little to feel the hole that formed there.

Chapter 12

Online, Mal-Chin's fans were organizing some form of petition in his favor.

Save Park Mal-Chin!

He found this out while checking the fake profile he created to mimic a fan account. Even months after his resignation from the group his fans were still upset. There was a small group trying to find him and someone had written a fan fiction smut about a made-up neighbor and him. That was too invasive. Mal-Chin thought about posting something reminding fans to give him some space and not make things worse by harassing the company.

Arin's smiling face kept gracing his screen as the big news this week was her new relationship. There were multiple paparazzi pictures of Arin and S.J. out together. Jadedly, Mal-Chin told himself that it was for the publicity. He had to admit she did look happy. His fans picked up a similar refrain remembering the time Mal-Chin and Arin's relationship was exposed then quickly ended.

He was pouting on the couch when Minseok messaged him and told him to expect company this weekend. *"You can't just invite people to my house without telling me."* Mal-Chin messaged back. He did not want company.

"I just told you," was Minseok's reply. Mal-Chin grumbled annoyed.

The first knock came at the door early. Mal-Chin stared at the door. He debated not answering it. Whichever one of Minseok's friends was out there could just leave. He was fidgeting with the hole in the sleeve of his favorite hoodie when the knock came again, louder this time. The cats scurried away hiding themselves somewhere down the hallway, probably his room. Mal-Chin got the feeling they were not going to leave. They would just have to put up with his hoodie and shorts combo. He opened the door and instantly regretted not changing into something decent.

"Seok told you we were coming tonight, right?" Sophie's big green eyes looked up at him as she spoke. The heavy grocery bags in her hands crinkled.

"He did," Mal-Chin let her in, simultaneously taking a few of the bags from her hands. "But not this early." He was mentally kicking himself for not realizing she would show up. At the same moment, he wondered why that mattered so much.

"Yeah, sorry," Sophie pulled off her shoes revealing gray socks with cats on them, "He asked me to bring some groceries by for a recipe." She looked at the bag uncertain. "Said you'd like it." Her guard was up. "Where's your kitchen?" Sophie kept looking down. Mal-Chin could not figure out what she was looking at. It was not the bags and it was too low to be his crotch. As a test, he flexed a muscle in his leg. Sophie's eye instantly found somewhere else to look. Mal-Chin turned to lead her into the kitchen with a cocky smile of his face. *Is she looking at my butt now?*

In the kitchen, Mal-Chin took inventory of what she brought and they were soon in the middle of a disagreement about who should be doing the cooking. Mal-Chin argued that he should be cooking because she was his guest and Sophie argued that she had come over to cook for him. They compromised on working together and Mal-Chin made a change to the menu. The two lapsed into a comfortable silence as they set about working.

Sophie held what she was cutting in her hand and pulled the blade toward her thumb. It looked as though she was going to cut her thumb off at any second. Mal-Chin showed her how he'd been taught, the standard method of putting the food on the cutting board and chopping. Sophie half stepped away from him when he got too close. It was confusing to him; she was so friendly and seemed to like having him around but did not want him close. He remembered all the times she skidded around people in the past. *Ah, got it.*

"Seok and the others must be running late," Sophie stated suddenly.

"Did he message you?" Mal-Chin asked checking his phone just in case. They began to wonder if Minseok had not invited anyone else. Sophie doubted it. That was more John's thing. She started asking random questions about what they were making. Her shoulders tensed up every time he moved too close to her. Mal-Chin answered her questions as he ate cut pieces of cut vegetables. He offered her one but she refused. Mal-Chin tried to be cautious about giving her enough space.

"Minseok and John," Mal-Chin began, Sophie tensed. How should he ask this? "They're not friends, are they?"

Sophie sat her knife down and turned to look at him. "That's a question for them." Her guard was further up now. It was not her place to tell that if he could not figure it out.

Mal-Chin nodded. "Do their families know?"

"John's does but Seok's doesn't. I know you are friends with his brother," the look Sophie gave him was sharp, "but don't say anything to him." She turned back to the cutting board. "He'll say something when he's ready." Sophie added, gesturing with the hand that was holding the knife without thinking.

"I won't. Be careful with the knife. Very sharp." Mal-Chin said. Sophie looked at it, gave him an apologetic look then went back to what she was doing. They lapsed into silence. Mal-Chin was dying to ask her a question. "If I ask a personal question? Would you promise to answer honestly?" He waited while Sophie scanned his face, everything on her went stiff for a second. "You can ask me one too. I'll promise to answer truthfully."

Sophie thought it over. The temptation to have an honest answer herself was worth it. "What is it?"

"Why don't you date?" Mal-Chin blurted out.

Sophie stopped what she was doing, looked at him then back at what she was cutting. Discomfort stoned her face. "I-um-I just don't like to."

"You promised a truthful answer." Mal-Chin reminded.

Sophie sighed and chewed on her lip as she thought. Mal-Chin was mesmerized by Sophie's lower lip between her teeth. Her eyes flickered around the room before finding something to look at. "Some people, I think, aren't meant to fall in love. And I'm one of those people." Something shifted in her eyes, looked almost broken, "So, why try? If you're unlovable, you're unlovable." She tried to shrug it off.

Mal-Chin just wanted to hug her. "Why?"

"You said one question, not two." Sophie joked pointing at him. She did have him there. "And I think I'll save my personal question for later." She went back to chopping as Mal-Chin tried to lighten the mood with some jokes. It was not working. A heaviness hung over both of them. How was he supposed to handle what she just admitted?

***

The smell of boiling broth filled the air by the time Minseok arrived. "Hello?" He called from the living room as he sat several bags down on the coffee table.

"You're late," Mal-Chin appeared in the kitchen door. Minseok noted that he looked to be in much better spirits than he was during their last visit. Sophie peeked around Mal-Chin.

"We're making *Jeongol*," Sophie added; mispronouncing *Jeongol* as jungle. Both men chuckled. Sophie and Mal-Chin disappeared back into the kitchen as Mal-Chin tried and somewhat failed to fix her pronunciation. Minseok followed them shaking his head.

"Where are the others?' Sophie finally asked.

"Oh, Anne, Eileen and Devon are on the way. Scotty couldn't find a sitter and I haven't heard from Faith." Minseok answered while he dug through the cabinets.

Electric burner in hand, Minseok left for the living room while the others piled the meats and vegetables onto plates. They heard knocks on the door as the rest of their small group arrived.

Gathered around the coffee table, the group looked at the boiling pot of broth. Minseok was spinning his beer bottle in circles. Eileen and Anne were silently questioning the boiling pot while Sophie was just staring at the chopsticks trying to remember how to use them.

"You just grab the meat from the boiling pot and eat it?" Devon finally spoke up.

"Yeah, like this," Minseok grabbed up a piece of thinly sliced meat with the chopsticks then dipped it in the sauce bowl in front of him and gobbled it up.

Mal-Chin leaned slightly toward Sophie, "What's it called?" He smiled knowingly at her. Sophie repeated the name of the dish with a proud smile. *So Cute!* It was still wrong but the pronunciation was slightly better.

The group quickly followed Minseok's lead. Minseok gave out quick tips to get them holding the chopsticks correctly. Eileen commented on it being super spicy, Devon disagreed. Sophie and Anne were giggling and trying to hold the chopsticks correctly. Mal-Chin fished a couple of pieces of meat out for Sophie. Anne started whispering to her and looking over Sophie's shoulder at Mal-Chin before the two of them were giggling again. They felt like they were back in college, when they used to sit in lectures and Anne would let her read incoming texts, mostly inappropriate, from Anne's crazy boyfriend.

"When I first moved here," Minseok said pausing to take a gulp of his drink, "I got homesick. So, Sophie showed up at my dorm with some of our classmates and a big plate of food. We ate, watched a k-drama and just hung out. It helped me, so I thought it might help you." He laughed, "A week later Dae-o visited."

"I remember that," Anne added. "That stuff was nasty, but you choked it all down."

"It was the first Korean food I'd had in months," Minseok added. "But yeah, this is much better." Sophie gave a bashful shrug. She tried.

"Thank you," Mal-Chin said. He remembered seeing Minseok gobble down the food Dae-o cooked him when they visited. Minseok acted like he had not eaten well since he left Korea. Mal-Chin reminded himself to let Dae-o know that his older brother had friends that were taking care of him.

"So, what did you miss most about Korea?' Eileen asked suddenly. "Minseok missed the food. What did you miss?"

Mal-Chin went silent for a moment. His eyes flicked back and forth. *How honest do you want me to be?* "I, there used to be people always around. Always something happening. Here it is quiet."

Minseok shrugged, "That makes sense. Seoul is a busy place, plus with your job." Minseok caught himself and looked at the group.

"Is there anything else bothering you?" Sophie asked. There was an edge to her question like she already knew the answer.

Arin. Beast. Scandal.

Mal-Chin stuffed his mouth full to avoid her question. He could not tell her about his ex-girlfriend's new relationship with a man he could not compete with. How a week after his scandal, he watched her dress while he was still tangled in his bed sheets. The realization that her goodbye was final. The way his heart broke as Arin's heels clacked out the door. He never felt so used. That did not even include hiding his scandal and being left out of his old group's album, which was even worse.

Sophie suddenly asked Devon something random, quickly changing the subject. Mal-Chin knew she was not dropping the question, just delaying it. It rattled him, like she saw straight through him. Even interviewers did not hit questions that spot on. Maybe she was not as naive as he thought. He excused himself for a moment.

"Did I upset him?" Sophie shifted.

"Who knows." Minseok shrugged it off.

"If you did it's that outfit," Anne whispered, "I mean, tight pants, tight top. The twins look huge."

Sophie blushed, "Well..."

"Yeah, Yeah. I think. If we weren't here, he'd....." Anne looked up as Mal-Chin came back with a striped cat cradled in his arms, "I think he should do something he doesn't get to do in Korea." Anne and Eileen exchanged a nod saying they agreed on whatever she was originally saying; Minseok and Devon looked uncomfortable.

"Very smooth" Devon mumbled.

"I found him in the hall. This is Ramyun." Mal-Chin said as he sat back down next to Sophie, who delightedly offered a hand to the cat. It sniffed her hand before giving it a head butt. In less than a minute, the cat was in Sophie's lap and she was cooing as she snuggled it. "So what should I go do?" Mal-Chin asked. He was looking at Sophie even though he was speaking to Anne.

The group began to brainstorm activities in town he could do. Anne Googled upcoming events in town and did not see anything until when the weather was expected to be warmer. Checking Lynchburg gave similar results. Eileen started making plans for them to go out as a group, she was planning an over complicated outing. This fell through quickly as Anne reminded her that the others would be working during her break. Mal-Chin mentioned bowling and the group began to question if the bowling alley was even still open. Sophie brought up Axe Throwing and they looked at her surprised.

The party began to break up after this. They all had good reasons for needing to go. Minseok, Sophie and Mal-Chin debated whether they should watch a movie as they cleaned up the mess. Sophie paused on her way out the door, "Hey, if you need someone to talk to, let me know." She gave him that look that made him swear she could see right through him.

The next day, Mal-Chin texted Sophie. It was not to spill his guts about his problems. He needed help buying supplies. At least, that was what Mal-Chin told himself. What Mal-Chin really wanted was the company. It was normal in South Korea to run errands with friends, but not here. A run to the pet store for food and kitty litter was needed. Sophie showed up after work in a gold sweater and brown pants that looked professional and soft. These after school errand runs soon became a normal thing.

Chapter 13

Mal-Chin hurriedly packed his bag with his phone up to his ear. His record company gave him just enough notice to book a flight and pack his things. Mal-Chin was heading back to Korea. Not permanently, the CEO wanted to call him in for a meeting. They could have done it over video call. Mal-Chin suspected this was a power move. Call him from halfway across the globe on a last-minute notice and watch him squirm. It was unneeded. The CEO scared him anyway.

"I need help," Mal-Chin said into the phone as soon as Sophie answered.

There was a long pause before she answered, "Are you ok? What happened?" Concern thickened her voice.

"I've got to go home. Can you watch my cats?"

"Oh, yeah. Is everything ok?"

"It's work." Mal-Chin threw his toiletries into a bag, "I've got to go now." He started to give instructions on where he left the key for her, where the cat's supplies were and how to get in touch with him if something went wrong. He threw his luggage into the car trying to think if he missed something. "I don't know how long I'll be gone."

"I see," Sophie hesitated.

"If I don't come back—" Mal-Chin started.

"I'll make sure your stuff gets sent back but I'm keeping the cats."

"Wait! What?" He stopped halfway in the car.

"I don't have a passport and that's a long flight for little kitties alone." Sophie's voice was coy as she said that. Mal-Chin could almost imagine Sophie cartoonishly batting her eyelashes as she said it.

"When I get back, you're getting a passport!" Was the last thing Mal-Chin said before hanging up.

That was the last conversation Mal-Chin had before making the trip back to Seoul. He took a more direct route this time, not having to worry about the cats' comfort. He felt guilty for just pushing the cats off on Sophie and not letting Minseok know he was leaving, but he was in a rush. During his flight, Sophie sent him a picture of the key and a video of the cats eating happily. He did not see it until he arrived and could not remember if it was too late to reply to her.

Nighttime in Seoul was strange after months in the quiet of Danville. People packed the sidewalks and the sound of cars filled the air. Mal-Chin felt the rush of energy, the crush of people. He was home. Luck graced him with a night landing. The media was busy following around other celebrities in the hopes of catching a dating scandal instead of camping out at the airport awaiting celebrities coming and going. He made it into his apartment without being noticed.

Mal-Chin's sports car pulled out of his apartment's parking garage. There was a stop he needed to make tonight. No one blinked an eye at a 20 something in a sports car here. Leaving the heart of Seoul brought less traffic and more curious eyes.

In the early years of Beast, the other members quickly started buying luxury items and fast cars. Park Mal-Chin bought a house. They called him crazy for such a purchase when he already lived in the dorm with them and owned an apartment. The house was for his parents though and they came to appreciate that decision. Especially after they gained an open invite. The house was half bought in the hope that Mal-Chin's parents would come to terms with his unorthodox career choice. They had talked about buying a house for years but could not afford it. As they aged, they appreciated not having to climb all those flights of stairs to their old apartment more and more. At one point, they talked about moving his grandmother in, but she refused to leave her home. Mal-Chin realized he should visit her sometime soon.

Mal-Chin took a deep breath before stepping out of the car. His parents never commented on the scandal. For all he knew, he was walking back into their disapproval. Despite the expensive gifts and Beast's success his parents never truly accepted his decision. Not bothering to knock, he let himself in. Scents of cooking food met his nose and led him into the kitchen where his parents were hard at work. The couple always cooked together. Mal-Chin's childhood was filled with memories of the pair in the kitchen giving the children small tasks to do. Mal-Chin leaned against the counter watching them silently as they mumbled to each other planning what to make even as they cooked. "Why are you fussing so much? I'll eat anything," Mal-Chin said with a chuckle as they jumped.

His parents turned surprised. His mother threw her arms around him and let go too soon. "Don't you know better than to sneak up on the elderly like that?"

"Don't you know better than to leave the door unlocked?" Mal-Chin replied with a smirk.

His mother tsked before going back to work in the kitchen. She wanted a full report of what he'd been eating in the U.S. At the mention of store-bought kimchi, she shook her head. He was ordered to stop by before leaving for some fresh kimchi.

"Oh, come over and we'll make it together," His father beamed at the idea.

"Is that my Chinnie?" A fragile voice called from the living room.

Mal-Chin's face filled with excitement, "*Halmeoni!*" He promptly abandoned his parents in search of his grandmother. Mal-Chin found Hayun sitting in their living room watching the news. He lost no time wrapping her up in a big hug and enjoying the soft pats to the back she gave him. He caught her up on what he was doing in the U.S. The whole time he was praying she had not heard what he was being accused of. The thought of his grandmother hearing that news about him hurt. Hayun liked hearing about the group of friends that helped him adjust. She was quite pleased to hear one of his new friends was Dae-o's brother. "How is that Suho doing?"

Mal-Chin chuckled as they moved to the table to eat, "He's good I haven't seen him in a while."

"Well, you tell him, that he needs to stop by and visit sometime. I'll make him a good meal." Hayun moved to sit down, "You sit next to me." She patted the seat next to her. Mal-Chin took it happily.

Dinner with family was nice. He caught up on all they were doing. His nephew's latest toddler antics made him laugh. Everyone compared the two; Mal-Chin had been a mischievous child and Hyeonuk was following the same track. The mention of his nephew was bittersweet, he missed the toddler. Seeing Hyeonuk would have made his day so much better. He focused on the fact that he was here with his parents and grandmother.

"Oh, *Halmeoni,* I heard a noise from the woods that reminded me of the stories you told us as kids." Mal-Chin started over a bite of food. "I kept hearing this creepy sound like a girl giggling in the forest behind where I'm staying and another day I heard this sound like someone yelling," Mal-Chin shivered remembering it. "It's so creepy out there at night." Hayun chuckled in amusement.

"You speak 4 languages and you're still scared by little kid ghost stories," his mother shook her head disappointed. "You're smarter than that."

"Umma," Mal-Chin whined, "Those were some scary stories," Mal-Chin replied innocently. He still hated horror movies as an adult.

"But what was it?" His dad asked entranced. "The United States has a lot of ghost stories."

Well, that did not help, "It was a coyote and a *scree child*" He made a funny face wondering if he said that right, "it's some kind of owl. That's what Sophie said at least." What Sophie really said was Screecher Owl, but her accent distorted the word.

"Sophie?" his mother looked up from her food.

"She's friends with Kang Minseok. When that group came over to eat, she was with them." He decided to leave it at that. They did not need to know anything else.

"I thought you had a new girlfriend," Hayun stated as she gave Mal-Chin the side eye. "The next girl I hear about better be a good one. I'm tired of my Chinnie getting his heart broke." Mal-Chin looked down embarrassed. "Bring home a good girl that's good to her family."

They cleaned up from dinner. Mal-Chin took anything that Hayun tried to pick up. Hayun reacted with playful frustration. Mal-Chin knew she didn't like to feel useless but that she appreciated her grand-children fulfilling their family duties. There was a long discussion about Hayun spending the night. She was set on taking a bus home.

The buses did not run close enough to her house for them to feel safe letting her go, but she refused to stay.

"I'll take you home," Mal-Chin smiled playfully, "I'm on one of the sports cars."

It was settled as easily as that "Oh good. Let's go!" She headed to the door. Mal-Chin chuckled following her out.

No sooner than they buckled up Hayun asked, "What happened? Don't lie to me."

Mal-Chin's mouth pressed into a line, "It's not true. I don't even know who my accuser is. I mean, I've gone to parties but nothing like that."

Hayun was staring at Mal-Chin as he drove. It made him more nervous than any of the detectives. "Thought so. How did you get into this situation?"

"I don't know. I was on tour and Kim-*nim* just dropped the news on me. I didn't think it would turn into this." Mal-Chin now regretted laughing the allegations off at first.

"What is going to happen to your career?"

"Well, it's down the drain right now. But once the investigation is over and my name is clear the CEO says I can relaunch as a soloist."

"Good. You do a good job so I can tell all those old biddies at the salon you're my grandson when they play your music again. They want to brag 'oh my grandson is going to school to be a lawyer' and 'my granddaughter just started an internship at Samsung' and I go 'Well, mine is on the radio. Your grandkids are his fans.'" Hayun laughed and Mal-Chin joined her. Hayun was motivation enough.

Hayun insisted they stopped for sweets on the way home. Mal-Chin reminded Hayun that the doctor told her to watch her sugar intake but she insisted. The ice cream parlors and cafes were closing so he ended up stopping at a convenience store. They sat at an inside table by the window eating their snacks. This reminded Mal-Chin of when he and his sister would spend the night at Hayun's house as children. Their grandparents would sometimes take them out for late night snacks with an order to "not tell your parents." Mal-Chin always felt like he was stepping into another world. They were usually the only kids out and the streetlights made the world look different, like it was different streets from the ones that he traveled during the day.

They loaded back into the car and started off for Hayun's house again. The radio played the latest hits. Hayun asked Mal-Chin if he knew the bands. When a Purple-Pink song started to play, Mal-Chin pressed his mouth into a line again. He could still taste the sweetness of his Choco Pie. The taste was starting to make him nauseous.

Sleep did not come easy that night. The adjustment to the different time zone and nerves made it hard for him to fall asleep. In the morning, he would have to work to remove any sign of sleep deprivation. He could not let anyone think he was struggling.

Chanyeol let himself into the apartment then buzzed around trying to help Mal-Chin prepare for the meeting at hand. They both guessed it was to do with the terms of his return but besides that they knew nothing. Being kept in the dark about plans for his career was frustrating.

Like usual, the two used a back entrance to get into the building and made their way to the office. Mal-Chin shifted uncomfortably when they were met by one of his exes outside the CEO's office, she was the CEO's personal secretary now. She was a front receptionist and Mal-Chin had been in training when they dated. When she started getting promotions and the secret relationship became hard to hide, they broke up. They worked hard to get where they were.

They were informed that the CEO would see them shortly and were left to wait an insulting amount of time. His heart stuck in his chest when he saw Purple-Pink and their manager exit. Arin looked into his eyes as she passed him. Mal-Chin looked away first. They belonged to a different company so he could not understand what they were doing here. Finally, they were led into the CEO's office. Mal-Chin and Chanyeol bowed respectfully to him before taking their seats. Stupidly, Mal-Chin wondered where Arin had sat. She was not what he needed to be thinking about right now. He tried to clear the thought from his mind. It did not matter. All that mattered was his career.

"You're in luck right now, Park," The CEO began, "You're out of the spotlight at the moment." He picked up an envelope and handed it over to them. Mal-Chin took it curiously, "I'm sure you've heard about this. It's a petition by your fans. We're being flooded daily with demands to bring you back."

Mal-Chin had to bite the inside of his cheek to keep from smiling as he looked at the paper. His fans had his back, even when no one else did. The display made him almost want to cry. He had seen the plans for a petition but thought it would only be a handful of fans if anything. Not this. "I'd seen mentions of it online but didn't think they would go through with it." A twist of excitement ran through him. Was he about to get his job back? Maybe the next time he spoke to Sophie would be to tell her to send his things home. He tried to settle his nerves. It could not be this easy.

"Well, I'll just assume you had no hand in that. I'm sure you realize we cannot bring you back into the company with an open investigation going on. It wouldn't be good for us to debut a new soloist only for him to go to jail." The CEO's words cut into him. Mal-Chin felt like a deflated balloon, he hung his head and just nodded. "Once the investigation is over, we can talk about debuting you as a solo artist." He put emphasis on the word solo. No matter what Mal-Chin did, he could never return to Beast. "Have you put any thought into what you'll do as a soloist?"

"I've been working some. I want to show a different side of myself, to set me apart from the group." Mal-Chin knew it was vague, but it had the right elements.

"Sounds good. Until then, we've got some rules you need to follow. You understand what will happen if you break them?" Mal-Chin nodded.

The rules laid out for him were:

1. No public contact with Beast including mentioning their music, watching their lives, or interacting online.

2. Not to be seen with a woman that he could possibly have a relationship with.

3. Not to use his official accounts until further notice.

4. Have a full album of songs and theme ready to be recorded as soon as the investigation is over.

Mal-Chin mulled over this list as they left the office. Chanyeol stressed the importance of following the rules. Mal-Chin did not need to be told this, he understood all too well. "Why were Purple-Pink here?" Mal-Chin blurted out in the elevator.

"I don't know. That's none of our business." Chanyeol let out a sigh, "Please tell me you're not thinking about trying to get back with Arin again. She's with S.J. It would be a bad move under normal circumstances but right now it's doom."

"Just curious." Mal-Chin mumbled. "Hey, let's get something to eat. It's almost lunch time."

"Can't" Chanyeol replied. "Beast has a full schedule all this week. They're keeping me busy."

Mal-Chin nodded getting the point. It was just a fast idea. He was hungry though. Mal-Chin had not had time to restock his kitchen and skipped breakfast. In the end, he ate lunch alone in the back corner of a ramen restaurant. He debated what to do with the rest of his day. No one was supposed to know he was here so he could not just go wherever. His parents decided to keep his visit secret from his nephew. That hurt but he understood the reasoning. His nephew thought he was still on tour so it would be confusing for Mal-Chin to return then leave again. That excuse could only last so long though.

Chapter 14

Today's gym visit was different in a good way. John asked to come along. Whether it was loneliness or just a whim to get active, Sophie never was sure. Tomorrow, John would be texting her complaining about how sore he was. Today, John was dutifully following Sophie around the gym floor and mimicking her movements as best he could. Sophie corrected large errors but figured her own form was not good enough to nitpick. Working out with another person made her feel uncomfortable. Sophie had gone solo for so many years that having an accomplice just threw her groove off. There were more rests, deciding what to do next, and a healthy amount of backing off weights so John would not feel the need to try to keep up. She did not mind. John was a good friend and had stuck it out through her many different interests so she could humor his sometimes interest in exercise. Workouts with him were usually fun too. John could make a joke out of anything, and the gym tended to bring out the best ones.

"Do you ever," John started as they trekked away on the elliptical going nowhere, "feel like you're just not good enough?"

Sophie thought it over for a second, "Yeah. Have you met my family?" John gave her a sympathetic look. John never met The Colemans, but he had heard the stories. "Why do you feel like that though?"

"It's Seok. He's got it all together ya' know? He's working on that internship at the hospital. On track for a gleaming career, excited about his work. Then here I am," he gestured to the elliptical that was already causing him breathe raggedly. "Working at a restaurant, with a useless degree and getting fat."

"I don't know. He was so proud when you got promoted to manager. As for the fat part, I'm not sure where that's coming from." Sophie's eyes scanned the gym floor. She looked at all the different shapes around them but did not find the form she was looking for. "Is it because of a certain visitor?"

John slowed down, took a sip of water then kept going. He scanned the gym floor, looked for something on the multiple TV, watched his feet pedaling away and once he was out of places to look, he finally answered. "No. Yes, maybe." He nodded. "I mean, you've seen him. I've never seen someone so handsome. I've looked at him. Couldn't blame Seok for it too." Then he added in a mumble, "Or for wanting better."

"But he wants you." Sophie added looking over at her friend. "Plus, I can't see Seok leaving you for his brother's friend." She adjusted the bottom of her ultra-support sports bra. The wire in it was rubbing a sore on the bottom of her breast. Sophie noted she probably was not the best for relationship advice. Was she approaching this the right way?

"I know. And I know I don't have anything to worry about. I just _"

"I understand."

"It's hard, ya know?" John tried to catch his breath before speaking again, "It's not even just about that. I know I don't have to worry about Mal-Chin. He's too busy looking at you. I just feel like Seok could do better."

"And Mal-Chin made you think that?" Sophie asked. "You really need to talk to Seok."

"I know, I know. But I don't want him to think I'm jealous. You know how he hates that."

"As long as you two have been together though." Sophie did not really understand what that meant, but John seemed to. Her fitness watch screen would not turn on leaving her to smack at the screen and squeeze at the sides until it did.

"Can we please get off this torture device?" John slowed to a stop. Sophie followed his lead. They went their separate ways. John going home for a bath and Sophie heading to her grandparents' house for Sunday dinner. No one cared if she showed up sweaty from the gym.

This was the kind of Sunday that Sophie liked, slow. Her aunt and uncle had not shown up yet for dinner. This was mainly caused by the fact that it was Robbie's weekend to work, and Jessica or Carol would not show up until close to time for him to get home. Sometimes, Robbie would stop by when he got off. Virginia's nephew had not showed up for a few weeks so they were positive he wouldn't today. They should be worried about him, Sophie knew, but this was not unusual behavior for him. When he was ready, he would show up again probably asking for something.

Sophie and Ford ate, not bothering to keep up a conversation. Sophie sometimes worried that she didn't talk to him enough, but other times wondered if he enjoyed the quiet time.

"Talked to Will last night," Ford stated.

Sophie took a long sip of sweet tea before asking, "What did he say?"

"He's gonna come in next weekend."

Now Virginia was excited and making plans for Will's visit, already debating what to fix and telling Sophie to make sure not to make any plans. Sophie just nodded. Silently, she told herself not to get too excited. Will promised to come in plenty of times and didn't.

"Is he ok?" Sophie whispered when Virginia went into the other room.

"I think they are arguing again," Ford huffed out. Sophie just shook her head.

Virginia's spiral of planning continued as she went on and on nit-picking everything. She wanted to make Will feel at home. To her, this meant having everything perfect. Virginia kept asking Sophie about the state of Will's bedroom to the point where Sophie was getting annoyed. Next, Virginia started in on Ford reminding him to not leave little messes in the living room. Once that was all done, she began to make a list of things that needed to be done. Instead of writing it down, Virginia rambled off the list and kept adding extra to it. Sophie lost track after the 10-minute mark.

Ford escaped to his garage. Sophie ate a piece of cake while she waited Virginia out. Having lost steam, Virginia took a seat and the two sat in silence for a bit watching T.V. but comfortable silences were not the Coleman family's strength. "You know," Virginia started. Sophie's guard was instantly up, that phrase never ended well for her. "I'm a little disappointed in you. Robbie sets you up with a nice guy whose good looking and you can't even answer his messages."

"I don't like him," Sophie admitted. Their definitions of nice and good looking were very different.

"But you can go running around with some stranger every time we turn around. Do you know how that made your uncle feel to find you sitting in a restaurant with some foreign boy? Robbie has been making excuses to Noah all this time." Virginia's lips drew into that annoyed pucker. Guilt flooded Sophie's chest.

"We were out as friends," Sophie answered exasperated.

"Don't get huffy with me! Now," she straightened in her seat, "the only reason you don't like that boy is because Robbie picked him out for you. You owe your Uncle Robbie a second chance with him. He's crazy about you."

"Well, I can't help it if I don't like him," Sophie restated. She was scrolling through her phone looking for a distraction.

"But you can give him a second chance. Text him now and tell him you're going to go out with him again."

"Granny...." Sophie couldn't bring herself to say no.

This would become the sticking point for this week. If Virginia was not fussing over having the house perfect for Will's visit, she was nagging Sophie about Noah. Sophie wished the weekend would arrive quickly. Once Will was in, all talk of Noah and extra dates would be out the door. Sophie would be on the back burner again, where she belonged.

Will did not come in.

Sophie became the target of Virginia's hurt feelings. Nothing she did was right, Virginia criticized everything from her hair to her belly suddenly looking slightly larger. Sophie could not see any difference in either one. Sophie's clothes were suddenly unprofessional for work, even though Virginia had not seen Sophie in work clothes since Fall.

Anything to keep from going home. Became Sophie's thought process for the week. No matter how tired she felt, she went to the gym or found a reason that she needed to stop at the store. Her best excuse was watching Mal-Chin's cats. The sweet creatures ate up her attention every time she came over. Sophie began to linger enjoying the positive attention. That ended as soon as Mal-Chin returned. She avoided the mirrors in the gym locker rooms and gym selfies were out of the question. All she could see was the turn of her tummy, how her face looked fat when she pulled her hair back. Every imperfection of her body stood out whenever she looked in the mirror.

"Maybe Granny is right," Sophie mumbled to herself as she washed her face one night, "Maybe I should go out with him again. No one else would want me." Her eyes burned. Her mind tortured her with every imperfection and flaw she had. Is this what her life would come down to? Settling on someone she did not like just because he was the only person who wanted to get in her pants? Being alone sounded much better.

Sophie squeezed her eyes shut and reminded herself that she did not fear being alone. That was the future she had planned for herself for several years now. Getting out of this house, buying her own cute little house in the middle of nowhere and living a quiet little life with no one to tell her how terrible she looked or how she was doing everything wrong. Maybe Sophie would get a cat. For a reason Sophie could not place her finger on, she was not content with this plan anymore. She told herself to get rid of the idea of having someone else in her life. No one wanted her. Sophie's mind was plagued with stories of people who lived alone whose bodies weren't discovered for years or their pets ate them. She awoke in the morning with a dark cloud over her head. All Sophie wanted to do was lie in bed, but she had students to teach, errands to run and a workout to complete.

Chapter 15

Will's visit came the following weekend. He showed up on a Friday night without warning. Virginia instantly fretted over the fact that she had not prepared his favorite meal. Will good naturedly laughed this off telling her it was ok. Dinner was quickly changed from just getting a plate and sitting wherever to eating at the table. "This just feels right," Virginia commented as they settled into their meal. Until Will went to college, they'd eaten this way for years; Sophie could not remember when or why they switched to eating in front of the T.V.

Virginia caught Will up on all the drama between Carol's family. Will was as uninterested Sophie had been. "Well, that's not good," was his only reply to the situation. Being away from them put things in a different perspective for Will. Sophie envied this trait. She wondered if the same thing was possible if she moved. He would never receive a scolding for being uninterested in the latest Coleman Family drama. But, southern men were not expected to gossip, women were. It was ingrained in their culture. At any social event, any meeting, you were expected to enthusiastically share the latest news. Sometimes, Sophie hated it.

"How's Vicki doing?" Ford asked.

Will stared out the window behind Sophie before finally answering, "She's good." That was Will's way of saying they were arguing, again. Sophie and Ford exchanged a quick look as Will told them about his current job and hobbies. Since Vicki moved into his Richmond apartment, Will no longer spoke of his friends or events he went to. It was all work and his girlfriend now.

"So, what have you been up to? Still Wonder Womaning it up out there?" Will asked.

"Trying to," Sophie sat up a little straighter.

"You look good. I gotta start hitting the gym again," Will leaned back patting his belly with a chuckle.

"She ought to look good. She'd got two guys after her," Virginia broke in.

"Really?" Will's eyebrows raised then a playful smile crossed his face, "I need to come back more often to keep an eye on you," He laughed.

"Oh you should meet the one, Noah, Robbie introduced him. He's handsome, has a good job and Robbie can't speak more highly of him. They went out once and do you believe she likes the other one?"

Will looked apologetically into Sophie's eyes then tipped his cup toward Virginia, "Man that was good!" Will patted his belly again before taking his empty plate to the kitchen. "So, what about the other guy?"

"We're just friends, --" Sophie started. Their conversation was cut off by Will's phone ringing. Brows furrowing, he stepped outside to take the call. They could hear his voice but could not understand what he was saying. When he returned he was on edge.

At home that night, Will would pick up the conversation about Noah and Mal-Chin again. He would be the only family member to ask why she did not like Noah and agreed with her reasoning. "Why do you like the other guy?" Will focused on his small sketch notebook. It was more so that he would not have to watch his sister fidget on the other side of the room.

"I like being around him." There was a long silence, Will was waiting on Sophie to finish instead of filling the silence. "He just wants a friend though." Sophie shrugged trying to release the knot in her throat with it.

"Why do you think that?"

That caught Sophie off guard. She watched the T.V. and thought about past relationships where she was left for exes, instantly asked for sex, or one-sidedly loved someone. Sophie had always been the person that was thrown aside as soon as something better came along. It was only a matter of time before Mal-Chin did the same. Sophie would not go through that again. All the imperfections that her family so often pointed out came to her mind and how little her parents seemed to care for her. *Why would he?* Sophie shrugged. "He's new here. He only knows a handful of people and he just needs a friend."

"I think you should talk to him." Will flicked his pencil at Sophie as he spoke, "Stop running."

Sophie did not answer, choosing to scroll her Instagram account instead. She showed Will a picture of Mal-Chin. He looked at it for a few minutes before commenting, "He looks familiar." Will wracked his brain for where he'd seen Mal-Chin before, "Like one of those k-pop dudes Vicki is crazy about. I think they're called Beast?" Will shrugged.

"Maybe he just looks like one of them." Sophie shrugged it off. There was no chance.

"Send it to Vicki, ask her." Will replied "He didn't tell you he was famous?"

Sophie shook her head as she sent a picture to Vicki, *"Do you know who this is?"* Sophie looked up at Will. There was no way Mal-Chin was the same person. "He said he was a camera man, I think." Even as she repeated it, it sounded ridiculous. A cameraman on an extended business trip in an expensive house driving a luxury car. *You're smarter than that.* Will's eyebrows raised at her like it was an obvious give away.

"Park Mal-Chin from Beast. We call him Chinnie. Are you finally getting on the k-pop train?" Vicki replied then added, *"Is this a new picture? What's if from?"*

Sophie froze, it could not have been the same Mal-Chin. That must have been a common name. *"Wrong person maybe? He lives here. We're friends."* Sophie replied. When Vicki did not believe her, she screen shot their conversation with the pictures.

Vicki rapidly sent out three messages. *"GIRL WTF!"* then *"THAT'S REALLY HIM"* followed by *"WHY IS HE THERE?"* Finally, she texted, *"Is this where he's hiding? Can I meet him?"*

Sophie felt like the world was slipping out from under her. Vicki must have been messing with her. A quick Google search revealed she was telling the truth. Park Mal-Chin, her new friend, was not a camera man, he was the entertainment.

"You ok?" Will asked.

Sophie was furiously researching Mal-Chin on her phone. She found thousands of shirtless pictures, butt pictures and cute pictures of him with flowers and in sweaters. In most pictures, his tan skin was so pale he looked fake. "He's—Mal-Chin is a member of that group." Sophie was scrolling through articles trying to find anything that explained his appearance here. "Why didn't he tell me? Why is he here?"

Will shrugged, "Maybe he was sick of being famous. Ask her."

Sophie just nodded. She was scared to ask. Putting her phone down, she tried to wrap her head around what she had just learned. *He's not who I thought he was.* She could add him to the list of liars in her life, Mal-Chin was too kind to be a sneak. Was that all an act too?

The week was tense. Sophie spent her time either tiptoeing around trying not to wake Will, rushing through exercising in case Will was up, and waiting on Will, or trying to find something to talk to him about. One moment, Will would be laughing on the couch and the next he was on the porch only to return with a scowl on his face. No one wanted to ask him what was going on. They did not want to upset him. At the same moment, they were worried about him as well.

If Sophie was not avoiding Will's problems, her mind was struggling to understand what was going on with Mal-Chin. She avoided him as she tried to sort out what she stumbled across. Sophie could not understand why he would hide something so important in his life. At the same moment, she thought of all the little things she did not mention to her family.

Chapter 16

Mal-Chin hurried out to his car the moment he was off the phone. He quickly punched Tight Squeeze Shopping Center into his GPS and took off. Sophie sounded off on the phone. "I'm out of people to call." She was almost crying, panicked when she called him. Mal-Chin did not question what was wrong or what she needed; he just came for her. Mal-Chin found her car parked far from the store front in the parking lot. Sophie needed help getting out of her car and into his. She was pale, so pale that her makeup looked too dark. They drove to her house with only the sound of the GPS. That much noise seemed to bother her. There was another car in her driveway. Sophie looked at it disappointed.

"Thank you, and sorry," Sophie stated as she climbed out of the car her voice almost slurred as she spoke. She was having to hold onto Mal-Chin's car for support. Mal-Chin hurried around to assist her. In one easy movement, Mal-Chin scooped Sophie up. She mumbled complaints before burying her face into his shoulder. Somehow, he got the door unlocked and closed behind them but the hallway in the laundry room was narrow and Mal-Chin banged her feet on the dryer. The hollow metal sound rumbled through the house. Sophie groaned in pain before wiggling in his arms, "You can put me down." A door opened on the far side of the house.

"You can't walk straight," Mal-Chin stated. They startled Will in the kitchen. He had come to investigate the source of the bang while still in his underwear.

"I'll be ok and I'm heavy." Sophie's words were slurred and muffled. Her head was buried in Mal-Chin's broad shoulder.

"You're not heavy," Mal-Chin replied he was trying to keep his voice low.

"Sophie?" Will's guard was up. "You ok?"

Sophie simply tapped her finger to her head. A blue vein throbbed across her temple painfully "Migraine. Mal-Chin brought me home and he won't put me down."

"That might be a good idea," Will added, "Let's get you to bed." Will led Mal-Chin to Sophie's bedroom. Mal-Chin gently set Sophie down onto her unmade blue and pink bed. Much to Sophie's embarrassment, Mal-Chin removed her boots and socks.

Mal-Chin looked over their living room while Sophie changed clothes. He might have been ok with removing Sophie's shoes but that's where he stopped. The Gregory's furniture was a strange mix of hand-me-downs from family members who had replaced their own; at the time they could not afford their own and did not care to replace it now. "This is one of those trailer things." Mal-Chin said more to himself. "Do they always look like this on the inside? How did you get it here?" Mal-Chin was inspecting the ceiling for a combining joint. Sophie shuffled out of her room unsteady on her feet. Mal-Chin was instantly at her side. It was Will that retrieved her medicine and water bottle thankful for not having to answer the questions. Medicine taken, Mal-Chin swept her up and put her back in bed. Sophie clung to Mal-Chin's shoulders as soon as she was in his arms.

Back in the living room, the two men discussed what to do about Sophie's car. They came to the decision to go back to retrieve it. "Should we leave her?" Mal-Chin's eyes turned back to Sophie's door, worry obvious in them.

"She'll be ok. Probably already asleep, and if not, she'd want the quiet." Will nodded, "The medicine she takes is pretty strong."

Will and Mal-Chin rode in uncomfortable silence. They were strangers with only one connection. "Um, can I come check on her later?" Mal-Chin asked as Will was climbing out of his car.

"Honestly, she'll probably sleep the rest of the day. I'll tell her to text you when she wakes up. Thanks man." Will had to adjust the seat way back to fit into the driver's seat of Sophie's car.

***

Sophie dutifully texted Mal-Chin when she felt well enough, *"Thank you. Sorry for the trouble."* Still weak, she pulled the covers around herself just wanting to be comfortable and warm.

"Sophie?" Will spoke softly as he cracked her door open. She'd drifted back off to sleep without realizing it. The sound of his voice was jarring to her still sensitive ears. She gave a mumbled response that she was not sure Will heard. "Your buddy is here. Do you feel like guests? He brought coffee".

Sophie grumbled a reply and sat up. When Will said "your buddy," Sophie thought he meant Minseok but it was Mal-Chin who entered. The mattress dipped as Mal-Chin took a seat next to her simultaneously handing her the coffee cup. Sophie tried to absorb the warmth of the cup before taking a sip. "I read," Mal-Chin's voice was a whisper, "coffee helps migraines." He took in the room awkwardly. Sophie knew she should be wondering what he was noticing about her still dark room, but she was too tired to care. Her chest swelled thinking how he had taken the time to get coffee for her. Sophie usually took care of herself during recovery. That meant fixing herself food, coffee, and a hot bath. She had to be careful in the hours following waking up. Her migraine would return if she was exposed to too much light or noise.

She leaned against his comfortably warm arm. "Thank you." Sophie sipped at the coffee enjoying the heat if not the strong bitter taste. The tingling feeling in her arms and legs slowly lessened as she sipped. "You didn't have to do this."

"Why wouldn't I?" Mal-Chin asked as he squinted at the stack of books on her nightstand. "It was nice to do something helpful for once." He picked up the book on the top of the stack. "Back home," Mal-Chin continued, "if I would have done that the media would have followed me and I wouldn't have been able to help."

"Are you a celebrity or something?" Sophie asked suddenly. "Vicki has said you're a member of her favorite k-pop group." This was not the time to have this conversation but, here she went. "I'm using my one truthful personal question."

"I am, was." Mal-Chin went stiff next to her.

"Um, where you – like—in trouble or something? Is that why you didn't mention it?"

Mal-Chin did not answer. The way they were sitting Sophie could not read his expression. "I – ah—got, uh, they said I did something, but I didn't." Mal-Chin hung his head. There was a long silence, then Mal-Chin took a deep breath and told her what happened. A bookmark advertising the local bookstore fell out of the paperback he was holding as he riffled through it. Sophie would later wonder where it went.

Towards the beginning of Beast's latest concert tour, their manager came to him with the news of a scandal involving Mal-Chin. It started with the rumor that Mal-Chin was throwing wild parties in his Seoul apartment. According to the rumor, these wild parties consisted of drugs, hard alcohol, and naked women. That alone was enough to ruin the reputation of an idol in Korea. The public had no trouble believing that the sexy member of a group that often sang about sex and partying would do something like this. Then, someone claimed that not only had they attended these parties, but they supplied the drugs and women. This person also claimed that Park Mal-Chin owed them thousands of dollars.

The scandal, combined with Beast's rising popularity, caused the media to go wild with the claims. The negative publicity began to hurt the whole band's reputation until the record label's CEO stepped in. The decision was made to remove Mal-Chin from the group. When it was announced, Mal-Chin told everyone it was his idea to save face for the company.

All public contact from his band members was cut off. He could not go out in public without the media hounding him, which made it harder for him to meet with the other band members and his friends. Everyone he knew needed to be careful around him. Being seen with a celebrity involved in a scandal could damage careers. There was no communication with his fans, even as they continued to flood his comment sections and fan mail with words of concern and wishing him the best. He watched the band members V-lives and noticed they avoided all questions about him. It was like he no longer existed to them.

Just as things began to calm down some, the news of an official investigation hit. It seems his accuser, a woman name Kim Eun Jung, had formally placed charges against him. Mal-Chin had no clue who this woman was and could not think of a reason she would do this. When the investigators were done with him, they'd cleared him to travel to the U.S.

"Do you have any proof?" Sophie asked.

"The drug tests they gave me showed nothing and when they checked my bank there was nothing paid to her," he sighed, "which doesn't help, because the claim is I didn't pay them."

Something about all of this seemed off to Sophie. Her post-migraine fogged brain was having trouble processing it. If Sophie tried too hard, she feared the pain would return. "Why didn't you say anything sooner?"

"I didn't want to talk about it. And I've lost everyone because of it." He placed his head on top of hers. "I didn't want to lose you too."

None of that fit his personality. Sophie noticed the way he got flustered just being around her; he could not act like that and throw naked parties. "We'll have to talk about this later. But I believe you." She felt him relax next to her. If asked, Sophie could not explain why she decided he was telling the truth. The edge of hurt and embarrassment in his voice sounded real to her. *Everyone needed someone to believe in them,* she guessed.

His fingers laced with hers. "Thank you." He lifted her hand and pressed it to his lips.

Chapter 17

In the week to follow, Sophie finished preparations for her SOL Tests. The largest stressor in her life would soon be over. The day before the test, she closed her classroom door with a weight on her shoulders. Sophie had done all she could, now it was just up to the students. That night, her yoga intention was that her students performed well on the test. Mal-Chin asked if she wanted to grab dinner after class but Sophie turned him down. She was too on edge to entertain. Some of the trust Mal-Chin had gained was lost. Even just an accusation of that type of crime put Sophie on edge around him. The fact that he lied about who he was and what he did only strengthened her distrust.

All night, her mind ticked off everything she thought she could have taught better. She made a mental list of which kids she was sure would pass, who would not, and who were on the border depending on their mood. Then, she tried to guess at a pass percent with that information. Mental math was not her thing. A rumor was going around that teachers would be replaced if the school did not pass this year. Sophie knew that would be her; she was one of the newer teachers. Virginia and Ford tried their best to give her confidence, but it did very little. Sophie thanked her luck that today was not a family dinner night. The constant chatter would have done little to ease her nerves.

The morning of the test, she got up and ready like normal. Rushing in would do her no-good today. Virginia gave her a last-minute pep talk on the phone as Sophie sipped a rare cup of coffee with her scrambled eggs. The talk did little to put her at ease. She took slow even breaths like she did in yoga; it helped quell some of the nausea. Maybe today was not the day for an extra boost of caffeine. The remaining coffee went down the drain.

"Hey y'all. You're going to do good. Take your time and remember to take a quick break if you need it." Sophie said as she popped her head into each classroom. The kids looked as nervous as she felt but they smiled and nodded when she spoke to them. Sophie plastered on a convincing confident smile before the kids arrived.

During the test, Sophie alternated between wandering the halls and sitting restlessly in her classroom. Test makers were afraid that she would help her students cheat, so she was not allowed in the testing room. Every time a door opened; she turned to see who was coming out. When the other grades switched classes, Sophie was trying to make sure they moved quietly. The guidance counselors, who were running the test sessions eventually made her come sit in the hallway with them. This kept her from wandering as she felt like she was doing something now. Other teachers and aides would stop by from time to time to see how things were going but there was little news. The administration even came by for a chat. Mal-Chin texted her offering to have lunch delivered. She turned him down.

The day seemed to drag on for an eternity. Just sitting in the hallway, watching classes change around her and hearing updates as students finished up. That was when the real nerves set in. Every finished test was a finalization, there was no turning back, no correcting answers. Some students finished faster than Sophie thought they should have. They could have just clicked answers.

After the test, Sophie showed her students a movie to destress. They needed the break. Their minds had worked hard enough today, and the math classes were still reviewing. Sophie let them pick from several movies that she had bought on an extremely good sale. Several students went to sleep. Sophie remembered taking SOLs, they were long and grueling when she had taken them on paper. Now that they were online she knew it had to be worse. The stress alone was enough to wear them down. All day, students showed up asking for scores. "I'll probably have them when you come to class tomorrow," was all she could tell them. She assured them that they worked hard and she was proud of them. The constant visits did little to calm her nerves.

"Ms. Gregory, come to the office as soon as possible," was the last thing said on the announcements. This had her shaking in her sparkly flip-flops, they usually just slipped the list of scores into her box in the back office and left her to add up the pass rate on her own. Did she fail that bad?

Her students were looking at her concerned. "I guess that's the scores," was all she said using her best calm teacher voice. It did little to hide her worry. That was ok though, it was good for the kids to see that she worried too. Mr. Worley offered to watch her students while she hurried up to the office. Sophie readily took him up on this offer and hustled up to the front. From the front window, she could see the car and bus lines already filled up waiting for students. Teachers with bus duty were already in their positions for the controlled chaos of dismissal.

Both the principal and assistant principal were in Mr. Motley's office when she arrived. They seemed pleased but Sophie could not be sure. "80%," Mr. Motley said. He waited while the pass rate sank in. Sophie's eyebrows rose; she had hoped for a passing score, which was 75%, but not that well. For a moment, Sophie thought she heard wrong. "You've got about 5 that can retake so that's good." Sophie nodded listening to the administration; she was barely aware of the bell ringing and the students leaving. Their voices and hurried footsteps echoing through the walls of the front office.

A spring in her step, she made her way back down the hall. At the intersection of the 3 grade level halls, she was met with curious teachers from other grades. The sixth-grade teachers took her papers looking through the list of students expressing surprise over some of the students that passed while one of the special education teachers gushed over Sophie's good work. Between the praise of her peers and her own excitement she was riding high. But every time the papers were passed to a new hand and more names were listed the feeling began to fade. Sophie had not looked over the papers yet and was just realizing she had no clue who passed and failed. It felt like Sophie was a child being told what was in her Christmas presents before she opened them. Sophie just wanted her papers back now, but she did not want to be rude. She could see the seventh-grade teachers milling around outside her room waiting for their chance. Finally, with the help of an older teacher who could be rather abrupt, Sophie made her way to her room. The other seventh grade teachers waited for her to tell them anything before bothering her. They went through the lists of passing scores together. This information could help them guess how the kids would do for them. It was not uncommon for students to perform similarly on each test. There were a few on the lists that disappointed Sophie. Mr. Worley walked out with her. Sophie was sure he would do better when his students tested the next day. She wished him luck before they parted.

Virginia was just as relieved as Sophie was. For dinner, Virginia made Sophie's favorite dish and dessert. Sophie had a feeling they would eat the same thing if she failed. Sophie texted Mal-Chin to say they had done well. His reply was *"Let's celebrate! We should go do something fun!"* Something fun became a topic of debate. They brainstormed ideas.

The next day was difficult. It turned out to be one of those days that left Sophie imagining she could feel her hair turning gray. She returned scores. There were students who were disappointed in their failure, even if they could retake. She did her best to let them know that she understood they tried their hardest and encouraged them. Some, she had to have a hard conversation about what happened, most of those avoided the questions. They wanted to talk over the movie that they started yesterday, and Sophie had to keep an eye on them to make sure they were not on their phones or trying to cause problems with other students. Since a student had written something awful on another's arm her first year she was paranoid about unstructured time. She tried to keep the noise down as there was other SOL testing going on. Hopefully they were not too loud.

Sophie waited around at the end of the day to see Mr. Worley's test scores. His were 78%, he said that he had more retakes. They planned out how they would remediate for retakes as they walked to their cars. Their choices were to either pull them during planning or to somehow arrange to pull them during class time. They preferred to try during regular class time so they could provide more individual help, but that would require finding someone to watch both of their classes. This would turn out to be the plan that Mr. Motely wanted and wrangled aides into their classrooms.

That night, she called Minseok about Mal-Chin. She knew she could not keep on avoiding him forever. Minseok confirmed that the general belief was that Mal-Chin was innocent.

"Why didn't he tell me he was a singer?" Sophie asked.

"Same reason I didn't tell anyone Dae-o was famous. It took the attention off. Plus, I think he liked not being known for a while." Minseok answered. "He wanted it kept secret."

"Aren't most people proud to be famous?"

"The media over in Korea is awful. One of the members of Fourth put on a little weight and they started saying I was about to be an uncle and she wasn't even dating Dae-o. They'd just been seen chatting in the street one day. They literally can't do anything."

"That's awful." Sophie answered. Sophie could not imagine living like that. Constantly hounded by cameras wherever she went.

Over the next few days the other grades tested. Sixth grade did not make the passing percent and eighth grade barely made it. Sophie just hoped their collective scores would set them over the edge.

Chapter 18

Even the cats were antsy at this point. At 10 pm, the CEO's secretary called and informed him of a video meeting with the CEO in about an hour. Mal-Chin kept checking the time to make sure he had it right. With the time difference, Mal-Chin was afraid he missed the call.

The sound of his phone ringing startled him. "Did you get the call about a meeting?" Chanyeol asked as soon as Mal-Chin answered.

"Yes, do you know what it's about?" Mal-Chin asked settling himself at his studio computer. Maybe being in the right place would help settle his nerves.

"No, but there's some new details in your case so that might be it." Chanyeol's voice lowered, "The new rumor is you're in the United States undergoing drug treatment."

The news shocked him into silence. He ran a hand through his hair feeling the need to get up and move. *Fuck.* "Does he know?"

"The detectives have been talking to everyone you know. It's on the news." There was a long pause. "Do you have anything to present? If he asks for it."

Mal-Chin shuffled through the papers on his desk, "I have lyrics but no music yet. It's all on paper."

"Good get that ready in time."

At 10:50, the secretary sent a link to the meeting. Mal-Chin checked the background before he entered the meeting. Chanyeol joined soon afterwards and they sat in awkward silence. Right on time, the CEO joined the meeting. He wasted no time with pleasantries. "Have you heard the newest allegations against you?"

"I told him before the meeting." Chanyeol answered.

"Do you know that there is now a formal investigation into the matter?" The CEO asked. His face and voice were calm but Mal-Chin saw the twitch under his eye.

"No, sir." Mal-Chin felt his stomach drop. "But there has not been any wrongdoing. I don't know who this woman is or why she's doing this."

The CEO let out a sigh. "This is what we are going to do. You are going to start posting again. Show people you are enjoying your time out of the country. Make some male friends, post pictures of you out doing stuff. But, keep the women out of it unless it's obvious she's with one of the other men. We can't have you fueling more scandals."

"Yes, sir," Mal-Chin replied. That was all he could say. "Will this hurt my chances of returning?"

"We'll see what happens. You may need to return soon. The detectives have expressed interest in speaking with you and you may need another stop by the office." With that, the CEO hung up leaving them stunned.

Mal-Chin ran his hands through his hair replaying everything. His head was spinning. Shuffling around the house, he looked out the windows finding only the darkness of a starless sky. The need to check multiple times overtook him and he found himself staring out the windows in the living room and kitchen like he would find something different.

Noise. Noise would help him focus. This silence was wearing on him again. He turned on the T.V. thinking that it would get him to sit still. While that worked, he found his mind going a million miles a minute. It ticked through everything in the call, plus every possibility in the future. He needed a better distraction. The cats were hiding, so Mal-Chin could not harass them. Beast was appearing on a T.V. show and they were already filming that. Talking to his old band mates right now seemed like a terrible idea. Bringing them down before a show was not good for them either. Mal-Chin settled on scrolling through his fake fan account on Instagram. This did little to help as he kept seeing pictures of his old life. John ranted about a rude customer, adding in silly voices and sassy comments that made it entertaining. Someone posted inspirational quotes about self-love and acceptance that he scoffed at before moving on.

The hollowness of the house was creeping up on him. Every noise seemed to echo like he was in a cave. His thumb tapped out a message before he really thought about it. *"Can I call you? I just need to talk."* As soon as he'd sent it, Mal-Chin regretted doing so.

Sofee lit the screen before it rang. Mal-Chin answered.

"Hey, you ok?" Sophie's soft voice came through the speaker. Something about her voice was relaxing.

"It's just too quiet here." Mal-Chin leaned back looking at the ceiling.

Sophie was silent for a long time, "Oh? Did something happen?" Mal-Chin gave a brief explanation of what happened. He ran a shaky hand through his hair. "Is there anything I can do to help?" Sophie asked. Mal-Chin could hear something shifting in the background. Was she in bed? He checked the time again. Late. Sophie would have work in the morning.

"Ah, I just. I don't want to be alone," Mal-Chin scratched the back of his head. "It's very late. I shouldn't have."

She let out a calming sigh, "Do you want company?"

***

Do you want company? That was probably the dumbest question Sophie could have asked. As rain began to splatter her windshield, Sophie was second guessing her decision. The rain quickly turned into a downpour. If she was not used to driving winding backroads, she would have needed to pull over. In the back of her mind, she registered that this was potentially dangerous, but she reminded herself of Mal-Chin's actions so far. Sophie had left the house without even the usual goodbye to her mother, who must not have noticed she left. A part of Sophie did not want anyone to know what she was doing. Sneaking around in the night to meet a man. How many cautionary tales had her family told about women doing this exact thing? This was not the same though. Sophie did not have to tell them what she was doing.

The porch lights were on. Mal-Chin ran out with an umbrella to meet her. They were barely inside when the first flash of lightning lit the sky. Sophie shivered. "I shouldn't have asked you to get out. You have work tomorrow, right?" Mal-Chin asked as he pulled his shoes off then hung up the umbrella.

"Tomorrow is Saturday." Sophie smiled.

"Right, American schools are closed every Saturday."

They settled awkwardly on the couch and Mal-Chin searched for something to watch. Sophie found herself just staring at his profile. The frown on his face was evident from this angle. She did not know what to do at this point. "So, did you want to talk or... um.."

He looked at her confused, "Or?" he blushed, "Where is your mind going?"

Her eyes got wide and her heart pounded in her chest. "Oh, uh, not there." Sophie shifted, "I don't know." *Well, it was now.*

"I didn't want to be alone." Mal-Chin rubbed the back of his head.

Sophie nodded. After a few minutes of silence, she finally asked, "So, what exactly happened, if you don't mind."

Mal-Chin leaned forward, putting his forearms on his knees and went through the whole story again. His leg was fidgeted rapidly by the time he was done talking. "I just wish this was all over." Sophie rubbed circles on his back and leaned her head onto his shoulder. His head was hung so low that she could not see Mal-Chin's face. Sophie could feel the sharp rise and fall of his shoulders as he sniffled. All Sophie wanted to do was wrap Mal-Chin in her arms and squeeze him until he felt better. So, that was what she did. Without moving her head, she snaked both arms around Mal-Chin. Sophie did not shush Mal-Chin or tell him everything was going to get better. Those were worthless words. The weight of his body leaned against her as he calmed. Gently, Mal-Chin grabbed her hand and pressed it against his mouth, his lips still shaking. The touch electrified Sophie's hand. They moved together as Sophie guided them to laying back on the couch.

"Am I too heavy?" He asked, his voice was off from his cheek smooshed against her shoulder.

"No, it's like laying under a warm weighted blanket." She ran a hand through his hair.

"Is this ok? You don't like being touched." Mal-Chin looked up at her, his brown eyes looked so innocent. Sophie wondered how he figured out her touch aversion.

"It's fine. And you need this." Sophie's fingers made little circles in his hair. "And," she added softly, "I don't mind with some people."

Mal-Chin moved around so that they were laying more comfortably. He somehow got one foot under her leg. She smoothed her hand over his back and placed a kiss on the top of his head. His ears turned red, so Sophie decided to just rub his back. A kiss was too personal. Mal-Chin's eyes closed.

"I didn't see you at the gym," Mal-Chin said suddenly. Sophie thought he was asleep.

"I didn't go today. We took a field trip to an arcade for the end of the school year. I was just tired."

"That sounds like fun," Mal-Chin's eyes closed again. "I love trips." He fell quiet again. Sophie's hip was beginning to feel uncomfortable where her leg was on top of Mal-Chin's, but he was so peaceful she worried that moving would wake him. Sophie's eyes closed as she tried to relax. Rain beating down on the roof and tapping on the windows put her to sleep.

Lightning flashed at the same moment that thunder roared outside. The windows rattled startling them both awake. Before she could fully register that they were still cuddled up, Mal-Chin was quickly sitting up. Rubbing his cheek, Mal-Chin scanned the room. Sophie sat up slowly, her body stiff and already missing his warmth. Whatever movie Mal-Chin had put on was over and the streaming service was displaying ads for other shows. Another flash of lightning and rumble of thunder, this time not as strong, broke the silence. Sophie scanned Mal-Chin's face. He would not look directly at her but kept glancing at her out of the corner of his eye. *Guess I'm no longer needed.* "I should go." She said the words but did not move to go. Driving in this storm was not how she wanted to spend her Friday night. Though, curling back up on the couch sounded good.

Taking her hand, Mal-Chin pressed her hand to his lips again, "Stay, please." Sophie found herself mesmerized by his dark brown eyes. There was a flame in them. He laced his fingers with hers. "It's very late and the weather is bad." Another window rattling clap of thunder pulled Sophie's eyes away. "I've got an extra bed."

"I don't have anything to sleep in," was all Sophie could think of saying. It was not a no, she didn't want to say no, it was just an issue.

Mal-Chin smiled softly, "You can sleep in one of my shirts."

This isn't just friendship but it can't be anything else. Sophie thought as she looked around Mal-Chin's bathroom. Her heart pounded a beat too fast now. She scanned her reflection in the mirror as she debated leaving her bra on. Usually, she did not sleep in it as the under wires tended to get uncomfortable. At a DDD cup, F when she brought sports bras, gravity was not kind to her when she was braless. It was natural but would it give him any ideas if he noticed? Maybe it would disgust him. She looked at the rest of her body in the mirror, noting the flab of her stomach and slight jiggle in her legs. A shiver ran through her as she imagined the disapproving look on his face. He would not be the first to have given her that look, but just imagining it on him was hurtful.

Well, you won't have to worry about him getting any ideas.

Mal-Chin's t-shirt was loose around her shoulders and chest, hiding the braless issue, but only barely covering her thighs. If she bent over, her undies would probably be exposed. Tugging on the hem did little to help, yet she kept doing it. The large shirt made her feel tiny. She folded her clothes up, careful to hide her oversized bra as best as she could then returned to the living room.

Mal-Chin changed into his pajama bottoms and tank top. She tried to ignore the fact that his chest looked perfect in the tank top. Mal-Chin's lips pressed together then slowly separated as he looked her over. Sophie could not read the expression on his face. More accurately, she would not admit what she was seeing. It was not disgust. That flame she saw earlier turned into a fire. He moved toward her then stopped suddenly. Mal-Chin rubbed the back of his head as his eyes changed, "Ah, I guess this is good night?"

"Yeah," Sophie agreed. "Thanks for letting me borrow this." She moved to go back down the hall.

Mal-Chin followed behind her. When they got to the spare bedroom door, they paused. "If you need anything, I'm down the hall."

Sophie nodded in understanding. Mal-Chin was standing too close. The fingers of one hand barely traced the line of her jaw. Her head leaned back so she could look up at him. That look was back in his eyes. Her heart thumped as Mal-Chin's gaze landed on her lips. He moved away, "Well, good night." Mal-Chin disappeared down the hall, leaving Sophie confused as she slipped into bed.

The skin of her jawline felt on fire and her lips tingled from the missed opportunity. Sophie tried to remember the last time she had been kissed. It was sometime in college, she remembered that; she also remembered it was partner who showed disgust in her body right afterwards.

Imagination is a terrible thing sometimes and Sophie's could be overactive. The look in Mal-Chin's eyes, the almost kiss; it was all in her mind. There was no way he wanted her too. Sophie curled up willing herself to go to sleep wrapped in the scent of his shirt and the crush of rain on the roof. Erasing the fantasy of his weight and warmth against her body in more than just a cuddle was difficult until she thought of Mal-Chin getting a handful of her soft belly. *No, no, no, don't even imagine anything more. You're his friend.*

Chapter 19

*S*he's just down the hall. Was the last thought Mal-Chin had before going to sleep and the first one he had when waking up. *She's just down the hall in your t-shirt that barely covers her full legs.* Was the next thought. Sitting up, Mal-Chin rubbed his face. He did not want to think too much about those legs again. His mind flashed back to almost kissing her in the hallway, to all the things he'd imagined doing to her once that shirt was off. Now his heart was thumping again. He cringed at the way he just ran off. As he passed the spare room, he slowed down trying to figure out if she was awake yet. Just knowing Sophie was in the house filled him with happiness. Sure, he wanted her in his bed, and more, but just knowing she was there was enough. He went through his morning routine with a spring in his step. A protein shake did not seem like the right breakfast for this morning. He put it aside in favor of a more traditional breakfast. Quickly, the kitchen filled with the smell of cooking food.

"Hi babies," Sophie's voice cooed. Mal-Chin tensed up. "Did last night's storm scare you? It scared me too."

He peeked into the living room to find Sophie greeting the cats with gentle pats to the head. To his disappointment, she had changed back into her clothes from last night. Maybe that was a good thing. Mal-Chin's mind imagined too much when she was wearing it. Sophie noticed Mal-Chin watching and greeted him. They migrated into the kitchen, where Mal-Chin turned down Sophie's offer to help. She settled herself at one of the counter chairs. Mal-Chin could feel her eyes on his back. The look on her face seemed pleased when he turned around. Every time he looked; she asked if he wanted help. "I want to fix you breakfast to thank you for staying," Mal-Chin finally said. That drew a smile to Sophie's face.

"Thank you. So, what are we having?" Sophie asked.

The menu for this morning was vegetable omelets, soy sauce seasoned tofu, and rice with red and black beans and kimchi. Mal-Chin admitted he wanted to make something slightly more American. They discussed their favorite breakfast foods. Sophie was a pancake fan and Mal-Chin hated scrambled eggs but loved omelets. They debated how scrambled eggs and omelets were practically the same thing.

She kept looking at him as they ate side by side. As discreetly as possible, Mal-Chin wiped his cheek thinking something must be on it. If she was not peeking at him, she was making funny faces while she struggled with the chopsticks. Mal-Chin made a mental note to pick up a regular fork and spoon set for her.

"I'm glad you're feeling better today," Sophie said as she fought a piece of tofu.

"Thank you," Mal-Chin replied. "I'm happy you came over." He pressed Sophie's hand to his lips again. The little smile she gave him made his heart skip again. They finished breakfast as they discussed plans for the day. Mal-Chin put last night's problems away. If he thought about them, a pit formed in his stomach. They decided to go to the gym together, which meant Sophie had to leave him, even if it was just long enough for her to change clothes and put on the illusion that she'd slept at home that night. While they did not really work out together, it was nice to think she was there with him.

Sophie wanted to go to the bookstore after a bath. Mal-Chin tagged along. Dog Earred Pages was a cute little building. It was a little farther up the street from the yoga studio. All the shelves lined one wall and there was a back area that looked like a sitting area where the used books were. Sophie bought several books informing the owner that she was stocking up for summer break. Mal-Chin tried to buy them but she wouldn't let him. The owner found this exchange funny.

"When do you get out for the summer?" Mal-Chin asked around a mouthful of food. They stopped at Link's Coffee House and were eating outside.

"Next week. The kids get out on Wednesday and we get out on Thursday. Then it's Memorial Day and I'm free till August" Sophie smiled happily. Mal-Chin was already planning events.

Chapter 20

The sun was bright and Mal-Chin's car hot as he pulled into the driveway that he thought was correct. When he saw Sophie's car blocked in by several others, he was sure of it. Mal-Chin was invited to the Coleman's Memorial Day cookout. He spent a good half an hour searching "What is Memorial Day?" to find out what they were celebrating and why. Mal-Chin did not want to come unprepared, but it seemed all he needed to do was dress for warm weather and be ready to eat. That second part was never an issue for him. Mal-Chin arrived 30 minutes early thinking to get there ahead of time, but it seemed that was normal for everyone. It was a small affair.

Several of the men craned their necks in his direction as he parked the car. Mal-Chin spotted Sophie helping Ford at the grill. When he stepped out of the car, someone yelled something about a stripper that he did not fully catch. Mal-Chin got the feeling that he was not supposed to hear that. But, Sophie was already hurrying across the gravel driveway to him, and that was all that mattered. Judging by her red tank and jean shorts, his white tank top and cloth shorts were the right choice. Mal-Chin barely opened his arms up to Sophie on impulse and she darted right into them, her arms wrapping around him for a quick hug.

"Very pretty, red," was all Mal-Chin said as a greeting.

"Thank you. Everyone's here." Sophie looked toward the group, "Um... my aunt and uncle invited Noah." Sophie's eyes searched the gathered group. Mal-Chin followed her gaze and found the man she'd gone on the terrible date with. Jealousy twisted in his chest. "But, my brother and his girlfriend are here too," Sophie cheerfully added. Mal-Chin followed her to where the cookout was happening. They were using the space between two houses even though they had a large back yard. There were several tables sat out, one small one was on a porch where two elderly women sat surrounded by the rest of the women. Sophie barely finished introductions before Ford ordered her to get cheese for the burger patties from the house. Sophie abandoned Mal-Chin with the women.

"I was expecting a tiny little thing when Sophie invited you," Virginia teased, "but you're good and solid." She patted his arm then gave it a squeeze, "Oh my." Mal-Chin only laughed. He was used to this kind of thing. It was funny from the elderly women.

The other elderly woman, Sophie had introduced her as her aunt but she was close to Virginia's age, asked him to come closer so she could get a good look at him. Papery soft hands patted his cheeks. "Oh, aren't you handsome!" She said when he smiled, "You and Sophie make a pretty couple." Mal-Chin felt his ears turn red.

"Oh," Carol said pointing limply at him, "You're the friend from Korea, the one that goes to yoga with her." Mal-Chin confirmed this as he stood back up. Somehow it sounded like an accusation. "We've got a friend whose husband is stationed in Taiwan and she moved there with her kids to be with him. Jessica, are they still over there?"

Mal-Chin tried to figure out what that had to do with him being from Korea while Jessica looked it up on her phone. "I've been there a few times. Nice place" Mal-Chin added trying to keep the conversation going.

"Now," Carol put her hand on her hip and leaned against the plain column she was standing next to you. "Are you and Sophie....." She crossed to fingers and Mal-Chin looked at her confused not knowing what that meant. "You know, seeing each other?"

Seeing each other? Mal-Chin wracked his brain for a meaning, "I would like to see her more often. She's very pretty." Mal-Chin smiled pleased with his answer. That accomplishment was short lived. Soon, Mal-Chin realized he misunderstood the question.

Carol and Jessica exchanged a look of annoyance, "Well, we brought Noah. My husband Rob," she pointed to the large man that only half greeted him, "thinks he'd be a perfect match for her so if you're not seeing her....." Virginia made a grunting noise and gave Carol a pointed look. Sophie emerged from the house with the cheese, a pack of hot dogs and a few other items. She handed the cheese and hot dogs to her grandfather then started putting the rest on a table set against the wall of the house. Noah spoke to her low enough that Mal-Chin could not hear what he said. Sophie chuckled uncomfortably before hurrying off. Sophie looked at Mal-Chin, her face showing slight alarm. The conversation changed to something else. Mal-Chin moved to be near Sophie. Lacing his fingers with Sophie's, Mal-Chin grabbed her hand and pressed a kiss to the back of it. That cute little smile lit Sophie's face. Mal-Chin wondered if Sophie knew she did that every time he kissed the back of her hand. Mal-Chin's eyes cut to Noah, who watched the short exchange. Noah needed to know to stay away. Mal-Chin had a feeling that the only "no" Noah would take was another man staking his claim.

"Are we ready to bring everything out?" Virginia asked her. Sophie stepped away from the table where she was trying to get Mal-Chin and Will talking.

"He's just starting the hot dogs so probably," Sophie was looking between Mal-Chin and her brother. Will was doing his best to calm a star-struck Vicki.

"Well, let's get to it." Virginia said getting up. The two disappeared into the house. No one else budged. The conversations continued to flow and Sophie darted in and out of the house. Mal-Chin tried to make himself useful, opening doors, carrying armfuls of drinks out. He caught Virginia expressing her embarrassment that he was helping. Styrofoam plates squeaked as they filled them with food. Mal-Chin snapped a picture of his plate hoping no one noticed. "*Happy Memorial Day America! Celebrating with the neighbors. They said I had to try to the lemonade.*" He posted quickly.

Sophie made sure he did not want the end seat before sitting down. Mal-Chin had been deliberate in his seat choice. With Sophie at the end of the table and Will and Vicki across from them, Noah could not bother her. Having her at his side felt good but he could tell she was on edge. None of the family spoke to her besides spitting out orders and watching her run to fulfill them. Mal-Chin quickly picked up on the anime conversation Conner and Will were having. Conner was amazed that Mal-Chin spoke Japanese. The other end of the table was talking about someone they mutually knew. From the conversation, it seemed they didn't like this person.

"Man that was good!" Robbie yelled over everyone gathered, "I'm gonna gain 10 pounds from all this."

"Uh-oh Sophie, you better be careful," Virginia called back from her table. The group had a good laugh.

"She's *trying* to lose weight," Noah asked with a smirk. "Does she know that she has to cut down eating for that? Hey, big man," he waved his arm at Mal-Chin "teach her how to eat right," Noah said with a laugh, Robbie, Jessica, and Carol joined him. Will's eyes cut to them and his jaw set hard, but he did not say anything. Mal-Chin looked at Sophie sympathetically. She turned a chip between her fingers before taking a sip of lemonade; her hair was hiding her face. The insult stung even to Mal-Chin.

"Girl! Don't listen to them. You gotta eat to keep them sexy curves," Vicki added swaying in her seat then nodding. This made the group at the other end of the table laugh more. Conner, for his part, looked embarrassed. Mal-Chin pressed Sophie's hand to his lips. Robbie went into Sophie's whole history of her weight struggles, how she'd been so tiny when she was younger then "bloated up" during high school and her never ending failures at diets. Carol finally hushed him to read something off her phone.

"How are we doing on buns?" Sophie suddenly rose from her seat. "I'll go get some more." She headed inside before anyone could tell her she didn't need to.

"Huh, someone can't take a joke," Robbie chuckled as soon as she was in the door. There was something dark in his eyes. Vicki grabbed Will's wrist. A silent conversation passed between them.

Mal-Chin looked around the gathered family. What kind of family just let this pass as ok? They must have known it was hurtful from Sophie's reaction. Mal-Chin could not understand the rest of the family just sitting there and letting them do it. "I'm sorry, I missed the joke." Mal-Chin feigned ignorance. Mal-Chin looked at Robbie. In American interviews, the host would sometimes ask rude questions or ones that were inappropriate. Mal-Chin would play dumb and ask them to explain the question. It would leave the host floundering for an explanation.

Robbie shifted in his chair, his eyes searched the gathered group, "Well, it's," Robbie cleared his throat. *Works every time.*

"I didn't get it either," Will answered. He looked hard into Mal-Chin's eyes. Collective anger passed between the two of them.

"That's what I thought. Just sounded mean." Mal-Chin stood from the table and went into the house.

Compared to the heat outside, the house was almost cold. The fact that the T.V. and lights were off only strengthened the feeling of coldness. Mal-Chin found Sophie standing in the living room on her phone. "Sophie?" She looked at him startled when he spoke.

"Oh, hey," She put her phone away, "I was just cooling off real quick." She smiled tightly.

Without a word, he wrapped his arms tight around her, "You know you're very pretty, right?" Sophie did not answer him, she just lightly wrapped her arms around him.

"They were only joking," came the muffled reply.

"That's not a joke."

"Baby?" Ford's voice called out. Ford was just stepping into the living room when the two separated. "I was coming to see if you were alright. Looks like he beat me to it."

"I'm ok," Sophie nodded. She took a half step away from Mal-Chin.

"You know how they are, don't listen to them," Ford looked at Mal-Chin apologetically, "Sorry you had to hear that." Mal-Chin nodded wondering how often these kinds of comments happened.

The three ended up sitting around in the living room in silence until Sophie took a deep breath, "They're probably wondering where those buns are. I should go." The two men nodded and watched as she left.

Some people, I think, aren't meant to fall in love. And I'm one of those people. So, why try? If you're unlovable, you're unlovable. Sophie's words echoed in Mal-Chin's ears. It made sense now. Of course she would think that her family shows her no love. Mal-Chin thought about the calm neutral expression that always graced Sophie's face. How long had she worked to master that expression? The image of her unguarded smile on the yoga studio floor popped into his mind. That's what he wanted to see more of, the real Sophie under the calm surface. "How long has this teasing been happening?" Mal-Chin asked.

Ford thought the question over before replying, "A while. I guess it started when she was in high school, maybe middle school." Ford nodded to himself. "Sophie was an easy target. Quiet, shy, her parents were too stuck on themselves to step in and Sophie wasn't going to. They don't like that she's pretty, smart and helpful." Ford let out a sigh. "I was hoping, with guests, it wouldn't be an issue today. She was so happy earlier."

"Why do you let them do it?" Mal-Chin searched Ford's expression but only found the same quiet calmness that Sophie carried.

"They throw a fit if you say anything against them. Gotta keep the peace. Sophie won't cause problems, but they will."

"It shouldn't be that way. She deserves better." Mal-Chin spoke carefully trying to keep the edge out of his voice.

Ford just nodded in agreement, "I know." Mal-Chin sat there in silence with Ford. He was worried he was about to get the infamous parent lecture from the movies. Ford just sat there in silence his hands resting on his stomach as he stared out the window rocking in the chair. There was something almost creepy about it. The way the light shone on Ford's blue eyes and the almost mesmerized look of his face. He finally looked at Mal-Chin. "Are you going back to South Korea?"

"Yes, eventually."

"That's too bad," was all Ford said before getting up and heading back outside. Mal-Chin pondered Ford's statement then followed the old man out.

"Now, it could only be better if we had a pool," Carol stated after the watermelon and ice cream was eaten. The heat and humidity of late afternoon had set in at full force. Robbie and his family had no love for warm weather. They were the kind of people that walked around in shorts until snow blanketed the ground. In the summer, the windows of their house were constantly fogged from the air conditioning being set as low as possible.

Mal-Chin pulled himself away from Robbie talking how much he used to lift to add, "I have one." That was all the invite the Coleman's need. Mal-Chin was suddenly their best friend. Noah, thankfully, declined.

***

All day, Sophie had felt grimy from preparing food for the cookout. Her arms and face felt like they were covered in a layer of grease. Sophie felt slightly refreshed as she took off her clothes and pulled on the emerald green two-piece bathing suit she bought on impulse. It was the only bathing suit that fit now. The bra style top had an underwire in it. For the first time in her life, she owned a bathing suit that supported her breasts and did not look like it was for a much older woman. Sophie swayed her hips in the mirror pleased with how it accentuated the inward curve of her waist. Outside the door, Vicki was bouncing around showing off the bathing suit Sophie loaned her. It fit tight but she liked it. From what she could hear, Will was expressing the same sentiment.

Sophie moved to join them then paused doubt raising in her. She had never owned anything that showed this much skin before, even if it was just a small strip of her stomach. She'd bought the suit in a moment of confidence but now that her family's teasing was playing in her head, she doubted herself. "Vicki?" She called as she opened the door. "How does it look?"

Vicki turned and gave her a big smile, "Oh my goodness! You look amazing!" Her smile turned mischievous. "Trying to show off for your guy huh?" Will made a noise of disapproval even though he could not see it.

Sophie pulled a long tank top over her suit and grabbed a towel. The group headed out; Lorraine opted to drive separately so she could leave when she was ready. Sophie had a feeling that Lorraine was just tagging along to see Mal-Chin shirtless. As they passed Virginia and Ford's house, the elderly couple pulled out of the driveway following them. Will and Vicki did not question how Sophie knew the way so easily. The whole family seemed to arrive at once. This was fine by Mal-Chin, who met them before they could get out of the cars. Virginia had packed up leftovers and snacks in case they got hungry while swimming. Mal-Chin and Sophie picked those up while Virginia took Mal-Chin's arm for support. Carol began telling this long rambling life story of a woman. The point of the story was: this woman lived up the road. Mal-Chin looked at Sophie confused about why Carol was telling him all this but Sophie just shrugged.

Mal-Chin was, in fact, shirtless. His chest was the perfection that it was in every picture, but his stomach was softer than the carb starved look typical of magazine pictures. Sophie had seen plenty of pictures of his perfect abs. This softer look with just a hint of definitions was sexier in her opinion. The other women in her family noticed the same thing as well.

Mal-Chin led them out to the pool. Conner lost no time jumping in. "Cold!" Vicki shrieked as soon as she was in. Vicki tried to climb Will's back. Which just caused laughs from the gathered group. Robbie cannon balled in, almost knocking Carol's floatie over and making Mal-Chin bust out laughing before copying him. Mal-Chin did not quite make the splash that Robbie did.

"Granny," Jessica said, "Have you seen my new bathing suit? I paid $80 for it *on sale*." Jessica asked as she unwrapped her towel to show it was a blue one-piece suit.

"That looks really good on you," Sophie stated.

"Fits your shape just right. You look real pretty." Virginia added. "It's so cute." She stated as extra.

"Show 'em yours." Lorraine ordered swatting a hand at Sophie. Her mother had seen the suit after Sophie bought it and was contemplating returning it. Sophie obliged pulling off the tank she was using as a cover-up.

Jessica's nose turned up at the end, "I like that color." Jessica grabbed a floatie and joined her mother.

"It's so..." Granny patted her tummy where it was covered by her high waisted bottoms, "at least it hides that tummy." Sophie felt naked now.

"You look nice," Ford added. "Now, let's get in that water." Ford rose from where he was seated and took the steps into the pool making little noises to say it was cold. Virginia questioned Lorraine about why she had not brought a bathing suit as they watched Vicki and the boys rough housing in the pool.

"Sophie!" Mal-Chin suddenly called. "Come join us." He looked back at her then swam to the edge of the pool. "You look good in green," he stated as she walked to the edge of the pool. He was looking up at her with a sparkle in his eyes that made her blush.

"Thank you," She sat down with her feet in the water next to him.

"I am going to have to pull you in?" He asked as he grabbed her arms and gave them a playful tug. With a giggle, Sophie slid in. Even on a hot day, the pool water was shockingly cold. Sophie shivered as her exposed skin hit the water. She thought the others were just kidding when they said it was cold. They were on the deep end and Sophie had to kick her legs to keep her head above water. This struggle was made harder when Vicki latched onto her back demanding that Sophie swim her around the pool. In response, Sophie ducked under the water hearing a muffled squeal from Vicki who let go.

"Get back here! It's not fair that you have built-in flotation!" Vicki yelled chasing after her.

"Vicki!" Will chuckled calling out before shaking his head. The two girls were splashing and giggling as Vicki chased her around. Neither one of them heard whatever Will said next. Mal-Chin was just watching them laughing.

Lorraine was the first to leave. As soon as the sky turned dark and the air cooled, she left with barely a goodbye. The rest slowly left soon after. Conner was reluctant to go, but he didn't really have a choice. Mal-Chin exchanged numbers with Carol and Robbie promising they could come over to swim again whenever they wanted.

Finally, it was just the four of them left. Sophie used the excuse that they were staying behind to clean up, but she just was not ready to go. Plus, Will and Vicki were having a good time. Mal-Chin disappeared into the house when his phone rang leaving Sophie the odd one out.

The plop of feet behind her drew Sophie's attention away from the night sky. The view was beautiful. Mal-Chin's house was just far enough out that the city lights did not obstruct the stars. She was seated on the edge of the pool her feet swinging back and forth in the water. Mal-Chin sat down next to her, so close they were almost touching. Their legs began to move to the same rhythm. "Everything ok?" Sophie asked without looking at him.

"I've got to go back tomorrow," Mal-Chin stated looking up at the sky. He was trying to find what was so fascinating to her. "Can you watch my cats again?" Sophie nodded. Mal-Chin laced his fingers with hers. "I wish you could come with me."

A nervous chuckle escaped Sophie, "You say that like," She stopped herself then shook her head.

"Like?" Mal-Chin prompted looking at her. That mesmerizing look was in his eyes again.

"Like you -uh- like me." Sophie looked away quickly.

"I do." Mal-Chin answered looking at her profile trying to read her expression.

"No, I mean, like, romantically." Just the word romantically brought warmth to her cheeks. Her heartbeat too hard. Sophie chewed on her bottom lip feeling stupid for even saying it. "Never mind," She moved to get up. Mal-Chin was still holding Sophie's hand and was not letting go. They stared at each other for a moment before Sophie awkwardly sat back down.

"Thank you for the clarity," Mal-Chin let go of her hand and used his fingers to turn her head so she was looking at him. "I meant I like you, romantically." Sophie looked at him with wide eyes. Sophie could not think of anything to say.

"Don't pick like that." She finally spluttered out completely flustered. He was too close, too serious. Her eye darted away trying to find something that wasn't him to look at.

"If I kissed you, would it prove I was serious?" Mal-Chin asked suddenly.

The question threw Sophie off for a moment. Her lips tingled with the invitation and her heart pounded. "I don't know. But, we could find out."

That was all the invite Mal-Chin needed. He kissed her gently, more gently than Sophie expected. One kiss turned into several and the two forgot everything except the pounding in their hearts and the softness of their lips.

"Oh! That's how it is huh!" Will's voice interrupted. Vicki was cheering her on. Sophie hid her face embarrassed. This was going to be a long drive home. Sophie began to wish she had a passport and could go with him. The feel of his lips lingered with Sophie the rest of the night.

Chapter 21

A discreet return to Seoul was not in the cards for Mal-Chin. SLS was leaving the country and, as with everywhere they went, the airport was a mad house. SLS's fan chant filled the air. Cameras flashed blindingly from all sides. Security was the only thing that kept the group moving. Pulling his mask up higher and the brim of his hat lower, Mal-Chin followed hoping he would be confused for a crew member. Mal-Chin heard a mumble of his name in the cacophony. SLS leaving may have been big news but Park Mal-Chin returning was also good for the gossip columns. Suspicion that his arrival was planned to coincide with their departure began to sneak in. No better way to say that he could travel freely than being caught at the airport.

"PARK MAL-CHIN! I LOVE YOU! EAT WELL!" Someone screamed over the den of noise. Mal-Chin was stunned for a second then he pulled his mask down, gave his signature smile, the one that made his eyes scrunch up, and blew a kiss in the direction the shout came from. He was met with squeals, which drew the attention of SLS. One of the members closer to him laughed. Mal-Chin was trying to keep his distance from them. One celebrity's scandal could easily bring a bad light on anyone involved with them. By the end of the day, the short exchange would only end up painting SLS as amazing people just for that acknowledgment.

They were corralled into a private waiting room. Mal-Chin to wait for his ride to arrive and SLS to wait on their delayed flight. Inside the waiting room, SLS spread out getting comfortable. Waiting was typical when you traveled often. They were talking quietly to each other or scrolling on their phones. Several were already eating the snacks from the free concessions. Mal-Chin sat in a comfortable chair off by himself. He was out of place here. A fallen star among suns.

Making a goofy face, he took a picture and sent it to Sophie to let her know he had landed. Next, he messaged his mother and the members of Beast to tell them he would be in town for a while. Suho instantly started arranging plans to meet up with him. The wait was getting long, and they were all getting restless. Mal-Chin's manager was there but he was waiting for the crowd to calm down before coming in. That was understandable; he did not want to face that mob alone. Eunho, the youngest member of SLS, sat down next to him and started asking questions about living in the U.S. Mal-Chin got the feeling Eunho was a little disappointed that Mal-Chin was in a small town and not a large city. The recount of an American cookout did interest Eunho.

"Hey man," S.J. added in suddenly, "We'll have to visit you if we ever come to that part of the country. Maybe we'll make you a special guest on our vacation show." S.J. smiled being genuine about the visit.

"Yeah, I've got a pool. And the town's got a walking trail by the river," Mal-Chin responded. He did not pay any attention to it until now with the rest of SLS staring at him dumbfounded. S.J. had spoken to him and he'd replied in English. A few made comments on how impressed they were. His English was just as good as S.J's.

"You sound like a country singer," one of the other members, who was lounging on a couch, added with an impish smile.

"I guess I picked it up from the people living there." Mal-Chin shrugged switching back to Korean.

"Oh, just to let you know," Eunho added, "No one actually thinks you did any of that stuff."

"Thank you." Mal-Chin dipped his head slightly as he replied. The mention of his disgrace caught him off guard. He met the group several times, they shared banter backstage at awards ceremonies, and knew they were a friendly bunch. The oldest member started fussing at the youngest for mentioning it. Even their arguments were friendly. Finally, SLS's flight arrived. The group was quickly hustled out to a waiting crowd of fans. With the group out of the way, Mal-Chin was able to slip out to meet Chanyeol. He hustled out to the waiting black van, quickly threw his things in and the driver whisked them back to Mal-Chin's apartment.

Chanyeol went over the official plans for the next couple of days. Mal-Chin was trying to pay attention but he had a running fantasy playing through his mind. In it, he was showing Sophie around Korea. They ate his favorite dishes, climbed the steps to temples, star gazed from the tops of a high hill and he took her on a shopping spree through Gangnam. All the touristy things that people loved to do when visiting Seoul played out in front of him. In it, not a single paparazzi camera bothered them.

Just as Mal-Chin's mind was spinning through all the delicious food he had been missing, someone rang his apartment call box. The detectives wasted no time coming to see him. Mal-Chin was grateful not to have his picture taken outside the police station. One detective wandered his house while the other asked the same questions they had last time. His answers did not change. Annoyance at answering these questions again began to surface. Getting angry now would do him no good.

"You granted us access to check your bank records. Do you have any other accounts that you didn't tell us about?" The female investigator asked.

"No." Mal-Chin shook his head. He wanted to add more but did not know what to say that would not come across as rude or condescending. The only way to end this quickly was to be as helpful as possible.

Finally done poking around Mal-Chin's apartment, the other detective asked, "Where are you staying in the United States?"

"Danville, Virginia. It's a small town. Boring." Mal-Chin answered unsure of why they wanted that information.

"What have you been up to there?" The male detective asked. Mal-Chin went through the basics of his daily routine; it was not very interesting. He left out the part about hanging around with Sophie. He got the feeling that that information would be turned against him.

That was when the female detective chimed in again, "Are you aware there's rumors going around that you're in a drug addiction program there?"

Mal-Chin hung his head. The mention of that rumor made his stomach turn. He spent years taking care of his body, trying to keep it healthy and strong. Doing drugs was the opposite of his goal. "I heard about that earlier in the week. I'm not. I'm just trying to ride this out outside of public view." The detectives nodded. Mal-Chin agreed to consent to a second drug test if needed and gave them a copy of his American address before they left.

Mal-Chin picked a random direction and started walking. Being able to just pick a direction and head off was liberating. No matter where he ended up, he would find something of interest to do. He was in Hannam-dong, a district growing popularity due the number of young celebrities living there. Seeing a famous person wandering the street without a mask or ball cap here was normal. *Still, couldn't be too careful,* Mal-Chin reminded himself as he passed a store with an SLS advertisement in the window. Fame was relentless. Sometimes Mal-Chin wished he followed his original path like his parents wanted.

Heat washed up in waves from the concrete as Mal-Chin walked. Midday in the city wasn't the best time to go for a walk. He ducked into a small café that he often visited. An iced Americano sounded delicious today. He ordered it and sat down in his favorite corner to cool down and hide from visiting eyes at the front. Hannam-dong was starting to get its share of tourist who were not here for the museum and view of the Han River. Mal-Chin began to daydream about walking the Han River with Sophie. The image was the same as their path down the River Walk Trail, he just changed the background.

"Chinnie?" A feminine voice spoke from beside his seat. His back was to the store front. Mal-Chin looked up at the perfection that was Arin. Her long silky hair was pulled into a low ponytail that looked professionally done.

"Arin. What are you doing here?" Mal-Chin asked. He looked away from her now.

"We were filming by the river," she gracefully swung into the seat across from him, "It's such a hot day that I thought I'd stop in and get a drink." She shook her cup at him and smiled. He used to think it was cute when she did that.

"I didn't realize you were working on a comeback."

"And I didn't realize you were back in town," Arin took a sip of her drink without picking it up off the table and turned her eyes up at him. Green contacts. They looked unreal, flat.

"I ran into S.J. on his way out," Mal-Chin tilted his head at her. Mal-Chin knew what Arin was up to, or at least he guessed.

"Yeah, they've got an interview in the U.S." Arin leaned back in her seat crossing her arms, "Some late-night talk shows or something." She sipped her drink. "He'll be gone awhile."

Mal-Chin just sipped his drink in silence. It did not taste good anymore. He messaged the Beast Group chat asking what everyone was up to while he was in. "I'm going to be busy. I don't have much time here," Mal-Chin said in answer to her unasked question. It was a no. They both checked their phones. There were replies flowing into the group chat about what everyone planned to do. Ryu, their youngest member, wanted to get Korean BBQ and soon the whole group agreed.

Arin's manager called to tell her she needed to return to the set. She went out the door telling him to calm down in a bored tone. Mal-Chin finished his drink ready to go back home now. The return trip felt longer.

***

Excitement filled Mal-Chin as the day grew later. He was visiting his family again. This time his nephew would be present. This warranted a new toy. In the toy store, he debated whether he should get an educational toy or just something fun. Well, he was the uncle so something just fun was the right answer. The shutter of a camera lens helped him along in making the decision. Fan or journalist, he did not want his picture taken. Toy in hand, he headed for his parent's home. Quickly, he busied himself helping in the kitchen and fretting his mother.

Mal-Chin's help came to an end as soon he heard little feet. Mal-Chin went off to the front door to greet his nephew. He squatted down and waited for the child to come to him. Hyeonuk looked at him, then his mother, Yeon-seo. Mal-Chin was beginning to worry he wouldn't have anything to do with him. When was the last time Hyeonuk had seen Mal-Chin in person? What if he was having the same reaction kids do when they meet their favorite TV character? Hyeonuk's face scrunched up in a smile. He and Mal-Chin simultaneously did a wiggle, and the boy went running to him. He wandered the house with Hyeonuk in his arms. In a few years, Hyeonuk would be too big for his parents to carry. Even then, Mal-Chin wanted to be strong enough to lift him. Hyeonuk showed Mal-Chin all his artwork that was hung about the house. They went into the kitchen and Mal-Chin let Hyeonuk peek into all the pots, careful not to let the toddler get burnt. The bites of food Mal-Chin snuck him got them kicked out of the kitchen. Mal-Chin's laugh was the only thing that kept the toddler from thinking they were in trouble.

Hyeonuk was squeezed between his parents at the dinner table and pouting because he wanted to sit with Mal-Chin. Conversation was slow as they ate but quickly picked up. Mal-Chin's sister told stories about work and silly little things Hyeonuk had done throughout the week. "You know," Mal-Chin's bother-in-law, Dae-sik, started suddenly when there was a lull, "you're a lot darker than when you left. Is that going to hurt your image?" Yeon-seo gave her husband a little pop and a look. Dae-sik looked back at her confused.

"Oh, there was a holiday in the States on Monday. Memorial Day. They had a cookout, and we went swimming," Mal-Chin's mind flashed back to the feel of lips on his and struggled trouble containing a smile.

"They? We?" His father joined in. "Who were you with? Was it the friend that you ate with that time?"

"Yeah. They're nice people. One of them is watching the cats while I'm here." He could not stop the smile that came to his face then. His parents looked at each other.

"Guess it's a supermodel," Dae-sik mumbled earning him an elbow from both Yeon-seo and Mal-Chin's mother. He yelped dramatically. Hyeonuk looked between them confused then laughed at his father getting in trouble.

Hyeonuk loved the gift Mal-Chin brought him. They played with it in the living room for a long time. Mal-Chin devoured every second of the child's attention that he could get. He even carried the sleeping toddler all the way to the subway station and did not hand him back to Dae-sik until the train arrived. If he had a car seat, Mal-Chin would have driven them home.

Chapter 22

Mal-Chin hated getting his hair cut, always had. It was too much sitting still. The pictures that were circulating online showed that he was in desperate need of one. Many of the fans liked his longer hair, but he did not. So, his first stop this morning was his stylist for a cut. He left feeling refreshed.

Weaving through busy streets, the van took him straight to the record label's main office. Instead of the back entrance that most of the talent used, he was instructed to go through the main entrance. Chanyeol was not anywhere in sight. Checking his phone showed no messages from the man. Reception told him where to go and let him pass into the elevators. Mal-Chin was dressed like the idol he was but the women at the front were unbothered. They were used to the barrage of handsome men coming through the lobby.

So this is how we're playing things huh? Mal-Chin thought. They were going to act like he was not part of the company. He tucked one hand into the back pocket of his black jeans and practiced his most intimidating stage face in the elevator door's reflective surface. He was debating how to react to this and practicing tough faces when the elevator door opened. Exhaust and a girl group climbed on together. Exhaust bowed in greeting to him and the girls followed suit. They were carrying bags of food and were heading to the roof. He smiled remembering the days of flirtatious meals with girl groups. One of the girls was trying her hardest, and failing, not to stare at Mal-Chin's exposed chest. He left the buttons open until right below his chest, exposing the full muscles there. For a moment, he debated closing it up, but he also did not want to embarrass this girl. He pretended not to notice. While the floors counted up, he complimented Exhaust on their newest album release. They were excited that Mal-Chin listened to it. They even mimicked one of the dances while they sang it for him.

The elevator reached his floor and he departed with a wave of the papers he carried, receiving another bow from the group, "Enjoy your lunch. Make sure your managers don't catch you all together," was the last thing Mal-Chin said as the doors closed. Beast had gotten into a good amount of trouble for trying to be playboys.

His stride took on a casual confidence as he headed down to the meeting room by memory. There were no hesitant stops, no glancing around. Chanyeol was waiting for him outside the conference room door. "They've got a new contract and deal laid out for you. It might not be the best, but we'll see what we can do."

Mal-Chin looked at the door and swallowed nodding. His confidence was fading now. *How bad could it be?* "I'm guessing I won't be on this label anymore." A secretary he did not recognize was the only person in the room as they entered. They were informed that there was a slight delay due to another meeting and were directed where to sit. The room they were in was small in terms of conference rooms. Coming here meant he was not meeting with the record label head but with one of the board members. He flipped through the papers as the secretary left the room, it was all policy and a copy of the song lyrics Mal-Chin had emailed Chanyeol.

Eventually, the door opened without warning. Mal-Chin's stomach turned into a hard knot as he stood and bowed respectfully to the man that entered. Mal-Chin recognized him, Choi Taeyeong was the head of a subsidiary group: SkyLimit Entertainment. They took the bands that the main label deemed risky but that might have a chance. Now, Mal-Chin really saw his situation.

The man rambled about Mal-Chin's situation, complimented his look and his music. All of which passed over Mal-Chin without registering. Mal-Chin thought the label had a main spot for him. The initial terms of his contract had not changed: get the investigation over with, not be seen with women, stop the rumor about being in rehab and no public contact with the members of Beast. Hopefully, this little trip home would help to end the rumors and eliminate one condition.

Chanyeol looked over the contract as well and added in a clause that none of Mal-Chin's music would be given to another artist without his permission. Somehow, by the end, Chanyeol worked out that Mal-Chin would retain some of the same back up dancers that Beast used and a full comeback schedule, including T.V. spots, music videos, and social media presence, when his first solo album came out. To Mal-Chin's surprise, the new record label promised him a higher level of creative freedom than he had with Beast. SLS flashed through his mind. That group did whatever they wanted and were a major success. Maybe this would not be so bad, even with a pay cut.

Mal-Chin left feeling confident but at the same time, like he had a huge weight on his shoulders. Between the pay cut, the lesser label name, and the initial conditions Mal-Chin felt like he sold away a part of himself. However, the idea of more creative freedom, being free from being just the "sexy one" was exciting. He took a breath trying to casually shake the feeling from him. In the elevator, he messaged the Beast group chat and told them of the no public contact order.

Mal-Chin knew this was a bad idea even as he pulled up to the restaurant. The car he drove was not his favorite, but it was less attention grabbing. Right now, Mal-Chin needed to be discreet. His newer luxury cars could be flashy enough to tip off the media and public that someone famous was nearby. He pulled the brim of his hat farther down over his freshly cut two-block hairstyle before he made his way into the restaurant. Mal-Chin did not use the front entrance like most guests, and probably the other members of Beast. He used the side entrance that was reserved for celebrities trying to be discreet. The hostess led him to the group's empty table. Minkyo tended to wait till the last second to get ready. Mal-Chin ordered a drink. Sophie texted him, *"There was a storm last night. Power went out for over 4 hours so I cleaned out your fridge. I'll refill it when I go to the store."* Mal-Chin sighed thinking about the wasted banchan he'd spent hours making. He was not looking forward to making kimchi again. The image of Sophie giggling in his kitchen floor in oversized kitchen gloves made him smile.

Jeong-hui, Ryu and Dae-o arrived first. They filled in the other side of the table, Ryu taking the outer most seat. "Should we order or keep waiting?" Ryu asked excitedly.

"We'll probably just get beef." Dae-o answered scrolling through his phone already bored. They briefly discussed if they could risk beef. They thought about upcoming performances and decided it would be ok. Any weight changes caused by it would be gone by then. Dae-o went off to order and passed Suho and Minkyo on the way. Suho took on the responsibility of cooking the meat. He gave no reason why but no one questioned their oldest member and leader. He wasted no time putting the food on the grill.

There was some awkwardness as they tried to avoid the subjects of their divided careers. They landed on the one of their friends being on the latest episode of Running Man and the antics he got up to. Mal-Chin caught that episode on his first night back. It was a good episode. Sometimes, it was nice to just be entertained. Jeong-hui and Ryu got everyone caught up in an argument about what type of dinosaur Dooley was. The answer was soon clear that none of them knew or would admit that they did not know.

"Dooley was a ceratosaurs," a female voice answered. The conversation came to an embarrassing stop. The members of Purple-Pink, who were all comfortably dressed, gathered at the end of their table. The speaker, Yujin, smiled looking over the table letting her hand rest on Ryu's shoulder. Yujin swung her pink hair over her shoulder, "So what are you up to besides being dorks?"

"Nothing, just," Ryu meekly gestured to Mal-Chin, who was smiling at his phone, "Chinnie is in town so...." He cleared his throat, "What about you?"

"We just wrapped up filming our newest music video. Thought we'd celebrate." Bora answered, half her hair was dyed blue. "Just looking for a little fun." Arin's eyes cut to Mal-Chin as Bora said this, but Mal-Chin was still looking at his phone and did not notice.

"Oh, can they join us?" Ryu basically pleaded. Yujin was practically rubbing his shoulder now.

Suho glanced around the table. His eyes moved as he tried to make a difficult decision. He finally shrugged, "I'm ok with it," the others agreed. Ryu was their youngest member and they often gave in to his wants easily. Luckily, he did not take advantage of it. Mal-Chin put his discomfort aside. The staff pulled another table over and the group resituated themselves. Arin somehow squeezed her way between Suho and Mal-Chin. He was over aware of her presence.

"When did that happen?" Mal-Chin asked leaning toward Dae-o and nodding toward Ryu and Yujin.

Dae-o shrugged, "He just suddenly liked her."

The group became livelier with the addition of the women. Always the showoff, Jeong-hui was the loudest member of the group. The women on either side of him were laughing and clapping at his antics. "Oi," Jeong-hui yelled from where he sat, "Mal-Chin. Why are you on your phone so much?"

"Nothing," Mal-Chin tried to put the phone away quickly. There was a commotion as the men started yelling about grabbing his phone. "No! No!" Mal-Chin said as he and Dae-o grappled for it. The group was laughing. Suho put an arm out wary of the open grill in front of them. Arin grabbed that spot on Mal-Chin's side. It caused Mal-Chin to jump and Dae-o suddenly had the phone. The phone was passed down to Minkyo, who unlocked it on the first try. Mal-Chin's eyebrows lifted in surprise. Suho was peeking over Minkyo's shoulder as they looked through it.

"Someone named Sophie has been texting him." There was a grumble of questions, "There's a bunch of heart emojis after the name." Minkyo chuckled.

"She's cute." Suho added as Minkyo scrolled through their messages. "And sexy."

"Who is that? You're new girlfriend?" Ryu asked. Arin went rigid next to him.

"She's just watching my cats." Mal-Chin answered nonchalantly. Embarrassment raised up his cheeks.

"That's a lot of kissy face emojis for someone just watching your cat." Minkyo answered to the amusement of the table. "And a lot of thirst trap pictures from you."

The whole table wanted to see the phone screen now. Suho displayed the picture Sophie sent him earlier. She was laying on Mal-Chin's couch with one cat cuddled up to her cheek, the other on her chest and the biggest smile on her face.

"Looks like she's decent at watching pets." Arin said. There was an edge to her voice that Mal-Chin recognized. "She's got a big face." There was a giggle from one of the other girls and Jeong-hui.

"Wait," Dae-o leaned around him to get a look at the picture, "Isn't that Minseok's girl?"

There was an awkward silence, "Like, you're brother?" Bora asked.

"Did you steal his brother's girlfriend?" Yujin asked, "This just got T.V. drama good."

"No, they're just friends." Mal-Chin answered quickly, "You should talk to him about that." Mal-Chin was focusing on Suho again who was scrolling through the messages.

Suho's lips poked out as he made a silent whistle then he scrolled more, "But, are you dating her?" Suho asked. Mal-Chin was thinking of the gym selfies they sent back and forth. Suho liked curvy girls and Sophie's gym clothes made her curves look amazing. Mal-Chin snatched his phone back thoroughly embarrassed now. Not to mention Mal-Chin flashing his muscles in an attempt to seduce her, which failed. They moved onto another subject.

Mal-Chin had too many drinks. His stomach turned into knots of disgust every time Arin brushed against him, even by accident. Months ago, his only worry was winning the supposed love of his life back. Now, he did not want anything to do with her. He was ashamed of all the years of break ups and getting back together even cheating on other people all under the guise of being in love.

Chapter 23

With the cat's curled up to her, Sophie was content. The house was peaceful. If she was not trying to get a good picture of herself and the cats, she probably would have gone to sleep. Sophie had been up since the power came back on before daybreak. The sound of the AC switching on was a relief after tossing and turning in her stuffy room all night. Beeping electronics and the lights suddenly coming on startled her into fully waking up. She came over to Mal-Chin's house as soon as there was enough light to travel safely. Running into a fallen tree in the dark was not how she wanted to start her day. The heat of the night pulsed in her head. Sophie checked the property and picked up what had fallen off the trees. The air still had a damp chill to it from last night's rain but the humidity would soon set in, then everyone would be miserable. Sophie's first plan of action was to empty out the fridge. The power to it was out well over time for the food to spoil. After resetting Mal-Chin's clocks and making sure the house was all locked up, Sophie headed for her grandparents' house.

There was another bad storm. It cut power to a large part of the city and county and done some damage. A tree had fallen at one of Virginia and Ford's rental properties and there was plenty of storm damage littering all the yards. Everyone in the family that could was called into clean up. With Robbie at work, that left Ford, Sophie, Conner, and Ford's brother Andrew to work. Jessica and Carol were easily affected by warm weather and wore out quickly. Andrew was already working on their connected yards when Sophie arrived. She waved to Andrew before she headed inside. "Well, it's just the two of us," Ford greeted her as soon as Sophie walked into the house. "Robbie wants Conner cleaning up at their house."

Sophie just nodded but Virginia reservations. "You're gonna hurt her."

"She's strong. I won't give her anything too hard to do," Ford answered annoyed.

"I'll be careful," Sophie assured. She was partially offended. There was always an argument over Sophie's strength. Virginia thought she was weaker than she was, and Ford thought she was much stronger. Before there was a chance for Virginia to argue anymore they loaded into the truck and headed off to the rental property. If they did not start there the renter would complain. This renter was becoming a pest. Ford ran the chainsaw while Sophie hauled off armfuls of sticks and branches. She was grateful for this job. The image of the chainsaw falling and butchering her legs flooded her mind. Sophie was suddenly grateful for paying attention during the Stop The Bleed Training she attended at work.

"Hey!" The renter called from his porch as she passed, he lifted his beer toward her, "I know a few men that could use a girl like you!" He let out an annoying laugh.

"Hpmh," was all Sophie said as she made her way to the woods edge to toss the stack of wood in. Later, Virginia would make the same noise when Sophie repeated the comment. The hard work came when Ford finished cutting the tree up. They had to load it onto the back of his truck so Andrew could use it for firewood when it dried. The truck's back came up to Sophie's shoulders, so it was hard for her to haul the logs into its bed.

The air, Sophie's hair, clothes and even the seats of Ford's truck felt sticky and damp. Ford talked on the phone as they cooled off in the truck. The little scratches on Sophie's hands and arms were beginning to itch as she finally sent Mal-Chin the picture of her cuddling with his cats. With an annoyed sigh, Ford turned the truck in the wrong direction as they pulled out of the driveway. Sophie knew immediately where they were going. She'd known from the beginning. This job was too much work for a middle school student.

Conner had not even started when they arrived, much to his own embarrassment. By the look on his face, Carol had been fussing at him about it. Sophie instantly got to work as Ford sat on the porch steps talking to Carol and Jessica about last night's storm. He needed a break, Sophie and Conner did not. Carol did not invite Ford inside. He was dirty and their living room was sterile white. Ford would use that as an excuse to explain it when they returned home. Jessica soon joined in to help, but her cheeks turned red quickly and she was sent inside.

Loading Ford's truck again was exhausting. The drive back to Ford's house did little to help them recuperate. Sophie and Andrew took the brunt of unloading as Ford was beginning to wear out. Ford was a strong man, but his age was starting to catch up with him. It worried Sophie every time she noticed it. She suggested Ford go inside and rest, but Ford just shook his head. He was insistent he would get his strength back in a minute. Sophie worked faster so he would not have to help.

Sophie had to practically peel her socks off her feet. Her clothes were damp and she wanted to go home to change but Virginia was fixing them lunch and Sophie was tired by this point. Her back ached. She wondered if she was old enough to have a back that ached now. The throbbing in her head filled her ears.

Sophie's phone rang in an unfamiliar tone. It was a video call from Mal-Chin's fake account. He'd been using his fake account to follow her online. At first, Sophie thought it was odd, but she was beginning to get used to it. The camera was shaking and she could hear several people talking in Korean. They seemed to be having an argument. "Mal-Chin?" Sophie called out worried. Was he in trouble? Hopefully, he had just butt dialed her.

"*Jagiya*! Sophie!" Mal-Chin replied, the screen finally stabilizing. He showed her two people in the background who waved uncomfortably before Mal-Chin began rambling in Korean. Sophie picked out her name once and Mal-Chin kept repeating a word that Sophie could not make out clearly enough to say. "Oh wait," he suddenly switched to English. "You did not hear any of that." He kissed the screen then hung up.

A confused giggle left her. Whatever he said did not sound like an insult. "What was that?" Sophie asked herself out loud as Virginia put a plate of food in front of her.

"What did he say?" Virginia asked. She took a seat at the table with Sophie even though she wasn't eating.

"I don't know," Sophie popped a carrot into her mouth as she stared at the black screen of her phone. *Should I message him?*

"He probably said all kinds of *terrible* things about you," Virginia offered. Sophie ruminated over this as she ate her lunch in silence.

Maybe he was laughing at her. Could she have misread the smile on his face? No one kisses a screen after an insult. Virginia was rambling on about how Mal-Chin was just using her as a plaything and an errand girl while he was here. The list of times Sophie helped Mal-Chin out, including watching his cats, was pointed out. According to her grandmother, Sophie was a huge fool. Ford just sighed listening to all this as he ate.

They barely finished eating when Ford suggested she go home, get a warm bath and a good nap. Sophie agreed, if only to get away from Virginia's nagging. A mix and guilt and relief filled her as she climbed into her car. While it was good to get away from the negative thinking, she knew Ford would not be napping. Once Sophie was clean, a nap sounded enticing. Her mind flashed to the idea of going to Mal-Chin's and curling up with his cats in the guest bedroom. This idea was quickly scraped; Sophie might have been watching the cats, but she did not think he would like her sleeping at his house while he was not there. Her mind turned over the things Virginia said. She fell to sleep with these thoughts running through her brain.

Chapter 24

She was so excited when she found the news article briefly relating Mal-Chin's return to South Korea. He looked so good walking through the airport. Was his skin tanner? He must have been near a beach. His hair was longer and silkier; she wanted to run her hands through it. Envy and jealousy filled her when she saw Mal-Chin blowing a kiss to a stranger in the crowd. That should have been her. She should have been the one to greet him on his homecoming. Instead, he left her no hints. It was almost like Mal-Chin did not want her to know.

Throughout his visit, she hung around his favorite places hoping to catch a glimpse of him. He was sneaky this time. She saw him heading into his recording label's office. She could have stared at the perfection of his outfit all day. Without a hat, she noticed that his hair was newly cut and back to its original black. She liked it. He looked like the star he was. If only she had time to snap a picture. The second time she saw him was later the next day. She followed him to the Korean BBQ restaurant. If asked, she would not have admitted to how she knew he would be there. The closest table to them was still too far away to hear him speak. It was, however, close enough to see him with Purple-Pink, and the worst of the group seated right next to him. She watched the fight over the phone with relative curiosity about its meaning. It slowly dawned on her that there was another woman to get out of the way. A new woman Mal-Chin must have been embarrassed by, if the way he grabbed his phone back was any indication. Probably some bimbo from whatever town he was living in. It would not be hard to get her out of the way though. Once they were together, Mal-Chin would forget all about any other woman. If he did not, she would take care of it.

Her next step was to make sure she was there when he left again. Obviously, his plan was for them to start over in the U.S. That was why he had not told her he was coming in. He wanted to send the message that she needed to find him. She was waiting on the day he flew out. Mal-Chin would be so proud of how smart she was when he saw her. She camped out near the entrance and waited for him to show up. He was dressed the same way he had been on the way in. Dark clothes, hat, black medical mask. She would know him anywhere. If Mal-Chin saw her, he showed no recognition. That was ok with her. He had to keep the act up a little longer. Keeping her distance, she followed him to his gate. She took a picture of the gate information trying to look casual then watched Mal-Chin board the flight. At home, she would search the information about the flight path and the city he landed in. Her best hint would come a few weeks later through his Instagram. It was only there a short while but it was long enough for her. She got a look at her competition.

Chapter 25

Mal-Chin left Korea with little fanfare. When his eyes scanned the airport, he purposely did not notice the woman that was watching him. Just like he did not notice her at the record label's office, or at the Korean BBQ restaurant, or any of the other times she was lurking nearby. It was easier this way. Bae Young-ae was banned from buying tickets to any event they were at. If he did not acknowledge her existence she would eventually give up. That was what he hoped anyway. *She's just after pictures. Keep walking,* Mal-Chin told himself as he headed to his gate.

It was a muggy afternoon when he landed in the U.S. To his surprise, Sophie's car was parked in his driveway. Mal-Chin figured she must be checking on the cats. A weight lifted from his shoulders as he entered the house. Sophie was seated on one end of Mal-Chin's couch with her head resting on her hand. The posture made her look bored. Her skin was now sun kissed and golden. Aruem had wedged herself belly up between Sophie's hip and the arm rest while Ramyun was curled up on Sophie's lap. They were all asleep. Mal-Chin put his things down as quietly as possible. He tried to figure out who had fallen asleep first. He saw the blue veins on Sophie's right temple and felt guilty that she came feeling bad.

Mal-Chin intended to let them sleep, at least until he was done unpacking and fixed food. Ramyun, however, had other plans. The cat uncurled himself and meowed loudly in greeting. Sophie took a loud breath. Mal-Chin snatched the cat up thinking he could keep it from waking her. He was too late. Sophie's head slipped from her hand. She jerked up with a start as her eyes opened. "Hey, sorry." Sophie said sleepily. Remembering Aruem was still curled up with her, Sophie looked down at her hip deciding against getting up. Her hand lazily stroked the cat.

"You looked comfortable." He smiled setting Ramyun down, who instantly started complaining. "Are you feeling ok?" Mal-Chin tapped his temple to indicate the line of her forehead. "What have you been up to?"

"I'm fine." Sophie smiled, "I've been gardening, and helping Granny decorate and repaper her kitchen. How was your trip?" Sophie asked. Areum got annoyed with Sophie lazily petting her and left to find another napping spot. Sophie reached up running a hand through Mal-Chin's hair. Her nails were chipped. "Your hair looks nice." He'd never liked anyone to play with his hair until this moment.

"You've kept busy. I missed you," Mal-Chin admitted. He took the opportunity to lean down and kiss her. "Oh, wait look at this!" He proudly produced a drawing Hyeonuk made him while telling her all about their visit, "See that's him in Korea and that's me here." Mal-Chin pointed at both stick figures. One was small and the other was large with circles on his arms that were supposed to be Mal-Chin's muscles. "And look, he made it dark on my side because he remembered that when it's night here, it's day there." He stared at the picture for a few minutes, "I try to teach him about the places I travel to."

An arm wrapped around his shoulders; Sophie's head leaned against him. "He's smart, and he's got a really good uncle."

"Is his uncle handsome too?" Mal-Chin turned to her suddenly with that mischievous smile.

Sophie stared at him for a moment, "Wow, you bounced back quick." She took the drawing from him, "You should hang this on the fridge."

Mal-Chin followed her into the kitchen. She was just staring at the fridge taking in the fact that Mal-Chin did not have any magnets. "But, really," Mal-Chin said watching Sophie try to figure out what to do. "You never say what you think of me."

Sophie froze, "I hadn't thought about that. I just figured you already knew you were handsome. That your fans told you all the time," She shrugged, "Why don't you have any magnets?"

"There's a difference between them and you. What did you think when you first met me?" Mal-Chin asked.

Sophie looked back at him, her eyes flicked around Mal-Chin's face, "Honestly, I was wondering why you kept looking at me funny. Then I thought you looked like you gave good hugs." She let her hair fall from behind her ear. "I liked your personality when I got to know you a little too."

Mal-Chin's ears turned red. Out of all the compliments he received over the years "possibly gives good hugs" was not on the list. Now it was at the top. It made him so happy he wiggled from happiness, which caused Sophie to giggle. He wrapped her up in his arms. "You can have all the hugs you want!" When he finally released her, Mal-Chin noticed the box of Moon Pies sitting in the middle of the stove. Mal-Chin picked it up, "Choco Pies. What are they doing here? Can I have one?"

"Those are yours."

Mal-Chin was absolutely delighted. Not only had Sophie remembered his favorite snack, but she bought him a whole box. He ripped open the box, "How did you know I like them?"

"You always do a little dance when you put one in the grocery cart," Sophie answered. Mal-Chin should have been embarrassed by that, but he was too busy biting into his snack. Sophie asked one of the questions Mal-Chin wanted to avoid, "What happened with your work? Do you still have a career as a singer?" Mal-Chin tried to avoid the question saying he was suddenly so tired. Mal-Chin could not bring himself to admit to her that he was with a lesser label. What would Sophie think? She was looking at him worried now. Sophie pressed harder for an answer but he kept using the same excuse.

"Ok, well, when you're ready, tell me. I guess I'll go so you can rest," Sophie said as she laid the drawing.

"No, don't go. I missed you. Sleep with me," Mal-Chin added. From the look on Sophie's face he said that wrong, in the worst way, "No, I mean. You were sleeping earlier. I was going to sleep." He could not think of the word he was looking for.

"So, you want me to take a nap with you?" Sophie filled in hesitantly.

Mal-Chin nodded in agreement, "No tricks. Promise. Maybe we could cuddle." Heat rose to his cheeks as the words came out of his mouth.

Sophie thought it over before nodding, "A nap sounds good." She followed Mal-Chin to his room. Her whole body tensed up as she looked around his bedroom. Mal-Chin so was busy pulling back the sheets and fluffing up a pillow for her that he did not notice for a moment. When he did, he stopped and just sat in the center of the bed. "If you changed your mind, it's ok."

Sophie's eyes wandered the room again then returned to him on the bed. She took a deep breath, "Which side do I get?"

Excitedly, Mal-Chin pointed to the pillow he just fluffed up, though she could have the other side if she wanted. She slid in still tense. Mal-Chin got comfortable on his side, "I won't be mad if you don't want to."

"I know," Sophie said as she laid down getting comfortable. They laid in awkward silence just waiting for the other to go to sleep. Mal-Chin's eyes were closed but kept peeking out. He realized Sophie was doing the same. Frustration was beginning to set in. Whether it was trips around the world with limited beds or the latest girlfriend, Mal-Chin never struggled to fall asleep with someone else in his bed. He was questioning if he had grown so used to Arin as his bed mate that someone else just felt wrong. Something from his drunken night flashed to Mal-Chin's mind. The memory of Suho and Minkyo trying to stop him from doing something but it was too hazy.

"When I um-" Sophie started suddenly then hesitated searching for the right words. Mal-Chin looked at her from where he lay on his stomach. She was staring at the ceiling, "The first time I-" she took a deep breath. "I was in college. My first serious relationship. He invited me back for a nap on our long break. Then we were kissing," her neck turned splotchy. Mal-Chin did not understand why she was telling him this. "I wasn't ready, but I told myself it was time. I guess I wasn't as mature as I thought."

"I'm sorry." Mal-Chin said as realization of what she was telling him set in.

With a shake of her head, she added, "It just," Sophie sighed, "this made me think of it."

"I'd romance you first if we were going to," Mal-Chin stated. Now he was the one embarrassed. "No surprise." They laid in silence again. Mal-Chin rolled onto his side to find that Sophie had already closed her eyes and was at least pretending to be asleep. He followed her example and soon fell asleep as well.

***

Sophie's first thought when she awoke was not the phone ringing or the fact that she was in a different room. All she could think of was how comfortable she was tucked into Mal-Chin's embrace, like she was meant to be there. Mal-Chin's hand was groggily reaching out for his phone. He sat up speaking in Korean. His voice sounded deeper but that must have been from sleep.

A change in tone let her know something was wrong. There was a nervousness in Mal-Chin's voice and body now. Sophie reached for him while she sat up. Alarm showed clearly on Mal-Chin's face as he turned to her. Mal-Chin held a finger up to his lips to shush her. She tried to tell him to hang up, but he was just staring at her confused. To Sophie's frustration, he was still talking to the person on the other end of the phone. She finally mimed a phone with her fingers and put it down on the bed. A light clicked on in his eyes. He pulled the phone away and hung up.

"Who was that?" Sophie asked.

"*Sasaeng*," Mal-Chin replied over his ring tone. He hit ignore.

"Is that your manager?"

"No. It's a fan that won't leave you alone." Mal-Chin explained.

"A stalker?" Sophie asked. The word itself sent a shiver down her spine.

Mal-Chin considered the word. "Yes. This one got my number somehow. It happens from time to time. She's smart. When I answered I thought I was talking to someone from the record label." Mal-Chin ran a hand through his hair. "She almost got my address."

"Block her," Sophie suggested. She was already thinking about all the shows where people used phone calls to track someone's location. Could private citizens do that?

Mal-Chin must have been having the same thought as he did something on his phone. He slipped out of the bed and considered her. Finally, he turned and started going through one of his drawers. "I think, I'm going to go to the gym. Didn't get much time in while I was in Seoul. Want to come along?"

Sophie shook her head, "No, rest day," Sophie explained.

"Oh, wait!" Mal-Chin said suddenly as Sophie got out of his bed. "I got you a present." He scratched the back of his head, "You know, for watching my cats." He shifted through one of his bags and handed her a rectangular box. He was proud of this gift. Mal-Chin chose it carefully.

Sophie looked at it then him. "Mal-Chin," she started looking at the box in her hand, "This is too expensive." Sophie turned the box over in her hand, all the product details were written in Korean but it was unmistakably the latest model of her fitness watch. She tried to hand it back to him. "I can't—"

"Your watch is in such bad shape and old," Mal-Chin replied. Disappointment was setting in, "Look at it first." He opened the box. "I even made sure to get a metal band." He carefully emptied the contents and took her wrist removing the old band.

Sophie felt a little embarrassed. Sophie's old watch was worn out but she did not think Mal-Chin noticed. "That's not something you just give someone though."

He smiled holding it up for her to see, "What's the point of having a rich friend if they don't get you presents?"

"I don't like you for your money," Sophie said. She was turning the new watch over in her hand. It was pretty. The face and metal band were gold but something about it looked different from pictures she had seen of them online. Sophie had contemplated shelling out the money to get this one.

"Oh, so you do like me. And I just thought that kiss was for fun," Mal-Chin smiled cheekily.

Sophie's heart stopped for a second. "Oh, shut up!" She looked away then a thought hit her, "Wait, did you buy me this because I kissed you?" She held it out to him. Just the thought made her feel used.

"No, I got it because you watched my cats. And you like me for more than my money," He answered matter-of-factly, "That you're a good kisser had nothing to do with it."

Embarrassment and frustration mixed up in her to the point that she did not know which one to feel. "Oh just," She pressed the watch back toward him, "just give me my old watch back and go to the gym."

"I'll give you back the old one after you've tried the new one at least three times. Three workouts." He held up three fingers for emphasis. Sophie let out an annoyed sigh and was about to reply when Mal-Chin started, "And I can't go to the gym until I change clothes, so you need to leave the room. Unless you want to watch." He gave her a cheeky smile.

Sophie's brain went blank for a moment as she stared at him wide eyed. "Bye," She shuffled out of the room while strapping the new fitness tracker onto her wrist. The front door closed behind her.

Chapter 26

The new fitness tracker worked so easily; a few taps and it was ready to go. It took a while for Sophie to switch the language to English. It displayed Sophie's text messages and even allowed her to switch songs from the screen. That was helpful at the gym. That perfectly harmonized love song by Beast just was not the right vibe for a workout.

When she'd spotted Mal-Chin at the gym, Sophie excitedly pointed at the watch and gave a thumbs up. Mal-Chin took his ear buds out long enough for a quick chat. By the time she left, Sophie was fairly convinced she would keep the watch. She knew she should not accept it, but Sophie liked it too much. If she thought about it, she would have realized that Mal-Chin could not return a used watch. Sophie didn't want to think about it. The idea that she could still return it made her feel less guilty for accepting the gift.

Virginia turned her nose up when Sophie first showed her the watch. Robbie quickly noticed it at Sunday lunch. He casually asked about the new expensive item. Sophie happily told him that Mal-Chin purchased it as a gift. Robbie shot Carol a look. In that instant, Sophie felt a pang of suspicion. Maybe she was reading the expression wrong. Jessica Googled the watch just wondering how much it cost. Sophie froze when Jessica said it was well over $400. How had she been running around with a luxury item on her wrist like it was nothing? Robbie made a noise at the price while the women checked to make sure it was the right item. They couldn't place a finger on it, but Sophie's watch looked different.

"Maybe it's an older model," Sophie suggested. She hoped that it was. Mal-Chin shouldn't be spending that much money on her.

Jessica's mouth turned down as she shook her head. "It's the same one. I guess it's the wrist band that's different." Jessica Googled the wrist bands. Her eyes almost popped out of her head again, "The gold bands are $40." Her nose turned up.

"You're kidding!" Carol took the phone looking through it. "There's no way that's the right one." They went through the whole process of Googling again on Carol's phone. This time they were closely inspecting the watch that was still on Sophie's wrist. Sophie could feel the floor shaking from the weight of Robbie's foot fidgeting. "Huh, guess it is." Carol was twisting and turning Sophie's arm like she did not have any bones. Sophie's skin was crawling from the touch.

"Wish my *friends* would just buy me pricy gifts for no reason," Robbie chimed in. Ford just shook his head.

"You've got to return that," Virginia added shock in her voice.

"Why, exactly, did he give you that?" Carol asked. She was looking down her nose at Sophie.

"He said it was for watching his cats," Sophie repeated Mal-Chin's explanation. It sounded like a lie.

From the look and snicker Robbie, Carol and Jessica exchanged, she knew something bad was about to happen. "Are you sure that's all you did for that?" Robbie asked.

Sophie looked at him confused as she nodded. She suddenly felt nauseous.

"It's just," Carol started then shook her short bangs from her eyes, "It's not a gift you just give to someone like that. He must have wanted something else." Carol tilted her head. "Someone might take that gift the wrong way." The accusations began to trickle out. They never came out and directly stated it, but the implication was there. Sophie must have slept with Mal-Chin for the watch. She felt so small sitting there. The watch felt heavy on her wrist, almost irritating it. "I mean, if he was going to pick someone to run around with, you'd think he'd pick someone," Carol paused, "Well, you know, more his level." That comment bit into Sophie. They were right, Mal-Chin was too good looking for Sophie. She wanted to think of the gift as being simply what it was: a thank you.

"Stop that!" Ford commanded. His brows furrowed deeply. "You all know better than that." Ford's blue eyes were sharp as he looked around the room. Everyone shifted; a tense silence fell.

"They were just joking," Virginia whispered sounding almost embarrassed. Sophie's cheeks were burning. She just wanted to rip the watch off her arm and hide. Sophie's hair fell over her shoulder, half hiding her face.

"We were. It was just a laugh," Robbie's face was a mixture of anger and surprise.

"Well you took it too far," Ford gestured with his fork, "There's things you just don't joke about and that's one of them."

Robbie was looking at Sophie, who would not meet his gaze. "Y'all take everything too seriously. Can't even make a joke," Robbie left the table slamming his chair into place then banging out the front door. Ford soon followed. From outside, they could hear Robbie's raised voice.

"You know they were just joking. No need to get upset about it," Virginia whispered to Sophie. Carol and Jessica moved onto another subject, already bored with the verbal lashing they had unleashed on Sophie.

Ford came back inside with a sigh and Robbie followed not too long after. He kept shooting Sophie dirty looks. "I think I'm gonna head on home," Sophie squeaked out through a tight throat.

"Just wait," Virginia stated. The first excuse was not interrupting Carol and Jessica's discussion of the whole life history of someone they knew. The next was a woman that married for money at a young age. Every story was making fun of these women.

When Sophie was about to break, they let her leave. Virginia packed a plate for Lorraine. Sophie could feel eyes on her the whole time. She knew they were waiting for her to leave so they could continue bashing her. Ford followed her out. "Baby," he started, "don't listen to a word of that. I'm sorry they said it but they didn't mean it." Sophie looked at him with glassy eyes and just nodded. The watch was burning her arm at this point. All Sophie could think of was that she needed to get rid of it. It was not worth having her morals called into question.

Quickly dropping off her mother's food, she climbed back into the car and took off again. She needed to get there before her nerves broke. Sophie took a few calming breaths that were not calming and soon found herself at Mal-Chin's doorstep.

Mal-Chin answered the door with a big smile on his face and a cheeky comment on his lips. It quickly fell away as Sophie thrust the watch back at him. Somehow, she slipped it off her wrist without thinking, "Take it back. Please." Just having it off was a relief.

Mal-Chin gave her a confused look as he let her into the house. She went in without even thinking. "We agreed to three workouts with it."

"I just- I don't want it." Sophie shook the watch at him, "Take it back." Her vision blurred and she blinked hard. Not now, whatever was causing the blur, not now.

Mal-Chin looked her over as he settled on the couch, "What happened?"

"Nothing. Just take it back. It's too expensive. I like the old one better." She practically stuck the watch in his face this time. Sophie was debating just dropping it in his lap and leaving. Yet, she could not make herself let go of it.

Mal-Chin's hand smoothed over her arm. The touch was tender, so amazingly gentle for such large hands. He slid the watch from her hands, "You were with your family," Mal-Chin started leading her closer, "Were they mean to you?" His eyes were sympathetic. Sophie barely noticed as he slipped the watch back on her wrist.

A sniffle escaped. The dam broke. Before she could protest, Mal-Chin pulled her close and wrapped her in his arms. She sobbed into his shoulder, "They just, hate me." She finally garbled out while trying to explain what happened. The words should have felt childish, but the way he held her tighter took away that feeling.

"They don't. They're just jealous. You're sweet and kind, and you have a good friend that sees you're special." Mal-Chin mumbled into her hair.

"I don't know," Sophie hid her face in his shoulder. Sophie was beginning to calm now. The smell of him, clean soap and men's lotion, and the feel of his warm arms around her was soothing. Just being in his presence made her feel better. "I'm sorry," Sophie mumbled. Embarrassment and exhaustion were starting to set in. His hold on her did not loosen. Sophie expected Mal-Chin to let go as soon as she calmed down. Just being held felt good right now. Was he waiting on her to ask?

"Why don't you take a rest?" Mal-Chin suggested. Sophie considered his question. A nap sounded good, but she did not want to go home. There would be questions from her mother about where she'd gone and why. Sophie did not have the energy to deal with it. "You can sleep here. My bed is comfortable, so is the extra bedroom."

"A nap would be nice. I'm sweaty though," Sophie thought about the fact she was still in her gym clothes.

"I've got a shower too," Mal-Chin added.

Sophie ended up cuddled to Mal-Chin, wearing one of his t-shirts and smelling of his soap. It should not have felt so good to shower in a strange bathroom, put on clothes that were not hers and climb into someone's bed but it did. Mal-Chin was right. His bed was comfortable, especially with his arms around her. She was quickly in a deep dreamless sleep.

Waking up was like surfacing after a long dive underwater. Instantly, she was aware that Mal-Chin had left the bed. His weight and warmth next to her was not easy to miss. She was not alone though. It took Sophie a moment to register the familiar rumble against her spine. One of the cats was curled against her back. Squirming, Sophie discovered the other curled up in the bend of her legs. Sophie could have just stayed in that bed with both cats. She wondered how long she could lay here before Mal-Chin got worried, or annoyed that she was still in his bed. Careful not to disturb the sleeping cats, she sat up. Areum, who was curled against her back, raised her head and gave an annoyed meow before getting up. Ramyun followed her lead, stretching as he got up. She patted their little heads and apologized for waking them up.

The smell of cooking food hit her as soon as she stepped into the hallway. Her stomach rumbled. It was not a surprise. After crying her eyes out then taking nap, she always woke up hungry. Like body-guards, the cats flanked her as she padded down the hallway.

Mal-Chin acknowledged her with a smile and nod as he stirred something in a frying pan. Aruem was weaving her way around Sophie's legs now and Sophie could not ignore the cat. "Did you sleep well?" Mal-Chin asked. There was amusement in his voice. Sophie hoped it was from her cooing at the cat and not something embarrassing she'd done in her sleep.

"Yeah. Thank you," Sophie shifted. She should be saying something. She could feel him waiting for her to say something. "Um, sorry. For all that earlier."

"You needed that." He stirred whatever was in the pan, "Hope you like spicy food." Sophie offered to help but Mal-Chin settled her on a bar stool with a bottle of water. Sophie did not have the energy to argue; she also did not feel like cooking. It was a nice sight. Mal-Chin's muscular back was covered in a tank top as he cooked for her. A wave of embarrassment washed over her as she remembered sobbing into one of those shoulders.

Mal-Chin placed a bowl of food in front of her and a soothing kiss on her forehead. The kiss felt like an ice cold glass of water on a scorching hot day.

She did not know what she was eating. It was some kind of noodles and spicy crunchy vegetables with a bowl of rice. They ate in silence. Sophie's mind began to replay today's events. "What was your favorite place to go on tour?"

Mal-Chin raised a curious eyebrow, stuffed his mouth full of the vegetable concoction and rice. He chewed slowly as he thought it over.

Licking his lips he replied, "Nice, France." He considered it again as he sipped his drink then nodded.

"Tell me about it?" Sophie asked. She was copying his method of eating the food. It led to a large mouth full and helped cool the burn.

"It was beautiful there. Blue oceans, everyone was so laid back. We went to the museums, rode those things," He pretended to grip something hand over hand and made a motion like he was sweeping a broom, "with the boards and you stand on them,"

"Paddle boards?" Sophie guessed.

"Yes, paddle boards. I kept falling off," He chuckled. "it was one our fan's favorite parts of the tour video." He got out his phone and pulled up the video. Sophie giggled watching him struggle and fall again and again off the paddle board. The cute pout on his face as he came up after the seventh time was endearing. They put a counter at the bottom of the screen. At one point, he fell off and Ryu looked at him completely bored. Mal-Chin scratched the back of his head and cringed. "We got wine drunk at dinner that night and were hungover when we got on the plane the next morning," Mal-Chin smiled at the memory.

"Sounds like you had fun."

Mal-Chin nodded. His face lit up as a far-off look came over his eyes. Sophie took a gulp of drink. His eyes suddenly focused on her. "I'll take you with me when I go back. Maybe we'll even go to Paris. You'll have to get a passport."

The idea sounded great. Wandering the streets of France hand in hand with Mal-Chin. It was a daydream she wanted to stay in for as long as possible. Her mind snapped back to reality. "Wonder what Robbie and Carol would say about that," the words came out almost bitterly. If they could not accept a watch, what would they think of a trip to another county?

Chapter 27

Sweat glistened on Sophie's arms, ran down her neck and dampened her hairline. Yet, somehow, she avoided the level of sweat soaked that many of the men's shirts were. This was the kind of day that men dodged out of her way when she passed with a barbell and avoided the benches close to her if they could. Sophie tapped her feet along to Metallica's *Of Wolf and Man* pumping through her earphones; the sound of her heartbeat added its unique rhythm to the music. Sophie did not care if anyone could hear the music. Her weight gloves absorbed the sweat from her forehead as she wiped it. Sophie's own reflection in the mirror dared her to keep going.

The family argument ended but the hurt remained. There was an awkward silence that followed Sophie anytime she was at her grandparents' house. She caught them whispering when she entered the room. Virginia went out of her way not to mention Sophie when Robbie or Carol called. The one-time Virginia did mention Sophie, Robbie started ranting on the phone.

The barbell smacked down on the leather of her bench with a thud. Sophie drank from her water bottle as her eyes looked herself over in the mirror. There was anger in the reflection that stared back at her. Anger at herself for causing the family drama, for just not being good enough in general. Bringing the barbell up as she went, she laid back on the bench careful to make sure her head rested comfortably. She was lifting heavier than normal. She wanted to feel anything except the stress that flooded her this week. Sophie concentrated on her form. She watched for traces of failure. It would not be good to get stuck under a weight while lifting alone. There was a shake in her arms, but no pause. That was fine by her.

A pair of hands took the weight from her as she moved to sit up. It made it easier for her to sit up, but she wanted to be left alone. Mal-Chin set the weight down then sat himself down on the bench beside her. Catching her breath, she pulled her earphones out and took a sip of water. "How are you?" Mal-Chin's eyes focused on her hand as she wiped the sweat from her neck.

Sophie just shook her head. She did not feel like explaining the whole situation to him. For one thing, it was embarrassing, and Sophie just wanted to forget about it for a little while. "Can I ask you something? What's it like living alone?" She rolled the barbell on the bench debating doing another set.

"Well, you can do what you want, when you want. No one bothers you," Mal-Chin nodded, "Which is nice. But, it can be very quiet and lonely. There's no one to greet you when you come home, and if something messes up you're the only one there to fix it." Mal-Chin put on his weightlifting wrist straps as he spoke then looked up at her with that cheeky smile, "My bed has room for two if you want to come stay." Sophie's brain went blank again; she hurried to put the weight up and heard Mal-Chin chuckle.

When she returned, Mal-Chin was doing split squats while holding two dumbbells. "Don't say things like that," Sophie requested as she wiped down her bench.

"Sorry," Mal-Chin set his weights down and took his foot off the bench. "Before you leave, why don't we have a real date?" At her confused face Mal-Chin continued, "You know, nice restaurant, flowers, all of that." Sophie just nodded her agreement with a shy smile. Her elliptical run was spent planning out what she would need. Mal-Chin picked a random day in the middle of the week. A day that just happened to be family dinner night. At home, Sophie realized she didn't have a date night worthy outfit and took herself to the store.

Then the night finally came. Sophie looked herself over in the mirror one last time. It was a special occasion so a new dress and shoes, while costly, seemed fitting. An Instagram post memorialized one of the rare occasions that she felt pretty. It also stood as a reminder why she was missing family dinner night. Virginia's reaction to the news popped into her head. Virginia had been mad and guilted Sophie about not being there to help her. The guilt trip almost worked. The need to feel like she was worth something more than being the family workhorse set Sophie on her path. She wanted this more than she should have. It was something she spent too long thinking she was not meant for.

For once, Sophie wished her mother was home. It would have been nice to have someone agree that she looked nice. The notifications binging on her phone as she headed out the door confirmed it in her mind. A knot formed in her stomach as she drove.

She was awestruck when Mal-Chin answered the door. Sophie was not looking at the man that she spent her days with but the celebrity that appeared in his Google searches. He wore a simple white button up with the sleeves rolled up to the elbow, a few buttons were undone exposing a dash of hairless chest when he moved. The shirt was tucked into a pair of black pants that Sophie suspected were jeans. "You look handsome," Sophie awkwardly stated.

Mal-Chin smiled and moved to run a hand through his hair, he stopped remembering the side part and slightly gelled style that he'd struggled to achieve on his own, "And you look beautiful." He invited her inside even though they'd be leaving again soon, "I got you something." He hurried into the kitchen and returned with a bouquet of flowers. These were not flowers bought from the grocery store, they were made by a florist. The colors matched perfectly and were professionally arranged. Sophie didn't want to think about the cost.

"Thank you, they're so pretty." Sophie was cradling them in her arms. A thought hit her, "Can I leave them here? They might get too hot in the car."

"That sounds like a good excuse to have to come inside later," Mal-Chin returned the flowers to the kitchen. Sophie missed them already. Curiosity about her phone got the best of her. She checked it while she was waiting for Mal-Chin to return but only got as far as comprehending the mass of notifications on her lock screen before Mal-Chin returned. "We should get going."

Mal-Chin picked the fanciest restaurant in town. Sophie questioned that choice; it was too much expense just for her. As they looked through the menu, Sophie kept shooting him questioning looks. Everything cost twenty dollars or more. With Sophie's permission, Mal-Chin ordered a wine that paired well with their dishes. "Did you learn that in France?"

"No, talk show," Mal-Chin told the story of how he was chosen to do a bit about different wines for Valentine's Day. It was his first solo appearance. Mal-Chin had felt out of place without his bandmates to interact with. In return, Sophie told him about how she used to have her students make Valentine's Day cards, which was a little childish for their age, and a student cut a big heart and walked around all day with it hanging from his face. By this point, both of their phones were going off constantly. Mal-Chin checked his quickly, so Sophie did the same. "What on Earth...?" Sophie muttered seeing even more Instagram notifications.

Mal-Chin said his was the crazed fan again. "Why don't we just silence these," Mal-Chin guided her phone to the table, Sophie noticed his palms were sweaty betraying his calm confidence. Was she making him nervous? For a split second, Sophie thought it was just first date nerves. That was, until she noticed his name showing in the previews of a message. She moved his hand out of her way. Mal-Chin moved into the chair next to her and used his fingers to turn her head to him, "Sophie, that color makes your lips look so pretty." Sophie looked at him in confusion before a soft blush spread across her face. "I just want to...." He pressed his lips to hers in a passionate kiss. Her phone was completely forgotten. His fingers played in her hair. The look on his face when he pulled away said that was not what he planned. He ran a hand through his hair, "I think...."

"That I need to pick up my flowers," Sophie finished. Her heart was pounding. She felt that kiss in places she should not have. Mal-Chin quickly paid the bill.

The drive to his house had never been so slow, but they got there faster than they should have. The first time his phone rang, Sophie had just gotten comfortable under him on the couch. She questioned if he needed to answer it between burning hot kisses. He just threw his phone on the coffee table. The second time his phone rang, Mal-Chin was squeezing a handful of her thigh, which they both must have liked from the noise they made. His pants were jeans, she could tell by the way they felt against her legs. Sophie was suddenly wishing she had worn a matching underwear set. She pulled at the back of his shirt until it was untucked. At the third ring, Mal-Chin pulled away with a sigh, "It's my manager. I have to." Sophie just nodded as she sat up. She fixed the bottom of her dress disappointedly knowing they were done. It was a mystery how Mal-Chin was so calm after that. The prattle of his voice floated from the kitchen. The way he spoke in Korean surprised her. Mal-Chin's voice was smoother and even a bit deeper.

Her lips pressed together as she sought out a distraction to the signals her body was sending her. She found her purse lying on the floor and grabbed her phone out of it. Finally, she checked all the notifications. The number of new followers was shocking, and the messages asking how she knew Mal-Chin were even more confusing. A few asked questions that made Sophie's imagination go over what would have happened without that phone call. *Stupid Manager.*

She got to the comments on her pictures next. Some were the regular comments from family and other followers that she expected but there were hundreds of strangers too. A few were sweet telling her she was cute, wanting to know where she got her dress. Then they turned mean, calling her fat, ugly, a slut. Ironically, there was even an argument about leaving her alone. Sophie's lips pressed into a line as she remembered that those were just the ones she could read. Where was this coming from?

Mal-Chin was watching her from where he stood on the phone. There was an apology in his eyes. Was he apologizing for the disruption? Maybe she looked as much of a mess as he did with his untucked shirt wrinkled and hair rumpled. There were a few faint lipstick smears on his neck. She looked at her phone then back at him. All the times he distracted her came to her mind. Even the kiss was a distraction. Whoever he was talking to was yelling at him, she worried she was the cause. She scrolled through the comments on her picture again and didn't find any comments from Mal-Chin. Her notifications were a different story though. An account named "@Chinnie_OG" with a verified check had started following her and commented on her post. That was before the other accounts swooped in. The comment had been deleted.

"@Chinne_OG" was Mal-Chin's official profile.

The couch dipped as Mal-Chin sat down next to her. "I was going to tell you when we got back. It was an accident," his voice was low with regret. "I was nervous so I was scrolling through my Instagram and wanted to look at your page. I just wasn't thinking. I saw that I wasn't following you so I hit the button and I should have known then. So, I saw how pretty you looked and that French model guy had commented on it so I had to too. I didn't realize I'd used the wrong account until too late."

"You should have just said something when I got here."

"I didn't want to upset you. I saw what they were saying and I just wanted to hide the ugly side of my fans from you." Mal-Chin found something between his feet to look at.

"I was gonna see it eventually. Why did it matter if I knew before or after we went out?"

"You wouldn't have to worry about it during our date. You wouldn't have had a good date," Mal-Chin replied. Her phone went off again, "I'm sorry. You might want to set your account to private for a while."

"What did you write?" Sophie refused to look at him. She was still reading comments about how she looked. Most of them sounded like things her family said.

Mal-Chin leaned his head back trying to remember exactly what he had written, "You look beautiful, *Jagiya*." He scratched the back of his head, "It means baby."

Sophie decided to ignore that last piece. It was nice thinking he had a nickname for her, but that wasn't the main issue here, "Are you in trouble?" She was turning the phone over in her hand now.

"A little. Idols usually wouldn't even post a compliment like that or use a nickname." He reached out to hold her hand, but she moved away from him.

"I should go," Sophie stood up without another explanation and picked up her purse from the floor.

"Sophie, *Jagiya*," Mal-Chin paused then sighed, "Don't forget your flowers."

As mad as she was with him, the flowers still ended up in a vase in Sophie's living room. It was a waste to get rid of them. Sophie could not remember the last time someone gave her a bouquet. Ford usually gave her a single rose on Valentine's Day, but a full bouquet was something special. Besides, it was not the flowers' fault.

Chapter 28

Mal-Chin was sitting on one end of the couch while Minseok and John took up the other side. They were having another movie night, this time at Mal-Chin's. It was John's idea; movie nights were much more fun when there was no neighbors arguing through the wall. Mal-Chin picked the movie. It was an action adventure; he refused to be scared in his own house. Minseok was using John's shoulder as a pillow and John was furiously typing away on his phone. The three casually chatted throughout the movie.

Slowly, Mal-Chin told them about his failed date and the mess he made. "I gotta be honest," John started, "I'm surprised you even got her to agree to a date." John looked away from his phone. "Like, good job, but she's mad as hell."

Mal-Chin just nodded, "I can't blame her." He scratched the back of his head. "How do I fix this?"

"Well, you could always apologize." John shrugged. "Though, it doesn't help that they are still bugging her. The poor girl, your fans were blowing up her phone the last I saw her."

Mal-Chin hung his head and started typing away on his phone. He erased and rewrote the same message several times before finally sending it. It was a genuine apology. *"Honestly, I know you didn't mean to. But the fact that that was a distraction bothers me,"* Sophie replied a little while later. Mal-Chin's heart thumped hard when he heard the notification.

"I don't feel bad about the kiss or what happened on the couch. I would do it again if you wanted me to. But I do hate using it as a distraction. I'm sorry." Mal-Chin did not get a reply this time. He kept checking his phone, but still found nothing. John's phone, however, was going off.

"Thank you," a reply finally came through. Mal-Chin let out a sigh of relief. At this point, he lost what was going on in the movie but it did not really matter. "Oh, Beast is going to be in the U.S for a while. I think they're going to stop in for a visit."

"Really?" John answered. He gave Minseok a look. "Are we still not telling?"

Minseok did not answer. The silence grew long; Mal-Chin finally filled it in, "Dae-o wouldn't be bothered by it."

Minseok nodded, "That's not the only thing I'm worried about." He sat up straight now uncomfortable. "I'm thinking of not going back to Korea." Mal-Chin just nodded in understanding.

"I still don't get why that's such a big deal," John answered rolling his eyes.

"I'm the oldest son. I've got a responsibility to my family," Minseok sighed out, "Mom and Dad won't receive that news well, and I don't want Dae-o to feel like I'm pushing that on him." He scratched the back of his head, "They were always tougher on me than Dae-o."

John patted Minseok's shoulder, "We'll figure it out. Maybe Dae-o is the best place to start though." Minseok agreed noncommittally.

A few days later, Mal-Chin excitedly greeted the members of Beast from his front porch. They filed out of the van looking tired but grateful to be on their feet. The house filled with life for the first time in months. They unloaded their suitcases and piled them into the living room. Beast had a week long break before their next American interview. As a group, they decided that instead of flying home they would pay Mal-Chin a much overdue visit.

There was one detail Mal-Chin had not worked out yet, which is what the group was debating now. If you included the twin bed in the studio and the couch, there were only 4 places to sleep and 6 members. The group set about deciding who would sleep where. They decided this the easy way. Years ago, Beast had not only shared bedrooms but shared beds. Whenever a decision about sleeping arrangements came up, they always defaulted to this set up: Minkyo and Mal-Chin, Dae-o and Suho, and Jeong-hui and Ryu. There was an argument over the fact that it wasn't fair that Minkyo got to sleep in a bed by default since they didn't want to kick Mal-Chin out of his bed. Suho proposed playing Rock, Paper, Scissors for the other 2-person bed. Ryu and Jeong-hui said it was only fair for the older two, Suho and Dae-o, to have the other bed. Ryu ended up on the couch and Jeong-hui in the studio after a round of Rock, Paper, Scissors. Minkyo went to take a nap as the rest of the group wandered around the house. They eventually settled into the living room. If it had not been raining, they would have gone for a swim. Minseok joined them for dinner. The siblings were eager to get together after not seeing each other for years. Minseok didn't mention John.

Mal-Chin was not looking forward to tomorrow. In the morning, the girls of Purple-Pink were flying in and were going to spend their few days of layover hanging out. Ryu and Yujin were getting closer. Mal-Chin hoped that this was all their visit was for. Mal-Chin hated the idea of Arin being in his American house. A part of him suspected Arin wanted to size up Sophie. Arin was good at finding women's weaknesses, and Sophie's were written all over her.

Chapter 29

Sophie did not want to be here. She tried to calm her nerves as she pulled into Mal-Chin's driveway. Her introverted side wanted to just sit this out, but it was important to Mal-Chin that she meet his friends. John informed her that Minseok was going to try to tell Dae-o about their relationship today as well. She needed to be there for support in case it went wrong. Maybe the group wasn't as big as she thought. Steeling herself for an awkward gathering, she got out of her car. Sophie thought she heard music coming from behind the house. She knocked on the door once to no reply. Contemplating texting Mal-Chin, she knocked again. The door opened. Sophie was surprised to find Minkyo there. He was a tall, slender, and almost delicate looking man. Sophie recognized him from pictures of Beast but could not think of his name. "Oh, Sophie-*ssi*," He gave her an awkward smile, "I see you, video call."

That took Sophie a second, her eyes widen with excitement, "Oh, you're one of the guys he was arguing with."

"Minkyo." He gave a little nod of his head in greeting then waved for her to follow him. Sophie thought they were going to Mal-Chin. Minkyo led her through the quiet house out to the pool area. K-pop blasted from a Bluetooth speaker. Water splashed from the pool and the sound of voices in Korean filled the air. Mal-Chin was nowhere in sight. Minkyo yelled something in Korean over the noise. Several men hurried over.

They crowded around her. Close, too close. They were taller than her and all talking at once. Sophie's shoulders pulled in, she played with the edge of her shirt to keep from pulling her arms up protectively. Sophie could tell they were trying to talk to her and did her best to follow along with their broken English. Dae-o was trying to translate for them all. One went in to grab her for a hug. Sophie instantly went rigid. The sliding door was thrown open. Mal-Chin yelled something at the group and they took a few steps back. Suho bowed his head in apology and the others followed suit.

"What did you say?" Sophie asked, she was beginning to relax a little.

"I told them you didn't like being touched," Mal-Chin explained. Now she felt doubly embarrassed. Mal-Chin made introductions. Jeong-hui, the one that tried to hug her, made an extra apology.

"I didn't realize this was a pool party." Sophie looked around. Everyone here was good looking. "I don't have my bathing suit." A part of Sophie was glad she did not have it on. She was thinking about how silly she would look next to these perfectly shaped women in their bikinis.

"You left it here, remember?" Mal-Chin answered. "Come on," He headed back inside. Sophie glanced between the group and Mal-Chin before following. "Are you ok?" He asked as soon as the door closed.

"Yeah, just wasn't expecting that. They seem really friendly," Sophie smiled trying to fight off the remaining shake in her stomach. "Thank you." She was following him down the hallway. Her mind was running through whether she offended them or not. Mal-Chin took her hand and was rubbing his thumb across her knuckles comfortingly. "How's Minseok and John?"

"Minseok was a little nervous earlier. They haven't really mentioned anything yet" Mal-Chin stated as he handed Sophie her bathing suit. "There's a bottle of sun block in the bathroom if you need it."

Sophie thought about slipping back out the front door and leaving. She could come up with an excuse to need to leave. When Minseok and Mal-Chin described this gathering they made it sound small. *What had Mal-Chin gotten in trouble for again? Wild parties?* From the glance she had gotten, there was a sizable group around his pool. She slipped out of her clothes and into her bathing suit as these thoughts ran through her head. No matter how much she wanted to run from these beautiful strangers, Minseok and Mal-Chin needed her there.

Disappointment was obvious on Mal-Chin's face when she stepped out. "Why did you put the shirt back on?"

Sophie just shrugged off the question. "Shouldn't you be outside hosting?" She headed down the hallway. It was more comfortable to have the tank top on. There was less to be embarrassed of if she kept covered.

"I thought you might need help with the lotion. Plus, I like seeing you in your bathing suit." Mal-Chin grabbed a few more drinks as they passed the kitchen. Sophie took a some from him to help out. They added these to the cooler once outside.

She was alone. Mal-Chin had run off to get in on whatever game Minseok, and Jeong-hui were trying to organize. Sophie took an awkward look around the backyard. John and Ryu were reluctantly joining in the game. They were playing some game involving trying to get on top of the pool floats and not get knocked off. Sophie wandered the edge of the pool watching this. She was trying to stay out of sight the same way she did at the gym. The pool chairs were taken so she could not really find a place to hide well. A woman with black silky hair dumped into her as they passed. Arin hit Sophie hard enough to make her stumble toward the water. Sophie would have ended up in the water if her balance was not better.

"Sophie-*ah*," Someone called from behind her. Sophie stopped to watch the group in the pool half amused, half worried they were going to break the floats. Sophie and Mal-Chin had wandered multiple stores trying to find the perfect floats. She did not want to go through that again. "Come, sit here." Sophie turned her head to see Suho swing his legs off the end of his lounge chair. She figured he meant that to be polite.

Minkyo moved from his spot on the next lounge over and sat down in the space that Suho cleared. Minkyo crossed his legs, threw a towel over his head and started talking in a high-pitched voice. Without warning, he pulled off the towel and started smacking Suho with it while yelling at him. Suho just laughed while trying to dodge the towel. Something about the whole exchange made Sophie laugh. "What was that?" Sophie finally asked Dae-o as she carefully sat at the bottom of his lounger.

"He was pretending to be you." Dae-o answered. Sophie was surprised by how clear his English was. "Then, told Suho that you were Chinnie's girlfriend and to stop flirting."

"No, No!" Suho waved his hands, "Not. Just nice." There was a splash and a woman squealed followed by a loud laugh.

Three of the women came over with drinks and started talking to the men in Korean. Sophie looked between them. Arin kept giving

Sophie a side glance that she could not read. Sophie was aware that she did not belong here. She looked around trying to find a place to sneak off to. Sophie scanned the area for John and Minseok and found them both happily still in the water.

"Are you Park's girlfriend? Or friend? Or what?" Bora asked; she had a British accent. Sophie had to think about that one. They had never really discussed it. Arin said something and one of the other girls laughed, Sophie just shifted uncomfortable. She might not have understood the words, but the way the woman's hands moved was enough to say she was picking at her weight. There was an awkward silence. Sophie's eyes flicked to Dae-o who looked away quickly. Sophie could not blame him for not wanting to translate.

"*JAGIYA!*" Mal-Chin grabbed Sophie around her waist and hoisted her up off the lounge chair. Sophie squealed in shock. He was cold from the water.

"Jesus!" Sophie exclaimed. She put extra emphasis so it came out sounding like *Gee-sus*. A laugh ran through the group.

"So strong," Arin quipped. Sophie tried to ignore that comment. Arin did not mean that Mal-Chin was just strong. Arin meant Mal-Chin was strong for being able to lift Sophie.

"Are you thirsty? I got lemonade and sweet tea. Just for you." Mal-Chin poked her cheek. "Or are you ready to go swimming." Jealousy twisted on Arin's face. Arin left, Yujin trailing behind her.

Sophie debated the prospect of drinking bottled tea. She loved the fact that Mal-Chin tried. "Well, I'm not thirsty but—"

Sophie let out another squeal as Mal-Chin swept her up off her feet again, "Then let's go swimming!"

"Wait! Mal-Chin! My phone" Sophie held her phone up out of the way as Mal-Chin ran for the edge of the pool. Flailing made no sense, but she did it anyway. If he dropped her, she'd just go right in phone and all.

"I'll buy you a new one," Mal-Chin answered. He was bouncing as though about to jump in with her in his arms. Suho took her phone with an apologetic look. All she could do was latch onto Mal-Chin's shoulders. At the last second, she flashed Suho with a wide unguarded smile. The water was shockingly cold as they momentarily disappeared under its surface. One of her flip-flops came off. For all the fuss she made, Sophie came up laughing. Several others jumped in and were quickly playing around. Sophie and Mal-Chin joined them. Sophie abandoned her wet flip-flops and tank top on the edge of the pool.

After Mal-Chin pulled several of the other smaller men under the water, Bora gave Sophie a nudge. "Let's get him. You distract, I'll dunk." It did not work. Bora grabbed him from behind and tried to pull him down. Mal-Chin made a comical face in surprise and stumbled but did not go down. Now, it was Sophie's turn. She lunged at him. Sophie and Bora got dunked and came up laughing. This did not stop them. The pair tried again excitedly yelling ideas at each other. Minkyo, having been dunked several times, was cheering them on. Somehow, Sophie got her arms around Mal-Chin's chest and Bora got his feet. Mal-Chin was flailing and putting on a big show while yelling for Suho's help. From the edge of the pool, Suho called something back and just watched amused. They finally got Mal-Chin under, taking Sophie with him. As soon as he came up, both girls swam away.

By the time Sophie finally pulled herself onto the edge of the pool, she was worn out. Sophie chose the spot where her soaked tank top and shoes waited. Bora joined her. They both fixed their wet hair as they watched the boys play fighting again. "They all want you to dunk them now. They're teasing Mal-Chin about it." Bora stated with a chuckle. "Are those real? Just curious?"

Sophie looked down at her chest, adjusted the material of her top. She could figure why they wanted her to dunk them. "Yes. Are you British?"

"I'm from London," Bora wrung the water from her hair, "It's a long story."

Minseok snuck in on the other side of Sophie. He dipped his feet into the water. His eyes remained of his feet. Sophie did not notice Minseok and John had disappeared sometime after Mal-Chin jumped into the pool. "You ok?" Sophie whispered leaning in to Minseok a little. "Where's John?"

"Can you drive me home later?" Minseok whispered back still looking down at his feet.

"Yeah, what happened?"

"I got scared. I think I hurt his feelings."

Sophie patted his back comfortingly. She made a mental note to slip away once she found her phone and call John. Bora tried to start a friendly conversation with Minseok but he was not in a talkative mood. "He's a Purple-Pink fan. Might be a bit star struck." Sophie tried to cover.

"Happens all the time. Hey, who's your favorite?"

This brought Minseok back to the moment. "It was Arin but," he looked at Arin. Having not gotten into the water, Arin was lounging on the other side of the pool. "She's kind of..." He cleared his throat.

"A bitch, yeah." Bora finished. Sophie and Minseok looked at her shocked. "The sweet girl thing is just an act."

Dae-o and Suho joined them. Sophie thanked Suho for keeping her phone safe then put it out of the reach of the water. Her mind went back to checking on John. She could just text him, but Minseok might see it. The group chatted for a while taking turns helping Suho when he did not know the word in English. Mal-Chin swam over to them after Suho patted Sophie's knee to get her attention. Suho had simply been trying to ask how Mal-Chin was doing. Without a word, Mal-Chin pulled himself onto the pool's edge in front of Sophie and kissed her. He lowered back into the water and folded his arms in Sophie's lap. Her whole face felt hot. "What are you talking about?" Mal-Chin asked innocently.

"You go play somewhere else," Bora told him. "This is English speakers only." She flapped her arms at him to tell him to go.

"But, Suho is here and I speak better English than him." Mal-Chin pouted up at Sophie as she just giggled.

"He has honorary membership. Now, go." Bora playfully pushed him.

"*Jagiya*! Help!" Mal-Chin cried.

Sophie playfully pushed him too, "Payback." Mal-Chin swam away pretending to pout but struggling to hold back a laugh. "Are they always like that?" Sophie asked leaning toward Bora a little. Sophie was watching Mal-Chin swim to the other side of the pool and start a conversation with Arin and Yujin.

"Yeah, and jealous. Look out for that too." Bora nodded. "So I gotta ask," Bora was watching Mal-Chin and Arin as they chatted. There was something one-sidedly flirty about the exchange. "Since we're talking about jealousy. Are you really ok with Arin being here?" Bora clarified seeing the blank look on Sophie's face, "She's Mal-Chin's ex. I thought you knew. Sorry."

There was an argument going on around Sophie in Korean. Even if she spoke the language, Sophie would not have understood what was being said. Her eyes were focused on Arin and Mal-Chin. Arin was slender with long hair and a heart shaped face. Sophie could not deny that Arin was beautiful. What she could not understand is why she was here. Actually, why were any of these people here? Maybe that was rude but it was a good question. Mal-Chin's scandal rang through her head.

Focusing on the slight waves in the water, she closed her eyes and calmed her breathing. Slowly, she came back to awareness of the argument happening around her. "Honestly, I'm kind of not." She leaned back on her hands. The look on Minseok's face said he did not believe that. "I mean, I know how I look. But, I know how I act too. That's more important." Secretly, she hoped it was more important to Mal-Chin too. "Do I need to worry?"

"She always wants him, but I don't think she loves him. Just his attention." Bora answered.

Dae-o and Suho talked in Korean for a few minutes. Minseok told her they were debating what to say. They finally came up with a definite answer of "We don't know." Suho tried to tell her something, going as far as reaching over and grabbing her hand to get her attention. When no one would translate he got frustrated.

Sophie left the group. They watched her go with an understanding that she was either going to cause problems or just needed a minute. Surveying the mix of alcoholic and non-alcoholic drinks, she picked a bottle of sweet tea and found a quiet place. Inside, the house was comfortably cool. Sophie sipped her tea as she called John to talk to him. It was easier than dealing with her own issue.

Chapter 30

Mal-Chin was having a good time. He always wanted to attend a pool party. Out in the open air, there was nowhere to hide from the media. Everyone looked like they were having fun. He was seeing Sophie's playful side again and she was bonding with his friends. He laughed watching Ryu, Minkyo and two of the members of Purple-Pink playing chicken. Mal-Chin was keeping an eye on the group from the opposite side of the pool from where Sophie sat. He was trying to keep an eye on Suho from a distance.

Arin could not be ignored much longer as she spoke to him from the pool's edge. How long before she tried to harass Sophie again to get his attention. Arin was speaking in a flirty tone that she used when she wanted him back. From across the pool, Mal-Chin barely registered an argument in Korean, but with all the other noise he ignored it. A piece of him wished he refused to let the women of Purple-Pink join them, but a party with all men would have been boring, and Ryu liked Yujin.

Thankfully, Arin had to run off to answer a phone call. S.J.'s face lit up the screen. Mal-Chin recognized the sickly-sweet tone she used to answer the phone. It never registered to him until now how fake it was. His eyes scanned the pool and yard. Jeong-hui had taken Sophie's place between Minseok and Bora. Minkyo and 2 members of Purple-Pink were clustered around the snacks and drinks. Where was Sophie?

Mal-Chin was crossing the pool when Arin's raised voice caught his ear. Mal-Chin reminded himself to stay out of it. Even as she hung up and dramatically threw herself into a lounger, Mal-Chin pretended not to notice. It was drawing the attention of his other guests. Yujin stepped in to assist her. He grabbed a snack and chatted with the group standing around there. They all wanted to know what was going on with Arin. Mal-Chin just said he did not know.

"Is she mad at your new girlfriend?" One of the women, her stage name was Lily, asked. She was looking at him innocently enough.

"No. Why would she be?" Mal-Chin scanned the group again still not seeing Sophie.

"Well," Lily rolled her eyes. "You know how vain Arin is and, well, as soon as your girlfriend took her tank top off every man here was staring. Not that I blame them. I've never seen a real hourglass figure before."

Mal-Chin just nodded. Arin was heading their way. "Where did she go?"

"Inside." Minkyo pointed toward the door.

Inside, everything was quiet. *Could she have left?* He rushed to the front door. His mind ran through every possible scenario that could have made her leave. The door flinging open startled Sophie. She was standing in the shade of the porch with her phone to her ear. A shake of her head told him not to come out. Whoever she was talking to, it was a private conversation. Mal-Chin lingered in the living room, not wanting to leave her.

An arm snaked around Mal-Chin's waist. The feeling was so familiar he knew who it was without looking. "Chinnie," the sickly-sweet sound of Arin's voice confirmed it. Resigned to see what she wanted; Mal-Chin turned to face her. Arin instantly buried her face in his bare chest and began to cry. "S.J. broke up with me."

"I'm sorry," Awkwardly, Mal-Chin patted Arin's shoulder.

Her chin rested on his chest, not a single tear fell from her eyes. "What am I going to do? He was paying for my hotel and now he's going to cancel it." *Well, that was a lie.*

He felt her hands begin to roam his back, "Maybe one of the other girls will let you stay with them." He took a half step back and she followed.

"I want to be with you." Arin looked up at him with doe eyes. "We've always been good together."

"No." Mal-Chin grabbed her wrist and removed them from him then, as carefully as possible, put them at Arin's sides. A cringe came to his face as he heard the door open. He watched as Sophie looked up from her phone, her brows knit with confusion. The position could not have looked good. Arin's chin on Mal-Chin's chest, her bikini clad body pressed against his, Mal-Chin's hands at her sides. A conclusion was beginning to form on Sophie's face, and it was not one Mal-Chin wanted. He dropped Arin's wrists. "I'm with Sophie now." He pointed to Sophie in the hope she would understand what he was saying.

Sophie shifted awkwardly; her eyes looked everywhere but them. Arin started crying again. Mal-Chin tried to make some distance between them. "Sorry for, um, yeah.... I've got to take Minseok home so, yeah." Sophie took long strides toward the back door, her head down.

Mal-Chin tensed up. "Sophie, wait." He was surprised when she stopped. "This looks bad but," He tried to find the right words. How could he explain this in a way that did not feel like a lie?

Arin let out a mocking laugh, "You think, he want you?" She said in her best English, "Ugly, nobody and stupid. He *want* you? No. Just fun."

Sophie's jaw set hard. Her eyes flicked between them with a coldness that cut into Mal-Chin. Sophie did not speak a word, she just turned toward the back door to leave. "Don't say that!" Mal-Chin snapped in Korean before he could stop himself. He turned to Arin. The tone froze Sophie in place as well.

Arin exploded. She started yelling at Mal-Chin and even smacked him a few times. Her head turned to Sophie. Arin grabbed her wrist and gave her a shake. "What did you say to him!? You think you're so much better than me? I would have never left S.J. if I knew he would act like this!" Not understanding a word of this, Sophie just calmly stared at her. The tremble in her hand was the only give away.

It was not Mal-Chin that stepped in. It was Suho. Mal-Chin had frozen. Hearing the noise, the group had run inside. Suho walked up to the two, calmly removed Arin's hand from Sophie's wrist and edged space between the two. "She can't understand you," was all Suho said. He looked over his shoulder at Sophie, who was slowly making her way out of everyone's direct line of sight. She was beginning to shake.

Arin's eyes cut to Sophie, who Minseok was trying to soothe without putting a hand on her. She shrunk away from Minseok when he tried to hug her. "Well, I'm sure she'll understand this," Arin gave Suho a smug smile before turning her full attention to Sophie.

"Leave," Mal-Chin's voice came out sternly. Whatever Arin was planning, Mal-Chin was not going to allow it. Arin looked at him surprised. "Leave Arin. Everyone else can stay, but you have to go."

"But Chinnie," the anger left Arin's face. It was like watching a balloon deflate. Arin's eyes got large as she tried to decide if she wanted to look hurt or pitiful.

"Someone take her home," Mal-Chin ordered. He passed Arin and wrapped Sophie securely in his arms. Sophie clung to him.

Mal-Chin was not sure who took Arin back to her hotel, and he honestly did not care, but all of Purple-Pink except Yujin and Bora went with her. Embarrassment, worry and relief mixed up in him as he followed the group back outside. Looking down at Sophie, who was still tucked neatly under his arm, he couldn't help but feel surprised. Arin always ran to him after a breakup, and he always let her run any other woman off. He smoothed his hand over Sophie's hair noticing how her shoulders were turning red. *What just happened? Did I really just choose Sophie over Arin?*

It was Jeong-hui that broke the awkward silence that had fallen, "Let's get food. Swimming made me hungry." The rest of the group agreed. Mal-Chin let Sophie go and slipped into the house while they were distracted ordering pizzas. From the window, he watched as they huddled around Minseok's phone animatedly ordering. Sophie edged to the outside of the group. Her motions reminded him of the way she behaved at the gym. On the outskirts, barely noticeable. He grabbed what he needed and quickly returned.

The group readily accepted Mal-Chin's credit card to buy the food. Confusion filled Sophie's face as she looked at the t-shirt he offered her. "You're turning red."

Sophie checked her shoulder before accepting the shirt, "Thank you."

"Aww, I wish my boyfriend would do cute stuff like that," Yujin said in Korean. Ryu was looking at her disappointed. Mal-Chin scratched the back of his head, his ears turning red. Bora translated for

Sophie, who just gave an embarrassed smile. *Boyfriend*. That word was so simple, yet it felt like a huge step.

Everyone helped bring in the snacks and drinks, worried that the heat would ruin them. Once the couch filled, the remaining guest took a seat on the floor. There was an argument over who was going to pick the movie. Dae-o had the remote but his choices were rarely good. The guys grappled over the remote as the girls giggled. In the midst of the scuffle, the remote landed on the floor where Yujin quickly snatched it up. "Why don't we decide," She smiled waving the remote.

"Yes, let them decide," Ryu echoed.

"Fine, just no sappy romances," Jeong-hui added.

They settled on a legal drama as the pizza arrived. Being on the end, Sophie answered the door, made small talk with the delivery boy before returning with the pizza. Somehow, the group resettled to have Sophie sandwiched between Mal-Chin and Bora on the floor and Suho behind her. Mal-Chin was beginning to not like how Suho was staying so close to Sophie, but he trusted his friend.

Chapter 31

Beast was traveling the United States. They were spending time, a lot of time, in the state of Virginia, which sent off alarm bells in her head. *Why there? Why so long?* It was a large place, but her senses told her there was more there. She leaned back on her bed looking at her photo collection. There was a new picture on the wall now. The picture of her biggest threat: The American, Sophie Gregory. She purposely chose the picture that Mal-Chin commented on of his "Baby." Jealousy ran through her every time she thought about that nickname. The pin through the woman's neck was obviously a coincidence if someone asked. The ones to her face and breasts, she couldn't explain. She had to get rid of this woman that had gotten under Mal-Chin's skin so easily. How could he have been so stupid as to openly comment on her pictures?

She stalked the woman's Instagram; simply to find out what she could about Mal-Chin. Of course, there were no pictures of him, just her lifting weights and posing in workout gear. Typical wanna-be influencer stuff. Sophie could not even pose well, no way could she have been a model. What was so special about her, besides a chest that must be fake and curves that had to be well edited?

There was some slightly useful information on her profile. Sophie knew Minseok. That only answered how Sophie latched onto Mal-Chin. She knew where Minseok's last location was. Hopefully he was still there. Pictures mentioning a local café and bookstore appeared sporadically. A quick online search turned up the town these were located.

With a smile, she checked her bank account and started planning. There was no direct flight to the town she needed, it was a small hole in the wall town, so that's why Mal-Chin's flight out had been somewhere else. The tickets were more expensive than she thought, even for the cheap seats, not to mention a hotel. Mal-Chin would, obviously, let her in when she arrived but it might take her awhile to find him first.

She chewed her nail as she tried to figure out how to do this. If only the record company had just settled and paid her, she would have the money to make it there. Though, that money was meant to help her and Mal-Chin start their new life. But, what was she to do? With this new woman in the way and an investigation that would eventually turn up nothing underway, she needed to act quickly.

Chapter 32

Beast stayed with Mal-Chin until they flew to their next interview. The visit felt like old times to Mal-Chin. Footsteps padded throughout the house all times of night. The television was always on. Voices and laughter filled the once silent house.

Mal-Chin was wandering the house one night, a terrible habit he picked up after one too many late night phone calls, when he was startled by a lone figure in his kitchen. "Thought I was a *sasaeng*?" Ryu chuckled. It was not funny, they both knew that, but they still needed to laugh.

"Just wasn't expecting you," he looked out the window, "This place is creepy at night. That forest looks haunted."

Ryu looked out and agreed. He took a sip of water from a bottle. "How did you do it?" Ryu's tone dropped.

Maybe Mal-Chin was half asleep but the question confused him, "Do what?"

"Be the sexy member?" Ryu lifted himself onto the counter to sit there.

Well, that was not what he was expecting. "It took me awhile to realize what they were doing. I didn't understand why everyone else had layers of clothes and I had tight pants and just a jacket with one button closed. Then, I started to question if I wasn't a good performer and if that was why."

Ryu nodded, "I remember you complaining about the clothes. They chose you because you're muscular. How did you get over it?"

"I started focusing on the fans that talked about liking me for my personality. I thought of it as being for them. I also got selective about what fan accounts I followed. Especially the perverted ones. Get rid of those fast." Mal-Chin felt violated just thinking of the stories people wrote about him online.

"I don't think I can do it. They aren't asking me for as much as you did but," Ryu trailed off.

"I know it's hard, but you'll figure it out. Try talking to our manager and the stylist. Maybe they can find something you're more comfortable with."

Ryu nodded, "Why me? Why not Suho? They always dressed him in less, it would have been easy for him to fill the role."

"They're thinking long term. His military consignment starts soon. You'll be around longer." Ryu just nodded in agreement. He looked out the window into the darkness.

The day they were leaving, Mal-Chin watched them pack wishing he was going with them. The vacation was coming to an end. As the members of Beast packed, Chanyeol pulled Mal-Chin outside. Everything in him felt the possibility of going home with the group. Mentally, he was packing his bags. Maybe the cats would be ok with a more direct route. He knew he would not be able to disembark with Beast, but they could still travel back together. They would all go home. Mal-Chin barely heard Sophie's laughter from the living room.

He wondered what would happen to her. Mal-Chin feared Sophie would be alone feeling unlovable again. The thought could not last too long. It ruined his daydream of going home.

"I just got a call from the detectives in your case," Chanyeol began. Now Mal-Chin was very excited. "Kim Eun Jung has disappeared." Mal-Chin did not understand what this had to do with him. "The detectives aren't sure what to make of the information just yet but might want to speak to you again soon."

"Do they think I did something?" Mal-Chin ran cold. He was in a different country. How could he have made her disappear? "Is she coming here?"

"They don't know. But keep an eye out and be prepared for any new tricks she might pull." Mal-Chin just nodded. They headed back inside, and before he knew it, Beast was piling into the car. Just like that he was alone again.

Mal-Chin had a new fear. Was there a stranger trying to find his house? He closed the blinds. Sophie watched curiously as he walked the house over. She followed him from room to room like one of the cats. "What's up?"

"I'm just worried that they forgot something," Mal-Chin explained away his behavior. The only thing Beast had forgotten to take back was him. Sophie wrapped her arms around him. Guilt filled him. That was not the cover up Mal-Chin should have picked.

"You'll make it back," Sophie stated, her voice muffled from being buried in his back, "It may not be as fast as you want, I know. But you'll go home. You'll be back with your friends before you know it." There was an edge to Sophie's voice, like it was about to break. Mal-Chin tried to tell himself that it was just the way her face was pressed against him. His eyes felt hot as he pressed the back of her hand to his lips.

"You've been the best part about being here," he admitted.

"Hmm... I thought the best part was Granny's cooking." They both chuckled at that. "Is that what you discussed outside? You were asking to go home, and he turned you down."

Mal-Chin squeezed his eyes shut. *Damn, how did she get so close?* "I had hoped." He waited for a reaction, for her to get mad or break down in tears. Instead, he just felt her body sag in what must have been disappointment. "But, it was just an update before he left. He also got on my case for having everyone here. I'm not supposed to be seen with Beast." Worrying about losing him was not as bad as worrying about his safety, Mal-Chin decided. Sophie was right, eventually he would return home.

"Another time," Sophie said. Mal-Chin mumbled the words back to her.

Chapter 33

When Sophie last saw Mal-Chin, he was seated in front of his computer headphones on and working on a song. She had fallen asleep on the twin bed in his studio with a book still in her hand. Sophie had a copy of this book at home, but she was reading from the copy Mal-Chin bought. Sophie would read him chapters at his request. But, that day, she read silently to herself.

Now, as Sophie climbed the steps of his porch, a dull throb in her head threatening to turn into something more, Sophie would not be surprised to find him still fiddling with the mini keyboard and that strange device with all the knobs. "I've been knocking," Minseok stated from where he sat on the steps. It was a hot day; Sophie hoped he had not been out here long. Neither one of them had heard from Mal-Chin in several days except for him to say he was busy. When Minseok came by today, Mal-Chin did not answer the door. That got them both worried.

Sophie banged again then took a deep breath in and summoned her best hallway yell, "PARK MAL-CHIN! OPEN THIS DOOR! OR

I'M COMING IN!" It echoed. She waited listening for any sounds inside that was not a cat. After a few minutes, she yelled again. This time she heard movement inside, too big to be a cat. The door flew open. Mal-Chin's tired face looked down at her with wide eyes. Without another word, Sophie stepped inside leaving the men to trail after her. Arms crossed; she surveyed Mal-Chin. His tired eyes were red and puffy from lack of sleep, his hair a mess, and Sophie was sure that was the same outfit he was wearing the last time she saw him. "Have you been in that studio this whole time?" Mal-Chin avoided the question, so Sophie marched off to his studio to find the desk covered in balled up papers, empty drink containers and snack wrappers.

"Dude, have you been living in here? That's not healthy," Minseok asked taking in the room.

"I've been working. I got an idea." Mal-Chin rubbed the back of his head.

Sophie was already cleaning the trash up, "Go get a bath. I'm going to check on the cats then we'll get something to eat." No one argued with her. Mal-Chin skulked off to the bathroom like a scolded child after insisting he had taken care of the cats. Minseok tried to find the cats as Sophie poured them a bowl of food. They materialized at her feet instantly. "Poor babies." They took all the attention Sophie offered.

After rooting through the fridge and finding nothing inspiring, Sophie resigned herself to ordering out. Joining Minseok in the living room, they blandly discussed what to order. "He's worse than when he first came here," Minseok stated almost in a whisper.

"He wants to go home," Sophie found a random spot on the wall to stare. "He was hoping his friends would take him home. But, that didn't happen. His manager took him outside for a talk. He'd gone out looking so excited then returned looking so let down." The dull pressure in her head was starting to turn into an ache. Sophie ignored this too.

"Maybe he should go back. He'd be happier," Minseok stated. He was tapping away on his phone. If John was there, he would have given Minseok a hard jab to the side.

"Maybe he should," Sophie echoed. Mal-Chin been so much happier when his friends were in. She closed her eyes not sure if the burn in them was coming from the growing headache or the hallow feeling in her chest.

Minseok's head snapped to her, "Oh, um, sorry. I didn't mean," He cleared his throat.

She shook her head, "It's fine. He needs to be with his friends. Besides, he was never going to be happy here. This was a punishment. What was that whole line about letting things you care for go?" Sophie smiled crookedly. Sophie knew that a few kisses and an invitation to meet Mal-Chin's friends did not make a relationship. She also knew that she really liked it when the members of Beast referred to her as "Mal-Chin's girlfriend."

"Doesn't that end with 'if it loves you, it'll come back'?" Minseok smiled proudly. He was still struggling with American sayings.

"He won't come back," her tone was deep, her voice coming from deep in her throat. The implication was there. Sophie's lips pressed into a line. Might as well stop thinking about it now.

Minseok was going to say something, but he looked over her shoulder and froze. Mal-Chin walked into the living room still drying his hair, his face subtly hidden beneath the towel. They dropped the conversation and returned to the talk of food. Nausea was beginning to set in – *just nerves* – and she was not hungry.

By the time they ordered, Mal-Chin had pulled Sophie into his lap and was holding her tight. Sophie let her eyes close, telling herself it was just comfortable. "You smell good," she mumbled to Mal-Chin. That caused a chuckle from Mal-Chin. Sophie offered to go pick up the food. She felt Mal-Chin's head move but could not decipher the motion.

"John's working. I'm going to go get it. I can bother him at work," Minseok hopped up. Sophie heard the door close as he left then silence.

Mal-Chin guided her head so she was looking at him. "*Jagiya*," he seemed to be debating his words. That intense stare of his was back again. Finally, he placed a gentle kiss to her lips. He lingered for a moment, their lips barely touching before pulling away. "I miss you very much when you're not around." He looked away from her confused stare as his ears turned red.

Her insides felt like mush. Sophie hid her face in his shoulder. It was not embarrassment; she wanted to cry. He had heard her, and Sophie felt awful. No words came out of her when Sophie opened her mouth to speak. She squeezed her eyes tight trying not to cry. In Sophie's mind, the last thing he needed was her blubbering into his shoulder because he liked having her around.

Mal-Chin smacked his lips, "Look at you. So cute." He wrapped his arms around her tightly. Sophie reciprocated by putting her arms around his chest as best she could. No matter how many times she hugged him, it was still surprising how large he was.

They were still sitting this way when Minseok returned with John in tow. "Aww! Look at our love birds." John teased as he came through the door, "And you wanted to knock and miss this sweetness."

"I was worried we'd see something else," Minseok answered annoyed as they headed into the dining room. Mal-Chin and Sophie followed them.

"How did you get off of work?" Sophie asked as she removed the thick slice of tomato from her sandwich. A stinging pain was forming in the crease of her eyelid.

"I told them I had a family emergency," John answered with a shrug. He looked around the group then nudged Minseok in the side, "Which one are we adopting? I guess it has to be Mal-Chin. He's the one that was having the crisis." He stole a fry off Minseok's plate.

Sophie pouted, "I see how it is." She pretended to be upset.

"You're too mom to be adopted." John clarified. Sophie thought this over around a bite of her grilled chicken sandwich.

Minseok changed the subject, "I gotta ask. How were you going to get in here if he didn't answer the door? And how the hell did you yell so loud." He looked at John, "She echoed. Twice!" John just nodded his head in approval.

They were all looking at Sophie, "Umm... Well..." Her eyes flicked back and forth before she just smiled mischievously and shrugged. Mal-Chin's head leaned back as he burst out laughing.

"Girl, you're crazy," John chuckled. The sound of their collective laughter filled the house.

After Minseok and John left, Sophie and Mal-Chin curled up in his bed for a nap. Sophie took an Excedrin when no one was looking and thought a nap would help. Mal-Chin just needed the rest. They slept well into the afternoon curled into each other's arms. Sophie knew she should be ending this, but she could not help herself. She craved being near him with an intensity that should have been alarming.

Chapter 34

The short-shorts and tank top combo Sophie picked for today's outing would have sent Virginia into a fit. Just around the house, this outfit bothered Virginia on occasion. The knowledge that Sophie was going out in public in it would have been too much for Virginia to handle. Temperatures in the upper 90's and a heat index in the 100's prompted little clothing. It was a good thing that Virginia was not in town today.

Robbie and Carol had invited her grandparents to the beach. There was only space for the six of them. This was a point of contention for several days until Sophie insisted it was ok to leave her. Virginia worried for days about leaving Sophie and Lorraine behind. Virginia acted like it was the biggest slight anyone could have given the two. Sophie finally convinced her it would be ok. Her grandparents loved the beach and deserved a vacation. Plus, a few days without them constantly asking where she was off to sounded nice. It was truly a vacation for her as well. The trip was a reminder that summer was coming to an end soon. The Coleman family liked to vacation at the end of the summer, thinking that the beach was less crowded then. Sophie would have to plan her school restock shopping trip soon.

Checking her suitcase again, Sophie started to get nervous. It did not take long for her and Mal-Chin to start planning their own vacation as well. Sure, they were not leaving town but they would not have their time interrupted. Sophie wanted to just pack her duffel bag, but it had not been large enough. A suitcase was too large, too official. Sophie said goodbye to Lorraine, who was slightly uncomfortable with Sophie's plans but promised to cover for her anyway. "You're an adult. Do what you want," was all Lorraine said. Part of Sophie felt guilty for this. She was sneaking around again while her grandparents were gone. Not to mention, the implication was obviously there. Sophie was spending several nights at Mal-Chin's house. In the mind of any Southern lady that meant Sophie is having sex with Mal-Chin. The multiple matching sets of underwear packed into her suitcase probably helped that theory.

Mal-Chin barely waited for her to park before running out to greet her. He carried her suitcase in. "My room or the other?" He looked back at her hopefully, but she was distracted greeting the cats.

"Yours is more comfortable," Sophie finally answered. She was going to add "If that's ok," but Mal-Chin was already putting the suitcase in his room. When he returned, she added, "It's really hot outside."

"Hmm. I just thought that was because you were outside," Mal-Chin smiled.

"Oh, shut up. Do you still want to go out or skip to swimming?" Sophie asked flustered.

"Let's go out. We can get ice cream to cool off." Mal-Chin replied grabbing his keys. Sophie gave the cats one final head pat before getting up.

They wandered the mall hand in hand. The anchor stores were still doing well but the halls were mostly empty, especially downstairs. The new owners removed all the benches in the hope of keeping the teenagers from just hanging out and refused any local businesses except restaurants from renting store fronts. The result was a mostly empty mall. The false walls with old pictures of Danville were a nice touch though.

They made a stop in the sporting goods store to get Mal-Chin some new wrist grips. Sophie debated looking around Victoria Secret, the only place in town that made cute bras large enough to fit her. Mal-Chin's ears turned red just seeing her look at it. When they got bored of walking around, they left the mall. The turn around the mall took longer than they expected, Mal-Chin wandered through a good portion of the stores just to see what was in them. He took a little too long looking at rings in the fine jewelry store.

Mal-Chin easily parallel parked on Main Street, just a few blocks up from the yoga studio. When the mall kicked out all the local stores, many moved to Main Street. Like it had been in the 50's and 60's, Main Street was becoming the place to shop again. Their first stop was not the bookstore but the shoe store next door. Mal-Chin tried on several pairs of sneakers while making small talk with the worker before buying a pair of Nikes and a blazer. Outside, Mal-Chin got Sophie to take his picture standing in front of the sign holding his purchases. Later, he would post the picture online. His fans had already figured out where he was, why not drum up a little business for the local shops?

They stopped at Dog Eared Pages next. It was quiet on a weekday. They were the only two in the store, which would usually speed Sophie through her shopping but not here. She took her time reading the summaries of books while trying to decide. Mal-Chin took the books she picked out under the guise of holding them for her. Sophie was not tricked by this. They had a playful argument at the register. The owner, a young red-headed woman, seemed amused with their argument. "Tell you what, you can buy the books if I buy dinner," Sophie said.

"Deal!" Mal-Chin happily paid for the books. "I'm ordering steak," Mal-Chin informed the owner as she handed over the bags. This set both women to laughing. Sophie talked to the woman for a few minutes like they were acquainted before the couple left. On the way back to their car, Sophie leaned up a pressed a kiss to his cheek.

After a stop at the Science Center to play around with the interactive attractions, and a turn through the butterfly garden, they considered walking the Riverwalk Trail. The consensus was that it was too hot, but they did lay in the hammocks outside the Farmer's Market until they began to sweat, which did not take long. They ate at Link's then returned to Main Street for fro-yo. Sophie snapped a selfie of them together to send to her grandparents. They were worried about her being alone. Even though Ford and Virginia did not know Sophie was staying at his house, they would probably like to know she was not lonely. Mal-Chin poked his lips out at the camera. Virginia replied with *"Looks good call you later."*

"So," Sophie started as she scraped the last of her fro-yo out of the little cup, "what should we do now?"

"Go back?" Mal-Chin suggested. He was out of ideas and coming in and out of the heat was starting to wear him out.

"Go swimming?" Sophie asked hopefully.

Mal-Chin leaned forward and gave that playful smile, "You really want to see me in the pool huh?"

Sophie looked flustered again, "No, it's just hot. Outside, it's hot outside. Besides, you wear that swim shirt thing when it's just us."

"I could just wear the shorts." Mal-Chin's smiled turned mischievous, "I've got a speedo too."

"Oh, you." Sophie looked away from him, "You're flirty today."

"I can't help it. You're the one kissing me in public," Mal-Chin quipped.

Sophie rested her chin on her hand then stated coyly, "I could do it again." Mal-Chin pretended to be scandalized this then offered his cheek to her. Sophie turned Mal-Chin's face to her and kissed him on the lips.

Mal-Chin just blinked twice and stared at her. A shy smile crept along his face. "You're bold today."

Sophie laughed all the way to Mal-Chin's house as he sang along terribly to the music on the radio and did over the top gestures. They did not make it to the pool. Instead, they crashed on the couch enjoying the refreshingly cool air. It did not have the stickiness that even the stores' air carried.

Mal-Chin put his feet up on the coffee table and Sophie settled on the end with one of her new books. Sophie stretched her legs out across the couch and was using Mal-Chin's lap as a rest for her knees. The familiarity of it made Sophie pause. It felt nice to have someone to be that comfortable with.

"Read it to me," Mal-Chin requested once she was a few pages in. Sophie looked up at him questioningly then turned back to the first page and began to read out loud. Mal-Chin leaned his head against the back of the couch as he listened. Sophie was a good reader, that probably came with the job. Her voice lifted and fell at the right moments. His hand found its way onto her knee which eventually turned into him rubbing little circles with his thumb. If he noticed the little stutter in Sophie's voice when he started tracing his fingers up and down her leg, Mal-Chin did not show it. The motion might not have been bothering him but it was doing things to Sophie that she was embarrassed to admit.

At least finish the chapter. Heat rose to her cheeks when his fingers explored the back of her thigh. "Umm," she squeaked out unable to concentrate on what she was reading anymore. Mal-Chin looked at her confused, he was in his own world for a moment. A world that put that flame back in his eyes. Sophie's gaze flicked between his hand and her leg; she bit her lip.

"Oh, sorry, I'll stop," Mal-Chin removed his hand. His ears were turning red.

Sophie guided his hand back to her leg, "Don't stop. I like it I just," she bit her lip again. A need was building between her legs.

Mal-Chin did not waste a second letting his hand wander her legs again, this time adding a little pressure. "Just?" He looked into her eyes. Desire sparked in them unrestrained. "I think I know, *Jagiya*, but I need you to say it." Sophie's eyes wandered to his hand on her leg. The extra pressure was causing heat to spread across her lower body. The fingers of Mal-Chin's free hand traced the line of her jaw, gently guiding her face up to look at him. "Tell me what you want."

Desire rushed through her. Sophie put her hand over his and kissed the palm of his hand. "You," Sophie's words were barely a whisper, but Mal-Chin heard her loud and clear.

A smirk crossed Mal-Chin's face as he ran a hand up to her waist, "I was hoping," He pulled her into his lap, "You'd say that." Their lips met in a passionate kiss. One of Sophie's hands ran through his short hair as she moved to straddle him, her other hand landed firmly on Mal-Chin's muscular chest and wasted no time exploring. She quickly realized she was not the only one needing this. His hand found its way up under her shirt and up her back as their tongues met.

Sophie leaned away to catch her breath; all she could think of in that second was reconnecting to him. First, she needed to lose a layer. Grabbing the bottom of her tank-top, she lifted it half-way before pausing, Mal-Chin was already rubbing the exposed skin of her side. Doubt played across her face. Sophie could not get the image of her own body out of her mind. "If you don't like it?" Her unsure eyes lifted to Mal-Chin's.

Mal-Chin was leaned back against the couch, taking her in with dark lust filled eyes like he was waiting for the show to begin. "I've been imagining what's under those shirts," he leaned forward, "since you came out of the bathroom in my t-shirt." Mal-Chin pulled his own shirt off.

"I hope it lives up to your expectations," Sophie whispered. She pulled her shirt up over her head and let it fall somewhere on the floor.

"So, sexy," Mal-Chin mumbled more to himself. His hands worked their way up her sides as he placed a kiss on her collar bone.

Sophie let her hands wander his bare back and shoulders, taking in every detail. "Are we?" Sophie started. When Mal-Chin looked up at her, Sophie took the opportunity to place kisses on his defined shoulder. "I think we need more space if we're going to do this."

"You're right," Mal-Chin answered. He gripped her legs before standing. Sophie clung to him as she continued peppering kisses along his shoulders and neck. Gently, he laid her down in the center of the bed before standing up, Sophie raised up on her elbows to look at him. She feared Mal-Chin had changed his mind. "Are you sure, *Jagiya*? We can stop."

"I'm sure. I don't want to stop. Do you?" Sophie sat up a little more.

"I'm sure." He hooked his thumbs into the waist band of his shorts, "Take your shorts off, but leave the rest." Mal-Chin pulled his pants down as Sophie unbuttoned and slid out of her shorts. The bed dipped as Mal-Chin crawled along it to be on top of her. Sophie's breath caught in her chest as she felt Mal-Chin's warmth on her. Her leg ran up his side as Mal-Chin placed a tender kiss on her lips. Her heart melted. The last of her nerves escaped her. Sophie was so focused on the feel of his hand over her stomach that it took her a moment to realize he unclasped her front closure bra. Sophie sat up enough to shrug it off.

Mal-Chin sat back on his heels as she laid back down. Sophie's head turned to the side; she did not want to see any disgust on Mal-Chin's face. A low rumble left him as his hand cupped one breast. She found a look of wonder on his face. "Do I live up to expectations?" Sophie asked, her voice came out weak.

"Better than I imagined. " Mal-Chin gave her breast a light squeeze causing her back to arch. "These are bigger than I thought." His pressed kisses to her breast, causing soft moans to come out of her. Sophie's body felt on fire as his kisses trailed down her body to her thighs. Mal-Chin took extra time on her legs. Sophie felt like she was about to explode from anticipation when he finally slid her panties down her legs and positioned himself between her legs. "Did I tease too much?" Mal-Chin looked up at her playfully. Sophie just shook her head no in reply. "Can I," Mal-Chin's eyes found hers, "I need to hear you say it."

"Yes, please." Sophie whispered. She reached down just wanting to touch him.

"So cute." Mal-Chin mumbled to himself. A soft moan left Sophie when he kissed between her legs. Her moans filled the room. Sophie's mind forgot all her worries and focused only on what Mal-Chin's lips and tongue were doing to her. Just when she thought she couldn't take anymore, her body shook with pleasure then relaxed into the bed.

Mal-Chin slipped back up her body to press another kiss to her lips. "You ok?"

Sophie nodded, "Yeah, but I think," her hands ran down over the material of his boxer-briefs, "I think you're overdressed." She gave him a giddy smile as she got a handful of his perfect butt.

"You're right," Mal-Chin pressed another tender kiss to her lips. "Hold on." Mal-Chin stood up to remove his boxer-briefs and slip on a condom. Mal-Chin took his time letting Sophie take in the full view of his bare body. Sophie could have stared at him all day until it was burned into her memory. She sat up on the bed to watch him fascinated by the way his body moved so comfortably completely exposed.

"Ready?" Sophie asked. Mal-Chin returned to her on the bed.

"Ready," Mal-Chin confirmed before capturing her lips in a passionate kiss. He leaned her back on the bed while her leg rose to wrap around his waist.

Outside, the summer heat roasted the ground. Inside, the heat was caused by their connected bodies. The air filled with the sounds of their moans and gasps.

Chapter 35

The room was dark. Mal-Chin could only make out the shape of Sophie snuggled up to him. He could not remember the last time he had sex, fell asleep with his partner in his arms and woke up to her there. It made him feel whole, loved. There was no rush for one of them to disappear into the night before they were caught on camera leaving. Mal-Chin wanted to get up and make a huge romantic meal, complete with flowers and candlelight and the other half wanted to lay here enjoying this moment. That was the part that won. Clumsily, Mal-Chin pressed a kiss to Sophie's forehead. There was a delayed reaction, like it took Sophie a moment to recognize the sensation. She took a deep breath; Mal-Chin felt the movement. Instead of sitting up, Sophie snuggled deeper into him and settled in like she was going back to sleep. Mal-Chin felt the smile form on her face as his hand traced her face.

"Can we stay here?" Sophie mumbled.

"As long as you want," Mal-Chin answered. Sure, Sophie fell back to sleep, Mal-Chin started planning out that romantic candlelight dinner again. It was making him hungry. Just as he was deciding on dessert, Sophie's hand found its way to his face before she pulled him into a tender kiss.

"How do you feel?" Mal-Chin asked between kisses.

"Good," Her legs moved, "Maybe a little sore." Mal-Chin tensed. "But like, a good sore," She clarified, "How about you?"

"Great. I could eat, but I don't want to get up," He chuckled.

Sophie took a deep breath, almost yawning, before answering, "I could eat too."

Mal-Chin sat up at that. "Then let's eat." He turned on the light, almost knocking off the damp cloth Sophie had used to clean them when they were finished. Grabbing a pair of boxer-briefs from the dresser drawer, Mal-Chin rambled about what they should eat. Sophie's eyes were on him. When he turned around, she looked away like he caught her. She was a beautiful sight, the softness of her nude body perched on the edge of his bed, her messy hair falling over her shoulder.

Now, with the lights on and the lust gone, Sophie moved awkwardly like she was uncomfortable with being naked in front of him. Mal-Chin left the room as Sophie rooted through her suitcase for something to put on. He could give her a few minutes of privacy if that was what she needed. In the kitchen, Mal-Chin started cooking by just throwing anything together that looked good. It was too late at night to order. The sound of her bare feet padding into the kitchen caught his attention. "Do you regret it?" Mal-Chin's voice dipped low as he asked the question.

"No." Sophie answered softly, almost confused by his question. "You're amazing."

Mal-Chin turned away from what he was cooking. She was leaning against the counter behind him. Studying her face, he looked for any trace of regret on it. Now in the kitchen, she seemed comfortable. Sophie opted to put her sleep shirt on and pulled her hair into a messy bun. They must have looked silly, cooking dinner already dressed for bed. "You acted like you were uncomfortable."

"Oh," Sophie shifted pulling on the bottom edge of her sleep shirt, "That wasn't. I just looked at you and thought you were perfect in every way," Sophie tried to smile at him. "Then, I looked down at myself and," Her lips pressed into a line, she crossed her arms over her stomach. "I just wished I," Sophie closed her eyes, took a breath, and found a spot on the wall to stare at. Mal-Chin tried to think of the correct words to say but found none. Sophie continued, "I just thought, you could have someone better."

"Better?" Mal-Chin wrapped his arms around her, "I like you the way you are."

"I know. It's just in my head." She looked up at him. Somehow, she managed to look so innocent. "I keep thinking I'm over it, but the thoughts come back."

"Let me remind you that they're wrong when they come." Mal-Chin put his hand on her cheek. He felt a stone in his stomach. Knowing Sophie was thinking that way was difficult. He pressed a kiss to her forehead.

"Sorry for worrying you." A smokey smell filled the air. Confusion then alarm crossed Sophie's face. "Something is burning."

With a start, Mal-Chin returned to his cooking. He frantically stirred trying to save it. In the middle of this, Sophie had to run into the living room to grab her phone where she left it on the end table. Mal-Chin could barely hear her voice over the food spattering in the pan. From what he picked up, it was her grandparents reporting on their day. There was a lot of "That's good" and "Sounds like fun." Mal-Chin could not help but notice the loneliness in her voice. She might have stayed home of her own choice, but Sophie was feeling left out. He felt that way every time a member of Beast called to talk. When she returned to the kitchen, she showed no trace of that loneliness. Sophie simply passed on what they told her.

Dinner ended up being simple: baked chicken, rice and smoky sauteed vegetables. It was a healthy end to a day of unhealthy food. They ate out by the pool enjoying music from Mal-Chin's phone with an underlay of crickets. It was a clear night. Mal-Chin was always in awe of how bright the stars looked out here. The view quickly became his favorite thing about those initial quiet nights.

His phone rang. Mal-Chin had thought to ignore the call until he saw Chanyeol's name. Did the man just instinctively know when they were having a romantic moment? "Kim Eun Jung was a fake name," Chanyeol blurted out as soon as Mal-Chin answered. The stress in his manager's voice was evident, "She's Bae Young-ae." For a moment, Mal-Chin did not understand him. It was not because Chanyeol spoke in Korean, Mal-Chin had not had time to forget that, the words just did not make sense.

"Bae Young-ae," Mal-Chin repeated the name back. The name alone sent a wave of fear through him. That was a name he could not forget nor could Mal-Chin forget Bae Young-ae's face either. Mal-Chin should have known she was up to no good when he saw her at the airport. He ran a hand through his hair, Sophie was instantly at his side. She did not know what he was saying but his body language was enough. "How did they—?"

"Her lawyer reported her missing. He had to list her real name in the police report. It's all over the news," Chanyeol answered. "They say they have no clue where she's at."

"She's coming here," Mal-Chin stated. He was overly aware of Sophie rubbing his shaking hands.

"That's what I'm worried about," Chanyeol acknowledged, "Do you have an alarm system? You need to get one."

"I will." Mal-Chin answered. He was thinking of how little good that would do him. Bae Young-ae could easily break a window or just hide in the woods until he came outside. She had hidden in Mal-Chin's parking garage in the past. He dropped the phone and just stared at the screen until it went black. The forest behind his house suddenly looked ominous. "We need to go inside." Mal-Chin stood up quickly and practically dragged Sophie behind him into the house.

With all the doors securely locked and all the windows well covered, he looked at Sophie. She did not know what was happening. Did not know they were in danger. Mal-Chin's stomach sank. What would Bae Young-ae do if she found Sophie? Especially if she caught Sophie leaving Mal-Chin's house in the middle of the night. He remembered the bruises Young-ae left on a member of the security staff at a show when they would not let her backstage. She even threatened to kill Arin when the news about them dating released.

"Mal-Chin?" Sophie's voice called softly. "What happened?"

"My stalker was the woman making the accusations and she's disappeared." The knot in his stomach was making him sick. "She's probably coming here."

"How did she find you?" Sophie's eyes flicked around the house.

"Once my fans connected us, they found out where you were and just guessed."

That made Sophie shift uncomfortable, "Oh. I'm sorry."

Mal-Chin shook his head, "She would have found me anyway. She was waiting at the airport when I left Seoul last time. I should have known." Mal-Chin put his head between his hands.

Usually, Sophie's touch was calming to him. Right now, though, it was not. It just made him aware of the danger she was in being close to him. Arin, the only girlfriend Bae Young-ae had known about, had bodyguards that protected her during every outing. Sophie would be alone. Even here Sophie was not safe. Was it safer for him to keep her close and be on the lookout or keep his distance and hope Bae Young-ae focused on him? Mal-Chin pulled her close. For now, this was the best he could do. If she was in his arms, she was safe. "Do you think—" Sophie stopped. Her hand was in his hair for the second time today. This time it was soothing.

"Think?" Mal-Chin prompted.

"Never mind." Sophie shook her head. Her brows knitted in worry. Sophie set about trying to find something to distract Mal-Chin. It was a worthless endeavor. His mind continued to play out the worst-case scenario no matter what Sophie came up with.

In the morning, Mal-Chin announced that he no longer wanted to go to SeaQuest. If Sophie was disappointed, she did not show it. She just helped make pancakes while they both did a little dance in the kitchen.

Chapter 36

Summer was coming to an end. At least, for Sophie it was. Teachers returned for the new school year on August 2nd. Which meant Sophie needed to collect supplies for her classroom. It needed to be redecorated and the regular supplies replenished.

This shopping trip took several days. The first was online to collect bulk boxes of supplies. 150 pencils for $12? Yes, please. $9.99 for a 500-sheet pack of paper? A life saver. Classroom sets of markers, cap erasers, glue sticks, even a new pencil sharpener was purchased online. This was just a drop in the bucket of costs. Every year, Sophie was embarrassed by the amount of money she spent on her classroom. Sophie would often lie about the actual cost to keep her family from being shocked. That was why when Mal-Chin excitedly offered to come along, Sophie turned him down. Mal-Chin would have tried to pay for it. Sophie did not know how to explain to him that she spent $75 on posters at one store and still went to two more to finish getting her decorations. At Target, she filled a buggy with cheap folders and notebooks along with more decorations and a few items from the dollar aisle. Sophie tended to purchase items here that she thought were cute only to discover later that she was not sure what to do with them. Her favorite part of starting the new school year was setting up her room.

Sophie was debating whether she needed the neon dry-erase markers when she began to feel like she was being watched. Taking a glance around, she was the only person on this aisle. She told herself it was just her imagination. Sophie's hair was up in space buns for the first time and she switched between liking it and feeling ridiculous. She worried that her face was too large for the style. This felt different though, the last time Sophie felt this way was when a creepy old dude at the gym was staring at her. It was not a good feeling. Bae Young-ae flashed through her mind for a moment. Quickly, Sophie shook the thought from her brain. There was no way that Young-ae could have known Sophie was here.

Guiltily, she unloaded her cart at the checkout and glanced around for any watching eyes. The poor cashier made small talk as she rang up Sophie's purchases. A cashier once told her that he hated working during Back-To-School shopping more than working Black Friday. Sophie always felt bad for the cashiers after that.

It wasn't hard to identify a teacher in late July. The cart full of school supplies was a walking beacon. The cashier's cousin was debating dropping out of the education program at the local university. It was Sophie's college. She remembered how difficult they made things, and how different actual teaching was. "It's worth it," Sophie told the cashier. Sophie's face lit up. Just getting her shopping done had her looking forward to the new school year.

No good big shopping trip was complete without lunch from Link's. She drank about half of her mango smoothie before the red headed woman that ran the kitchen brought out her ham and cheese panini. The woman asked about Mal-Chin remembering them from their past trips. Mal-Chin was very hard to forget. With as much k-pop as they played, several of the workers must have been fans of the genre.

Sophie thought of her grandparents. She should have gotten take-out and brought them something. They liked the hot dogs Sophie brought them last time. She wondered what they were doing. Her grandparents had a habit of not eating until Sophie joined them during the summer. Thinking back on it, she missed plenty of lunches with them while out with Mal-Chin. Honestly, she had not even thought about that until now. This summer had been one of the best Sophie had but now she was wondering if she was doing something wrong.

The feeling of being watched returned. Sophie finished her lunch quickly and left.

At her grandparents' house, Sophie pulled out all the new cute decorations she bought. Virginia enthusiastically went through them. Virginia always wanted to come to the school to help Sophie set up, but she had never done it. The closest Viriginia got was going through the decorations with Sophie.

Virginia's eyes suddenly turned glassy, "You know," she started. Sophie was instantly on edge. "I never thought you'd abandoned us but you did. We've barely seen you all summer because you've been running around with that boy all summer. I guess we'll never see you when you go back to school."

Sophie twisted the handle of the shopping bag in front of her. "I won't." She looked down her lips pressing into a line. "I didn't abandon you. I've come over every day like normal."

"Yes, but you either leave early or don't get here until dinner time. You're so wrapped around Mal-Chin's finger that you can't spend time with anyone else. Just because he's showing you a little attention doesn't mean he cares about you. You're just a bit of fun for him."

Virginia might as well have slapped Sophie in the face. Sophie thought of that embarrassing day Mal-Chin pulled her into his arms and let her cry when Sophie tried to return the watch, how he always grabbed her hand when she was fidgeting with anxiety. In the few months Sophie had known Mal-Chin, he'd shown her more love than she'd felt from her family. Just thinking it made her feel guilty. "Granny, he—I" Sophie could not find the right words.

"Oh, he doesn't love you. I knew you'd fall for the first man that showed you any interest. Why would he want you? Look at him. He's handsome, fit and rich. What would he want from you?" Virginia's words were cold.

Sophie pressed her lips together wanting to cry. Virginia was right at some level; Sophie was not good enough for Mal-Chin. "I love him." Sophie stated trying to keep her voice even. "He's kind to me. I don't know why he likes me, but he does." She looked at her grandmother. "Why do you suddenly not like him?"

It was Virginia's turn to stumble for words, "It's not that I don't like him. It's just, Sophie, he's not right for you. It's just, Mal-Chin he isn't, well you know." Virginia looked embarrassed.

"I don't," Sophie stood picking up her bags, "and I don't want to know what you mean." She shifted uncomfortably. "I'm going to take these home."

"Oh, baby, don't be upset. I'm just trying to tell you the truth." Virginia said as Sophie headed out the door.

Sophie's heart was pounding before she even made it off the front porch. Her skin had turned blotchy with nerves. The short drive home was not enough to calm her down. She had been in such a good mood today but, now, she was even more upset at Virginia for ruining it.

She stood up to her grandmother. Regret instantly flooded her. She should not have done that. Now, the whole family would be against her. What was she going to do? Dumping the bags of hand sanitizer and anti-bacterial wipes onto the living room floor, Sophie made a quick run to her bedroom. She sat on the side of her bed and let her legs fidget. Tears blurred her eyes and a knot twisted in her stomach. She bent forward and attempted to calm herself, which was not working.

Sophie stayed at the house, calming her nerves, and trying to figure out her next move. Virginia's admonishments were usually met with silence. Sophie just took the fussing and stayed in the awkward aftermath. She never left before. What did Sophie do now? Did she just go back when she calmed down? Wait for Virginia to call her? That was not going to happen. At least, Sophie had not expected Virginia to call. About an hour and a half later, Virginia called. Virginia did not apologize or act like they had gotten into an argument. She simply asked if Sophie was coming back down.

Chapter 37

"Are you ready to talk now?" Mal-Chin asked as he pulled the sheet over their bare bodies.

Sophie instantly snuggled into him, "I'm tired now." They were swimming on a sweltering day out of a need to beat the heat when another need had gotten in the way. She felt his chest rumble with a chuckle. It was a sound he only made in bed. Sophie liked it. It was a sound just for her. "This has been a good summer. I don't want it to end," She confessed, "and Granny is just being Granny."

"We have plenty of time left. We'll have a good autumn and winter too," Mal-Chin replied. Sophie felt him take a deep breath like he was relaxing. There was an unspoken knowledge there. They both knew he might not be here in the fall or winter. There was also the understanding he might still be here next summer. Selfishly, Sophie wanted to keep him as long as possible. Mal-Chin was not happy here. He might have found temporary happiness with Sophie, but this was not his home. It never would be. Sophie fell asleep to the sound of him humming a tune. The tune was new but was quickly becoming familiar. Mal-Chin hummed it every time they cuddled.

Voices in the living room woke Sophie up. Whoever was out there was excitedly talking in Korean. Sophie sat up looking around the room. Her still damp bathing suit was on the floor but her regular clothes were in the bathroom down the hall. Now, she was trying to decide how to get them without looking suspicious. Thinking it was the best option, she borrowed one of Mal-Chin's shirts. It was the best coverage she could get until she got to her real clothes.

Peeking into the hall showed no one, though the voices were louder now. Had Mal-Chin closed her in to keep her hidden or let her rest? Sophie debated this question for a moment. This was an awkward time to be caught but her car was obviously in his driveway so, at some point, Mal-Chin would have to explain where she was.

As quietly and quickly as possible, she crept down to the bathroom. Unfortunately, this was the same moment that Suho turned down the hallway. They both froze. Suho's head turned toward the wall, he wiped his nose, cleared his throat then turned and walked away. Embarrassment flooded her as she ducked into the bathroom. Doing her best to look presentable, she took her time getting dressed, making sure to brush through her hair well. Hopefully, Suho would think they had just been napping. One look at Sophie's swollen lips told a different story though.

Dressed in her college t-shirt and shorts, Sophie crept back out of the bathroom. Meekly, she joined Mal-Chin by his side. Several members of the group shifted or rubbed their neck or arm. Sophie looked at Mal-Chin apologetically, she should have stayed hidden.

Kim Chanyeol's face was red but not with embarrassment. He looked Sophie over with a critical eye that made her feel more uncomfortable than she had originally been. It was like he was taking stock of all her flaws. She took a half step toward Mal-Chin. Chanyeol yelled at Mal-Chin and gestured toward Sophie. Dae-o looked away like nothing was happening when she turned to him for clarity. Jeong-hui and Ryu were looking at her sympathetically.

A hard knot filled her stomach, "Ok first off," Sophie snapped before she could stop herself. Her Southern accent came out heavy, Chanyeol looked at her surprised, "You *ain't* got no reason speakin' to him like that. *And* if you're gonna talk about me you best be doin' it in a way I can understand." Sophie crossed her arms and her brows knit. There was a shocked silence. "One a y'all," she gestured at Mal-Chin and Dae-o, "tell him what I said."

Mal-Chin very politely relayed the message. "Sophie, he is my manager," Mal-Chin informed her, "That means he's my boss."

"I know, but he still don't mean he can be talking to you like that," Sophie insisted. Her brows furrowed.

Chanyeol looked at Sophie then Mal-Chin, "He not be with you," he stated in English.

It was Sophie's turn to look confused. She looked at Mal-Chin, who just hung his head trying to not look at her. The other men did the same when she turned to them. "What does he mean I can't be with you? Why does he get to decide that?" Her voice sounded thin. The air felt like it was draining from the room taking Sophie's anger with it.

Mal-Chin looked at her but did not answer her. "It's normal for idols to not be allowed to date," Dae-o gently filled in.

Sophie felt the ground being pulled out from under her. She was still looking at Mal-Chin. "Mal-Chin. Why is he telling me this?"

Mal-Chin squeezed his eyes shut. He refused to meet Sophie's gaze. "It's in my contract. I can't date. I'm not even supposed to be seen out as just friends with a woman." He took in the pressed lips and tiny tremble of Sophie's chin. Her neck was turning splotchy red. She looked around the group confused. Beast was trying their best to distance themselves from the situation. "I'm sorry. I thought," He shook his head.

"You didn't think," Sophie said harshly, "I guess I was really a plaything." She mumbled more to herself. "So that's it?" Sophie looked at him then glanced at Chanyeol. Neither met her gaze. Without another word, Sophie headed for the door. She snatched her purse up and stuck her feet in her shoes, absentmindedly thanking her good luck they were flip-flops and easy to pull on. Her vision was blurring as she opened the door. Her throat hurt.

There was no dramatic scene of Mal-Chin chasing her down or calling her name. Sophie simply got into the car and left as the first tears ran down her face. She made a mistake one that she promised never to make again. Sophie let her walls come down and now the bricks were falling on her head. Sophie spent the rest of the day hiding at the house pretending to have a migraine. The weak cracking of her voice aided in this lie.

<h1 style="text-align:center">Chapter 38</h1>

"Chinnie *hyung*!" Jeong-hui called from the pool, "I'm going to dunk our leader! Watch me!" Jeong-hui jumped onto Suho's back and tried to pull him under. Mal-Chin watched just to amuse Jeong-hui. His friends were in for an extended visit and he could not even enjoy it.

"I don't think it worked," Suho stated unfazed by the attack behind him. Suho fell back with a smile dunking Jeong-hui. This brought a laugh from the members of Beast but not Mal-Chin.

Mal-Chin had just stood there as Sophie left. He did not try to follow her or explain himself. Mal-Chin just let her go. It was useless to try and explain himself. Eventually, he would have to leave Sophie anyway. Mal-Chin just wished he picked an easier way of telling her. The image of Sophie's face returned to him in the moments he least expected it. Her face had gone blank with confusion before understanding cracked through the surface turning her eyes glassy. Mal-Chin worked hard to win her heart only to tear it into little pieces. A part of him acknowledged Sophie would never try again but Mal-Chin did not want to take that responsibility or think that highly of himself.

Checking his last message to Sophie did not help either. *"I'm sorry you had to find out this way. It's a part of my job that sucks. I was going to tell you."* There was no reply, maybe she did not even read it. That hurt, though Mal-Chin could not blame her. With a sigh, Mal-Chin hopped into the pool and dunked his head under the water. When he came up, he almost overturned Minkyo's float. This caused the skinny member to give him a push in retaliation. In a matter of moments the group was play fighting. For a while, Mal-Chin was distracted.

That night, Jeong-hui and Dae-o analyzed his music. He left to grab a snack and returned to a soft melody playing. It flooded the room with a sense of calm. The two members sorted through Mal-Chin's notes. A lump formed in Mal-Chin's throat. "This sounds really nice. What is it? Sounds like a lullaby," Jeong-hui asked.

Mal-Chin's mouth turned down. Sophie's sleeping face appeared in his mind, "I don't have lyrics for it yet." His voice cracked.

The two other men tensed. "Well that's too bad. You should get Minkyo to help you with it. He's good with that kind of song," Jeong-hui advised before clicking to *Baby,* a fast paced song. "Where's the lyrics to this? That's a good beat. Are you going to try to rap?" Both began to nod their heads along to the beat. Jeong-hui hit pause, "You know what would be go here? Like a-" he made a beat. "Yeah, that would sound good and maybe some drums."

"I was thinking of adding some guitar to it," Mal-Chin stated as he returned to his seat. None of the music sounded right to Mal-Chin again. They spent a frustrating amount of time cramped into the little room functioning as a studio.

The rest of the week, the group did their best to distract Mal-Chin. They went biking on the Riverwalk trail and kayaking on the Dan

River. After both trips, they sat on the bank of the river enjoying the view of the sun on the surface of the muddy water. Ryu bought them all iced coffees to sip while they relaxed.

Suho and Minkyo insisted on going to the gym with him. They wanted to try new routines. This always worked to ease Mal-Chin's mind. It backfired when they caught a glimpse of Sophie running on the elliptical. She looked away from Mal-Chin quickly. Before he could look back, she was gone. This was the last time Mal-Chin saw her at the gym. Mal-Chin did not know if Sophie was avoiding him or if something was wrong.

Dae-o's idea was to go drinking. He invited Minseok and John, to attend. Minseok picked a popular bar on the outskirts of town. The number of motorcycles outside made Mal-Chin think of all the biker gangs he had seen in movies. The group tried to match each other drink for drink, shot for shot. Dae-o could drink all of them under the table. He became the goal. This led to the whole group getting extremely drunk, and not remembering how they got home.

Mal-Chin stumbled out of bed the next morning to the smell of Hangover Soup being made. The T.V. in the living room was playing previews from the streaming service he did not remember turning on.

"This is getting exhausting," Suho stated from the kitchen. Mal-Chin stopped out of sight listening to him.

"I know," Dae-o joined in, "but we're leaving soon and we can't leave him in this state."

"He's worse than when we sent him here. I thought he was doing better," Suho added, "Even his parents thought this would be good for him. It's obviously not."

"I don't think you were expecting him to meet Sophie. That's what's bothering him now." Minseok's voice joined the conversation.

"What happened? She won't tell me or John anything." There was a long pause. The silence was almost awkward.

"You spoke to her." Mal-Chin rounded the corner, "Is she ok?"

"Not really. She was supposed to go to Girl's Night and didn't show so John called to check on her. She just said she didn't feel well." Minseok scrolled through his phone with a shrug.

Dae-o looked over his shoulder at his brother, "Why were you invited to Girl's Night?"

There was a long silence. Minseok and Mal-Chin exchanged glances. "American men can be real assholes sometimes so they invite Minseok or John as protection," Mal-Chin explained. *How did Dae-o not know?* Minseok gave him a relieved look as Dae-o just accepted this answer. Suho shook his head.

A memory flashed back to him. His arm was around someone's shoulders, as they helped him to the van. He complimented the person's strength and gotten a giggle in return. Followed by a memory of someone tucking him into bed, a kiss to the forehead before them saying something he could not remember and leaving.

"She was here wasn't she?" Mal-Chin looked around the group.

"Dude, we were all so drunk. Who knows what happened." Minseok answered. "Fairly sure John's going to have a nasty hangover when he wakes up."

Mal-Chin wanted to ask more questions when Jeong-hui came in yelling about soup and dragging a sleepy Ryu behind him. Chanyeol joined them soon after. He was the only one not hungover but looked exhausted. Mal-Chin vaguely remembered him picking them up from the bar last night. He could only imagine what it had taken for the short pudgy man to get them all into the van. The thought made him chuckle to himself.

Chapter 39

When Sophie finally pulled herself from her bed, the first thing she did was go to her grandparents. She went in pursuit of comfort. The tears poured again as she tried to explain it all. This gained her hugs and kisses to the top of her head from Virginia. They were gentle with her for a few days. When Mal-Chin's text reached her, she did not know what to say, so she just ignored it.

The taunts began as soon as Robbie and Carol learned the news. It started over family dinner the next day with jibs about the relationship. Carol offhandedly commented about the fact that he was so handsome and Sophie was "well... you know." Virginia joined in the jokes. Sophie just wanted to get away, to change the subject.

"What gets me is," Robbie sucked the remaining food off his fingers before continuing, "we set you up with a nice American boy but no, you had to chase after the mail-order boyfriend—"

"Don't call him that," Sophie spat out at that comment. Sophie mentally stabbed him with a fork.

Robbie continued like he had not heard but anger twisted on his face, "And now look at ya. Shoulda listened to us," he chuckled.

"That Noah was no good for her," Ford stated gesturing with his fork, a piece of pork loin skewered on the end. That took some of the wind out of their sails. Robbie suddenly switched to bashing Noah's work ethics and a number of other complaints. Sophie wracked her brain for a reason to get away until she remembered that it was supposed to be Girl's Night with her college friends. She made a big deal out of going and how she needed to get ready. No one thought twice about it being an escape. Virginia encouraged her to get out. On the way out the door, Carol made a comment about her meeting a "good man" while she was out.

At home, Sophie broke down into the kind of ugly sobs that turns a face red and stretches the lips out. Lorraine tried to comfort her but realized that Sophie just needed to be left alone. In the end, Lorraine just closed Sophie into her room to deal with it. John called her later that night. Music and voices from the night club boomed in the background. Sophie just made the excuse that she was not feeling well. John offered to have Minscok come check on her, but Sophie insisted she just needed to be left alone.

The next morning, Sophie decided to avoid her family as much as possible. She set about trying to spend too much time at the gym but she caught sight of Mal-Chin. It was better to disappear. Mal-Chin was looking at Sophie like she was the only person in the world. Sophie could not handle it. Sophie's days festered back into the dullness that she was accustomed to. Even the extra yoga classes became routine. She found herself scrolling mindlessly through her phone more often. A few times she'd picked it up thinking she needed to text someone only to put it down remembering she had no one to talk to.

On her last Saturday of summer break, things got interesting again with a phone call. Mal-Chin's voice excitedly yelled through the receiver in Korean. Sophie guessed he must have been drunk. The sound of other loud voices in the background made her think that they must have all been drunk. Sophie coldly reminded him that she could not speak Korean.

"Oh, right, right, right," He slurred out his accent sounding thicker, "I miss you."

Sophie softened, "I miss you too." It was safe to say. Mal-Chin probably would not remember it in the morning. "Where are you?"

"Clucky's" Mal-Chin slurred out. Sophie was considering just hanging up but hearing Clucky's changed that. Clucky's had a bad reputation. Rumors of brawls, drugs and pure chaos had marred the bar since Sophie was a child. Even her father, who was a biker and hard partier, thought twice before stepping into Clucky's. Lorraine once told Sophie about women fighting just to get a better spot in the line for the bathroom.

"Are the others drunk too?" Sophie sat up. She tried to hide the worry that flooded her mind. Why would John and Minseok let them go there?

"Uh....." Mal-Chin spoke to them in Korean. "Yes. Except John, because he didn't answer."

"You spoke in Korean. John doesn't know Korean," Sophie reminded him.

"Oh, oi, John. Are you drunk?" There was a pause. "He say no. Come join us. I want hug."

Sophie sighed looking down at her nightgown. She wanted no part of this, but they did not need to be Clucky's. Drawing too much attention was sure to get the table full of handsome, even pretty, Korean men in trouble. By the time Sophie was dressed, she had convinced

Mal-Chin to call Kim Chanyeol to come get them as well. Mal-Chin only agreed if Sophie showed up. As much as Sophie was not fond of Chanyeol, she did know he would need help. A drunk John alone could be a handful.

To her surprise, Sophie got carded at the door. In a tank top and shorts, there was no way she was passing for underage. Chanyeol did not get carded, which seemed to insult him. Inside, the bar was sticky from the summer heat. The whole place reeked of alcohol and sweat. The pair scanned the room for Mal-Chin and the others but had no luck. Sophie finally flagged down a waitress in her 50's. "Oh them," the waitress pointed to a back corner yelling over the blasting rocked music and boisterous guests, "they're kinda cute huh? Even if you can't half understand them." Sophie just smiled at the comment, thanked the woman and headed off in that direction with Chanyeol close behind her.

The mix of bikers, rednecks and preppy 20 something's looking to party must have made Chanyeol's head spin. His eyes were constantly darting around the room. Sophie wondered if he was scared. Sophie probably should be too but years of her father dragging the whole family to parties had desensitized her to the situation. Luckily, the divorce ended all that. Sophie's comfort with this situation made her realize how messed up that was. The thought that her dad might be there crossed her mind. A few of the bikers looked familiar.

Empty bottles and glasses were scattered all over the table when Sophie finally found them. There was not room for anything else. John and Minseok looked plastered. "Sophieeeee!!" Mal-Chin yelled. His face was flushed red. The rest of the table joined in.

"Hey guys." Sophie was trying to keep her voice cheerful for some-one who had been pulled out of her bed after midnight only to face the man who smashed her heart. Sophie put her hand on the curve of her waist trying to look casual. She mimicked the movements of all the bikers' wives she grew up idolizing: Calm, comfortable and able to control a room full of drunks with ease. Sophie's back burned with the feeling she was being stared at. "Having fun?" She had to raise her voice to be heard over the music. A chorus of "Yes" was her answer. Minkyo shook an empty glass upside down over his head.

"The waitress said no more drinks," Jeong-hui pouted, it somehow showed his dimples.

"I can understand why," Sophie mumbled more to herself. "Well, let's get you all home."

"But, you just got here," John stated, not helping the situation at all. The others quickly agreed insisting she needed a drink before they left. Mal-Chin somehow slipped his hand into hers at this point; it felt right. The notion twisted in her chest. They were trying their best to make a good argument. Chanyeol spoke to them in Korean and the group gave up. Suho eagerly offered his credit card to pay off their bill. Sophie was not going to argue with that one. Some of those drinks looked expensive.

A couple of bikers helped get the group out to the cars. The way their eyes traveled Sophie's body made her stomach turn. Sophie had a hold of Minkyo, who mumbled something then hopped onto her back for a piggyback ride. His feet scrapped the ground as she walked.

"Ah! Sophie! So strong!" Mal-Chin called from behind her. Her laugh filled the air. "So much muscle," Mal-Chin flexed causing her to laugh more. Dae-o, the only one who seemed halfway sober, helped her unload Minkyo into the van. John and Minseok went into her car; she was worried one would accidentally expose their relationship in a drunken state.

One of the bikers, handed her a couple of empty to-go bags, "Just in case," The woman said it with a knowing lift of her eyebrows.

"Oh, thank you." She handed a few of the bags to Dae-o.

"You're Fred's little girl aren't you?" one of them asked out of the blue.

"Yeah, from his first marriage," Sophie confirmed. She shifted her weight to one side suddenly uncomfortable. A look of disappointment came over the biker's face. His eyes were no longer wandering all over her.

"Ha! My Sophie girl! I knew you looked familiar!" The woman wrapped her in a hug. Sophie could smell the alcohol and cigarette smoke on the woman as she awkwardly returned the hug. "Oh, look at you! I remember when you were this big," the woman indicated a height around her knee. "But look at you! You look just like you mama."

"Yeah, Lorraine was a pretty woman.," One of the men commented. This made Sophie more uncomfortable, she had gotten that comment as a child and had the same feeling. "Do you need us to follow you?"

Sophie shook her head, "No I'll be alright. We can pull right up to the door."

The woman looked at the group, "You sure, sugar, that's a lot of large men." She eyed the men in the van suspiciously.

"I'm sure. They're good guys. Plus, they'll probably be asleep before we get there." Sophie nodded. The group of bikers watched Sophie pull out of the parking lot with concern on their faces.

The group was not asleep by the time they reached Mal-Chin's house.

Sophie unlocked the door while Beast did a drunken performance on the porch, Minseok and John cheered them on. It was a credit to their talent that they were able to get through it so well as they stumbled and flailed. They finally herded the group inside, where Ryu quickly came up with the idea to go swimming. Chanyeol talked him out of it somehow.

Sophie was beginning to think she would have to manage the group all night when they finally settled. It was like trying to handle a rowdy class; frustrating but manageable. She turned on a movie and plied them with snacks to keep them all in one place. Chanyeol snuck off to wherever he was sleeping, Sophie later guessed he must be in Mal-Chin's studio, leaving Sophie to deal with them. Minseok and John curled up on one side of the couch, Suho fell asleep on the other, using the coffee table as a footrest. Jeong-hui and Ryu helped Minkyo stumble into the guest bedroom the three were sharing.

Mal-Chin started leaning on Sophie heavily as they sat on the floor. "Why don't we get you to bed?" She asked in almost a whisper, trying not to wake the ones sleeping on the couch. All she needed was for John to wake up and start sing-yelling again. Mal-Chin just nodded sleepily. If he had not been drunk the motion would have been cute.

With a little help from Sophie, Mal-Chin got to his feet. He put an arm around her shoulders for support as they stumbled to his room. Mal-Chin was heavier than she thought. He started undressing as soon as he sat down on the bed, Sophie looked away. What was once a welcome sight was now off limits to her.

Dae-o spoke to Mal-Chin in Korean, the sound of his voice surprising them both. They had turned on the light coming in not realizing that Dae-o was sleeping on a floor bed in there. Sophie apologized for waking him before finding Mal-Chin a pair of pajama bottoms to throw on. Dae-o ended up having to help him do that. Sophie tucked him in intending to head home now. It was late, she was sleepy.

Mal-Chin's hand grabbed hold of her shirt. He mumbled something and gave her shirt a childish tug. "Stay... just a minute." Sophie sat down on the edge of the bed with her back to him.

"You're not the prettiest girl I've dated," Mal-Chin started. Sophie's jaw clenched. A dull pain spread across her chest that was quickly filled with a cold emptiness. She already knew that. Just about her whole family reminded her she was not pretty enough. Yet, coming from him it felt like a slap in the face. "And I was just using you as a distraction. You were so sweet and kind and – and lonely."

Dae-o shifted and made an excuse about seeing if he could get Suho into bed before leaving the room.

Her throat stung, "Well, you don't have to worry about any of that anymore." Sophie moved to get up just as an arm snaked around her waist. It was not tight enough to hold her but she stayed anyway.

"But I like looking at you. You're cute and sexy. And you make funny faces without meaning to. And your eyes are so green. You're the best part of being here and I don't know if I could have made it without you."

"You could have," Sophie squeaked out. She meant to sound cold but sounded broken instead.

"I fell for you. And, your family, they, they don't care about you the way they should. Why don't they love you?" There was a long silence. Sophie did not have an answer to that question. "I wish I could take you away from here. I wish I could wake up next to you every day." He sat up and wrapped both arms around her. "But I don't think we can." He buried his face in her shoulder. "I just want you to know, before I leave—that— that someone loved you."

"I love you too," Sophie mumbled back.

"While I'm here, while we can. Let's love," He leaned slightly to try to look at her. The silence grew long. "Sophie, please."

She turned her body to face him and looked into his alcohol glazed eyes. The swelling in Sophie's chest sunk away like a deflating balloon. Without saying a word, she got him laid back down. "You should get some sleep." That came out colder. The hopeful look faded from Mal-Chin's face. He repeated her name. "You're drunk why don't we talk about this when you're sober."

"I couldn't say it sober," Mal-Chin admitted. He wiped his hand across her cheek finding it damp.

"You'll have to try," She told him. Sophie leaned over him slightly. He puckered his lips almost ridiculously at her. She kissed his forehead, which caused him to get a giddy smile on his face. "Good night."

Sophie passed Dae-o in the hall, who was helping a half-asleep Suho find his way. In the living room, she repositioned Minseok and John so they were laying comfortably on the couch. Minseok instantly snuggled into John like he was a teddy bear. Careful not to wake them, she covered the couple up with a blanket.

"They look happy," Dae-o stated. His gaze was soft.

Sophie looked at him surprised then back at the pair, "They are."

"I wish he would tell me." Dae-o sighed then turned away. "Get home safely. Thank you for coming to help." He walked back down the hallway leaving Sophie. She turned off any lights left on before letting herself out and locking the door behind her. For a few minutes, she just sat in the driveway looking at the silent house. The darkness and silence began to pervade her car leaving a creeping feeling of being watched. With a sigh, she backed out of the driveway and made the drive home.

Chapter 40

Bae Young-ae found Sophie. It was a stroke of luck, Young-ae had gone out to pick up supplies at a store with self-checkout so she would not have to fumble through a conversation with cashiers. Young-ae passed an aisle and backed up. There Sophie was with a cart full of junk and contemplating another item. She must have liked spending money to have a cart so overloaded. Just another gold digger after Mal-Chin's money. That was alright, Young-ae would run her off soon enough. For now, she needed Sophie to help her find Mal-Chin. *Just wait,* she thought, *I'm on my way, my love.* When Sophie looked around, Young-ae ducked down the next aisle out of sight. The last thing she needed was for Sophie to realize she was being followed. Young-ae kept her distance as Sophie headed for the check out.

Young-ae's years of following Beast around had taught her how to keep a low profile without losing sight of her target. Her hope was that Sophie was heading to Mal-Chin's house. That was not the case. Sophie pulled into a house where an old woman was sitting on the porch. Over the week, Young-ae followed Sophie everywhere. Which turned out to, boringly, just be the gym and a few yoga classes. Even-tually, Young-ae stopped seeing Sophie at her regular times and could not quite place what that meant.

Her target changed to Minseok. He went out to lunch with Sophie and John. A few days later, Dae-o came to the door of Minseok's apartment. Young-ae took Dae-o's presence to mean the other mem-bers were in town. This was good news for her. If Beast was in town, Mal-Chin would be going out with them. The next logical route was to follow Dae-o. To her surprise, he did not return to wherever they were staying. Suho was waiting for him at the entrance to the town's walking trail. They went to a coffee shop where Sophie was waiting for them. It almost looked like a date. Though, the bun on Sophie's head didn't look fancy enough for a date. Young-ae could not go inside, it was too small and too empty at this time of day. She would be exposed instantly.

Young-ae pretended to check her phone, glanced around, then took a seat outside. Even in the shade, it was too hot to be sitting outside. How did the air always feel heavy here? This was her only option though. Her plan at this point was to pretend she was meeting a friend that was running late, an old but decent strategy. Through the window, she watched whatever conversation was going on inside. Truthfully, she had no clue what they were discussing, but that was not her main point here.

After what felt like a lifetime, they exited. Young-ae got into her rented car to follow them. She watched as Sophie shrunk away from Suho's hug then as the two men climbed into their car, she prepared to follow. They took Young-ae exactly where she wanted to go. Mal-Chin was even standing on the porch.

She took a quick glance at Dae-o and Suho standing in the driveway and knew it was too early. Driving further down, Young-ae expected to find another road to turn down, but all she found was a dead end. *Damn*. It was not even a rounded end. The road just stopped. Turning around would look suspicious but she had no other choice. Young-ae had to turn carefully to not end up in a ditch. Luckily, they were all so caught up in what looked like an argument that they did not notice the rental slowing down to watch.

Chapter 41

The school year started on a cool August morning. The school's parking lot was practically empty as Sophie began to unload her trunk full of supplies. It would take her several trips to bring everything in. There was a general calmness in the air, yet Sophie felt the return of students approaching. Empty hallways always felt strange. Schools were not meant to be this silent, this dead feeling. Once the students arrived, the school would be alive again. The distant thud of boxes and shuffling of feet were the only clue that others were already there. A strange feeling washed over Sophie as she opened her classroom door. She felt it every year yet still could not place a name to the feeling, something like curiosity, anticipation and coming home all mixed together.

The feeling quickly faded. Sophie got to work, taking advantage of the quiet time. Someone was unpacking next door. This caught Sophie off guard, Mrs. Davis usually dragged in later on workdays, and worked to music. "You're here early," she called from where she stood near her door putting up her bulletin board.

There was a pause. "Yeah, I figured my first day I should get started early," A man's voice answered. Sophie looked over in shock. A man younger than her in an ill-fitted suit stepped out into the hallway. He was looking at Sophie curiously.

"Oh, hi," Sophie stepped down from the student desk she was standing on, "Sorry. I thought Davis was here early. Are you the new math teacher?"

"Yeah, Jason Cook. Nice to mee ya'. I think they moved Davis down the hall." He looked at the bulletin board she was working on as Sophie introduced herself. "Need a hand? That's kinda high."

"I'm ok, do this every year. Just don't let Mr. Waller catch you." Sophie answered as she stapled fabric onto the board. Jason watched asking Sophie questions about it and just generally talking. This was his first teaching job and he was eager to get started. He wanted to discuss all things teaching as Sophie worked and even asked for advice on where to get the best supplies.

As other teachers began to trickle in, Sophie took a rest to catch up with them. One teacher commented on Sophie's double French braids, she never wore the style outside going to the gym. "Guess I'm overdressed," Jason remarked as he noticed everyone's jeans and t-shirts. Even Sophie was wearing capris and a school t-shirt.

"I did that my first year too. You'll look good for the picture at least," Sophie added. Jason made the short trip back to his classroom, only a step and a turn away, and got back to work in his own room.

Sophie tended to do her best work in the morning. She made quick work of putting her bulletin boards back up even if she had to stand in the seat of a desk to reach the top. It was easy when she used the same design every year. Posters were next. She tried to hang as much as she could before the janitors arrived and caught her using a student desk as a step ladder. Mr. Waller had threatened to write her up for an OSHA violation a few years ago out of concern she would fall. An older teacher had broken a leg after a fall out of a chair Sophie's first year here.

The annual beginning of year meeting started with breakfast and catching up in the cafeteria. One affectionate teacher ran her hand over Sophie's French braid complimenting the style. Sophie's hair felt like there was something stuck in it for an hour. They went through the yearly policy changes, reminders of the Tiered approach to teaching, and introductions of new teachers as well as a list of teachers who moved rooms. Beside her, Jason furiously took notes while the rest of the table picked at the remains of their food. Mr. Motley and Mrs. Hall made a good attempt to make the meeting interesting, adding in jokes as they went. That was the best part of these meetings.

At lunch, Sophie found herself alone. The men, including Mr. Worley and Jason, went gone together, the teacher at the end of the hall was eating with family and the rest disappeared. Sophie thought about delaying lunch an hour before time to leave and eating with her grandparents then just not coming back, but she was hungry.

Sophie scrolled through her phone deciding where to go and almost texted Mal-Chin in the process. Her mind caught on what she would say to him: *Hey let's have lunch, hope you don't get lost getting here!* Or *Hey, remember that thing you said when you were drunk?* She sighed. Sophie missed him. Mal-Chin had not messaged her, so she figured he had forgotten the conversation or not meant what he said. Though drunk people liked to tell the truth, at least Sophie did.

Sophie shook the thought out of her head and took herself to lunch. At first she decided to go to the good Mexican restaurant in town but ended up at Subway instead. The idea of grabbing something and getting back to her room suddenly sounded better than eating out on her own, an activity that usually did not bother her. While she ate, she played Beast's music on her phone. Sophie had learned to pick out Mal-Chin's voice. This had been helping to ease her longing for him but today it did not work.

The day dragged on after lunch; this was always her worst part of the day. She slowed almost to a stop in the afternoon on workdays. This was a good time to unpack her teacher's desk, as she could sit to do it. This was, ironically, the same time of day that Mr. Worley amped into full swing. She could hear him across the hall aligning desks and tearing into supplies. Sophie was watching the clock at this point, ready to head out the door. Jason kept popping in to ask her questions or just have a short chat. It was a bit annoying. He really should have been asking the teacher across from him, the most experienced of the other 2 math teachers, these questions. But Sophie's door was just a step from Jason's, so it made sense. She made a mental note of everything left to accomplish by Thursday. It seemed like too much to do before the parents arrived for Open House night, but Sophie always got it done.

Without thinking, she opened her phone to the text thread with Mal-Chin. Her chest felt tight as she looked through the messages. Sophie took a deep breath and tapped in a message before climbing into her car.

Chapter 42

Sophie Gregory found herself sitting nervously at a table in a small Italian restaurant just a few buildings up from the gym. She had taken the time to do her full makeup – lipstick and eye shadow. When Sophie left to get ready, Virginia was huffy, which only served to add to Sophie's rattled nerves. Virginia was adamantly against this meeting.

Sophie tried, and failed, to check her reflection in the window. She did, however, get a good look of Mal-Chin crossing the parking lot. The fact that he was incredibly handsome smacked her again. Somehow, she'd forgotten. Maybe she was used to it, or maybe it was because he was wearing jeans that fit just tight enough and a white button up that looked simple yet expensive. His hair was fixed too perfectly, like he spent a good amount of time, and maybe too much hair spray, trying to make it lay just right. Sophie recognized the style as the way he tended to wear his on stage instead of the regular banged cut he usually sported. The whole outfit reminded her of their date that ended in disaster. There was some kind of tension in his shoulders. Was he nervous too?

You're not the prettiest girl I've dated. Those words smacked her in the face, hard. Like the rest of her family, she was doubting why someone like him would like her. She tried to shake the idea out of her mind, to focus on the other things Mal-Chin said that night. *Sweet and kind.* The last thing she wanted was for him to see a sad expression on her face. She watched the ice in her sweet tea swirl as she spun her stirred in it.

***

Mal-Chin did not notice Sophie when he passed by her window. He looked for her when he entered and a waitress had to direct him to the corner she was seated. Mal-Chin noticed her hair first the way it was slightly wavy and tucked behind her ear instead of hiding her face. The calmness of Sophie's face caught his attention as well. Those lipstick reddened lips showed no hint of nervousness, but she was stirring her sweet tea with her straw almost absentmindedly. Mal-Chin had learned over the last few months that Sophie's emotions were in her hands, not her face.

He wanted to just stand there and stare at her. The ease of her movements told him that she did not think anyone was looking at her. Everything in him needed to be close to her though so he crossed the room to their table.

Surprise filled Sophie's green eyes. It reminded Mal-Chin of the day they met at the gym, back when she was just another gym-goer trying to avoid any attention. A smile crossed Sophie's face and sparkled in her eyes in a way that made Mal-Chin's heart melt as he seated himself. He missed that smile.

They made awkward small talk as they decided on what to order. The distance between them felt great. Mal-Chin felt Sophie wasn't telling him everything. By the sadness in her eyes, he guessed it was her family. She quickly changed the subject to his recent visitors. Mal-Chin detailed their visit and the fact that they left a few days after their night of drinking, "They've been pushing me to call you,"

Sophie's lips just pressed as she nodded taking in that last piece of information. "That was a crazy night," She added.

"Did you really give Minkyo a piggyback ride?" Mal-Chin asked, a grin on his face.

Sophie giggled, "Well, he kinda just hopped on, but, yeah." Mal-Chin laughed with her, still having trouble imagining it. "Um.. do you? Remember anything else from that night?" Sophie asked pushing a penne noodle around the plate.

Mal-Chin took a sip of his drink, glanced around then nodded, "Yes, some of it. I remember saying something I shouldn't have to you." He rubbed the back of his head, his ears turned pink, "I also remember something about confessing how I felt." It was his turn to find a distraction. Sophie confirmed what Mal-Chin said and filled in the blanks. The sadness in her eyes confused him.

Sophie expected him to falter back on his words. Deep down she wanted to believe it was all true, but she knew it could not be. Mal-Chin made a drunken mistake. "You were very drunk when you said it. I understand if—"

Mal-Chin grabbed her hand it was oddly comforting, "It was all true. Every word." He looked into her eyes. She never noticed just how dark brown his eyes were, dark enough that she could not tell where his irises ended and his pupils began. "I did use you as a distraction, but I fell in love with you." Mal-Chin watched her try to read his eyes.

"That was the most romantic thing anyone's ever said to me," Sophie looked away but a giddy smile lit her face for a second, "and you were too drunk to remember it."

"I remember enough," Mal-Chin ghosted a kiss over her knuckles, "I remember telling you I wanted to be with you as long as we could and, you kissing my forehead. But I don't remember what your answer was, though I can guess." He focused on her hand, examining the new burn mark on one finger.

"I said wait till you're sober, but you never messaged me and I thought, maybe, you didn't remember or you didn't mean it." She looked at him now.

"Well, I do. I was just waiting on you." He smiled, "So how about it?"

"Um.... What about? You're career?" Sophie asked, "He said it was me or your career."

Mal-Chin gave her a blank look for a moment then smiled, "The thing about my manager is he can be easily persuaded. Plus, I think you impressed him the night we were all drunk." Mal-Chin smiled almost proudly. "You did a good job, there was no," he searched for the right word, "no one paid us much attention."

Sophie nodded, "Ok. So, what happens when you have to go back?" Her eyes looked pained already.

He shifted in his chair. Mal-Chin had been trying to figure this out for the last few days. He did not think she would be happy as a housewife – house girlfriend? —, and Sophie did not speak any Korean so finding a job would be difficult, except maybe in one of those posh private schools. Not to mention she had never been to South Korea before and it would be like stepping into a different world. They would have to be careful going out anywhere because Sophie would quickly be thrown into the spotlight. With the chaos that just a comment on her picture caused, Mal-Chin could not see that ending well.

"We'll figure it out when the time comes," Mal-Chin stated. Maybe, just maybe, he could teach Sophie Korean in time. He watched her, trying to figure out what she was thinking.

Sophie did not know how to reply. She wanted to be by Mal-Chin's side. In her mind, she could see holidays spent together, quiet winter nights cuddled up on the couch, waking up on cold mornings to the warmth of Mal-Chin next to her and the sound of their joint laughter filling an apartment that she could not even imagine. Sophie imagined something in between the opulent apartments they showed in kdramas and a regular house. But, she could also feel the heartbreak of him boarding the plane back to Korea to never been seen again. Was it better to love someone knowing heartbreak was ahead or to know you missed something special to protect your heart. Sophie could not get broken again.

"I—" she hesitated, the words stuck in her throat, "Mal-Chin, I love you." Sophie watched the bright smile form on his lips, there was something tense in his shoulders, it made her change her mind, "I—Let's date, be together, whatever you want to call it."

They did not want to be separated but they also did not want to occupy a table for too long. They ended up driving down to an entrance for the Riverwalk trail. They used one at the end of a car lot where they could look over the artificial waterfall created by water turbines. The falling water made a relaxing noise and the cool river air was refreshing against the humid heat that set in during the day. They stood by the railing; occasionally, Mal-Chin would raise their interlaced hands and kiss the back of hers. It still gave her a fuzzy feeling.

Mal-Chin watched a man successfully pull in multiple fish before the stranger wandered off. A couple on bikes rode farther down the trail drawing Mal-Chin's attention. Sophie suggested they walk down the tree lined path, and the two headed that way. It was darker than they expected, the path lights gave off a dim yellowish glow. They only got glances of moonlight shining off the water. Sophie suddenly remembered walking here at night was not considered safe. They returned to the man-made waterfall.

They stayed there until Virginia called asking Sophie where she was. Virginia expected Sophie to have called in tears of despair by now. Hearing the chipper tone of Sophie's voice mixed with the fact she was still out upset Virginia into another one of her huffy moods. Sophie had lost track of time, she raised Mal-Chin's arm and read his watch to get the time then looked surprised. She kept apologizing and saying she was heading home. Her neck splotched over with worry.

Chapter 43

Throwing the bed sheets off, Sophie sat up and clicked on the bedside lamp. Her eyes squinted as they adjusted but she did not wait long to pull herself from the bed. The living room felt cooler, yet she was hit with a sense that something was off. The silence and the darkness of a sleeping home always gave her house an eerie feeling in the late hours of the night. She sipped water glancing around the darkness. Years of her parents watching horror movies had left her with the knowledge not to put your back to a dark room for long. Sophie still could not shake the feeling of being watched.

Her body felt heavy as she slowly made her way back to her bedroom. Sophie needed sleep. Tomorrow was Open House, and she would need all of her energy to make it through the day.

The next day felt like it would never end, but once it was over, time seemed to have flown by. Sophie was terrible at Open Houses. Kids she could handle, parents were completely different animals. To her great relief, they always seemed to appreciate the quick walk through of what to expect. Two of the teachers on the hallway had long presentations to give and always had a line out the door. Sophie could never figure out what they talked about so much. Mr. Worley was a staple in the community of the tiny town surrounding her school so most of his visitors were chatting about family or church events; he had also taught a good portion of the parents as well. Her favorite part of these days were past students who stopped by to say hello or were there with younger relatives. She was always surprised with how much they'd grown. Her first class of students would graduate this year and she was excited to hear what they were planning to do after graduation. Sophie excitedly informed Jason of every past student they had a chance to discuss and what type of student they had been.

"Good afternoon, parents, staff and students!" Mr. Motley's voice piped through the speakers. Sophie was packing up before he could say anything else. "Open House is now over. Please finish your conversations and make your way to the front. Teachers, you may leave if you have no parents." The hallway had been empty for a good 20 minutes. Sophie did not check before closing up her room.

At first, she just thought it was a trick of the light from the setting sun. Her car seemed to be leaning to the driver's side. It looked like something was spread across the hood as well. Another teacher was looking it over. Sophie stopped dead in her tracks and looked around the parking lot. Her car was leaning because the tire was flat. Worse than that, Korean words were into the hood.

"What happened?" The sixth-grade teacher who had stopped asked as Sophie inched closer.

"I don't know." Sophie looked at her tire.

"Man, that looks slashed." A male teacher answered, he materialized beside her car while she was not looking. Sophie also discovered more Korean etched into the driver's side door. Her heart rate went up. Sophie could only think of one person that would do this. By this time, multiple teachers had stopped to look. The principal even walked over on his way out. He called the school assigned police officer, who returned and casually looked the car over before taking pictures and promising to look into the school's security camera.

One of the perks of working in a southern rural town was that there was always a man nearby with tools in his truck. In this case, Mr. Waller was the first to retrieve his tools. With a shake of his head at the damage done, he pulled out the spare tire from her trunk. It took three men to fix the tire: One to do the actual work and two others to discuss it. The principal excitedly told Sophie where she could get replacement tires and which ones were the best.

"So, who hates you enough to do this?" the resource officer asked.

Sophie was sending pictures of the writing to Mal-Chin. A chill ran up Sophie's spine. There were new teachers, new cars. She could not keep track of all the cars.

"My boyfriend's stalker," The words felt strange even as she said them.

The officer's brows raised, "Really? Damn." He did not question it. The idea of explaining it already sounded too crazy to be true. *I'm dating a k-pop singer whose fan flew across the globe to wreck my car.* Sure, that sounded reasonable. Her coworkers did not even know about Mal-Chin.

Within minutes, Mal-Chin was calling her. Mr. Waller had just finished changing the tire and she was giving him a one-armed hug as the group began to disperse. "Go straight to your mechanic or home. That spare won't last too long," Mr. Waller warned.

"I will. Thank you," She climbed into the car as she answered her phone.

"Where are you?"

"At work. Just leaving," the edge creeped into her voice. Now that she was in her car, out of the view of others, her nerves were beginning to kick in.

"Are you going home? I'm going to come meet you."

"Granny made dinner, so I was going to go there first," Sophie explained. All she wanted was to be with her grandparents. Ford could look over her car and tell Sophie how to fix it. Her coworkers' advice was all mixed up in her head. Sophie pulled out onto the highway. The knot in her stomach climbed into her chest; threatening to suffocate her. "What did it say?"

"I'm going to meet you at your grandparents," Mal-Chin answered.

"That's not what I asked."

There was a deep sigh from the other end of the phone as a car door slammed, "It was her. Bae Young-ae. She—" he made a noise, "I'll tell you later."

"I'd rather you tell me now so I'm not freaking out in front of my grandparents," Sophie passed cars as her foot pressed harder on the pedal.

"She's threatening to do the same thing to you," Mal-Chin's voice was tense.

Sophie's hands tightened on the wheel. "Do the same to me?" She drove faster. Her mind went to deep scratches all over her face and body, her belly split open. Blood oozing from her. Sophie's skin felt tight. Like the wounds were already there and healing. Would it scar? Somehow, walking around the rest of her life covered in scars was worse than the actual injury. The knot in her chest was soon joined by nausea. If her belly was split, she would not have to worry about scars.

Breath in 1....2....3.... Hold 1....2....3.... Out 1...2....3.... It was not working. Sophie's mind thought of where she could pull over if she needed to vomit. There really was not a safe spot to go on the highway. Pulling over would leave her open if she was being followed. Sophie needed to get home.

"Sophie?" Mal-Chin's voice brought her back, "Should I come get you?"

"No, I just," She was already at the stop light in Tight Squeeze, "I need to call my grandparents." Sophie hung up.

Her mind played through what she was going to tell her grandparents before she called them. They did not need to know what the carvings meant; they might not even realize it was words. When she did call, she asked to speak to Ford. That set off alarm bells that something was wrong, Sophie heard the worry in Virginia's voice.

All the men in the family came to look her car over again. Ford and Andrew were waiting in the driveway when she arrived. Robbie showed up soon afterwards. Even Mal-Chin gave it a knowledgeable once over when he arrived. The four discussed it as Sophie just sat on the porch steps and stared into the distance having trouble wrapping her mind around it. Virginia was rubbing her shoulder trying to comfort Sophie but all it did was twist Sophie's stomach more at the unwanted contact.

Chapter 44

Mal-Chin offered to drive Sophie home with the promise she could borrow his car until hers was fixed. When she hesitated to drive it, Mal-Chin ordered a rental car. Something small and nice. He quickly convinced her to just stay at his house. Mal-Chin wanted-ed Sophie close where he could keep her safe. While Sophie packed, Mal-Chin wondered how useful he would actually be in keeping her safe. Sure, he was strong but Mal-Chin always had a bodyguard to protect him. He never had to fend off an attacker. Could he do it if he had to? Mal-Chin froze the last time a fan rushed him.

Once it was late enough, Mal-Chin slipped out of bed. It was diffi-cult to leave Sophie sleeping there alone. Having Sophie by his side, in his bed, just felt right. If she was right there, Mal-Chin was sure she was safe. Mal-Chin was careful to close the door behind him on the way out. All he could do was hope that Sophie would not wake. He worried that she would understand the conversation even if it was in Korean.

As the phone rang, he plopped down on the couch without even checking to make sure the cats were not there. They had probably found something of Sophie's to curl up on. If anyone loved Sophie more than Mal-Chin it was Aruem and Ramyun. Most of her days here were spent with at least one of the cats on her lap or at her feet.

Mal-Chin played out the conversation he was expecting before calling the number. When Kim Chanyeol answered, he started with "Pay the money." That was not what he was expecting to say. "Whatever price she wants, I'll pay it."

There was a long silence as Chanyeol either tried to figure out what Mal-Chin was saying or found a quiet place to talk. "What are you talking about?"

"Bae Young-ae, she wanted money to make the accusations go away, right? Tell her I'll pay it if she signs saying she'll leave me alone." Mal-Chin could barely see his reflection in the T.V. screen. It was a vague form, just the basic shadow and a hint of color.

"Park, this doesn't make any sense. Why pay out now?" Chanyeol's voice was annoyed.

"She's threatening to kill my girlfriend." Mal-Chin looked down the dark hallway. He feared Sophie was awake. "Keyed her car, slashed the tires." He looked down, "Wrote on it that she was going to slit Sophie's throat if she didn't leave me alone."

"Paying that money is just like admitting you were guilty. You'll lose everything," Chanyeol stated, "Your career will be over. Not to mention, any link to your girlfriend would break your contract."

"I know. Just pay the money. She's here, she's ready to kill." Mal-Chin ran a hand through his hair.

"Bae is bluffing. There's a big difference between stalker and killer. I don't think that's a line she's willing to cross," Chanyeol answered. Even over the phone, Mal-Chin could tell he was uncertain.

"We don't know what she'd do. She broke into my house, ruined my career, now she's followed me here. If she's desperate enough—" the words caught in Mal-Chin's throat. He did not want to think of what Bae Young-ae would do. If she was willing to make accusations, follow him across the globe and key a car, what else would she do?

"Then let the American police handle it. You're not risking your career over this." Chanyeol hung up.

Mal-Chin wanted to throw his phone across the room, watch it smash into pieces. However, he did not want to replace it. He leaned back against the couch annoyed. There was no going back to sleep now. His heart was pounding. That conversation did nothing but make him even more upset. He wracked his brain for who to call next.

He tried his lawyer but it looked like Chanyeol got to him first. The lawyer told him the same thing: do not pay, call the police. Sophie had already done the second part, what else could they do? Mal-Chin could not just sit around and wait for Bae Young-ae to decide to act.

Chapter 45

Young-ae was surprised when her phone rang. International calls were expensive. This whole endeavor was getting pricey. It would be worth it in the end. Money would not be a problem once she was done. Young-ae was more surprised to see "Chinnie" on the screen along with her favorite picture of him. Her heart did a flip. He was reaching out to her. Mal-Chin was finally coming after her. Young-ae answered quickly. Her plan was to surprise him for his birthday, but this was better.

The tension in his voice was evident throughout the conversation. Mal-Chin must have been just as anxious to finally be with her. Young-ae convinced him to meet her. They could talk in person for the first time outside the distraction of fans and managers. Just the idea of it made her giddy. Young-ae spent a good portion of the day preparing to meet him.

Young-ae hurried to their meeting spot, a table outside of Link's. Confusion flooded her when Mal-Chin arrived. His shoulders were tense. The look in his eyes reminded her of the time she surprised him in his apartment. Was he mad? "Chinnie!" Young-ae wrapped her arms around him as soon as Mal-Chin was close enough. He might have been upset now but they were together; it would all be ok. Mal-Chin gripped Young-ae's arms and removed them from around him. She was shocked, he had given out hugs to fans before. Why was he refusing her? "What's wrong? Are you worried about someone seeing us? We're in the U.S. the media hasn't found you." Young-ae's arms fell by her side as he released them. Anger bubbled up in her, "It's because of *her* isn't it?"

"Leave her alone," Mal-Chin stated. It was not harsh, but a command. "She has nothing to do with this."

Young-ae was confused again. How could Sophie not be involved in this? "She's distracted you. You've been telling me for years to get you out and now that I have, you've forgotten. How could you forget?"

Understanding slowly spread over Mal-Chin's face, "You thought I wanted this?"

Young-ae nodded, "I heard your message. It took me awhile to put it all together. But I have. And now we can be together forever." She tried to hug him again but he stepped away. "I know this wasn't the way we were supposed to meet up, but I guess you were just as desperate to see me again. Love can do crazy things."

"I don't love you." Mal-Chin's jaw set hard. His words cut Young-ae hard.

Numb, that was all Young-ae felt at this point. "I've been your fan for years. You told me-"

"I've told thousands of fans that," Mal-Chin set the full strength of his angered gaze on her. "You call yourself a fan! You stalk me! Destroy my career! Now you're harassing my girlfriend!" He took a couple breaths trying to calm himself. A few people in the café were staring. "You're not my love. You're not even my fan. You never were. Go back to Korea," Mal-Chin spit the words out, "And leave me alone." He stalked away back to his car.

Young-ae watched him go. The sidewalk opened up under her feet. She had been a devout follower since she first laid eyes on Mal-Chin. How could he not love her? Beast always said they love their fans more than anything. Young-ae sat back down. Someone came out to try to check on her. She waved them away. A memory of the fan meet where they exchanged I love you's played through her mind. He looked at her so sweetly with that sparkle in his eyes. There's no way Mal-Chin could fake all that.

Go back to Korea. Those words stuck in her mind. Young-ae's funds were running out, she did not even know if she could afford a trip to return at this point. Back in her cheap hotel room, she tried to decide her next move. Young-ae's first step was to turn online for help. She had to make some money. The online fan base was always ready to buy up any merchandise they could get their hands on.

Chapter 46

"Are you sure?" The stylist asked looking over the picture on Sophie's phone. Sophie nodded. She was beginning to worry but the stylist seemed excited.

"Yeah, it's just been getting on my nerves lately." Sophie ran a hand over her hair.

The two chatted about Sophie's family. The stylist had cut Sophie's hair for so long that she was a trusted friend. They discussed Will, work and even Mal-Chin. "I knew you'd turn up with a sexy thing eventually," The stylist commented as she looked at the picture of him over Sophie's shoulder. Sophie just smiled giddily. "Look at that smile!" The stylist put a hand over her heart, "I've never seen Sophie make that face before," she said as she turned to the other patrons there was a rumble of laughter. Sophie told her about Mal-Chin's stalker and what happened to her car. The woman just shook her head, "Girl, you never know with these sexy men." As the stylist spun Sophie away from the mirror, Sophie's eyes landed on her repaired car through the salon window The new coat of paint shined in the light.

A tickle on the nape of her neck, the cold of the scissors brushing her skin. That's all she felt with the bottom layer. It was not until the stylist was cutting the upper layers that the difference in weight became obvious. After what felt like a lifetime of pinning up, snipping, measuring, and curling, the stylist spun her around. The thick curtain of hair now felt fluffy and airy. Sophie could not imagine her hair as anything but drab and straight. The sensation of it hitting her neck felt odd, almost tickling. It was a long-angled bob that had been curled to a stylish wavy look. It was hard to tell who was more pleased, Sophie or the stylist. The cut softened the diamond shape of her face, and somehow made her eyes look bigger. Other customers were laughing at the two of them for acting so excitedly. The amount of hair on the floor was shocking. Sophie always forgot how thick her hair was until she saw it on the salon floor. They could have made a carpet out of it. She played with the soft, freshly cut ends; it felt like something was missing. Now the other customers, all her mother's age or older, were laughing at her surprise.

In the middle of all this, Mal-Chin texted her, *"Hey, did you wear any of my shirts home?"*

Sophie thought that was a weird question. She slept in them when she stayed but always returned them, *"No. I think I have 1 that you gave me at the pool party, but nothing else. Why?"*

"I'm missing the one with Beast's last tour logo."

Sophie thought it over as she paid, *"I never wore that one. Have you checked behind the clothes basket and the dryer?"* She did not hear back from him so she hoped that meant he found it.

All the way home, Sophie was riding high. She felt pretty, fashionable. A knot did not form in her stomach until she climbed the porch steps. Virginia was already staring at her open mouthed. Sophie had never seen that expression before. It soon turned into a smile, "It's so short!" Sophie smiled her shoulders drawing up only to wiggle. Virginia examined her hair, fixing the waves, taking in the length, and scrutinizing the unevenness – the only part she did not like. "You look like a mature young lady," There was a hint of pride in Virginia's voice that hit Sophie in the heart.

Sophie took the seat next to Virginia. They sat in silence for a while just enjoying one of the last warm days. "Mal-Chin has a birthday coming up," Sophie said as she scrolled through her phone, "I was kinda hoping we could do something for him. You know since his family and all are in Korea."

Virginia considered it all for a moment. "When is it?" Sophie smiled and they started discussing what to do for a party. Virginia came up with the idea to surprise him. By the time dinner was ready, the two had everything planned out even down to how to decorate the cake. Sophie had one secret in mind that would take a while to arrange. Her grandparents agreed that it would be a good idea if she could pull it off. Sophie was up late into the night arranging it.

When she visited Mal-Chin, Sophie acted like she did not know of his upcoming birthday. It was not difficult. He was too busy playing with her hair, which eventually led to the playful touches, and they ended up in the bedroom. They'd lie in bed afterwards just talking about their days.

T he days turned cold as the weeks passed in a blur. Now that Sophie was working again, his days became lonely. Sophie would visit in the afternoons but she was usually tired from work or contacting parents. He dived into creating new music half to pass the time. A creeping notion that something terrible was going to happen would twist his stomach when he least expected it. A flash of his meeting Bae Young-ae would come into his mind. It could not be that easy.

Mal-Chin was moping on the couch while flipping through social media today. His fans were celebrating without him. It was a celebration for Mal-Chin, but he could not attend. His fake fan account was full of pictures and video compilations of him. He checked his messages again, still nothing from his friends or family. Mal-Chin would have to celebrate his birthday alone. Even a live with his fans was out of the question. They must have missed celebrating as much as he did.

Mal-Chin sat up with a start when the front door opened. It was locked; he'd been careful of that lately. A sigh of relief left him when

Sophie came through the doorway. Her hair was wavy and she was wearing the full face of make-up that she reserved for special occasions. If she was pretty without makeup Sophie was absolutely gorgeous with it. "*Jagiya.*" Excitement filled him.

"I heard," Sophie started playfully, her purse swayed as she turned, "that it was someone's birthday." She smiled at him, "Thought we should celebrate."

A thrill of unwholesome possibilities ran through him. It was just Sophie here. What was she thinking? "Celebrate?" He implied. Mal-Chin's arms wrapped around her.

Sophie saw the fire in his eyes, "Oh, no, not like that," Sophie nibbled on her lips, her hand landed on his chest. "Not yet."

He played with her hair. "You know, I do really like this hairstyle," He leaned forward, "I can see your pretty face better, and" he gave her a peck on the cheek before placing kisses on her neck. "And I can do this easier." Mal-Chin spoke the words against her neck.

"Oh, get changed, Granny is expecting us." Sophie flapped her hands at him.

Mal-Chin repeated the movement at her with a laugh as he headed toward the hallway. "Oh! Granny!" Mal-Chin called from the hallway; he was already stripping. Sophie was cooing at the cats before Mal-Chin even reached his bedroom.

The whole ride, Mal-Chin switched between playing with Sophie's hair and trying to grab the gift bag in the back seat. They pulled into the driveway just as Carol, Jessica and Conner showed up with several pizza boxes. The group helped carry the pizzas and gifts in. The whole affair was noisy, they spread throughout the dining room and living room to eat, then assembled into the living room to open presents. Mal-Chin got a new water bottle from Lorraine, a sign with music symbols that said something about "Man Caves" on it from Carol and

Robbie – Sophie explained what a man cave was later—, a new gym outfit and a stocking cap from Virginia and Ford. Mal-Chin quickly put the stocking cap on.

He opened Sophie's present last. It was a hoodie to replace the worn out one he wore all the time. Mal-Chin could not figure out how she got it here so quickly since it was a Korean brand. "Oh, that's where my old hoodie went." Mal-Chin laughed.

"You lost that too?" Sophie looked surprised.

"You didn't take it?" Mal-Chin asked. Sophie just shook her head no. "Huh, where did I put it." Mal-Chin looked lost in thought. The group began to talk, first about losing things and the odd places they found them, which turned into Carol complaining about Connor losing things. Sophie did something on her phone then signaled to Virginia and they disappeared, only for Mal-Chin to catch them re-decorating the dining room table with a plastic tablecloth for cake from the local bakery and ice cream. They had barely gotten him seated at the head of the table when the video messenger sound rang on his phone. "Answer it," Sophie excitedly prompted. Sophie almost pulled Mal-Chin's phone from his hands.

The members of Beast appeared on his screen yelling at him. They wished him a happy birthday and the group was excitedly talking to him in Korean, Mal-Chin summarized some of it for Sophie's family as he laughed. Sophie held her phone screen where he could see it just as her video chat rang. The biggest smile Sophie had ever seen lit Mal-Chin's face as his family appeared on the screen. They chatted for a while; Mal-Chin showed everyone how adorable Hyeonuk was the whole group got introduced to the ones on the screen. Sophie used two cups to prop their phones up while they sang Happy Birthday to him. The blend of Korean and English kept in rhythm yet sounded disproportionate.

Mal-Chin struggled to blow the multiple candles out, which caused everyone to tease him, until they noticed the redness on his face and the wetness on his cheeks. He tried to wipe it away. Sophie rubbed Mal-Chin's shoulders trying to comfort him and he buried his face into her stomach, his shoulders shaking as he cried. Sophie placed her head on top of his trying to comfort him as Virginia started rubbing his back as well. Hyeonuk could be heard crying through Sophie's phone while Hayun spoke comforting words to him.

Mal-Chin calmed himself down and looked up at Sophie with an adoring smile on his face. She returned the look as she wiped the remaining tears from his cheeks, he leaned his head into one of her hands. Lorraine and Virginia exchanged a knowing look, Mal-Chin's parents and Hayun did the same. Virginia patted Mal-Chin's shoulder comfortingly. He looked back at her age spotted hand. Something about a grandmother's touch was so comforting, even if Virginia was not his grandmother. Virginia blinked the tears from her eyes then spoke, "Let's have some cake and ice cream. Sophie, you cut. Carol, ice cream?" Carol, red eyed, sniffed and nodded. As Virginia passed Sophie to take her seat she quietly added, "You did good." Sophie just smiled.

Mal-Chin took this time to assure Hyeonuk he was ok then laughed at the fact they brought their own cakes to celebrate, both shaped like cats. When Sophie slid the cake away from him to cut it, he reached his hands out after it, "No! Come back!!!" He pouted comically.

Sophie laughed, "I've got to cut it," she started cutting.

"You want ice cream?" Carol asked, taking the plate from Sophie, moving his slice further away.

"I can have both?" Mal-Chin looked excited; Carol took that as a yes.

"Don't! No. Don't!" Suho yelled. It was too late; they were already handing the plate back to him.

The group laughed at the look of wonder on his face as Jessica handed him the plate. He had a large slice of cake and two scoops of ice cream. He made a woah noise before he started eating. When Sophie was done cutting, Mal-Chin pulled her chair close to his. He was doing a little wiggle dance that made the chair squeak.

J.E. suddenly felt the need to warn them, "Just so you know, there's a reason he doesn't eat sweets, and that's like a bomb about to go off."

"Is that what the wiggle is about?" Sophie chuckled side eyeing Mal-Chin, who was happily eating away.

"Yeah..... Just wait." J.E. and the group around him laughed.

"It's not that bad," Mal-Chin stated around a mouthful of ice cream.

"It's very bad. He'll be up all night," His mother added, translated through Dae-o.

"We'll just give Sophie some caffeine then let her take him home and they can annoy each other," Robbie added. Robbie went into telling them how Sophie came bouncing into the house hours after she had a soda a few years ago and proceeded to talk their heads off.

Mal-Chin's family suddenly started asking Sophie all the basic get to know you questions, asking about jobs, hobbies, anything they thought they needed to know. Mal-Chin's head began to spin as he tried to keep up. It was like having two separate parties going on around him. The Korean one on screen and the English one all around him. He was having to switch between languages rapidly and try to translate the English to himself while also hearing the Korean. Sophie's hair made a good fidget as a knot formed in his stomach, and it was not from the massive amounts of sweets he just ate. Maybe the sweets were making it hard to concentrate.

Mal-Chin wanted to retreat to somewhere quiet, but he did not want to leave. Just as he thought he could not take it anymore; the party began to break up. Both sides had members that either needed to go to work or were tired from work. Beast had a photo shoot later in the day and needed to get ready for that.

Sophie drove him home. They shared a sweet kiss that turned into something more before they even pulled out of the driveway. "Stay the night." Mal-Chin's fingertips were running up and down the length of her arms.

"I was going to stay tomorrow after I took you out for dinner," Sophie stated enjoying the feeling of his fingers on her arms.

"Stay tonight and tomorrow. All weekend, stay as long as you want to," He watched a car pass, "Just stay with me."

The presents in the back seat were long forgotten by the time they climbed out of Sophie's car. They were too busy hurrying to get inside and out of their clothes. Mal-Chin struggled to open the door with his lips stuck to Sophie's. She broke the kiss to help him out but ended up just distracting him by peppering kisses along his neck.

Distracted as they were, they did not notice the figure seated on the couch in the dark. She made her presence well known by clearing her throat.

Chapter 48

All the passion drained out of the pair. Darkness clung to every surface. A ray of moonlight trickled in through the dining room window. It was just enough light to make out the form of the intruder. Being careful to keep himself between Sophie and the intruder, Mal-Chin turned on the light. They squinted as light flooded the room.

Of course, it was her. Who else would break into his house in the middle of the night? Bae Young-ae had a deranged look in her eyes as she sat comfortably on his couch. Young-ae's eyes were blank yet a glint of fire was in them. It was the same wild expression he had seen the day she showed up outside of their concert claiming to be Mal-Chin's girlfriend.

"What are you doing here?" Mal-Chin asked in Korean. He was nudging Sophie closer to the door.

"I told you, I'm here for you." Young-ae picked up the knife that was sitting on the end table. "You're mine remember?" She turned the knife in her hand. Mal-Chin's stomach turned. That was his missing knife.

"I thought you were going back to Korea." Mal-Chin replied. He was trying to pick his words carefully.

"I am." Young-ae stood up, "I'm going back with you." She started toward them. "We've got some loose ends to tie up first." Her eyes flicked to Sophie. Disgust played across Young-ae's face. She rounded to the side, effectively causing Mal-Chin to step Sophie away from the door. Mal-Chin tried to keep them a safe distance apart. That is what he thought his bodyguard would do. If he could not get her out the front door, Mal-Chin would find another way. His mind went blank. *Where can we go?* His eyes flicked to the dining room for a second. If he could get her to that door, she could escape. But Young-ae was blocking their path. From past experience, Mal-Chin knew she was fast.

Sophie mumbled to him; Mal-Chin just nodded his head. He hoped she was not drawing too much attention to herself. Mal-Chin replied as quickly as possible. Young-ae was stalking closer. Her eyes were on Sophie now. "What is she saying?" Young-ae demanded.

"She just wanted to know who you are." Mal-Chin held out a hand. Young-ae was pointing the knife at the two of them. A new look came to her eyes,

Sophie took a half step out from behind Mal-Chin. His arm crossed in front of her still trying to keep a barrier. "Why is she here?" Sophie asked.

Mal-Chin looked at Sophie skeptically before telling her about the confrontation at Link's. Sophie shook her head and gave Young-ae a sympathetic look. "Ask her if she's here because of that," Mal-Chin relayed her message.

Young-ae's face twisted in anger. "What do you think? I was just going to surprise you, take you home then we could start a new life together. But, no, you didn't want that," Mal-Chin translated quickly.

"That's painful, to feel like your plans aren't going right," Sophie added. She put her hand on Mal-Chin's arm, whether to steady herself or comfort him was unclear.

"Don't touch him!" Young-ae lunged forward. Mal-Chin backed them up, so they were still out of Young-ae's reach. He could feel Sophie trembling even as her hands left him. "He's mine! He's always been mine!" Young-ae gestured with the knife. "I was his biggest fan, his best supporter!"

Sophie took another half step away from Mal-Chin. Even as her hands trembled, her face remained calm, understanding. "And you want that back. You want to continue being his biggest fan and supporter. It must hurt feeling like you can't be." Mal-Chin could not figure out where Sophie was going with this as he translated the conversation. He made a move to follow her, but she motioned for him to stop. The sound of Mal-Chin's own heartbeat filled his ears.

Young-ae let the arm holding the knife fall to her side. "I just want him back." Her full attention was on Sophie now.

"But, hurting us won't help that will it? You'll be banned from seeing him ever again in person, probably end up in jail." Sophie edged a step closer. Mal-Chin just wanted to scream at Sophie at this point. He could not keep her safe if she was moving closer and closer to Young-ae.

Young-ae shook her head. "I can't be around him. His company blocked me from everything, and he was calling out to me with every new song." Her eyes turned glassy.

"But if you do this, if you hurt him, it'll only get worse." Sophie edged closer holding her hand out palm up, the fingers visibly shaking.

She was reaching toward the knife. "Maybe, we can help you." Sophie was so close she could almost reach the knife.

"I don't want to hurt him," Young-ae mumbled. Her eyes locked onto Sophie with a fury they had not held before. "I hurt you!" Young-ae yelled in English. She was on Sophie before either could react. Mal-Chin froze.

Chapter 49

One second, Sophie was about to calmly take the weapon from Young-ae's hand, the next she was on the floor with a weight on her stomach and searing pain in her arm. It took her senses a second to catch up. Sophie had been stabbed. Young-ae was on top of her raising for another blow. Sophie's hands went up by reflex. She tried to deflect the blow that was aimed at her throat only to receive a fist to the face. They were grappling for control, Sophie desperately trying to stop the onslaught of slashes and Young-ae trying to find a clear shot at Sophie's body.

Do something, get her off. Use those muscles. Sophie's mind furiously told herself. Her feet dug into the hard wood floor looking for leverage. With her hands on full defense, she could not use them to help balance. Something hot was dripping onto Sophie's face, sometimes momentarily blinding her. For such a small woman, Young-ae was heavy. Sophie lifted her hips trying to throw her attacker off balance and push her off.

All it did was give Young-ae an opening. The knife nicked Sophie's neck. A scream burst from her lungs. It echoed. "Sophie!" Mal-Chin's voice cut through. Young-ae hesitated only a second before thrusting down with the knife. Sophie's eyes squeezed shut, there was no way she could block the attack.

The weight on Sophie disappeared in an instant. Sophie opened her eyes in confusion. Shaking bloody hands were the only thing she saw. Young-ae and Mal-Chin were yelling. Adrenaline coursing through her, Sophie climbed onto shaky legs and ran to help. She slipped in something as she hurried to grab the knife from Young-ae. Together, the two were able to wrestle the weapon away and Mal-Chin restrained her by holding her wrists behind her back. In the scuffle, Mal-Chin let out a grunt but Sophie paid little attention to it. Sophie was losing focus.

Finally taking in her wounds, Sophie flopped down on the floor. Her body shook all over. *Call for help, call for help.* Her mind kept telling her, but she fumbled with the phone. Blood smeared across the screen as she tried to type. Her shirt worked decently to dry her hands enough to dial. Sophie was beginning to feel heavy, head spinning. If she could just lay down.

"Sophie!" Mal-Chin called again. He was holding onto Young-ae, who was out of fight. Sophie still feared the attack would continue if she was set loose.

"Don't let her go!" Sophie yelled as she finally dialed 911 hitting the speaker phone button because she didn't think she could hold the phone much longer.

A lifetime passed before help arrived. Sophie lay down on the floor and was trying to figure out how to pack the wounds. At this point, she could not think of how to pack it. The pain was starting to set in. Hot oozing liquid dripped from her arms and neck pooling on the floor under her. Every wound seemed too deep, too much blood flowed out. Sophie's mind imagined nicked arteries and cut muscles. She kept hearing Mal-Chin switching between calling her name and telling the operator he was restraining the attacker.

I'm not going to make it. Her mind became foggy. Sophie was trying to remember how much blood she could safely lose. Tunnel vision made it hard to focus. Sophie barely registered being loaded into the ambulance. She closed her eyes and opened them again to an EMT patting her cheek trying to keep her awake. "Hey, stay with us. I think she's lost too much blood." Her eyes closed again.

"Oh, god! Her face!" Virginia's voice cut through the haze. *My face? What's wrong with my face?* Sophie tried to raise a hand to feel it but her hand was pushed back down.

Something cool and rough swiped over her face then her arms, "It just dripped," Minseok's voice stated. "We've been so busy with her wounds that we hadn't gotten her cleaned up yet."

"Seok? Granny?" Sophie's eyes blinked open blurry. Her throat was sore.

"We're here baby," Virginia said. "You're at the hospital. You're ok."

"Did she slice my face?" Sophie reached up touching her face finding only the scratch of bandages on her hands.

"Your face is fine." Minseok patted her check. "Your family is here. You're safe." Sophie nodded and looked around the room. Her grandparents were taking up the two seats while Lorraine was leaning against the wall next to them. Mal-Chin was nowhere in sight.

"Where is Mal-Chin? Is he ok?" Sophie tried to sit up, but Minseok stopped her. Her head spun.

"Careful, you lost a lot of blood."

"His arm was cut. They're fixing him up in another room," Ford said, his voice sounded off, deeper.

"He's alone. Someone needs to check on him," Sophie requested taking in everyone's faces. She tried to sit up again. Even going slower, her head still spun.

"I'm going when I leave you and John's on the way," Minseok replied, "You were the main focus for now."

After a while, the police came by. The story spilled out of her the best she could remember it. Sophie tried to run a hand through her crusty hair but the bandages made it impossible. She did not want to think about what was causing the crunchy feeling in her hair. The police were patient. The questions went around in circles checking over every detail until Sophie was exhausted. Finally, they informed her that her story matched Mal-Chin's. They were waiting for a translator to talk to Young-ae but they were pressing charges. Sophie just nodded.

She began to shiver under the thin hospital blanket. Someone had changed her into a flimsy hospital gown, even her bra was gone. Ford laid his jacket over top of her. The smell of his after shave was comforting.

Robbie arrived pale faced, with him came a pair of clean clothes for Sophie. It looked like they had woken him up to get him here. Everyone was looking tired at this point. Sophie had no idea what time it was. Time moved different in a hospital day and night blurred together. There was no conversation besides the basic, "How are you doing? What did the doctor's say?" Minseok returned about this time with news about Mal-Chin. He was stitched up and discharged but the police told him he could not visit Sophie.

"We'll take him home," Virginia offered. Sophie just nodded in thanks. Now that she knew he was safe, Sophie could rest.

The hospital released her in the early hours of the morning. Lorraine brought her home, where Mal-Chin was waiting for her. The first thing Mal-Chin did was wrap his arms around her, careful not to disturb the bandages. Next, he washed the grime from her hair. She was worried about the stitches on his arm coming loose but he promised that he was ok. To her horror, the crunchy feeling was caused by blood. The site of blood tinted shampoo going down the drain turned her stomach. Sophie went cold all over, colder than she'd been at the hospital. Mal-Chin helped her change into her sleep shirt then the two curled up in bed together. Sophie did not think she would be able to sleep, but she was wrong. Safely wrapped in Mal-Chin's good arm and dosed with pain killers, Sophie fell asleep. She slept most of the day.

Chapter 50

The attack hit the news faster than Mal-Chin expected. Once local reporters realized that Mal-Chin was a celebrity, the local news quickly jumped on the story. ***"Danville woman attacked with knife"*** read the local newspaper headline the next morning accompanied by a picture of the rescue squad in his yard. Mal-Chin slipped out of bed as soon as Sophie was sleeping calmly, she jerked and kicked in her sleep for most of the morning. A call to Chanyeol was needed but hopefully it would be a short one. If the story reached Chanyeol before Mal-Chin did there would be hell to pay.

Even though it was late in Korea, Chanyeol answered, "Park? What's going on?" Chanyeol's tired voice slurred out. Mal-Chin explained the whole story. "She tried to kill the girl to get to you?" Chanyeol was fully awake now. "How much of this has hit the news?"

"Not much, just the basics. Names, what happened." Mal-Chin looked toward Sophie's room hearing a noise "And that I'm a k-pop star."

"Let me call your lawyer and Mr. Choi. I'll be there as soon as I can. Don't talk to anyone until we figure something out." He could hear Chanyeol moving around. A car pulled up the gravel driveway.

"Right. Hey, can you," Mal-Chin suddenly felt like a child, "can you bring my mother. I'm going to call her." Mal-Chin hung up as the side door unlocked.

Will came running in. "Where's Sophie?" Mal-Chin informed him that she was still sleeping. Will nodded. The two tip-toed around trying to not wake her. Will's brows furrowed, "What happened?"

Mal-Chin went through the whole story again with him. Will wanted every detail, not just the basics of who had done it and why. "She tried to take the knife away? What was she thinking?" Will shook his head.

"I kept asking myself that too." Mal-Chin hung his head. "It was like a movie scene. She was trying to talk her down."

Well into a very awkward afternoon, Sophie stumbled out of her room looking pale. Will hugged her tight and apologized for not being there earlier. He also gave her a quick lecture on the fact that no one had called him. This did not last very long; their main concern became making Sophie comfortable. She complained of being sore. Mal-Chin quickly produced the pain reliever the doctors prescribed. Sophie quickly concerned herself with Mal-Chin's wound until her medicine began to work and drained her energy.

"Are we on the news?" Sophie asked after some length of time. She had been scrolling through her phone.

"That's how I found out," Will answered.

"Everyone I know is messaging me," Sophie said as she typed away on her phone. By that night, the attack hit Korean news.

Mal-Chin and Lorraine went to scrub his living room floors in the morning, leaving Sophie home under Will's care. Sophie protested saying Mal-Chin would reopen his wound or the water would mess the stitches up. Mal-Chin did not want to go into the house, but he knew he needed to. The longer any blood sat on his floor the harder it would be to clean up. The cats were also hiding in the house somewhere; he had not seen them since before his birthday party. Mal-Chin worried they ran outside during all the commotion and gotten lost.

On their hands and knees, the two began to scrub. The work quickly had Mal-Chin hot. The more they scrubbed, the redder the water turned and the worse he felt. He grabbed the bucket suddenly throwing down the Brillo pad he was using. "I'll get us fresh water." Outside, Mal-Chin felt better. The air was cool and eased the queasy feeling in his stomach. He emptied the bucket watching the abnormal color of the water absorb into the grass and fallen leaves. Lingering in the backyard, he took it all in.

Mal-Chin had frozen. His mind was not able to process what he was seeing. Mal-Chin watched as Young-ae sliced Sophie while doing nothing to stop it. The nausea returned to his stomach. He was the man. Mal-Chin should have been the one keeping them safe instead of watching as Sophie tried to talk Young-ae down. The pavement patio was cool but not unbearably cold for Mal-Chin to sit on. He squeezed his eyes closed, took deep breaths through his mouth. A strange acidic salty taste filled his mouth.

"I think we're going to need something stronger," Lorraine stated. She sounded out of breath. Mal-Chin had not heard her come out. How many other sounds had he not heard or just ignored? He just nodded his head and got up. "Why don't we take a break? Your arm has to be hurting." Lorraine patted him on the shoulder, "It's a lot to take in."

They returned home to find Will and Sophie gone. Mal-Chin's heart rate went up. Had she had an accident? Maybe her stitches had popped open. Lorraine soothed him explaining that they were probably just at her Virginia's house.

Mal-Chin found Sophie curled up in Ford's favorite spot on the couch and half asleep. Robbie was glaring at Mal-Chin from the seat he pulled over from the dining room. Concern filled Sophie's face as she sat up. "Are you ok?"

"Yeah," Mal-Chin rubbed the back of his head before sitting next to her. Instantly, she leaned against him. "Just, a lot."

"You're pale." Virginia added. "Do you need something to eat? How is your arm?"

Mal-Chin shook his head. "No, we were just cleaning the house." He could not imagine eating right now. Sophie kept squirming next to him trying to find a comfortable way to rest against him. Tension left her body when she finally got comfortable.

Virginia insisted on changing his bandages. Virginia attempted small talk as she worked, "So how did the clean-up go?" Sophie was trying to assist but her bandaged hands were of little help.

"It's not as bad as I thought but it's not coming up easily." Mal-Chin stated. He wanted to forget the blood-stained sponges and red water. Sophie stilled next to him.

"We got some kinda cleaner at work. It'll take it right up. I'll see what the name of it is when I go in," Robbie informed him.

Mal-Chin just nodded before turning his attention back to Sophie, "You worried me. I came back and you were gone. I thought something was wrong."

Sophie slowly explained that they came to Virginia and Ford's house because her bandages needed changing and Will was grossed out by it. Will looked down embarrassed. Virginia changed them with no problem. Afterwards, Virginia fed her oldest two grandchildren as much as they could eat. For Sophie, this turned out to be a worryingly small amount of food. Sophie simply said she was not hungry. Throughout this whole conversation she was snuggled into his side. It was comforting. "Is the medicine hurting your stomach?" Mal-Chin asked. Sophie just shook her head no.

"Let me ask you something," Robbie started. He scooted to the edge of his seat.

"Robbie," Virginia warned.

Robbie's eyes shifted to his mother before returning to Mal-Chin. There was anger in his eyes. "What were you doing while all this was happening?" Robbie gestured toward Sophie, who held onto Mal-Chin tighter.

Mal-Chin looked down. His face was hot with embarrassment. "I froze."

"So what you're," he pointed at Mal-Chin, "telling me is you stood there and watched while that crazy bitch was slicing her up?" Sophie made a noise and tucked her head into Mal-Chin's shoulder. He felt a shiver run through her and into him. Virginia made a noise of discomfort.

"I didn't mean to. I just," Mal-Chin looked at Sophie, "I just couldn't move."

"It happened so fast," Sophie added, he could feel her words against his skin.

"Just froze," Robbie repeated, "What kind of man just freezes? Just stands there and watches a woman get attacked. What, were you afraid of getting hurt? I knew you were no good. You're no man." Robbie was turning red in the face as he spoke. His brows were furrowed.

Sophie glared at Robbie, the look so sharp it could cut, "Stop it." Her leg began to fidget, not with anxiety but anger. Robbie's eyebrows lifted.

Ford joined the conversation at this point, "I've seen plenty of men freeze up in a fight." He nodded, "It happens. You still saved her. If you hadn't been there," something swam behind the vivid blue of Ford's eyes. He pressed his lips into a line and found something else to look at. An uncomfortable hush fell over the group. Sophie pressed closer to Mal-Chin. There could not be air between them now.

"Let's, let's talk about something else," Virginia stated watery eyed. She was doing a one-handed flap like she was trying to slowly remove a bad odor from the air. There was a long silence as they tried to think of a subject. Will flipped channels until they found a show that they had seen before. The group sat and made comments on it. Sophie asked about the cats. Mal-Chin quickly confirmed they were ok.

After a while longer, Sophie untucked her head from Mal-Chin's shoulder and rested her chin there instead. "Can you take me home? I'm really tired and I left my pain meds."

"Oh, baby why didn't you say anything." Virginia said with a start, "I've got some ibuprofen." She moved to get up.

"I can't remember what they gave me," Sophie excused, "and I could really use a nap."

With that said, Mal-Chin got her out the door and into his car. Sophie could not stop fidgeting. Once inside the house, Mal-Chin found her medicine, which she refused. "Can we just cuddle," Sophie requested. Never one to turn down a cuddle session, Mal-Chin quickly agreed. A sniffle escaped Sophie as they lay down. This soon turned into a soft cry. All Mal-Chin could do was hold her close and lay gentle kisses on the top of her head. He could have cried too. She fell asleep in his arms this way.

Mal-Chin barely stayed at his home since the attack. He made short trips to check on the cats and grab clean clothes. Sophie's home felt safer right now. The police still had not figured out how Young-ae had gotten into his home and even new locks did little to make him feel secure. A knot formed in Mal-Chin's stomach when he thought about staying here. He could still see the bloodstain on the floor even though it had been thoroughly scrubbed clean. He kept expecting to hear a terror laced scream every time the house fell silent.

Mal-Chin had no choice but to return to the house. His mother and Chanyeol arrived. The media descended on him soon after. They camped out in his front yard. Mal-Chin was stuck inside this house just like he had been stuck in his Korean apartment. Every motion was monitored. If they even opened the front door to look out, the journalist rushed for the door. The back yard was not safe either. His mother stepped out for a breath of fresh air and was hounded by a journalist. That was the first time the police were called. Anywhere he went, he took a confusing route in the hopes of losing any following car. It was exhausting.

Park Mal-Chin attacked by crazed fan, Bae Young-ae.

Ex-Beast member hurt in knife attack.

American woman saves Park Mal-Chin!

These headlines flooded his social media feeds. Fans were going crazy with worry. Outrage flooded the comments section of these articles. Every fan page, and even the fan pages of other bands, were discussing the news.

How could the police mess up this bad? – **PMCforever**

Where was his security? They should have been sent over as soon as they found out Bae Young-ae was there. Also, don't all Americans carry guns why didn't this Gregory chick just shoot her? – **Jeonghui'sdimples.**

*This crazy bitch sliced his arm open! Hope he doesn't get a scar. -***Sarang-haeSJ**

The attack cleared Mal-Chin's name to some degree. Once news that his attacker was Bae Young-ae and that she had started his scandal, the public turned sympathetic to him. Though, questions of who the unknown woman was who had taken the brunt of the attack swirled. There were rumors circling that Sophie Gregory was a bodyguard. The journalists were on the lookout for her. Mal-Chin did his best to keep them away.

Mal-Chin did a Vlive to prove he was ok. He put on his best smile, waved, and made jokes with his fans. Mal-Chin went as far as retrieving a container from the fridge to show them the food his mother fixed. Questions about Sophie or the case were ignored. As a distraction, he started replying to questions in English. This caused the comments to be flooded with *"English King!"*

Mr. Choi reached out. He offered to send a bodyguard down to keep the journalist at bay. Mal-Chin informed him that he did not know where a bodyguard would sleep, his house was full. They talked over the situation for a while before coming to a decision. The security guard would arrive, and they would just have to make room. Maybe he would not mind sleeping on a floor bed.

"As soon as this whole mess is cleared up you can return and we'll start launching your solo career," Mr. Choi stated. "With your record cleared, there's nothing holding you. Be working on backtracks for those songs. We'll work out any issues when you return. Only," he paused, "the American woman. You're going to have to come up with a convincing story to explain her."

Mal-Chin hesitated. His lips pressed into a line, "I don't think I can give the explanation you want."

"That's what I was afraid of. You can't bring her with you. Find an acceptable answer," There was disappointment and a hint of sympathy in his voice.

Mal-Chin found himself seated in his studio struggling to come up with ideas. He kept humming the tune to a song he did not have lyrics for yet. Tapping his pencil on a notepad, Mal-Chin struggled to create anything. Sophie's picture, now the background of his desktop computer, became a distraction. He would find himself staring at it as he composed, often getting nothing done. When his mother bought him snacks, she began to comment on Sophie's eyes. Mal-Chin was sure he heard his mother mumble something about green eyed babies on the way out the door.

Chapter 51

Sophie hustled down the hall with warm worksheets fresh from the copier tucked under her good arm. The warmth of the paper was almost soothing, like a blanket fresh from the dryer. Early this morning, Sophie carefully picked her outfit to cover the bandages on her arms and be easy to change her bandages in later. She'd even gone as far as to put make up on her neck where a bruise showed. *Can't let the kids see how bad it really was.*

She was not supposed to be here yet. The doctors had not cleared her to return and she was still worn out from the medicine. But, Sophie could not take being at home much longer either. Her family was either tip-toeing around her or just being annoying. Mal-Chin started bringing his mother to visits and she kept asking Sophie uncomfortable questions about how many kids Sophie wanted or when she planned to get married. Mal-Chin's mother was friendly enough and they got along well, but she seemed to constantly be sneaking questions about Sophie's future into the conversation.

The other teachers welcomed her back showing genuine concern for what happened. She knew that at lunchtime they would want the full story. Sophie would tell as much as she could. It slipped Sophie's mind that they did not know Mal-Chin was famous. Mr. Worley and the Special Education teacher that worked with her made sure to tell her to let them know if she needed help. Her mind just was not ready to comprehend the massive amount of work that needed to be done.

There was a murmur from Sophie's classroom, this class was usually quiet and sleepy in the morning. She stuck her head in the door and smiled at then and said, "I'm back." Half of them relaxed and the others smiled softly. Throughout the day, Sophie received mixed reactions. Most of the students were happy to see her, a few did not seem to care and one or two girls came to Sophie squealing about Park Mal-Chin. They all were wearing Beast t-shirts. "Ms. Gregory! Why didn't you tell us!" One girl asked, she was already taller than Sophie and tucked her chin in to look down at her. "I can't believe you would hold that information back from us, your favorite students!"

Sophie just laughed at this. For some reason this group of girls had instantly attached themselves to her at the beginning of the school year. "You wouldn't have believed me."

"You're right, you're right." Another chimed in with a nod. "Did you kiss him? Is he a good kisser?" She added batting her eyelashes comically. "What's he like?"

"He's really nice," Sophie said with a big smile on her face.

"Did you do something more with him?" The tall one hopped in excitedly.

Sophie looked at them in wide eyed shock, "That is a personal question. Ya'll shouldn't even be thinking about that stuff!" She playfully shooed them into the room before sharing a laugh with the other teachers in earshot. All class period, they kept giving her giggly looks like they knew the answer.

Until planning, Sophie ignored the stack of papers on her desk. Grading them was going to be a hassle. Her hands were already hurting from drawing the same anchor chart multiple times, and there still was one more class to go. She plotted ways to get the work checked quickly while replacing the bandages on her arms. *Trade and Check?* They were already telling her it was too hard. *Give everyone that finished a 100?* They would not learn anything, but it would give them a better grade. *Get help?* No. Her co-workers already had done enough to help; they handled all the worksheets and lesson plans while she was out so she would not have to worry. Sophie could not ask her family. Will and Mal-Chin had been falling over each other since the attack trying to help her to the point it was frustrating.

This moment, changing her bandages and contemplating the laziest way to grade, was the moment her co-workers decided to get the full scoop. Embarrassment flooded Sophie as they got a glimpse of her injuries. She tried to keep calm as she rewrapped them. Jason found something else to look at. The story flooded from her as practically as she could make it. A knot formed in her stomach as she spoke. She just wanted to move on from this all quickly.

As soon as the last load of buses left, Sophie packed her things taking with her the mound of paperwork and her favorite pen. She was exhausted and just wanted a nap but as she put the last of her items into her bag she received another visitor, this one unwelcome. Administration and Mrs. Barbour walked in without a warning. Mrs. Hall closed the door behind them as gently as possible. Sophie sat down in her desk chair. Closed door conversations were never good.

"Ms. Gregory," Mrs. Barbour started, "how are you feeling?" She had been picked for this conversation because of their supposed working relationship. Mrs. Barbour's presence alone set Sophie on edge.

"I'm ok. Little sore, tired." Sophie searched the faces of the three trying to gauge what was going on, even though she knew. A glance out the door window told Sophie that her co-workers were wondering what was happening as well.

"Well, that's to be expected," Mrs. Barbour stated as she slides into the nearest desk with ease. Mr. Motley and Mrs. Hall followed her lead, Mrs. Hall was uncomfortable. "We were coming by to talk to you about Saturday's........ incident." Mrs. Barbour crossed her legs.

"We're all glad you're ok, let's start by saying that," Mr. Motley added with a slightly grim smile. "You're a good teacher and colleague and this school would suffer from your loss," Mr. Motley's eyes shot to Mrs. Barbour when he said that. Sophie's stomach turned at that.

"That brings us to our main point. Ms. Gregory," Mrs. Barbour paused, "Your actions Saturday, the resulting news headlines and the people that you were involved with are bringing some... scrutiny on you and the county schools." Sophie just nodded, her voice caught in her throat and she did not know what to say. Mrs. Barbour continued, "We just wanted to make you aware that the school board is looking into your actions that night and whether they were aligned with the code of the handbook. If you are found to be at fault in anyway, you'll be asked to leave." That was a nice way to say get fired.

"But, they can still find that you did nothing wrong. Then you'll be fine," Mr. Motley added with a confident smile. "Let's be realistic."

"I didn't-" Sophie swallowed, "I just threw a little surprise birthday party for my boyfriend. I took him home and got attacked. I didn't do anything." Her throat felt thick.

"Well, I thought you should just know that. In the meantime, keep working. Your students have some catching up to do from where you were out." Mrs. Barbour rose from her seat. Sophie clenched her teeth; she was only out four days. Sophie knew teachers that took longer off for vacations. "Have a good day. I hope you recover quickly." Mrs. Barbour headed for the door giving administration a quick look.

"We just want to go over one or two things real quick with Ms. Gregory before we leave," Mr. Motley stated, "Could you close the door back on the way out please?" As soon as the door closed, they turned to her.

"Ms. Gregory," Mrs. Hall started in, "You're a capable teacher. We know you're not at fault for any of this. Unfortunately, Mrs. Barbour doesn't seem to think so."

"So, do I have to leave?" Sophie finally asked, "What about Monday?"

"Get here before the kids," Mr. Motley laughed, "We're going to do everything we can to keep you here." Sophie nodded trying to stay calm. She laughed at their jokes as they let themselves out. She felt heavy all over.

For a moment, Sophie just sat there and stared at her desk. Her bag on the desk caught her eye. Part of her wanted to cry, the other wanted to rage but she did neither, she grabbed her purse and left the papers still packed and ready to go sitting on her desk. Sophie ducked her head and headed straight for the exit, not looking at anyone, not speaking to anyone. She reached her car before she fell apart.

Without even thinking about it, Sophie found herself pulling into Mal-Chin's driveway. Strangers with cameras were instantly swarming her car. Sophie turned her head from them. The flashes were hurting her eyes, threatening to set off a migraine. She could not put her car in reverse, someone was behind it. Attempting to get out only caused them to crowd in closer. Her whole body tensed up.

Chapter 52

Someone yelled over the sound of the journalist. They rushed to Mal-Chin as another man kept them at a distance. He was bombarded with questions as soon as he stepped out the door. Everyone was trying to find out who Sophie was and why she suddenly showed up at his house. Mal-Chin threw his jacket around Sophie, hiding her face from the journalist, which caused a lightning storm of flashbulbs, and ushered her inside. By the time they were inside, Sophie was shaking all over. She clung to Mal-Chin.

He meant to yell at her. To tell her how foolish coming here was until he saw the splotchy redness of Sophie's face and neck. Mal-Chin held her tight. Outside, the journalists were asking who she was, while his bodyguard tried to run them off again. "What are you doing here?" He finally asked softly.

"I just, I don't know." Sophie let him go. "I'm sorry. I was just upset and," she looked embarrassed. Sophie about jumped out of her skin when a hand landed on her shoulder. Mal-Chin's mother looked at her sympathetically before offering a bottle of water and telling her to take a seat. Sophie thanked her, taking the water bottle with shaking hands. The color drained from Sophie's face as she froze. Mal-Chin's eyes followed hers to the spot of the attack. They'd cleaned up as best as they could. His mother and Chanyeol assured him the blood stain was gone but Mal-Chin thought he could still see it. Sophie must have too.

Practically carrying her, Mal-Chin got her settled on the couch. "I know two cats who have been missing you." Mal-Chin ran off to find the cats.

"Hey! Don't leave her in here alone when she's upset like this!" His mother chastised.

Mal-Chin scooped the cats up from their hiding place, Aruem hissing at him as he did so. He dropped both into Sophie's lap. She mumbled something and snuggled them. "I'm sorry. I just had a bad day and," she looked embarrassed. "I kind of just drove here. I should have thought about it."

Sophie explained what happened after work today. By the time she finished telling the story, she was leaning against Mal-Chin. Sophie could have fallen asleep. When she closed her eyes, she could see Bae Young-ae's wild eyes staring at her. The healing wounds on her body throbbed at the image of the attack.

The investigator in charge of Sophie's case called. The ring of her own phone made her jump. Sophie answered right away. The investigator told her they were offering a plea deal to Bae Young-ae. Apparently there was also a case being opened by immigration and South Korea was pressing charges for false accusations and stalking. Sophie's hand ran across the bandage on her neck as she spoke; Mal-Chin moved her hand away, "If it keeps me from having to go to court, I guess it's ok."

Mal-Chin shifted uncomfortable when Sophie told him this. "That's great," was all he said. He did not like it. Young-ae was getting off easy.

As Sophie left, Mal-Chin watched her with a sigh. How many days did they have left of this? His mind filled with ways to keep her with him but none of them worked out. Sophie's picture hit South Korean news quickly. Online, people were doubting the frightened woman in the photographs could have been the same one who took on Mal-Chin's stalker. The comments on her pictures quickly took a mean turn. They picked on her fuller form some people even decided her breast were fake. Arguments began to break out between haters and Mal-Chin's fans, who were already crowning her their "queen." Mal-Chin realized that trying to bring Sophie to Seoul would just throw her to the wolves.

The weeks began to pass by at an odd pace. Mal-Chin buried himself in working on his music as his house turned silent again. The newly appointed bodyguard drove them to the airport. "Mal-Chin-*ah*," his mother started, "You tell your Sophie that I hope to see her soon." The implication was obvious. She wanted Mal-Chin to bring Sophie home to Seoul.

Mal-Chin nodded, "I will. *Umma*," He hugged her goodbye. "Tell everyone I miss them."

Mal-Chin looked forward to the sound of the bus turning around at the end of the road. Even if she did not visit, that meant Sophie was home. A rug covered the floor where the attack had taken place. Putting it out of sight seemed to ease their nerves.

They were cuddled up on the couch one Friday night when the anticipated call arrived. Mal-Chin answered his phone already knowing what the call was. Chanyeol excitedly confirmed his belief, "You've been cleared you're coming home!"

"That's great," Mal-Chin tried to be excited. He'd wanted this for so long but now, watching Sophie flip through shows, he wasn't so sure.

"We've already got your flight lined up. We'll send a packing crew to get your personal items. You can leave the rest, maybe rent the place out or have a summer home." Chanyeol went into the details of his new arrangement. The transition back to Seoul would happen just as fast, maybe even faster than his departure. Mal-Chin listened without registering the full details. He was looking at Sophie, who was using his chest as a pillow as she scrolled through a streaming service. Mal-Chin scripted out the words he needed to say.

Sophie looked up at him with curious eyes as he hung up. "Everything ok?" She finally picked a show. Mal-Chin was not ready for this.

Mal-Chin nodded; his hand ran through her short hair. He was trying to take in the small details of her. The softness of her hair, her weight and warmth, the little flecks of brown in her green eyes. "That was my manager. It's time for me to go back."

Sophie sat up, "That's great," she tucked one side of her hair behind her ear, "when do you leave?"

"Wednesday," Mal-Chin answered. Sophie sighed the word out. It was too soon, too fast. He cupped her cheek. "You know I love you."

"I love you too," Sophie's eyes squeezed closed. Pain crossed her face before she took a deep breath and looked at him again. "But?"

It was Mal-Chin's turn to steady himself. He looked away from her unable to bare the teary eyes that stared back at him. Sophie knew. It was written all over her face. "I need you to know that. Sophie, I love you. Don't let anyone make you think you're unlovable. You're not."

"Mal-Chin," Sophie's voice was thick, like it hurt her to speak. Her pained eyes searched his face. Something inside of him was breaking worse than telling his fans he was leaving. His jaw set hard but still trembled. Sophie must have seen the answer in his face. "I had thought, maybe," she gave a bitter laugh and pulled her sleeves down farther onto her hands, "I don't know what I thought. I knew you had to go back." Sophie looked away and wiped her eyes with a sleeve.

"I wish I could take you with me. I can't," Mal-Chin moved to wrap his arms around her.

Sophie moved out of his reach, "Don't. Clean break. It'll be easier that way." She stood up from the couch. "I hope everything works out." The words were choked out of Sophie before she made a quick exit. Mal-Chin watched her walk out the door, heard its definite click as it closed behind her and he broke. His arms arched to be around her. Leaning forward, Mal-Chin knotted his hands in his hair as the tears fell hot and fast.

Chapter 53

Preparations for the album began a week after Mal-Chin returned to Seoul. He was grateful for the distraction even if it required early morning workouts after sleepless nights. Sophie's face appeared in his mind whenever he was not busy, so Mal-Chin stayed busy. He spent over a month just editing music and getting back into a camera-ready body. All those months of eating like a Southerner had done some damage to his shape. SkyLimit Entertainment started an official YouTube Channel for Mal-Chin. He began posting videos to regrow his fan base and hint at an upcoming album. The videos were simple. He cooked meals, filmed workouts, and did crafts. Mal-Chin thought about reading books but his manager said that would be boring. He thought about how much Sophie would have liked that. Whatever would potentially entertain his fans, Mal-Chin did.

Mal-Chin's make-up artist tried to cover the scar on his arm. The stylist covered it in makeup and when that did not work, just stuck a skin tone band-aid over it. The scar was the only blemish on Mal-Chin's perfect skin. Fans were constantly posting screenshots when the slightest hint of the scar showed. Mal-Chin tried to remove it. He was able to fade it significantly but gave up after a while. He debated covering it with a tattoo but the thought of big pricked that many times with a needle made him queasy. Besides, he could not think of an image he would permanently want with him.

Today, Kim Chanyeol let himself into Mal-Chin's apartment while he was eating a simple lunch of rice and grilled chicken. The cats looked expectantly at the door when it opened only to skulk away uninterested when Chanyeol came in. Mal-Chin was recording later and they were going to film the process for a special release after the album came out. They discussed the plan for today as Mal-Chin prepared to leave.

The last few sessions in the recording booth felt strange. He was used to the other members buzzing around on the other side. Being in a studio just did not feel right without Jeong-hui analyzing every detail of the song. Behind the camera, Dae-o and Minkyo were visiting. Their presence put him more at ease. Unsatisfied with one of yesterday's recordings, Mal-Chin started by rerecording the sexy, fast-paced song, *Baby*, that he knew would get a music video. It was perfect for an eye-catching video.

He listened to the track replay as they brought in the next song. That was unusual. They usually had everything ready when he entered. Mal-Chin's heart leapt to his throat when he saw which song it was, "I thought we agreed not to use this one."

The producer shrugged, "I think it'll round the theme of the album out well. Plus, the Mr. Choi requested it."

"I don't want to use this one yet," Mal-Chin pressed. He was looking at the song in front of him. Mal-Chin did not know if he could sing it. Now or ever. Frustration set in. What happened to creative freedom?

"I mean, if you want to screw things up on your first album," the producer shrugged. Minkyo and Dae-o were peeking over the producer's shoulder trying to see what it was.

With a sigh, Mal-Chin put his headphones on. Sophie's lullaby flooded his ears. His voice cracked before he finished the first line. They restarted. It kept happening. The music would play, Mal-Chin would think of Sophie, his voice would crack, or muddle and they would have to stop. The producer was becoming frustrated, Mal-Chin just wanted out of this booth. He sipped water trying to hold back the tears that threatened to fall.

"Why don't we take a break?" Minkyo suggested. Everyone agreed. Mal-Chin slinked out of the recording booth feeling drained. The three retreated to the hallway where they found a quiet place to sit. Thankfully, the camera man did not follow. Minkyo and Dae-o's presence kept this moment from being filmed. They did not speak but sat there as Mal-Chin covered his face leaning back against the wall.

"Maybe you need to save this song for later," Dae-o suggested.

"No, I can do this," Mal-Chin wiped his face and returned to the recording booth. He powered through forcing himself to keep his voice calm. He knew the video would show his teary eyes and hurt expression. All he could hope for was that it came across looking romantically teary eyed and not pained. The recording session dragged on for what felt like too long. They finally finished and left Mal-Chin to his own devices.

Mal-Chin wanted to celebrate with a snack, but his trainer had him on a strict diet. He settled for a juice from the café down the street and a smiling selfie for Instagram. Without thinking, Mal-Chin flipped to his fake fan account and made his way to Sophie's profile. A smile that did not seem quite right was plastered on her face. It was her eyes, Mal-Chin decided, they looked darker the way she used to smile when they first met. Was it the light or was she hurting too? Mal-Chin rubbed the back of his head. When she learned that Sophie was staying behind, Mal-Chin's mother smacked him on the back of the head. The pain was temporary. Right now, he thought he could still feel it. It was the only time his mother ever hit him.

His alarm went off. Mal-Chin's evening workout was looming. Just like when Mal-Chin first moved to Danville, the exercise was a needed distraction. Luckily, Mal-Chin's afternoon sessions were solo. His coach left him a list of instructions and all he needed to do was keep track of what he was doing. This was the last thing on his schedule for today. Afterwards, the worse part of Mal-Chin's day would begin. He'd have dinner, settle on the couch with a movie and try not to think of Sophie.

The following month flew by. Long days turned longer as dance practices were added to his schedule. He was given a team of 6 younger male dancers. They slowly bonded over their grueling days of practice. It helped that Mal-Chin frequently brought the group snacks and meals. They all knew the story of the woman that fought his stalker. They did not know the desire for Sophie that inspired the fast-paced sexy song they were dancing to. No one asked him about it. Sophie was a taboo topic in his life. That is, unless he was around his mother who constantly lamented the loss of future green-eyed babies in her opinion. Hayun even started asking questions ; his mother sung Sophie's praises to Hayun. It did not take long for Hayun to agree, even if she didn't like that Sophie was not Korean.

The stylists dyed his hair blond. The color made his skin look tanner. He liked it. The industry standard was porcelain pale and skinny. His muscular build and darker skin made him feel more manly. He stood out from the crowd. Mal-Chin was still playing the sexy image, but he did not feel trapped in the role now though. He could write heartfelt songs and appear soft or fast paced songs with a pop rock twist and appear strong and intimidating. The future was wide open for him.

The day finally came to shoot his concept photos. They were always the first thing released to hype up a new album. This is where the process felt real to him. He was no longer a voice behind a microphone. Now Mal-Chin had to embody the character he laid out for the album. The photographers dragged him into the wet cold sand of a rough beach. Mal-Chin tried to hide from the cameras how cold he felt while his pants were wet to the knees and his flimsy shirt was standing wide open. Day 2 was, thankfully, indoors. They had him in a suit with no undershirt surrounded by flowers, mostly roses of different colors. Now more comfortable, he made jokes with the staff and did silly poses. They were filming all this too for a behind the scenes release after the album came out.

There was only one step left until release: the music video for *Baby*. This would be a multi-day process. It was always hard work, but it was Mal-Chin's favorite part of preparing for a comeback. Before he knew it, the album would be out and the real work would begin.

Chapter 54

"Ready?" Will asked as Sophie took one last look around her packed room. Sophie did not want to forget anything. Sure, Chatham was only a 20-minute drive away, but she did not want to keep making trips here to pick up what she left. Sophie intended to hand over her keys to the house as soon as she could.

She nodded, "Yeah." Sophie moved to get a box but Will stopped her. They needed to get the heavy items into the U-Haul first. Sophie's moving party consisted of 4 people: Will, John, Lorraine and herself. This meant Sophie was going to be responsible for most of the heavy lifting. Her hands were still slicky from the oily scar fade product she was using. Sophie regretted putting it on as she tried to wipe it on her pants.

This move was carefully planned. All last week, she spent her nights packing items, she even stocked the apartment fridge on her usual Friday grocery run. Sophie planned the move-in to coincide with a warm day of her Spring Break. She wanted today to be as stressless as possible and moving small items ahead of time sounded like a smart idea. She wore a short sleeve comfortable shirt. The scars on her arms were on full display for the first time since the accident. Sophie even switched to long sleeved shirts at the gym to hide the scars.

The move was overdue. Sophie needed the space, needed the room to grow into the adult she was. It had not been clear to her until the Fall. Ever since the need was clearer and clearer. Virginia criticized her for taking too long to recover from her heartbreak. Carol loved to lament the fact that Sophie had marred her body for a man that left her so easily for a job. She needed to get away. "Well, don't expect us to help you!" was Virginia's only statement when Sophie announced that she finally rented an apartment after months of searching. Ford expressed concern until Sophie told him about the building's security measures.

They maneuvered her new bed out the front door and she barely registered the sound of a car door shutting. Sophie was backing down the steps when someone grabbed her end. "I got it! I got it!" Ford lifted the end as he motioned for Sophie to get out of the way. Unable to move until they passed, Sophie looked toward the driveway. Ford's truck was there with Robbie standing next to it waiting to help. Behind it, Virginia was sitting behind the wheel of her car with the rest of the Coleman Family. Sophie smiled, *So much for not helping.*

With all the help, loading did not take long. They filled the U-Haul and put several delicate items in Sophie's car. Lorraine was going to hold onto an antique lamp that used to belong to Sophie's great-grandmother. What The Colemans were not expecting was having to carry everything up to the third floor. Her apartment was a cheaper room in a luxury apartment building. It was small with only one bedroom and a living room just big enough to call it that. The view was great and the counter tops were fake stone, so that was a perk. The building had been a school at one point, explaining the too high ceilings and the chalkboard by her door. Sophie thought it was an ideal place for an actual teacher to live and she was looking forward to doodling on the chalkboard. Realistically, she could have rented a small house with multiple bedrooms for the same price, but the apartment was in better shape. Sophie liked the security of needing a passcode to get in. Sophie was almost paranoid about security since the attack. A part of her worried Young-e would come back to finish the job.

Carol and Virginia set themselves to unpacking and decorating as soon as they stepped into the apartment. Lorraine gave herself the task of opening the front door and watching any items left there while the rest got busy bringing in boxes. They took turns resting, especially Ford who was wearing out quickly. Sophie wished she could just stay outside and unload her sparse boxes. Every time she entered the apartment she was hit with questions coming from every room in the apartment. Virginia and Carol wanted to know where to put everything, what was in each box and how did each unpacked item look. It was not until the men were bringing in the heavier pieces of furniture that Sophie had a chance to inspect the women's handy work. It looked good, really good.

"This place is nice," Carol commented as she looked for somewhere to rest. Sophie did not have a couch yet. Robbie took a quick break to give his advice on home security, which Sophie did her best to understand. She was fairly sure her renter would not let her install a door camera outside her apartment, the cameras in the hall would have to do.

Sophie promised to take her original crew out to dinner when they were done. Now that it was doubled, she could not go back on that promise. Carol and Robbie were handing out every tip they had about house care. Robbie, who'd never rented a house, was suddenly the expert on how to handle landlords. Will cut in explaining to just make sure to communicate with them. They switched to other topics. Jessica began talking about buying a tiny house to put in her parents' backyard. "Y'all ain't ever getting rid of me," Jessica joked. The bill was more expensive than Sophie expected but she did not mind.

Will offered to spend the night, but there was nowhere for him to sleep. With everyone gone, Sophie was well aware of how empty the house felt. Her mind flashed to Mal-Chin. How he had been here all those months in that house. Had he felt the same way? Sophie's heart broke for him just thinking about it. No wonder he wanted to leave. At first, Mal-Chin crossed her mind almost daily, but as the months passed, it slowed until he was now just a painful passing thought. Sophie did something she promised herself she would not do anymore. She pulled up an old Beast video so she could see him. He was younger and smaller than Sophie remembered him, but it was still Mal-Chin. In the video, his bright smile was on display. One of her recommended videos was of Mal-Chin cooking a meal. It looked new. Sophie watched it finding just the sound of his voice to bring more comfort than she felt in months. Maybe she should have found a way for her brother to stay. Will would have given her someone to talk to.

The first night in the new apartment was rough. She woke at every pop and creak of the old building. The top floor provided her the luxury of not having the dreaded loud upstairs neighbor. Unfortunately, she was near the staircase. A few times Sophie heard shuffling in the hall as people took their dogs out for nighttime bathroom breaks. One dog went out yapping and came back the same way. The sound echoed down the quiet hallway. It was an eerie feeling, to know someone was right outside her door even just in passing. About 4 in the morning, she peeked out the blinds. All she found was a silent picnic area, an empty dog run and the darkness that blanketed the field and walking trail behind it.

It took Sophie a week to settle into the apartment. She looked forward to coming home to the peace of her own home and the extra time that it gave her. The couch finally arrived. It was brand new and matched the pastel Modern Victorian design of her apartment. Sometimes, she would fall asleep on the couch and wake up guessing it was time to go to bed.

***

A month after moving in, Sophie hosted her first party. It was a small gathering with her usual group of friends. They came to congratulate her on the move. What she was not expecting was for Minseok to bring his brother along. It was awkward for both. "Seok told him. Over dinner last night," John whispered almost giddy as they refilled their drinks.

"How did it go?" Sophie asked even though she already knew the answer.

"He wasn't surprised, but he was happy," John nodded. "Is it ok, that he's here?"

Sophie looked at Dae-o and just shrugged. The apartment was small enough that whispered conversations were difficult. "Yeah. He's not the one I miss. I'm proud of Seok."

John smiled looking adoringly toward Minseok, "Me too."

John rejoined the group squeezing into her living room as Sophie cleaned up a small spill in the kitchen. "He's got an album coming out soon," Dae-o suddenly stated. Sophie had not seen him come around the counter.

"That's good," Sophie nodded, "I'm glad he's doing well." She meant it. Mal-Chin was finally getting what he wanted. His career was back on track, it sounded like, and he was back with friends. Just the mention of him sent a wave of emotions through her. Sophie was happy for him but just the mention of his name made her feel lonely. It did not help that Sophie was now known as "the girl that saved that singer."

Something in the way Dae-o shifted told her she was wrong, "You should listen to it."

"That wouldn't be good for me," Sophie admitted as she munched a chip straight from the bag. "I don't think I'll ever stop loving him."

"You're not the only one," Dae-o stated before leaving Sophie to figure out what he meant.

Her sixth year of teaching was ending when the album finally came out. Sophie was embarrassed to admit she was keeping an eye on its release date. For a few weeks, she refused to listen to it. The idea of hearing Mal-Chin's voice again, especially singing love songs, was too much to handle. She did not try to watch the music video either, seeing him was worse than just hearing him. Every time it made her long for the warmth of his presence, the calm she had found in his arms. He still had a strong hold on her. It was annoying even to Sophie at this point.

The day finally came when Sophie had to know. Sophie pulled up the album on her phone and played every song. They were good, she even found herself grooving along to the fast-paced pop rock song. A song came on that sounded too familiar. All the enjoyment left her body. Mal-Chin's voice was so heartbroken. The music was what drained life out of her. It was the song he hummed to her when they cuddled. She grabbed her phone to check the title. *Unlovable*. Tears poured down her cheeks.

Chapter 55

The album, *Let's Love*, finally released in late spring. Mal-Chin manically checked his YouTube and music streaming plays. A successful solo release was all that kept Mal-Chin going these last few months. The music video was doing much better than the songs on streaming services. The chest baring outfits mixed with body rolls and a sexy concept was what sent the video over the edge. Fans new and old were flocking for their 3 minutes of eye candy and coming back for more.

Welcome back my king! – **Chinniesbodyguard**

I was never a Beast fan but Mal-Chin this is amazing. – **TinaMini**

The things I would do for this man! -**Justhereforthedogs**.

Chanyeol had negotiated for a full variety show tour when the album released, and that was what he got. Mal-Chin put out a cheering guide for *Baby* ahead of time. On the day of his first performance, he was surprised to hear fans in the audience following the cheer guide as he performed. It added extra strength to his performance.

Unfortunately, he did not win the show prize. Mal-Chin left to the cheer of fans and that felt better than any award.

After the behind-the-scenes video of the recording sessions released, streams for *Unlovable* increased to the point where SkyLimit Entertainment asked Mal-Chin to create a video for the song. He agreed. The final product had been a teary eyed dimly lit piece that perfectly matched the song. It had a completely different feel from his other video or any of the work he had done with Beast.

Beast and his family threw him a celebratory release party after all the rush of variety shows was over. They congratulated him on a successful solo launch over bulgogi and Mal-Chin's favorite banchan. They toasted to his future career and ate too much. It was during this party that Dae-o accidentally let it slip he went to Danville. Suho tried to cover it up by changing the subject but Mal-Chin heard them. "Did you see Sophie? How is she?"

Dae-o shifted in his seat, "She's fine. She knows about the album." Mal-Chin tried to press for more information but could not get anything, "It was a short visit," Dae-o clarified, "And I was there to see Minseok. He finally told me about John."

Mal-Chin's eyebrows went up. "He did? Good!"

Jeong-hui passed around more drinks, "One more thing to celebrate. Drink! Drink!"

A few days later, Mal-Chin received a request to appear on a talk show. They requested a performance of *Unlovable*. Mal-Chin was on edge until he stepped on stage and heard the crowd cheering for him. The hosts were super friendly. The inevitable muscle squeezing took place. It was his least favorite part of appearing on these shows, but he put on a good face for the cameras. They asked the basic questions about living in America, his new album and music video. Then the interviewer asked a question he was not expecting, "We've heard rumors that you had a specific source of inspiration for many of the songs on the album. Who was that?"

Mal-Chin smiled, his ears tinted pink, "Well, my fans are always my inspiration and there is a song on the track that is just for them." He gave the camera a playful wink and the audience squealed.

"Your fans certainly are amazing, but I've heard there is another source as well," The interviewer pressed. This was a subject that was usually off limits in interviews. Confirming a relationship was a big deal for idols. It was scandal causing territory. Contracts could be lost over relationships. Mal-Chin knew Chanyeol was probably sweating backstage. Mal-Chin tried to think of a good work around. Sophie's heartbroken face kept flashing through his mind and it must have shown on his face.

"There was someone, yes," the crowd reacted with surprise, "It was the American woman that was involved in my incident back in the Fall. She was kind, compassionate, and there for me when I was alone," his vision blurred with tears, the crowd reacted to his sparkling teary eyes. The screen behind them displayed a collage of pictures of Sophie, some pulled right from her Instagram. "I was so stupid. I let her go because I was afraid." He tried to cover up his pain with a joke, "My mother actually smacked me in the back of the head when I left her." The crowd and interviewer laughed along with him. "It really hurt!"

When they went to commercials Chanyeol met him backstage fuming. Mal-Chin might have just ruined his career. All Mal-Chin said in return was for him to book him the first flight back to Danville. Chanyeol looked shocked but did as he asked. As soon as his performance was over, he was on a plane back. Unknown to him, a clip of his confession in the interview was circulating the internet as soon as the show ended and was going crazy. His album would get more listens on every platform and his music videos doubled their views.

Mal-Chin was on a mission as soon as he stepped off the plane. Sophie moved. Mal-Chin knew this from her Instagram posts; he spent the better part of the trip scrolling through it. What he did not know was where she was. Mal-Chin knew where to go to find out though.

John and Minseok had moved into his house when the lease on their apartment was up. They were renting it for enough to pay the yearly taxes on it. Mal-Chin thought it was a good idea, he had someone to take care of the house without the worry of strangers coming in or leaving it empty. He drove straight there and found only a sleepy John there. "Where is she?" He asked unceremoniously.

"Well, nice to see you too," John answered, "Who are you looking for?"

"Sophie. She moved. Where did she go?" Mal-Chin felt desperate. He did not want to waste a second.

"Who just gives out people's addresses? That's weird." John crossed his arms. The look on his face said try again.

"John, please. I've got to talk to her. I can't—" Mal-Chin pressed his lips together his eyes burnt. "I can't keep going without her," Mal-Chin almost whispered the words. A weight lifted from his shoulders. Mal-Chin suppressed the knowledge for so long that finally admitting it felt like a great secret.

John gave in.

The drive to Chatham was only a short 20 minutes but felt like hours. Maybe he should have rested first. The brick apartment building was so unassuming that he passed it several times before realizing it was his stop. A familiar red car was in the parking lot. Mal-Chin thanked his luck that Sophie was there. *Did John tell her I was coming?* He looked up at the windows wondering if she was looking out at him now. Maybe she would rush down to meet him; maybe she was out with another man. Mal-Chin ran to the call box. The first time he didn't speak hoping she would just let him in. No answer. He rang it again. This time calling her name. No answer.

Chapter 56

Sophie waved as another regular passed her in the gym. She switched to one closer to her new apartment, conveniently located next to the grocery store she now used. The space was smaller than her old one, and everything was a boring shade of gray, but the people were friendly and no one seemed to care about the scars on her body. All of Danville and the surrounding county knew her story. The members of her old gym were constantly asking what happened to Mal-Chin and staring at the scars. No matter how much product she put on, they just did not fade.

She chatted with a man while they rested. He knew some high school friends of Sophie's and the two slowly became acquainted. They chatted about their workouts and basic pleasantries. "What are you doing this weekend?" He asked suddenly.

Sophie prepped her weights and straightened her purple half ponytail. She had given up on losing weight and was growing muscle. Confusingly, she looked smaller. "Um, let's see." She moved so that her

barbell was in her lap. "I'm spending time with my grandparents.....
and... book club is this weekend."

Dejected, he looked down at his feet and nodded, "Sounds busy. I
just thought we could go do something." He gave Sophie his number,
so she could text him when she was not so busy. "I know your last
relationship didn't end well. But, it's time to try again."

Sophie looked up at him. She did not need to say anything, her face
delivered the message clearly: *That's my decision. How dare you make
it for me.* She started doing glute bridges. He walked away. Another
man instantly approached him laughing.

Sophie left the phone number in a trash can.

The smell of Pinesol greeted her as soon as she stepped into the
apartment. She had mopped the floor on the way out. It made sense.
The floor could dry undisturbed while she was gone. Her phone
dinged as she was getting into the shower, but she decided it could
wait. After washing her hair, Sophie watched more of the purple hair
dye run down the drain. Sophie knew she should be doing more to
preserve it, like she had done with the dark red, but the purple needed
to come about before the school year started.

She heard the call box buzz while she was getting dressed. Sophie
ignored it. No one had spoken so it was either the wrong room or
a stranger trying to slip in. It rang again as she stepped out of the
bathroom. A thrill ran through Sophie as she heard her name called.
Sophie knew that voice. She could never forget it.

It rang a third time. "Sophie, I need to talk to you. Please, let me in."
Even through the box she could hear the desperation in Mal-Chin's
voice.

She just stared at the box. She must have been hallucinating. She
hit the button to answer. "Take the steps on the right to the third
floor then turn left." She forced her voice to be even. *I'll hear him*

out. Then he can leave. Her living room was not large enough to pace the way she wanted. Instead, she paced from the front door, down the hall past the bedroom and bathroom and to the large windows in the living room then back again. Unfortunately, this meant that when the knock finally came, Sophie was already at the door. She uncovered the peep hole and glanced out. Mal-Chin looked amazing with blond hair, though his face looked more angular. Her hands shook. She took deep breaths to calm herself and stared at her chalk board. John and Anne had filled it with doodles on movie night. Sophie erased some of the more mature drawings.

The door opened soundlessly. Mal-Chin stared at her; Sophie stared back. He was as handsome as ever. Sophie could feel the warmth of him, the safety of him even as he stared at her with wonder filled eyes. Sophie softened. Any notion to get rid of him that she entertained was gone as she let Mal-Chin into the apartment. "The blond looks nice on you." She led him down the hall intending to take him to the living room. "So, what did you need to talk to me about?"

"I love you. I shouldn't have left you," Mal-Chin blurted out. Shyness crept over his features as Sophie took him in.. "Leaving you was the worse decision I've made. Worse than leaving Beast or canceling my schedule to run here and openly confessing my love on TV.

Sophie froze. They were just going to have this discussion in her small kitchen. "Isn't – Isn't that bad for your career?"

"Maybe. But, fuck it. Who cares?"

"You do. Be honest." Sophie looked him directly in the eyes now. Mal-Chin nodded like a child caught in a lie. "I listened to your album, well, most of it."

Pride shined on his face, "You did? What did you think? Most of the songs were for you."

Sophie tucked her hair behind her ear. Her stomach was doing flips as she looked out the window. Someone was walking their dog in the field out back. "I remember the one you used to hum to me, *Unlovable*, it was so beautiful and I- um- I didn't look at the lyrics but, yeah." She chewed on her lip as her throat tightened up. "Why are you here, really, Mal-Chin? Why did you say whatever you did in that interview?"

Confusion then hurt filled Mal-Chin's face. His eyes flicked around the apartment without taking it in before they landed back on her. "Because when I go to bed at night I imagine telling you good night and when I wake up in the morning I think of your sleeping face next to me. You're the first person I think of when I want to share something and when I read I hear your voice reading to me." Tears filled Mal-Chin's eyes. "Every time the cats do something cute I just think 'Sophie would love this'." He looked away out the window.

There was a long silence. Sophie's throat would not let her get any words out. Her eyes squeezed trying to hold back tears. Finally it burst out of her, all the hurt, all the loneliness she was hiding. Mal-Chin's head snapped back to her just in time to catch her wiping her eyes. She hid her face in her hands. "I thought," she cried, "I thought..."

"I know, I'm sorry. You were perfect then and you are now," Mal-Chin wrapped her in his arms.

"No, I thought I was the only one that felt that way. I missed your voice, and the way you laugh. You're so warm, so safe feeling. I even miss the little rumble your chest makes when you'd hum to me. I've never met anyone that made me feel the way you do. Like I've been in the cold and suddenly standing in the warmth of the sun." Sophie looked up at him. What are you doing? She took a step away, out of the safety of his arms. "I can't, not again."

"Sophie, *Jagiya*," He let his arms linger in the air for a moment. That name, *Jagiya*, Sophie missed the intimacy of it. "I know it's going to take some time. I know I made a huge mistake, that I hurt you. Give me another chance, please."

Sophie took him in before sinking into her couch. Her mind needed all its power to think, not to stand. "That night you got drunk. You made a plea for me to come back to you, to stay together as long as we could." Mal-Chin looked down. "You also said you couldn't say any of it sober." She looked up at him.

"But I said it." He stated.

Relief washed over her, "But you just said it." A soft smile graced her face. "Let's try again. Let's love each other again."

Mal-Chin sat down next to her, "I don't think we ever stopped." Sophie leaned against him; a giddy giggle escaped her that he soon copied.

They did not think about tomorrow, or next year, or even an hour from now. They just enjoyed the moment. Eventually, Mal-Chin would return to South Korea and they would figure this all out from there. For now, they were thinking about being a couple in a small apartment who could not go another a second without each other.

Chapter 57

Sophie thought back to that day 4 years ago when Mal-Chin had shown up at her apartment on a whim. It crossed her mind when one of his songs came on the radio or his face lit up a store front on the drive home. Today, it was students dancing to his song, *Wild*, in the hallway. They had an audition to be back up dancers for Exhaust and were practicing diligently. They stopped and bowed respectfully to her as she approached, "When is the audition?"

"Saturday, do you think we'll make it?"

"I hope so. You've been working really hard on it."

"Please cheer for us, Gregory-*nim*"

"Always am. Keep practicing but don't forget to take breaks to eat." Sophie nodded to the students before continuing.

Sophie had trouble getting a job at this school. It was an expensive private school that wanted a native English speaker to teach their English Language classes. The Southern accent was not popular with the staff, or wealthy parents, until she proved her teaching chops.

By the time Sophie reached her car, her feet were begging to be released from the high heels that the school mandated she wore. The good part about them was, she wasn't as short compared to the high school students now. Sophie slipped on the pair of tennis shoes she kept in the passenger's side floorboard. There were not many cars in the teacher's parking lot. Most took the subway or bus home. Sophie's husband insisted she drive to work, not trusting people on the subway system. At the time it was annoying, he wanted to buy the most expensive car he could get his hands on. Eventually, Sophie talked him into something sensible. Just because her husband was rich, did not mean she needed to flaunt his money. She also worried that driving too nice of a car would ostracize her from her co-workers. Some talked down about her when they did not think she was listening.

On the drive home, Sophie debated what to make for dinner and tried to remember her husband's schedule for the day. She was fairly sure he would be working late tonight. That meant taking him something. Korean work schedules were terrible. Sophie learned this the hard way. Schools only got 2 Saturdays per month off and her work days ran longer. She felt bad for these kids who were coming to school, then going to a cram school or other after school event.

At home, she changed clothes before setting to work on making a light dinner. He was on a fairly strict diet so Sophie was trying to meet his needs. Most days he packed several small meals to take with him, but Sophie still liked to make dinner.

The walls of their luxury apartment were practically empty when Sophie first moved in. Sophie quickly filled the walls with family pictures. There was one of their engagement on a beach in France. Sophie had known it was coming, he flew her whole family there, but she was still surprised. Carol posted pictures online, which caused a scandal. Sophie's husband had asked that they not post anything,

Carol feigned forgetfulness. A large picture from their wedding hung above the couch. Sophie was wearing a mermaid style lacy wedding dress standing at the altar with her husband in a Dior suit, looking as handsome as ever. It was from their Korean wedding with his friends and business associates. The picture on the wall was taken right after the bowing ceremony. In the picture, they were smiling lovingly at each other while her hand rested on his chest. In actuality, he had just gotten up from laying down on the floor to bow the lowest, a sign of showing the most respect, and she was wiping dust from his suit as they laughed. Only her grandparents, Lorraine and Will attended. The members of Beast were there too, but they were not photographed. They had a smaller wedding in America for her family.

With dinner done, Sophie carefully packed up eight plates and made the trip to the office. The front staff greeted her with a smile and bow of the head. Sophie was a regular visitor and they let her through without a question. When she first came to South Korea, she worked here for a little while helping the celebrities practice their English conversations. Sometimes they just wanted a native speaker to look over the English lyrics. Sophie had caught some interesting misuses that way.

SJ was just getting onto the elevator when she reached the door. "What did you bring him today?" SJ looked at the bundle in her hands. SJ spoke in English, he liked to practice the skill with her whenever he got the chance. Sophie did not mind having a conversation in English, it put her at ease.

"*Bibimbap*. You're coming in late. Did you get snacks?"

SJ just nodded, "This new choreography is giving even Max a hard time."

"Some of my students are your back-ups. You're treating them well right?" Sophie asked.

SJ laughed, "That's mostly who the snacks are for. I think the whole building learned their lesson after that lecture you gave our manager. I think he's still scared." They both laughed. A few years ago, Sophie let the full fury of Southern anger out on SLS's manager after he pushed one of her students too hard. The poor kid was showing up at school exhausted, starving and barely able to focus. She finally came over and given them her two-cents on the topic. Her husband was surprised that they did not kick her out. They were silent for a few minutes as they watched the numbers count up. "I heard you were offered a modeling job and turned it down."

Sophie nodded, "Yeah. It was for an underwear company. I wasn't comfortable with that." Sophie had done a Valentine's Day photo-shoot in a cute pink dress for a magazine with her husband but lingerie was different. Her husband was relieved when she turned it down. SJ's neck turned red. They got off on the same floor. Sophie wished him good luck as they parted.

Sophie made the trip down this hallway so many times that she did not even need to think about what room she was going into. It did help that the door was slightly cracked. The sound of shuffling feet overlayed with the rock-like guitar of his new song greeted her ears.

Mal-Chin's back was to her as he focused on his dance moves in the mirror. Sweat beaded on his forehead and damped his hair. The room was warm with movement and smelled slightly of sweat. A camera was set up in one corner as they were filming today but no one stopped Sophie from coming in. When they had gotten so publicly engaged, SkyLimit Entertainment quickly dumped Mal-Chin from their label. That should have been the end of his career, but SLS's company swooped in and signed Mal-Chin up. He became the ultimate tease. Mal-Chin oozed sex appeal and flirtation but flaunted his wedding ring any chance he got. It was an unorthodox strategy, but it worked very well. So close you could touch, but just out of reach. The magazine had asked Sophie what she thought of his sexy moves and photographs. She just smiled coyly and said, "I like seeing them too." The comment made Mal-Chin blush and sent his fans into a frenzy.

Mal-Chin caught a glimpse of her in the mirror. A smile brightened his face. This was Sophie's favorite part of the day. She did not think he knew it, but that smile was like coming home to her. Even if they were separated only for a short while, it greeted her. "*Jagiya*!!!" Mal-Chin yelled even as he continued to dance away. He would not stop dancing until the choreographer gave them a break or he messed up. A laugh ran around the room. They were used to this but laughed for the camera.

"*Nuna*, did you bring us food?" One of the back-up dancers asked as soon as the music ended. *Nuna* had taken Mal-Chin some getting used to. It meant big sister, but it could also be a flirty way to say girlfriend. "What did you try this time?" The choreographer grabbed the camera and was filming into the bag as the dancers unpacked in.

The group gathered around as she handed out the containers of food. "It's *Halmeoni* Hayun's *bibimbap* recipe," Sophie answered sheepishly. The back-up dancers were already digging into it before she could finish her explanation. Since moving out on her own Sophie realized she liked cooking and hosting. It was fun when the work was appreciated.

She offered to run the camera so the choreographer could eat. "No, you've got to eat with me," Mal-Chin whined. Sophie just giggled. They opted for sitting the camera on a table to catch them eating.

"*Nuna*! It's so good!" The youngest of the dancers stated.

Sophie did not stay long. They had work to finish, and Mal-Chin tended to get too distracted if she was there. They loaded up all the containers, Sophie kissed Mal-Chin's forehead, and waved to the back-up dancers before heading out again.

After loading the dishwasher, Sophie spent her alone time curled up on the couch with the cats watching k-dramas. Sometimes she would pull up an American show just for comfort, but she tended to lose track of time when she did that. Sophie liked the bit of alone time. It let her recover from the bustle of the day without having to worry about Mal-Chin running into one of her anti-social moods.

The front door beeped as it opened almost as soon as Sophie stepped into the shower. *It's like he knows.* Sophie smiled to herself. The bathroom door opened as she washed her hair. "Hey Sweetie," was all she said. Mal-Chin climbed in with her. When they first started showering this way, it was more exciting but now it was just a regular part of their life when Mal-Chin was preparing for a comeback. He was usually too tired for anything else. It was just another way to be close to each other. "Why don't you wait, and you can take a soak?" Sophie asked as he shifted on tired legs.

"Because I want to be close to you, and I'll want more if we're in the tub," Mal-Chin answered. Sophie was scrubbing his back. She chuckled softly.

"You're too tired for that." She answered after a moment. Mal-Chin just agreed even as he placed kisses on her shoulder. They dried off together, Mal-Chin insisting on drying her hair. Instead of watching TV they snuggled up in bed and chatted until they were too tired to stay awake. Sophie fell asleep curled in Mal-Chin's arms.

Acknowledgements

I want to start by thanking my family, who supported me through this process. My amazing cover artist and brother, Nick deserves and extra shout out for creating a lovely book cover. Wendy let me use to the name of Link's Coffee House which helped set the scene for several sections of the book. Many of the stores mentioned in this book are real and locally owned. I'm grateful to all the stores that I mentioned even if I did not put your name in . The lovely town of Danville, VA. was the perfect backdrop for this story . I want to thank Paul as well for offering advice as a published writer, hope I did not bug you too much! And to my Beta Readers, Julie and Angie, I'm not sure this book would have made it to this point without your great questions and comments.

Thank you for reading! I hope you enjoyed the book!

About the Author

Gina Marie Adkins is a middle school Language Arts teacher. *Unlovable but Maybe Not* is her debut novel. . When Gina Marie is not teaching, she enjoys knitting, weightlifting, yoga and reading. She lives in Danville, Virginia with her family and 18-year-old cat. Please check out her Instagram @ginamarieadkins or her Facebook page.